I KNOW WHERE I AM WHEN I'M FALLING

Amanda Holmes

To Livia,

With so many great memories of sculpting together!

Love,

Amanda Holmes

This edition published in 2014 by
Oak Tree Press
www.oaktreepress.co.uk

An imprint of
Andrews UK Limited
www.andrewsuk.com

Copyright © 2014 Amanda Holmes

The right of Amanda Holmes to be identified as the author of this work has been asserted by her in accordance with the Copyright, Designs and Patents Act 1988

All rights reserved. No part of this publication may be reproduced, stored in or introduced into a retrieval system, or transmitted, in any form, or by any means (electronic, mechanical, photocopying, recording or otherwise) without the prior written permission of the publisher. Any person who does any unauthorised act in relation to this publication may be liable to criminal prosecution and civil claims for damages.

All characters appearing in this work are fictitious. Any resemblance to real persons, living or dead, is purely coincidental.

Excerpt from *The Unbearable Lightness of Being* used by kind permission of Milan Kundera.
Excerpt from "The Rain Horse" by Ted Hughes used by kind permission of Faber & Faber.

for
Ben, Rozzie, Alex and Elliot

Acknowledgements

Special thanks to Ananya Bhattacharyya, Elizabeth Geoghegan, Anna Jaquiery and Yelizaveta P Renfro for their close reading and insightful suggestions. I'm particularly indebted to Peter Gurnis and Carrie Callaghan and to my tireless agent Brie Burkeman, without whose assistance this novel would not have been published. Many thanks also to Gail Arias, Helen Gasperetti, Robyn and Stephen Goodwin, Alice Jolly, Walter Van Dyk, Atli Stannard, Charlie Weber and my brother Robert Holmes for their extraordinary support. Finally, I am deeply grateful to my husband Ben Duffy, close reader and life long partner; for the perceptive feedback from my daughter Rosalind and my mother Judy; for the buoyancy of my sons Alex and Elliot, who kept me going forward; and for the faith my sisters Claudia and Stephanie always had in this novel.

Anyone whose goal is 'something higher' must expect some time to suffer vertigo. What is vertigo? Fear of falling? ...No, vertigo is something other than the fear of falling. It is the voice of the emptiness below us, which tempts and lures us, it is the desire to fall, against which, terrified, we defend ourselves.

Milan Kundera

I KNOW WHERE I AM WHEN I'M FALLING

One

Truth is like God. You cannot see it face to face and live. So when I look at the truth about Angus Aleshire it is often in sidelong glances. I might begin with the paintings. Or with a man who jumped ship just off Peddocks Island, in the winter of 1982. But that's just speculation. The truth is, I haven't seen Angus since.

Except of course, in my dreams. In my dreams I sometimes spot him in a crowd, standing by a bank of elevators, at a party, or waiting for me to notice him at a restaurant table. In my dreams, as in life, he often shows up unannounced.

But dreams are only fancy. They aren't true. I was once in a position to know the truth about Angus more than anyone else. There were also things I didn't know. Angus lied. I lied to myself. Unraveling lies is like picking up the dropped stitches in an intricate and fragile tapestry. It's an enormous risk. The tapestry gives me a precious though incomplete picture of Angus. Dwelling on the dropped stitches, reduces that picture to tatters.

But if I'm going to tell our story truthfully, I must start from the beginning. In 1969 when Angus was fifteen. That's when we met, at Sunday services, which spilled at noon into the parking lot of Old Lincoln Parish. The Chambers, the Aleshires and the Garsides, and the Lamberts, all of us including Grandpa, flocked outside after church, and old Mrs. Cronk was wheeled in her chair by Miss Cronk, and Pastor Jackson with his clean round face, smiled on the steps out front.

The Aleshires lived in a New England farmhouse in Hingham Massachusetts, a property with plenty of land, up a gravel driveway and behind a magnificent hedge. Their house was set on a hill, overlooking the harbor full of boats.

In 1969, my family moved a mile up the road. Our house was tall and messy, with rooms leading off in funny directions, and staircases piled with books. It hummed with life and movement. Lights blazed. Laughter and conversation burst into the evening air. Tempers flared; music blasted.

The Aleshires had three children, and Angus was the oldest. He did well in school. He was gifted at music, intellectually curious and athletic. He could do anything he put his mind to. But he also had a way of stirring things up, and disrupting the family dynamic, of undermining authority and tearing down people's facades. It was always a battle of wills between Angus and his mother, although she challenged his potential, and I could see she was also quite proud of him.

At the church picnic she once told a story about sailing up in Maine. The family got far out when the weather suddenly turned. The mainsail came loose and trapped at the top of the mast. It looked quite desperate, as the weather came in. "Until," she said, "valiant Angus shimmied up the mast to fetch the sail back down." Hearing that story was when I fell in love with him.

My father Timothy was an ethics professor. He wrote Bible commentaries and lectured at various seminaries. My mother, Nora directed plays down at the Community Center. Whenever one of her plays was about to go up, laundry piled near the washing machine, and her scripts and books of stage blockings and notes for the actors joined other ongoing projects on the dining room table, the audio tapes of Timothy's lectures, Lydia's collection of marbles and shells. Freddy's guitar, next to its case, lent against the bookshelves. Folded blankets piled on the settee. And when Nora became pregnant a fourth time, it was as if to underscore the implication that nothing would ever be complete in our house. Life was underway and anything might happen.

We had always called my parents by their first names, although I don't know why. They were always Nora and Timothy to us, never Mom and Dad. As children we were pure complexioned with healthy auburn hair, small proportions and lively bones. Our natures played off each other, one picking up where the other left off. I was the first, overly sincere and a champion of causes, practicing piano or curled up in the window seat with books; Lydia, two years younger than me, was petite and trendy, while Freddy was the true musician. He could play any instrument he picked up, especially guitar, and his rebellious nature played out in his humor and the way he dressed: long hair and striped trousers that looked like pajamas.

Sorrel was the last of us, twelve years younger than Freddy – "our little surprise" Timothy called her, making her appearance in 1971. At first she resembled a porcelain doll carried on high in my father's arms, but later she wore her smallness less easily. She was observant and slightly furtive, saving impressions for later use.

We saw the Aleshires every Sunday, but rarely socialized outside church. Picture Angus as a soft-faced boy of fifteen, with pants that were always becoming too short, playing the opening and closing hymns on the Sunday School piano. In between playing the hymns he rocked back and forth on a chair in my father's Bible class. I remember the way he forced relevancy on the least of discussions. How come the cool kids were always the bad kids, he wanted to know. Wasn't it true that good was synonymous with boring?

"But how can something be good and boring both at the same time?" I put in, for I too was a member of the Bible class, and I was a champion of virtue.

"Most of the good kids are the biggest wimps and losers of all," Angus continued, sitting back in his slender long-legged body, a single wave of hair across the forehead. "If you never take risks, it's easy to get by. You just give people what they want."

My father had a gentle manner and eyes that smiled from the corners. "Well," he said. "Sometimes it's risky to be good, too. To stand up for principle, you know."

"Perhaps we should define what we mean by good," he replied.

"All right," said Timothy. "Tell me what you mean by good."

Angus turned his head to one side, leaning on his elbows, thinking hard. "Goodness is integrity," he said at last, throwing out a witty smile. "And to have integrity you have to follow a reliable set of rules. But only with the certainty that they are based on something authentic."

The others in the class sat in neutral silence, under a fug of adolescent malaise. "People are sometimes more self-righteous than they are genuine," Timothy said, delighted to have found such an engaging interlocutor in Angus, "and that's why Jesus preferred sinners to hypocrites."

"But wait!" Angus cried, his face filling up with new considerations. "These terms you keep using like sinner and hypocrite. It's all a question of semantics. Because as I understand it you consider a hypocrite to be sinful."

"The parable of the prodigal son is about this very question," Timothy said, bringing in his Bible reference. "It teaches us that being good means more than missing out on the fun. And we need to make sure that our good behavior is not just a self-righteous façade. It has to come out of a heartfelt desire to do what's right."

But it was really the piano that brought Angus and me together. There weren't many kids our age who took it quite so seriously. "That was a rousing rendition of Onward Christian Soldiers," I remarked after Sunday School one morning. This was before Sorrel was born, so I must have been fifteen, and Angus sixteen. He was sitting in the back seat of the family car, looking through the window grinning at me, as I stood in the parking lot.

"Where do you take lessons?"

"At the South Shore Conservatory," I said.

"Same here," taking the opportunity to brag about his teacher: "a concert pianist who handpicks his students. Who is your teacher?"

"The great Mrs. McNaught," I said."An extremely old woman who drives down from New Hampshire twice a week to teach. She even drove down when she broke her arm."

Angus laughed. "What are you working on now?"

"Bach Inventions and a piece by Edward McDowell."

"Edward who?"

"He wrote *To a Wild Rose*."

"Do you want to come over for lunch?" he asked.

∼

We sat in the back of the station wagon, suddenly shy without the barrier of the car door between us, looking anywhere but at each other, with the other Aleshire children packed in like sardines, and then we sat in the enormous turquoise kitchen, sipping vegetable soup. His little sister Beth was a blond girl of about ten, who sometimes inexplicably burst into tears and was very keen on making me feel at home. "Here Ruby, would you like a sandwich? Would you like some apple juice? Wait, I'll get you a glass." Cheryl Aleshire was a broad beamed woman, bending a practical head to the passing out of napkins and plates. "Don't expect Angus to help you, Ruby," she said. "If you wait, you'll go home hungry." The table was silent, everyone busily helping themselves to tuna fish, tomatoes, sliced rye bread and mayo. Angus's brother Duncan caught my eye and smiled. He was about my age and had these cute dimples, and tight curly hair. Cheryl turned to the sink, washing out a glass, sleeves pushed up, hands sunk into the suds. "So what's your favorite subject in school, Ruby? Drama, I suppose."

I noticed that some of the kids started their lunch as others finished, and when they were done each of them cleared away their own plates, left the room and vanished into the house.

Angus led me to a parlor decorated with New England antiques and ticking with clocks. The sweet aroma of adolescent boy lifted off his sweater, as we sat side by side on the sofa. Please God, I thought, let this moment never end. A linen shaded lamp shed its light across the book in his hands.

The pictures he showed me were puzzles, M.C. Escher prints: figures walking round a tower, up and down stairs that folded, in a cunning twist of perspective, back upon themselves. In another print, birds flew off the page, while in their negative space fish swam downstream.

As usual, Angus had a challenge. "Which do you see first? The fish or the birds?"

"The birds," I said. "You?"

"Both."

Angus Sidney Aleshire. A name to fall in love with. A name bequeathed with care. But there was very little of the Scotsman in his dark skin and black hair, his strong nose and high cheekbones. "You don't look a thing like your parents," I said, taking in the shrewd curve of his mouth.

He looked me straight in the eye. "I was adopted."

"No! Really?"

"Sure. I was adopted when I was five. Want to see the piano?"

I followed him into the piano room, where he practiced a couple of hours each day. No one in the family was allowed to interrupt when he was practicing – and that was Cheryl's rule. Play was strictly organized in the Aleshire home. There were music lessons, skiing lessons, sailing, hiking and riding, tennis games, hockey practice. "It's one of my worst memories," he said, as I slid beside him onto the piano bench. "Waiting on the platform at South Station with my new family, while my grandmother's train pulled away." He leafed through a pile of sheet music. "My name back then was David."

The piano room was white and bare-floored. The piano was a baby grand – grander by far than our old family upright with its missing notes. The windows of the piano room faced a lawn. He set up the first movement of Beethoven's Pathetique. His fingers on the keys were broad and brown with clean flat nails. He began the opening measures with feeling and control. I tried to imagine what he was like at five, adopted by the Aleshires, as I listened to the music, and looked across the huge expanse of lawn.

The following Saturday, I checked out two recordings from the Hingham Public Library, one by Vladimir Horowitz, the other by Glenn Gould, both playing the Pathetique. I sat on the floor with the music spread in front of me. I preferred the Horowitz version, and listened again and again, while following the sheet music. But it was a long time before I allowed myself to place that music on our piano, sit at the keyboard and form my hands around those first, exuberant, wide mouthed chords.

Two

Frank Aleshire sat behind us at the Cohasset Ice Arena, dressed in a red-checkered shirt. He had a hearty face, and short hair, which stuck out in thin, layered ridges at the back of his neck. "Hey there. You folks enjoying the game?" Our family had stopped by as promised, to watch Angus's hockey game, to watch him float past on the ice with a stick, and get into sudden violent scraps with the puck, raucous shouting matches with teammates, to slam against the walls, and charge top speed in the opposite direction. For my own part, I was only waiting until the end when he might skate over, grinning, his black hair showing beneath the helmet.

You know," Frank said. "You've made a great impression on him."

"And he on us," Nora replied. "We're all very fond of that boy."

"Such a thinker!" Timothy put in.

Frank chuckled. "Sure," he said. "Gus can turn on the charm when he likes." The hockey arena echoed with the cries of the players, the glide and whoosh of skates, the crack of stick hitting stick. I sat alone at the far end of the bleachers, hugging my jacket around me, but close enough to overhear the rest of their conversation. The change in Frank's tone alarmed me.

"We've been having an awful time," he confided to my parents. "He doesn't respect the difference between right and wrong. Undermines authority. Calls people out. Always in trouble at school, for back talking or showing up late, and missing important assignments."

"Frank," said Timothy. "You know if there's anything we can do..."

"We think he needs more challenge," said Frank. "Cheryl and I are hoping we can get him into a private school next year. That would be one solution. We'll have to see, I guess."

"Nora," I ventured, when we were driving home in the old station wagon with wooden sides. "Angus told me he was adopted. But is that really true?"

"Yes," she said. "It's perfectly true."

"He said he was five years old," I told the family. "He said it was one of his worst memories, watching his grandmother's train pull away."

"I'm sure it was," said Timothy. The windshield wipers thumped out their regular beat across the window. "What happened to his real parents?" Lydia wanted to know.

"I think his mother died of cancer," Nora said. "The Aleshires have done a lot for that kid."

"Yikes," said Freddy. I'd forgotten Freddy was even there. On car rides he had a way of disappearing into the back seat, and looking out of the window.

"I shudder to think what he must have gone through," our mother continued. "Can you imagine Angus at five?"

I could. And he must have been gorgeous.

∾

Angus liked to stop by unannounced. He poked his head in at the Community Center when Nora was conducting her drama workshops and he'd stand there grinning from the door. Nora sat in the middle of the hall on a straight-backed chair, her belly growing ripe with the baby due in four months' time, and she had this laugh, which she couldn't seem to let out all in one go. It bucked and rolled and tossed her about, and then flowed out like fast running water. "Oh, hello darling, what brings you in here?"

"I'm on my way to practice," he said, hockey gear jammed in a bag.

Nora turned briefly back to the stage, where her favorite student Ari Braun was going through a scene with me. "Ari," she called, "I want to see the thoughts on your face, darling, before you speak. Remember that it's thought, action and then speech."

"Timothy said I could stop by Friday," Angus continued, "for a game of chess."

"Sure. Why not?"

"But it's Freddy's twelfth birthday on Friday..." I threw out from the stage.

Then Nora remembered. "Oh, that's right. We're going out to supper at the Aloha. But we'd love to include you."

It was on account of one of Freddy's favorite dishes there – the Pu Pu Platter – that all of us, Grandpa included, squeezed into the semicircular Polynesian booth, in the low ceilinged dimly lit Aloha Restaurant. And to my joy, Angus came as well. Five different conversations were conducted at once. Everyone ordered fruity drinks with miniature parasols propped inside them. We passed around plates of batter-dipped shrimp, eggrolls, and chicken wings. We cracked open fortune cookies, and unraveled the messages inside. "Your hard work will soon pay off," Timothy read, putting on a funny accent. "Openness is a quality that has its rewards," read Lydia. "Help," read Freddy, unraveling his fortune. "I'm being held captive in a fortune cookie factory."

I remember we thought up names for the baby that evening, trying on identities, on the baby's behalf, a dressing up box full of characters, which changed according to costume.

"Victoria!" Timothy suggested, looking round for reaction.

"Nah..." we all cried.

"How about Sebastian," suggested Lydia.

"Oh dear," Grandpa muttered, blotting his mouth with a napkin.

"Maybe we should call him David?" I suggested.

"What do you think of Elimelech for the baby's name," Freddy put in. It was a name from Sunday School, from the book of Ruth and everyone laughed, so that only I saw the expression on Angus's face then. Our eyes met, and fused together and everything else fell away.

~

The Aleshires went to their cottage up in Maine for several weeks each summer. But we remained in Hingham, taking weekend drives to the Cape, while Nora grew bigger by the day, until at length she sat on the wicker sofa on the sun porch, red faced and miserable, and completely lacking in energy. "I feel like an unexploded bomb," she wailed.

Sorrel was born at home, with the help of a midwife, at the end of July during the summer I turned sixteen. I remember how we sat in the living room waiting for the birth, Freddy and

Lydia and I, and how Freddy kept on going outside, hoping to overhear birth pangs and baby cries, while I was reading *Swan Song* by John Galsworthy, and Lydia was poised to tape record our thoughts, just at the crucial moment. She recorded Freddy's voice, still unbroken, "I hope you are a boy. I really want a brother...so I hope you feel terrible if you're a girl..."

Sorrel was a name from a Noel Coward play, which Nora had kept up her sleeve in case the rest of us objected. And how could we, once we saw the baby? Because she did look a lot like a Sorrel, with her determined and compact face, her big green eyes. Timothy made the telephone calls to all the relatives and friends. "It's a girl," he said. "Sorrel Elizabeth."

We gathered around our mother's bed, laughing in amazement and joy, because our sister Sorrel was in Nora's arms, tiny and primal, as if she had come from the sea, and just a few minutes old. Then the baby turned her mouth down as if with disappointment. "Oh darling!" Nora said. "They're only laughing at you because you've got cream all over your face."

Timothy had wallpapered Freddy's old bedroom in a duck, drake and bulrush pattern for the baby, and painted Nora's chest of drawers to match. Freddy meanwhile, moved into Lydia's room, and Lydia moved into my old room, and I was now on the very top floor, in a room all by myself, with dormer windows. The excitement of the baby, the feedings, the wakeful nights, the burping and the changing used up the rest of the summer. We all had time for reinvention. Freddy was no longer youngest. Lydia was no longer youngest girl, and three sisters in the house is a lot more than two.

∼

I practiced the piano, Bach Inventions and Schumann's Scenes from Childhood. I spent several days with a paint pot, covering the old fashioned walls of my room in mint green paint. I put up my George Harrison poster from *All Things Must Pass*, and I had a little desk, which doubled as a dressing table, and a tiny bottle of patchouli oil, and several strands of colored beads. Then I lay on my bed, thoroughly pleased with myself, reading the next book in the Forsyte Chronicles by John Galsworthy, looking through the skylight, daydreaming about Angus, watching the clouds and planes pass overhead.

Timothy worked from home all summer, pecking out pages on his typewriter. Grandpa went to the library to pick out biographies. The baby cried. Freddy played his guitar. The cat sprawled in a streak of summer sun, which fell across the carpet, and Lydia and I went swimming at Little Rocky Beach.

The water was covered in light, the stones patched in shadow. We crossed the road, and walked to the rickety wooden staircase, towels over our shoulders. The air smelled of seaweed. The flinty shore of Little Rocky Beach trailed with shells and horseshoe crabs. Sailboats bobbed on the water, like ornaments on a glass table.

Lydia was a mermaid, at home in her body, scooping into the sea, only to emerge again several meters out. "Come on, Ruby! It's warmer now than yesterday. I remember because there was a chill in the air and it isn't like that now."

I was white skinned with auburn corkscrew hair, standing with my feet curled round the stones. "Let's swim out to the boulder," I said. And then we swam, making for a particular favorite boulder, which when the tide was high became a tiny cap above the sea. It was beautiful in high tide, that boulder. But when the tide was low it became an ugly cone with markings, naked and exposed.

∼

First sign of autumn: tiny Concord grapes ripening on the pergola. They were tough skinned and sour and got squashed on the terrace or eaten up by Hetty the dog under the shadowed table. Sun quieted and breezes picked up. The air smelled sharp, of seaweed and low tide. I was entering tenth grade and moving up to the high school meant an enormous change I wasn't looking forward to. But a week before school was to start, the energy of August paused to catch its breath in a protracted anticipation of the coming year. Approaching the house after a swim at Little Rocky, we looked across the garden to see Nora and Timothy sitting under the pergola. Nora was nursing Sorrel and guess who had showed up unannounced? I could hardly move. There wasn't a moment in his presence that he didn't burn a hole through the center of my consciousness.

"Angus! What are you doing here? And why are you all dressed up?" Lydia asked, for he was tanned and polished looking, dressed smartly in a navy blue suit with narrow legs. He had combed his hair in a curl across the forehead and wore a clever smile. "I'm leaving for boarding school this afternoon," he said, never looking in my direction. "I came to see the baby. And to say goodbye."

He wrote me a letter that September, though. He wrote it in code, with funny drawings, and a little ribbon of piano keys decorating the borders. Deer Roo bee, eye M sew HA + P a boat ewe.

Three

Angus was expelled from boarding school that November, for truancy and alcohol possession. The Aleshires then sent him to another private school, more locally accessible. When he was expelled from that one too they arranged for psychological counseling. I heard from Duncan that he'd got back in touch with his biological grandmother and was going out to Pittsfield to live with her. But he was back again soon enough, and enrolled once again at the local high school. I sometimes saw him in the cafeteria, or in the hallway with another girl, throwing me a look of veiled recognition as I hurried along with an armload of books. He sauntered now, and wore a pair of hippie jeans so covered in patches it looked like they might disintegrate. He never carried books or school supplies. He was a free agent, disappearing up the slope behind the school cafeteria where the cool kids went to smoke pot.

By this time I was in love with Henry, a tall skinny kid with the beginnings of a beard and a fondness for the writings of Kahlil Gibran. We kissed in front of the lockers before class. We walked home arm in arm and kissed on the sofa, listening to Neil Young records.

My piano teacher Mrs. McNaught brought in an accompaniment to Mozart's 5th Piano Sonata- written by Rachmaninov. There were two baby grands, positioned end to end in the front parlor at the South Shore Conservatory. For weeks our lessons started the same – with Mozart's 5th Sonata, me playing the Mozart, Mrs. McNaught the Rachmaninov. She perched at her piano looking at me across an expanse of polished wood and when I went too fast, or played too many mistakes, "Whoa!" she cried, as if I were a runaway pony. "Whoa, whoa whoa!"

Angus had stopped attending church. The Aleshires had to pick their battles. So it became my task to play the hymns for Sunday School. His brother Duncan and I often chatted in the church parking lot after services. Duncan was quiet and serious, hardworking, a lover of horses, camping, and the outdoor life. He told me Angus had recently been picked up by the cops for breaking into a house on Main Street.

Duncan had his driver's license, so we took a drive and sat in the parked car and talked, overlooking Hull Harbor. Angus, he said, was a pain in the ass and Duncan was sick of putting up with him. He invited girls to his room when their parents were out, and smoked weed in the house. In one of their knock down drag outs, Cheryl Aleshire threw a lamp downstairs, narrowly missing his head. But Angus just stared at her, stony faced while she raged. Then he walked out, with his head held high. I wondered, what had gone so terribly wrong? Why was he always acting out. What had become of the Angus I knew, with a gift for the piano, thoughtful analysis of biblical passages, the boy who sped across ice with a hockey stick?

That winter, he showed up on our doorstep. The muscles in his face were tense. His hair was longer, pulled back to a ponytail, making his head seem narrow. He wore a leather bomber jacket and jeans, the hems of which were wet and stained. "Hey," he said when I opened the door. "Is your dad at home?"

"Sure," I said. "Come on in." It wasn't unusual for people to consult with my father. Counseling others was what Timothy did best and when he appeared at the kitchen door, his face lit up in welcome.

"Angus," he cried. "How good to see you again!" And with that they disappeared into the study. Angus sat on a wooden swivel chair opposite my father, as I started to head up the stairs. Then on second thought, I sat on a step beyond their view, to eavesdrop.

Lydia joined me. "What's going on?" I put my finger to my lips. From our vantage point we could see Angus's reflection in the glass of a bookcase, but we had to strain to catch any words.

"I'm not going back to my parents' house," he said. "My mom doesn't want me back. And she's threatened me with a Stubborn Child complaint, if I trespass on their property."

"Your parents love you, and they have been doing their best under very challenging circumstances," our father's voice responded. Angus drew in a lungful of air, and sat back in the seat. "The last thing your parents want is for you to be placed in juvenile detention," Timothy said.

"You want to make a bet?" he challenged. "If my mother files that complaint it will make me a ward of the state and keep me away from their property. And you want to know something weird? That law, the stubborn child law, is based on the Bible. It's a law of hate and intolerance and it's taken almost exactly from Chapter 21 in Deuteronomy. If you don't believe me, look it up."

Then, "I don't know what to think," Angus said, in a softer tone. "Would you say it was right for your family to call you a trespasser? But maybe they're right. Because the fact of the matter is, I need to find a new place to live. It isn't working out. And I can just tell, if I could get away from them, if I could start off somewhere fresh..."

I had never heard of a stubborn child complaint. Up in my room I leafed through my Bible to Chapter 21 of Deuteronomy, and was dismayed to read these words: *If a man have a stubborn and rebellious son, which will not obey the voice of his father, or the voice of his mother, and that, when they have chastened him, will not hearken unto them; Then shall his father and his mother lay hold on him, and bring him out unto the elders of his city, and unto the gate of his place.*

Four

Angus moved into a spare room on the ground floor of our house after the weather had broken. He pulled up in a borrowed van with his father Frank, full of belongings and plans for the future. Pastor Jackson, the Aleshires, a juvenile probation officer and my parents all sat round the kitchen table carefully discussing the arrangement. The plan was that Angus would find a part time job and stop getting into trouble. Since the high school wouldn't take him back any more, Timothy offered to drive him to Quincy twice a week for night classes. This way he could earn his high school equivalency and build towards a future. In return for room and board he would do odd jobs, and a bit of gardening work for us. It was 1972 and Angus was almost eighteen.

Timothy and Freddy helped unload books and stereo equipment from the van, a laundry hamper of clothing, a beanbag chair and an Indian print bedspread, a ten-speed bike and ice hockey gear, some rolled up posters, a box of LPs, and a stack of motorcycle magazines.

Sorrel sat in her highchair picking up dry Cheerios with her fingers. Nora had the clam chowder on while Lydia and I were busy making grilled cheese sandwiches. "Why don't you stay for lunch, Frank?" Nora suggested. "We'd love to have you."

There was a meeting of eyes between father and son. Frank declined. "Hey, it looks terrific, Nora. But I think I'll get on back." He gave Angus a meaningful pat on the back. "Okay, Gus. We'll be in touch, old buddy."

Frank and Timothy had a final word or two, standing in the driveway man to man, while Angus, cautious and quieter than usual, joined us for lunch in the kitchen.

Afterwards he walked with Timothy down to the grove at the bottom of our property. "It's not that we don't like the trees," Timothy explained. "In fact we like them very much. We want to see a bit more of them. What we don't want to see is a forest."

When Angus laughed he tilted his head back, eager to make a good impression, wanting to come across. Sure. He understood perfectly. Of course. He'd clear out the brush and the brambles, thin out the top-heavy branches.

I had assigned myself the task of reading Dante's *Divine Comedy*. I curled up in the window seat with my Penguin edition, every so often looking up to see Angus with the wheelbarrow, going back and forth from the grove. I had the impression of his figure amongst the brambles, and his red sweatered arms moving through the branches, black hair, a strong straight profile, physical confidence and easy comfort within his body. I saw him at the top of a very tall ladder and wondered if he would fall.

By midafternoon he had cleared out all the dead wood, and raked around the trees. Freddy went outside to help. At least, he stood on the outskirts strumming on his ukulele, riffing and one upping Angus while he worked. Hetty the dog trotted around, sniffing at the pile of brush. The ground was soft and dirty, the sky stippled in clouds. "What's the weirdest face that you can make?" Freddy wanted to know, with Angus breaking into laughter. "Oh man! Make another..."

Before supper, we set up the Scrabble board. I drew my knees up under my Indian skirts, frowning at the board, at a remove now, because of my boyfriend Henry, and my new ideas of identity. *Bloom, mired* and *rig, pies, wine, bend, join*. Words across the Scrabble board.

"Go, Rube. Your turn," Freddy said.

I scrutinized my letters and when I put them down, Angus threw me a skeptical grin. "Cobbed?"

"The corn is cobbed," I explained with mock earnest.

"Ah, come on!" leaning on his elbows looking hard at the board. Then he tilted his head, picked up his letters, and with fingers strong and brown, and an amused flicker of triumph, he placed down every last tile.

"Hey! That's not a word!" Lydia cried. She was fifteen, tiny and tempestuous, wearing a peaked velvet cap, her hair in two auburn braids.

"Of course it's a word. And it's sure as hell better than cobbed. That's triple word score and double that for using all my letters."

"I think you'll find that the word is *in*corrigible," I said.

"Nope," he said. "You're wrong. Corrigible means correctable. You want to look it up?"

A sudden race and playful challenge: hands and fingers fumbling for the dictionary, rifling through pages; outcries of mirth as the dog barked, tug of war, a childish foreplay, over the dictionary pages.

Angus could never be idle. He walked up the high street with his friends Nacho and Kevin, went into the city for concert tickets, because Led Zeppelin was playing at Boston Garden; acquired odd possessions, which absorbed him for weeks: a broken down MG that he spray-painted yellow and which he left for several weeks in our driveway. He read books about Buckminster Fuller, sat at the table drumming his fingers on the table and eating bowls of cereal. Then he settled down on the sun porch and carefully glued toothpicks into a model of a geodesic dome. He left little scraps of toothpick and glue all over the table. And the MG ended up being junked.

But when the vacuum cleaner broke, he stared at the pieces for a very long time with a concentrated and patient expression on his face, and then he set about fixing it. He played chess with Timothy, sitting in the living room as the sun came down. He sat at the table reading magazines about Evel Knievel and his next daredevil jumps on a motorcycle, and told us all about sound systems and musical equipment, and the fine points of motorcycle engines. He gestured expansively, riffing with Freddy or my boyfriend Henry, whoever would take him on and test his mettle, carrying out a thought or an idea to see where it took them and if it was funny.

"Hey Angus. Want to play some duets?" I asked.

"What kind of duets?"

"Fauré's *Dolly Suite*. I just started learning them."

"Oh, I remember those."

"Come take a look, then." He sat beside me on the piano bench as I opened up the music. "I'm playing this," meaning the second one: *Mi a ou*.

Angus sat at the base end, less than fully invested. "Okay," he said, looking across the music. "You ready?"

We began the first few measures, hesitant at first, our fingers side by side on the keys. Gabriel Fauré surely knew a thing or two about mischief and seduction and I liked to imagine the notes describing kittens with a ball of yarn. But although it had been my suggestion, playing with Angus made me nervous, and my imaginary ball of yarn became a little tangled as the notes slid away beneath my hands.

He shot a glance in my direction. "You need practice~"

"Just keep going," I said, "... to the part where they're basking..."

"What are you talking about?"

"I always think of kittens when I hear this piece ~"

So we played through to the three languishing measures on the top of the last page and then the finale became a kind of contest, and I gave it my best, thumping out those final chords so decisively and yes, a little messily, that Nora and Lydia came in from the kitchen to listen.

I assigned myself more reading. After *The Divine Comedy* I would read Machiavelli's *The Prince*. After that there were mountains of important books on my list, and hardly a minute to lose. I sat on the floor of the local bookstore reading Phillip Larkin, or scribbling "The Waking" by Theodore Roethke into my journal. What did he mean by *wake to sleep and take my waking slow*?

Left to his own devices, Angus might have passed up his night school classes altogether. But Nora insisted on an early supper and Timothy always appeared dressed in his jacket at 7 o'clock sharp, tapping his wristwatch. "We don't want to be late now."

Then he had to face the tedium of some forgotten assignment, a paper that wasn't finished or a looming test. Not that he needed to try in these classes in order to pass them. He could do the work with his eyes closed, which only underscored the foolishness of the exercise. "Won't you let me skip even once?"

"I don't think it's useful to open yourself up to that debate, Angus. It's so much easier not to make a decision about whether or not to go every week," Timothy reasoned.

They drove to Quincy, past the Hingham Marina and past the church, Timothy determined to do what was morally right, Angus disappointed in the lack of meaningful challenge. Sometimes

I went along to keep them company. "Don't you ever question things?" Angus asked.

"Of course," said Timothy.

"But don't you see the hypocrisy in these night classes, or am I the only one who can see the hypocrisy?"

Timothy frowned. "I don't quite catch your meaning..."

"It's a bullshit qualification. A marker that doesn't mark anything. Everyone in this night school is a total loser. You know I don't belong with them."

Timothy considered this a moment. "It's a step though, isn't it? A step towards university, perhaps. You have a fine mind and imagination; you have musical talent and athletic ability. Once you have your high school credential, you can do anything you put your mind to."

"I can put my mind to something else without a meaningless credential. Do you think I'm going to be any smarter after I finish these night classes? The teacher is a total idiot. You've got to see that I'm right about this."

They passed Building 19 and the old Drive In Movie Theatre, Timothy firmly concentrating on the road ahead. The water glistened in the early evening light, until at length they crossed the Fore River Bridge near General Dynamics, where the sound of the tires on the metal grid beneath them took on a rumbling timbre. I can still hear Angus's protests, "I'm the kind of person who can see the bad side in people and you always look for the good. You think of the good as the real part and the bad as the part that needs correcting."

"I think I see it as an opportunity," Timothy responded. "To prove you can complete something. So go forward and put the past behind you and try to see the glass as half full, instead of half empty." There was a long silence. Then, "Saint Paul faced a similar question, you know. Brethren, he said, I count not myself to have apprehended: but this one thing I do," and Timothy paused here for emphasis: "forgetting those things which are behind, and reaching forth unto those things which are before, I press toward the mark for the prize of the high calling of God in Christ Jesus!" Angus and I caught each other's eyes in the rear view mirror and grinned.

"So you see Angus," Timothy continued chattily, bound and determined to finish off his quote. "Let us therefore as many as be perfect be thus minded, and if in anything you be otherwise minded, God shall reveal even this unto you!"

If you had been there, you would have laughed along with us. Because Timothy's sincerity had a charming levity as he recited these verses. For him the power of goodness was absolutely indisputable.

We passed an Irish bar, a Chinese restaurant, an old auto supply store. It drizzled lightly and a few people hurried down the sidewalk underneath umbrellas.

"You want to know something weird though," Angus put in. "It's not so much a question of a glass half full or half empty. Because the glass is half full *and* half empty."

Timothy pulled to the curb in front of Quincy Public Library. "And therein lies the challenge," he said. "Think about it, all right? And I'll meet you back here in a couple of hours."

So Angus got out of the car, leaning in to catch his eye before slamming the door shut. "Sure. Thanks, man."

Picture his saunter as he heads over to the school building, and before showing up for class, cuts down a path behind the dumpster at the back of the school parking lot, to smoke a joint of Sensimilla, sucking in the sweet and earthy smoke and holding it into his lungs.

Five

He stayed out of trouble all that year, unless you count a few late nights carousing, and a prank involving band instruments, stolen from the high school and eventually returned. One night he broke into the church just in order to play the organ. He told me all about it at the time, about how Pastor Jackson had entered the sanctuary while he was playing and sat in a pew at the back of the church. And had said nothing. Perhaps he was charmed at the impulse. Perhaps he thought that Angus might begin attending church again. In Timothy and Pastor Jackson, Angus had very strong allies. Not to mention Nora who listened to him for hours, as he talked about the temptations he had and the exhilaration he felt taking a hit on the center of risk. He called it an adrenaline rush. It was largely because of Nora that Angus met with his probation officer regularly, and attended psychological counseling sessions. He finished the night classes, earned his high school equivalency and got a part time job at a fast food place in Weymouth, mopping the floors and cleaning the fryers and counters.

"The people," he said. "My God! The people who go in there at night! The lowlifes! This guy, the manager, his name is *Chad*," pronouncing the name with a care that made it sound ludicrous. "He wheels this bucket across the floor. I swear to God, he's been there for years and he's as dumb as dirt. And when he explains how I'm supposed to mop the floor, he leaves a thin, slimy coating of industrial strength soap. That place could never be clean in a million years."

"It sounds dreadful," Nora said.

"A kitchen should be clean. And that place is a health hazard. You don't think I should support an organization like that, do you? Is that the kind of work that I should do?"

The weather turned warm so we ate our meals on the sun porch overlooking the garden. Nora loaded the table with sandwiches, a pitcher of lemonade and ginger ale, garden salad, a big bowl of potato chips, and more often than not we were six or eight teenagers round the table, everyone's boyfriend and girlfriend, band members, playmates, laughing and talking at once.

The shade of endless mornings stretched across the driveway. My boyfriend Henry hitchhiked down from the new development almost every day and different girls came round to sit beside Angus or trail off behind him, silently, to see the Rickman dirt bike he had recently acquired. He always had a scheme: heading out to Brewster Woods to shoot the bike over ditches and burn up the ground; organizing jam sessions with Freddy, bringing musicians together. "You should hear this kid play guitar," he boasted on Freddy's behalf. "He's fourteen years old and he's the best guitarist I know."

Lydia had babysitting jobs and a crush on a boy named Richard. She walked in her flip-flops down to the harbor and waited for him to finish his lawn-mowing job on Ship Street. She sat on the grass without turning round, and sooner or later she heard the thud of his feet as he ran down the dock and dove off the end into Hingham Harbor.

Grandpa sat in his chair with his hands up to his face, having a snooze. Sorrel played on the living room floor hammering colored pegs into a tiny cobbler's bench.

Henry was out in the driveway with the hood of the car opened up. He had decided to explain to me how the engine worked. "And that right there is the carburetor," he said, as Angus passed, looking tanned and ragged in a pair of cut off shorts and a tie-dyed shirt.

"Man!" Angus cried. "That's not the carburetor!"

Henry's face softened in submissive perplexity. "What do you mean?"

"You're wrong," said Angus, allowing a beat to pass, before he broke into laughter. "Ah, I'm just kidding, man," hitting Henry lightly on the arm, pleased at having sown a few seeds of doubt in his mind.

Later that afternoon, after Henry had gone, I sat in my window seat, biting the end of a pencil. *Sentiment twists repentance*, I wrote. *Sentiment twists repentance to its own polite history...* Then I looked up to see Angus in a chair across the room, watching me fixedly. "I'm writing a poem," I explained.

"One day when we are married, I'll massage your back for you. And then you'll massage my back for me. And then we'll go to sleep. All right?" he said.

I laughed. "All right."

"Lydia, could you come over here for a minute and try this on for me, darling..." Nora had her sewing machine set up and she was trying to convert a velvet curtain into an Elizabethan doublet for one of her plays.

"I'm off then," Timothy said, meaning to the church hall where he would conduct a weekly Bible seminar. He leaned over her, giving Nora a kiss. "Goodbye Thumbelina!"

"I have a question for you, Nora. How do you handle your life without going nuts?" Angus asked when Timothy had gone.

Nora frowned, holding pins in her mouth, fitting the curtain to my sister's body. "What do you mean?" asked Lydia, as she stretched out her arms obligingly. Nora was under pressure and might have reason to be annoyed.

"Well, there's this persona you've erected for others. The housewife, mother and daughter in law bit. But who are you beneath all that?"

"*Persona* isn't a word I'd use," she said.

"But is it your calling to be a mother and a wife?"

"It isn't as simple as having a calling."

"What about the stage? Is that a calling for you? Don't you want to direct something more serious than these community projects? Why keep yourself in a little box?"

"Oh Angus," she sighed. "I have too many things to do, to think about all that. I have teenagers to raise, a two year old child, an elderly father in law..."

"Haven't you heard about Women's Lib?"

"Of course she has!" I put in from my window seat. "But maybe she doesn't see her life as a little box."

"Hingham is a total box," he said. "Don't you feel the urge to break away? To travel? Because I feel a calling to go across the country and see the Grand Canyon. Go to the West Coast and the Rocky Mountains. I want to have a sailboat of my own. I want to own property someday too. Maybe build a plane. And buy some land out west and build a geodesic dome."

Nora laughed. She loved a good laugh. We watched with amusement as her laughter bubbled up from the deep and toppled over in cascades of joy, and when she had finished, "Oh dear," she said, wiping her eyes. "A plane *and* a geodesic dome. Don't limit yourself or anything, darling."

Angus was crestfallen. "I'm sure you are capable of achieving your goals Angus," I put in.

"So long as you don't get bored by the demands of ordinary life. We all have to guard against that," Nora said.

"I don't see the point in an ordinary life," Angus answered. "It's depressing. It saps my spirit to think about it."

"Well, sweetheart, even the most extraordinary lives have their moments of tedium," Nora said. "Do you think that Michelangelo enjoyed lying on his back for years while he painted the ceiling of the Sistine Chapel? Don't you think there were days and weeks when he thought he couldn't continue another moment? You have to get through the tedium, if you want to aim towards a higher goal."

"It doesn't make sense," he said.

Nora sighed. "You have enormous potential," making another effort. "And we want to see you fulfill it. I like to think of potential as another word for hope. In Hebrews it says that faith is the substance of things hoped for, the evidence of things not seen. Maybe that's what we mean, Tim and I, when we say that we have faith. We mean that we recognize your untapped potential." And she looked directly at him across the table, her eyes shot through with amber flecks.

"I get the feeling that for you guys the person you are inside is true and solid enough to interact with the world on your behalf," he said, warming to his subject as he went along. "You have this idea that your inner self has your best interests at heart. But I'm not like that. I can see the weaknesses in myself and I can see them in everyone around me."

I frowned, considering this. "But we wouldn't be human if we didn't have weaknesses."

"So why are the people in charge such total losers," he continued. "The high school principal with the heavy Boston accent and the mole on the tip of his nose; or the guidance counselor who tries to sort out everyone else's life. He's a high school guidance counselor for Christ sake! And he has so little self-confidence that he combs thin strands of hair over the bald spot on his head. And how about the losers who teach at Quincy Night School, or the bullies who end up working as cops and probation officers?"

"How about President Nixon?" Freddy put in from the corner of the room. He was looking for a track by Jeff Beck or Pink Floyd and the floor around him was littered with album covers.

"Exactly! Can't you see that there is more fear than confidence in everybody, and a whole lot more stupidity than you care to admit? Because once you recognize that everyone is ready to lose it in one way or another, the game is pretty much up. What is the point? Faith is the substance of things hoped for, because everyone needs something to believe in, and something to give them hope. But they might just as easily be waiting for a reason to pack it all in."

Grandpa hovered in the doorway, tut-tutting loudly, putting his eye to a chink in the door, spying on us. "We can see you Dad," Nora called out. "We know you're there."

Grandpa darted away at that. "Oh, oh," he said. "Doddup."

"What does he mean by *doddup*?" Angus asked.

"I think he means 'right oh,'" I volunteered. "But he's said it for so long that over the years it's turned into *doddup*."

"What?" And Angus laughed until his eyes shone with tears.

"Oh goodness," Nora said, with a new thought. "He did drive me mad this morning. I didn't make his breakfast on the dot of nine, so he was hovering around and grumbling."

"You should make him do it himself," Freddy put in.

"Yes, darling. Except that his rigid schedule is what keeps him going, I think."

The one thing Nora didn't appear to handle very well was the discovery, a few days later, that Hetty the dog had gnawed on the wooden rungs of her ladder back chairs. "Look at that!" she cried. "Why did she do that? Oh, really. I give up. My poor chairs! What am I going to do! Whatever happens kids, don't let Timothy see them!"

Angus went immediately to the hardware store after that, to pick up wood filler and two kinds of stain, and he spent the better part of a day sanding the chair rungs, filling them, painting them and making them look new. He crouched on the ground in front of the chair, a tiny paintbrush in hand, as he finished the details.

My focus was shifting to literature and writing. I practiced piano less and less. Besides, Angus played it so much better, that my lack of technique embarrassed me. He often sat improvising, usually beginning with the warm up of Beethoven's *Ecossaises in E Flat*, while in the adjoining kitchen, Nora chose clean cups from the dish rack, and shoved over a pile of books and papers to accommodate the tea tray. His ease before the instrument made me self-conscious about my own limitations. He played *Bridge Over Troubled Water, Mr. Bojangles, Rocket Man*, and sometimes he sang along, for his own enjoyment more than for any one else's, in a thin but pleasant voice, chin lifted up, and eyes closed.

Six

The weather turned muggy. I lay on the carpet stroking the cat, staring at the cat's face and marveling at his huge marbled eyes and perfectly sweet markings. I had plans for my future too. Sure I did. I was entering into my senior year of high school that September, and hoping to apply to the literature program at Boston University. I was convinced that things would become clear if I read all the books I could get my hands on, and once in college, I might also get a handle on the books I'd like to write. But oh, how painful beauty could be! How painful the thought of leaving such beauty behind!

Summer was high and the world slowed down. The shades in the living room were drawn to keep out the heat. "What is the sun?" Grandpa wanted to know. "Is it a planet? Is it inhabited?"

We took excursions to the beach in Scituate in our new Pontiac convertible, everyone sitting on laps and squeezed in together, breathing the cooler air off the salty Atlantic. The boardwalk was lined with rosehips and a steep wooden staircase led to a warm stretch of sand. The tide was low, a silver line of distant shallows. "Put on plenty of sun block," Nora instructed, from underneath her floppy hat, as though sunburn was the most hazardous challenge facing us. "Weather like this will burn you to a crisp."

Sorrel sat on her haunches with a yellow bucket and a red spade, digging in the sand. Angus stretched out and closed his eyes to sunbathe. His chest was brown, muscular and deep. He was handsome all right, but oh, so vain, I thought to myself. Lydia crouched beside him and squirted a swirl of Coppertone onto his forehead. "Whoops," as a trickle ran towards his eyes. "Sorry."

"What the hell..." wiping it off with disgust, propping himself up on the beach towel and grimacing. What, was she crazy? He was already several shades darker than she was. She would never be as brown as him at the end of a thousand summers.

"She was only trying to help," I interjected, and I felt the sting of his irritation as he took me in, red from the sun, my hair a haze of unruly corkscrews. The purple chords of my bathing suit were tied around my neck underneath my t-shirt.

"Sorry Mr. Big Stuff!" Lydia said, watching him as he proudly settled back down to sunbathe. "Good Lord!" and she ran towards the water's edge to jump in the waves with Freddy.

"Sorry," he called out.

"Love means never having to say you're sorry!" I quipped, laughing as I ran to the water's edge, feeling the sand between my toes, my hair spiraling up and tightening in the ocean breeze. And when Angus came in for a swim later, I flew away across the beach, though the sand gave way with my every step, and when I reached the bend near the private beaches and guest houses, I was pleased with the impetus that carried me away from him, at one with my heartbeat and the thud of my feet on the wooden ocean-side steps.

The hydrangea dried out. Some of the blossoms were pink and others were purple and still others faded to white. Timothy started the barbeque grill and the smell of lighter fluid mingled with the aroma of sizzling meat. Iced drinks were squeezed with lime. Sorrel played on the lawn, and Grandpa pruned the rosebush.

"Ruby!" Nora called in her soprano intonations. "Come and help me make the salad. The boys will cook the meat, and you and I can make the salad."

Ah yes. The salad of life. We would toss our refreshing salads while Timothy forked sausages onto a plate.

"No meat for me thanks, Timothy. I am becoming a vegetarian," I announced. I had recently read *Diet for a Small Planet* and was convinced that grazing cattle on fields, which could just as easily be planted with soybeans, was thoroughly wasteful and immoral. "I'll be having salad," I said. "And maybe a little cheese."

"Cheese contains animal fat, you know," Angus teased from behind his mirrored shades. "It's called rennet. All cheeses have it..."

"Not cottage cheese, or ricotta."

"Oh really! You want to make a bet?"

"Cottage cheese doesn't have any rennet, Angus. Rennet is a coagulant and it goes into other kinds of cheeses but not cottage cheese..." I declared. "And they sell this new stuff called tofu at the health food store on North Street. It's made from fermented soybeans and it's full of protein. They sell edible seaweed too. I think it looks interesting."

"Seaweed? Oh my God! You're eating *seaweed* now?" Angus threw his head back, laughing and laughing. It was a jollity well worth carrying over through the washing of dishes in the kitchen, and into a lot of raucous behavior with the dog, while the sun glinted off windows, flashing its sheen of brightness.

He went every morning for at least a week to a new job welding dumpsters for a factory in south Cohasset. "That job totally sucks. What can I say? You work all day. You put on this helmet and it's hot and loud and greasy and uncomfortable. They give you this welding torch and this helmet with a vise and you're in a metal drum. You're crouched inside it welding, and the sparks are flying and you're sweating and tired and sick. You can feel yourself getting sick right to your bones. It's burning hot, it's loud and it's dirty and it stinks. And at the end of an hour of this, you take home seven dollars." He had a burnished look in his eyes, an agitation in his movements.

The following evening he didn't come home. Nora waited up for him, dressed in her terry cloth robe, and finally when the telephone ran she lifted the receiver and listened. "Angus, where are you, darling?" Timothy and I stood waiting. "What do you mean, trespassing? Where are you now? And you say they're letting you go? Give me the address, then. Right," she said. "Timothy will come in and get you."

"What happened?"

Nora sat down and addressed Timothy, as though it was part of an ongoing deliberation. "He broke into the backstage area of Boston Garden during the Linda Ronstadt concert. They've decided not to detain him."

The air was hot and motionless, hanging over the South Shore like a woolen blanket. I went with Timothy into Boston to pick him up at the police station, and on the way home, none of us said a word.

In the morning, my parents sat with Angus in the kitchen, frowning at each other, puzzled, but determined to work it out, until Angus bowed his head, and clasped his hands before him on the table and talked about how sorry he was for his mistaken urges to do things he knew were wrong; about how his heart pounded and his nerves were shot, and how he couldn't control it. "I hate it when I'm like that. You have to believe me. But at the same time I feel driven. Like doing it will bring me release. It's almost a kind of comfort."

"You've been here before and you've pulled yourself out of it," Timothy reminded him. "Tap into that again. We all know it's possible."

But only a few weeks after this, Angus went to a party and came home with a horrible cut and second degree burns on his foot, apparently having run through a campfire and broken glass. Nora took him to the hospital for treatment. They gave him stitches. But he was high on something else and when he got home he insisted on picking the stitches out. "I have stitches in my skin!" he cried, picking at them with scissors, while we all looked on in horror. "I have stitches in my skin!"

By now his chores had fallen by the wayside, he argued constantly with Nora and insulted Lydia when she tried to help. "You don't know what you're talking about," he told her. "You know what's missing from you, Lydia? It's your mind."

Lydia burst into tears.

How dare you talk to her like that!" Nora cried.

∼

"Ruby."

The curtains of my room were drawn, yellow and green curtains, torn at the hem. The air was green and cream and yellow in my darkened bedroom, and hanging from the center of the ceiling was a candlelight fixture with a golden cherub decorating the wire. A girl's room, the room of a girl becoming a woman. Angus knelt by my head, and I felt the roughness of his fingers, stroking my hair. "I came up to tell you I love you," he said. "Can't you tell that I love you?"

I was groggy with sleep, hair mussed up on the pillow.

"Look at you," he said. "Look at you! You're like the water nymphs in that poster. There's nobody as good as you. Everyone else in the world is full of shit compared to you. Really," he said. "It's true."

"It is not." But he bent to kiss my lips. His mouth was soft and warm and I parted my lips, enjoying the danger of having him there in my room, crouching beside my bed. His breath was slightly boozy and I folded my arms round his neck. "Angus, you shouldn't be up here, though. What if Nora finds out? Or Henry. I can't cheat on my boyfriend."

"Henry doesn't have to know about this."

"But I know. Don't you see?" Then I kissed him again, quite unable to resist it. He pulled back, and we gazed at each other in the sweet intimacy of the darkened room. I looked into his eyes, noticing their glassy appearance, as he stroked the hair away from my forehead, smiling. "Anyway, you're high," I said. "Why do you get high all the time? And even though I like you... of course! I love you..." curling my arms around his neck. "You are very sweet," pulling him closer, for another gentle and sleepy kiss. "It's nice of you to tell me this. It's very very nice..." And I raised my hips towards him, underneath the girlish bedclothes, inviting him.

"Oh, man. You're right. I have to go. Jesus. I have this wicked erection." And while I was laughing he bent to kiss my forehead.

"Goodbye then," I said.

Before he closed the door behind him he turned around. "You're right, Ruby. I don't deserve you. But I will deserve you one day. You'll see."

A rolled up carpet stood in the hallway as my parents cleared out his room. Timothy was installing a new lock on the door, bent over the chore in his shirtsleeves, looking concerned, while Nora loaded magazines and papers into boxes. I thought at first that it had to do with the carpet and that Nora had wanted it moved, and that Angus hadn't done it. Then I was afraid it had to do with something else: Angus coming up to my room. "Has he done something, Timothy? What's wrong? What has he done this time?"

"We've asked him to leave," my father explained. "We can't keep cushioning him, honey. He has to learn. That's the way with some, unfortunately. They have to learn the hard way."

Nora in her flower power skirt, tight lipped with fury, turned on her heels and stalked off to the bathroom. "Nora?" The toilet flushed. Then it flushed again. "What's going on?"

She was dropping small brown bricks into the toilet and flushing them down. "Hashish, Ruby," said my mother, in a voice laced with rage. There were several plastic bags of it, on the floor beside her. She flushed the toilet. "He was selling the stuff right under our noses. We gave him a chance," she said. Flush. "When I think of how we've trusted that boy. How we vouched for him to the Aleshires and that dreadful probation officer." Flush. "How we stepped up to helped him when he needed us. And this is what he did with our trust." Flush.

Seven

Timothy conducted monthly services at Bridgewater State Hospital, a correctional facility for the criminally insane. One Sunday afternoon, finding himself in need of a pianist at the last minute, he asked me to come along. It was a sprawling complex of institutional brick, not unlike the local high school, except that it was surrounded by barbed wire fence and topped with loops of razor wire. We pulled into the visitor's parking lot, and together walked up the path, through the front entrance, to the lobby.

The reception area did not resemble high school. The ceilings were lower and the corridors leading off behind steel doors were more constricted and menacing.

A guard ushered us past the security checkpoints and through the metal detectors. Then we crossed a courtyard, entered a second building, and found ourselves in an auditorium set up with rows of metal chairs. An upright piano stood against one wall, along with a small podium large enough for Timothy's Bible.

We distributed hymnals on all the metal chairs then I went to the piano and opened mine onto the stand and tried out the first few notes. The piano had a loose action and tinny sound.

Timothy paced, checked his watch and cleared his throat. "All right?"

At last a guard opened up the doors at the far end of the room and ten or fifteen ordinary looking men filed in. A small man with his head shaved bald, closed his eyes peacefully, while another grinned, mouth upturned, two long lines creasing his cheeks. One guy with small ears and a hooked nose had a kind of complacent overlay to his expression. All expectation appeared to have been muffled beneath a veneer of good behavior. But after all, there wasn't much room for individual expression in this place, and they were all dressed in identical jumpsuits. I sat at the piano as the men filled several rows.

After a few moments, Timothy caught my eye and nodded. I turned towards the piano, and breathed. Timothy cleared his throat again. "Good afternoon! It's a privilege to be here with all of you today." A murmured response rippled through the room. "Let's begin our service by singing Hymn number 410." He read the first verse. *Praise My Soul the King of Heaven*, and then I played the opening refrain on the tinny piano, and the inmates shuffled to their feet.

They sang like everybody else in a church service, except of course there were no female voices. My heart pounded and while I played, my mind caught hold of several floating strands of thought: Get through this Ruby, without mistakes; don't think about the crimes these men have committed. They must be disturbing crimes like rape, perhaps, or murder. But don't think of those. These men are criminally insane. That means they can't be held accountable. But then, why do they look so ordinary?

The sermon began with a reading from Luke.

And he said, A certain man had two sons:

And the younger of them said to his father, Father, give me the portion of goods that falleth to me. And he divided unto them his living.

And not many days after the younger son gathered all together, and took his journey into a far country, and there wasted his substance with riotous living.

The parable of the prodigal son had always been my favorite, its message inseparable from the poetic rhythm of the King James translation. What economy in the phrase "Wasting his substance with riotous living." No further description was needed than that. And afterwards, the turn to full forgiveness, in a father's warm embrace sounded beautiful and oh, so simple.

Bring forth the best robe, and put it on him; and put a ring on his hand, and shoes on his feet:

And bring hither the fatted calf, and kill it: and let us eat, and be merry:

For this my son was dead, and is alive again; he was lost and is found.

Except the story of the older brother, which Timothy went on to read, troubled me deeply. He labored in the fields while the younger son was gone. And when the younger son returned, he got the short end of the stick because he lacked intensity and passion. He was a drudge, and even a good drudge who believed in God, wasn't good enough. He missed the party. No one thanked him for his pains. He shouldn't have tried so hard because it got him nowhere. I didn't want to be like the older brother.

We heard from the Aleshires that Angus had moved out to Aspen, Colorado. He was heavy into bicycle racing, and loving the mountain climate. His old room on the first floor of our house still had a whiff of his presence about it, even without him there. But Timothy repainted it, as a woman from the church, who had recently ended an abusive marriage, needed a place to stay for two or three months, while she got herself back on her feet.

Eight

That which hath been is now and that which is to be hath already been.

And God requireth that which is past.

Timothy lined up the salt, pepper and ketchup bottles on the kitchen table for me, to represent past, present and future, a few days before I headed off to France. "This verse from Ecclesiastes is one of my favorites," he said. "And what this all means you see, honey, is that there is nothing but the present! The past, that which hath been is now, you see? And the future has already been..." moving the ketchup to where the pepper shaker had just been, "but that which has already been is now. You see? There is only one thing and that is the infinite now! Just make sure your present is God-filled," he finished.

But did God require our past from us or did He require us to have a so-called past? I didn't get it. I only knew that the past was all around us. As indeed was the future. But in 1976, heading off to France, my concept of that future was wide-awake and open. Angus was simply a poignant shadow, a kind of wistful question mark, part of our family history.

Freddy's band had taken off and he was playing every week in gigs across New England. Lydia had gone to secretarial school, and fallen in love at least a hundred times. Sorrel started kindergarten and had a giraffe patterned backpack in which she kept her plastic ponies. And I was halfway through college, twenty-one and living in Paris by the time I got a letter from the Arizona State Penitentiary written on yellow notebook paper in a familiar half printed script.

April 8, 1976

Dear Ruby,

This morning I heard the Cat Stevens song with your name in it, and thought of your smile and your sense of humor and you sitting on the sun porch embroidering flowers on the pockets of your jeans. The fact is, I still remember you and your family a lot. You guys gave me a chance to get back on track, and I screwed up that chance. Nora used to tell me that potential was another word for hope. At the time I didn't understand, but now I think I do.

I might like to add an idea of my own. Potential is also the power of 'yet'. Don't give up on me, Ruby. I still have a future and I believe there is a 'yet' out there. Now more than ever.

I've been here five months. I live in a small cell and spend a lot of time playing chess. I miss playing the piano, but I do a lot of reading. It's not that I think I'm unintelligent or uneducated by larger standards but now I have nothing but time to learn and read so much more. I just finished The Red and the Black. Have you read that book? I remember how you loved to read.

There's also a gym where I'm allowed to work out with weights, run round the track and sometimes shoot a few hoops. I'm in good shape. I was heavy into bike racing before being arrested and plan to get back into that one day. I love Arizona. The desert climate suits me better than New England.

But all this is small talk. It is as though I think that through endless painstaking printing I can escape myself and the situation I've put myself in. Sometimes when I think of you I feel like I put off resolution because I couldn't finish it. I didn't believe enough in my ability to change. There seemed no point unless I could do it correctly, and back then I didn't think I could. Can't you remember? You and I sitting there in the sun porch talking about the latest band, the latest book, while our eyes were saying so much more. You know it's the truth.

So this isn't such painstaking printing after all. You may think that knowing you didn't make a difference to me. But it did. Right now is that critical age when people grow and learn about themselves. I feel like I'm in a clear crystal ball watching the world, and it almost seems like I could predict the future. I know one thing for sure. When I get out of here, I'll make some very different choices. I understand if you feel skeptical about that so, write back only if you feel inclined. I will reply.

Love. Angus.

I was staying with a friend of a friend of a friend at a studio in Montmartre. The first night I slept in a little book-lined loft. My host, an angular pale-faced photographer named Gilles, spoke in a French so quick and charming, that I could answer nothing but *oui*. He asked if I would pose for him and I happily complied. A couple of rolls of black and white film later, I ended up in bed with him, and woke up in heaven, as it were, to take my coffee on the little walled terrace. A cat trod lightly across the mossy wall, while Gilles sat at his desk sorting through slides. I was filled to the brim with the eternal now. So what was this meddlesome piece of the past doing, trying to shove things over and take a place in my story?

I wore my lemon kimono until noon, and then got dressed and walked to the park where the flowerbeds were patterned in plump red zinnias. Accordion music tumbled to the streets from one of the cafés, like something from a dream.

Oh, European dream! A blue sky washed you with white streaks of cloud. A girl rode past on a scooter, with a fresh baguette under one arm. A man stood next to his chair in the park and stretched his leg in midair, grasping his foot with one hand. European dream, you were the perfect backdrop to a fresh young life, a backdrop that even in spring was tinged with gentle melancholy.

France was a mood I yielded to and doing so lent depth and dimension to every feeling I had about myself. Until reading Angus's letter, that is. Suddenly with his letter, new selves seemed like inventions, safe haven cover-ups for deeper felt desires.

After all, there was no particular man in this European dream of mine. There had been the usual heartbreaks and sexual exploits, the twists and turns through the maze of young love, taking me to and then away from what I thought I wanted. But Angus was my real and wide-awake life. I had a choice of boys. But he was the boy I always had my eye on.

Dear Angus,

Lydia forwarded your letter because I'm not in Massachusetts, but in Paris. How did we get here? How did it happen? What are you in there for? What you say about using your time to read fills me with tenderness for you. Perhaps you will have your whole life to travel and see things, but while we are young our minds are really flexible and filled with an unidentified hunger, it seems good to be reading and learning things from books.

I have been so sheltered until now. That is why I took these few months off for the chance to speak French and to write some of my own things, and explore the world beyond Boston. Last night there was a party as my friend Gilles had an opening at a photography studio. This morning I'm taking my coffee and croissant in a café round the corner from where I live. There's a big wooden table in the sun, the smell of fresh bread and croissants and with thoughts of you, I feel more strongly than ever the desire to live a productive and beautiful life. You have so much potential, and I feel so interested to see what the world will make of you and me. I miss the piano too, and haven't played for ages. But perhaps when I return to Massachusetts, I'll take that up again.

I won't give up on you. None of our family ever has. True, when Nora found all that hash, she was very hurt and disappointed. I thought it had to do with you coming to my room, and I think she may have suspected something. But that's the thing about you, Angus. You make people suspicious, even when there is no cause for suspicion. I would love to hear from you again. You could write to me here, although I'll be returning to Massachusetts in a month. Lydia is still living at home, working as a receptionist in Boston and intending to travel next year. Freddy's band is doing really well, and has quite a following in the Boston area. I'm sure he will write to you about it. Sorrel has started kindergarten and loves to dance. Grandpa is still alive...

Can I make a few recommendations from my French literature shelf? If you're looking for long and luxuriant, read Marcel Proust. You will adore Swann's Way. But if you favor short and satisfying, read Return of the Prodigal Son by Andre Gide. In his version, the prodigal tells his brother that he left home because he imagined other cultures, other lands, imagined himself like a new being rushing along them. Does that sound like you, Angus?

Yours from another culture, and another land,

Ruby

In June I returned to Boston. The family waited at the airport like a snapshot. Lydia had got wind that she was sexy, and taken measures to push things along with makeup and clothes for greater effect. Nora seemed eccentric and bossy craning her neck at the flow of arriving passengers. Timothy appeared distracted and tweed jacketed and Freddy had a kind of vagabond quality about him, with a pair of suspenders holding up his jeans. I saw them like a family I didn't know. Until Sorrel, who had suddenly stretched out, burst through the crowd to embrace me, "There she is!" and I was no longer someone who had dropped into Logan Airport by accident, from a sophisticated and surprising world. I was still just Ruby.

Grandpa, with his ancient old man's head, waited back at the house in his cardigan with wooden buttons. He met us as the car pulled in. Everyone got out, helping with suitcases, chatting at once. Hetty the dog wound around my legs wagging violently.

"Oh Hetty! Look at you! The hair round her muzzle has all gone white!"

Grandpa pecked at the side of my cheek. "Oh oh oh," he said. "How are you dear," as though I had only been gone for a week, instead of an everlasting spring, where I had moved from girl to worldly young woman.

Massachusetts was relentless in its pursuit of clarity and happiness, stridently full of itself. After Paris, the town of Hingham looked more American than ever, bedecked in the red white and blue for the 1976 Bicentennial celebration. I walked the rooms of the family house, just to make sure that all of it was there: the nutmeg aroma and the tatty wing chairs in the living room, the sun porch where we had our meals at the long country table, the sofa with its faded checkered cover, and the kitchen with blue and white tiles and blond wood floors, the egg cups and the toast racks, the mess of the kitchen with Sorrel's hair ribbons and Lydia's blown glass baubles hanging on hooks around the welsh cupboard; and Nora's bag stuffed full of scripts and teaching supplies.

Grandpa sat under the pergola in his wicker chair, asleep with a library book on his lap. Timothy mowed the lawn, still wearing his jacket and tie. Nora made a shepherd's pie and we ate the meal on the sun porch off the mismatched family china of botanical prints and polka dots. Plates were passed and everyone talked and argued.

Nora was deep in play rehearsals for the end of school production of *The Heiress*. "Oh they are so bad. All of the principals are bad," she said, scooping salad onto Sorrel's plate. "How I wish someone like Ari had auditioned for this show."

"I'm sure it's not as dreadful as you make it sound."

"But it is, Tim. And you know, Ruby, I was actually laughing at stupid things because I have really given up. I gave notes to the father, which he didn't or couldn't execute; the other three stumbled and paraphrased their way through. The Morris falling over his words..."

"They must be quite intimidated by you."

"If anything I'm not stern enough," Nora went on. "And one of the reasons I don't get stern for too long is that I'm anxious not to make them tense and nervous because I think that actually makes them worse. Lydia, put some shepherd's pie onto Grandpa's plate, would you darling?"

"The play will be fine," Timothy said.

"But I don't want to go anywhere near that show anymore," Nora went on. "It will be a complete disaster. Oh, it's a very far cry from when I had students like Ari. And Ari, by the way, has been so looking forward to your return, Ruby."

"What is it?" Grandpa asked, with his nose up close to the plate.

"Shepherd's pie, Grandpa," Lydia said.

"What?"

"Shepherd's pie!" we chorused.

"All right, all right," he said. "No need to shout. Oh oh oh."

"I meant to ask," I ventured at last. "Did anyone ever hear back from Angus again?"

"Oh," said Lydia. "He sent me a letter. And also one to Freddy. They came after the one he sent to you."

Timothy looked troubled. "He's in prison you know, honey."

"Yes, Timothy, I heard. What were the charges, Lydia?"

"Stole a piano from a country club," Freddy put in from his end of the table. His eyes had a red-rimmed glaze to them, and when I glared at him questioningly he broke into a grin and had to look away.

"Oh, I'm sure that wasn't all," said Nora.

"No," said Lydia. "Probably not."

"The trouble with Angus," Nora put in with authority, "was that he knew so much that he thought he knew everything."

"Good riddance," Grandpa growled, in between slurps of mashed potato.

The rest of us exchanged glances. "He hears a lot more than he pretends to," Nora murmured under her breath. Then Timothy cleared his throat, and with that the conversation swept off like a flock of birds, into a different direction.

Nine

That September I moved to a Boston brownstone with a formal entrance and wide carpeted staircase a few blocks from Boston University. My room was on the second floor, half the elegant back parlor of a nineteenth century house. At the far end, a window looked onto trees, garages and an alley. The bathroom, which I shared with the occupant of the other half of the parlor, was a cubicle jutting into my living space, with enough room on top for a loft bed and narrow bookcase.

Life became classes, the library and coffee shop. I was beginning to outgrow all the student parties, shouting over pounding music, too much beer and pot smoke, with everyone leaning together on crowded balconies. So I took Nora's suggestion and looked up Ari Braun, who was studying voice at the Longy School and had recently realized he was gay. He carried *The Complete Works of Shakespeare* everywhere he went. We sat on the banks of the Charles together, while Ari read sonnets and told me how much artists suffer.

"Oh artists suffer terribly," he said. "Because no one understands them."

"Surely that's an oversimplification," I said, irritated, in spite of myself, by his sincerity.

"Oh no," said Ari. "It's a special torment to feel things deeply." He closed his Shakespeare volume and stared across the river, while an obliging breeze ruffled his hair. Ripples loosened across the water, spreading out and dissipating.

"I don't think it's the norm," I said. "It's not the norm for artists to suffer terribly. That's only a cliché to satisfy failed artists. Successful artists are understood and appreciated by their public. How else do they sell their work? There are lots of people who suffer more than artists."

"Like who?" Ari challenged.

"How about the criminally insane," I suggested, pleased to have that reference up my sleeve.

Ari had wanted a more poetic conversation. "I've never heard you use that word before," he said. "*Norm*. I don't know what it means. Can you explain, because it's ugly."

"I mean it isn't typical. Now the criminally insane are really beaten down by life," I continued with authority. "My father took me once to a jail when he needed someone to play the piano. And I learned that those who can't control their minds suffer more than artists."

I hadn't learned anything of the sort, of course. All of it was posture. But I was impatient with Ari as well as with myself. I wanted to be an artist too. The only trouble was, I hadn't suffered very much. So I thought being an artist might be more like trying to paint a rainbow, difficult when you didn't have a complete set of paints.

What did I expect out of life back then? I didn't know precisely. I was twenty-one, artistically inclined but not sufficiently drawn to any particular discipline to commit myself wholeheartedly. Most of all, I wanted meaning. I wanted something authentic, something greater than myself to call me forth and mold me to its purpose.

I discovered the practice rooms at the top of the student union. You could use a piano there for as long as you liked. So I dug out my Schumann and Fauré, and the second movement of Beethoven's Pathetique, and I climbed the stairs.

Sometimes with Ari and sometimes alone I took the T to Harvard Square and wandered round the Fogg Museum, or browsed through Tango's bookstore, looking at chapbooks and rare poetry editions. Oliver Gordon, who ran Tango's, looked to be about sixty with rumpled clothes and a salt and pepper moustache. One afternoon I saw him pasting a notice into the front window. "Help Wanted. Inquire Within."

The job involved cataloguing titles, making coffee, and typing correspondence on a small portable typewriter. Oliver asked about my interest in literature and listened to my answers, adjusting his smudged glasses, which were held together with a paperclip. He pushed back his mop of salt and pepper hair in one continuous gesture. Tango, the bookshop namesake, he told me, had been a gentle giant of a cat with an enormous Hemingway skull.

"I'm more of a dog person myself," I said.

Oliver chuckled. "Hmm. A dog person. So, you call yourself a dog person, eh? Well, we don't have any particular fondness for dogs in here."

I went in twice a week. I helped him sort his clutter, and typed up correspondence as he handled various papers, penciling notes to himself and organizing his books. There was a small brick terrace in back, where I sometimes sat on my breaks, to look at the sky and imagine this place as a secret garden, without the trashcans and stash of rusty pots.

Oliver had met everyone. The Black Mountain poets, and the Language poets and the Confessional poets and he loved to recount anecdotes about parties and readings, and the revelries of bygone years, as I cleared away the cups with cold coffee dregs resting in their bottoms, all of it scattered about the place. I made room on the sofa, which had been so buried in books there was nowhere to sit down even if you wanted to.

Sudden gusts of activity brought drifters to the shop as well as regulars, a girl with a spider web tattoo on her arm and broken shoes, dusty academics, young writers in dreadlocks and second hand clothes, as well as the famous and acclaimed -Tim O'Brien, Denise Levitov, Bill Knott and Jack Gantos.

One woman, (I thought of her as the *weird sister*), always came in to ask about Russian translations. She had plucked her eyebrows into absurdly thin arches and powdered her face so that she looked like a doll with dyed hair and capped teeth. "Lillian Silverman," Oliver said. "In her day she was a brilliant scholar. And a well-known beauty." There was also Adrian Skinner, a gangly poet who came in for long conversations and to check up on his chapbook sales. Adrian reminded me of those Victorian illustrations of the North Wind. He sat on Oliver's sofa, legs spread before him, lighting up cigarette after cigarette and nodding his head very quickly, sucking in breaths of smoke and air.

There was also a boy. His name was James Gillespie, and he was a young poet who regarded Oliver as his mentor. He had a fine boned, evenly proportioned face, and wore his hair unfashionably short. He was quiet and spoke with a kind of cured stammer, pulling out of his words to let his sentences hang there, like a jacket caught on a peg, without resolution. Beckett's *Malloy* is. Oh. It's an interesting book.

Harvard Square was active with students and shoppers. The air had a light Indian summer quality, the smell of newsprint and fresh autumn leaves. After class, I caught the crowded subway there, and when I came up the steps and saw Oliver making his way with a carrier bag of books, the sight filled me with joy, and I gladly took a detour round the Yard.

He kept peanuts in his raincoat pocket, which he fed to the squirrels as we walked the paths. A squirrel gamboled towards him. He tossed a peanut across the path, and straightened himself, giving me a cockeyed smile. A squirrel took up the peanut and scampered away. Oliver's transactions with squirrels, as with everyone else, were simple transactions, without any show of sentiment.

One Friday, after work I managed to get to the depot on Arlington Street just before my bus left for the South Shore. I clambered on board as it pulled from the curb. "Ruby – over here!"

The bus lurched and I turned around to see James Gillespie. He was sitting by himself. "Hey!" I said. "What a surprise." The bus smelled like exhaust fumes and old cigarettes. It began to move as I slid in beside him. "Are you going to Hingham?"

He nodded. Then, "Actually Cohasset. I'm living at home with my parents temporarily."

"Really? Because my parents live in Hingham."

"Look." He handed me a couple of books: Bukowski and Burroughs, as the bus made its way to the highway on-ramp.

I glanced through them with brief interest. Then, "So how long have you known Oliver?" I asked.

"Oh, we met at a reading a couple years back. He used to have a small press and I submitted some work. I hope he revives that press. In fact maybe you can encourage him."

"He hasn't said anything about it to me," I said. "Or maybe he has, but I didn't realize the press was his."

"Anyway, I've been away for several months. I just returned, in fact. From Nepal."

"Really?" Silence. "And what were you doing there?"

"Climbing..."

"Up Everest?"

"Also hiking. Oh." He closed his mouth, then opened it again. "It's beautiful. The glaciers," he said. He mentioned swimming in an icy river, and chuckled with a new thought, making a funny clicking sound at the back of his throat. "At night I lay in a tent near the fire, watching rats. They ran round a ledge like lights."

We fell silent as two businessmen behind us discussed a new presidential candidate called Jimmy Carter. Jimmy, I thought, for a president? He wouldn't stand a chance, with a childish nickname like Jimmy! "He's too non-committal..." I heard one man say.

James spoke again. "And what about you?"

"Oh, I traveled a bit in France last year and now I'm in my final year at B.U., studying literature. Right now I'm writing a paper on the Metaphysical poets. Andrew Marvell, as it happens. I love how he tries to reconcile body and soul ~ "

"Had we but world enough and time..."

"Well, sure. There's that. I guess I'm more drawn to his other poems. "Nymph Complaining for the Death of Her Faun". On the face of it, she's mourning a pet faun, but I believe she's really mourning lost innocence. I also love his ones about the mower."

"I don't know those."

"This mower is cutting the grass, you see, and then he accidentally cuts himself with the scythe. So at first he's the mower and then he's the mown. *And there among the grass fell down, by his own scythe the mower mown.* I'm researching that," I said.

The bus approached Hingham Center so I gathered my books and coat. Then James stood up too. "Would you like to go for a walk?" he asked.

Hingham Common was mute and picturesque, its well-appointed houses soundless, decked in patriotic bunting. I held my coat over one arm, feeling the miscalculation of having brought it. The warm suburban air carried the smell of sun and rotted grass clippings. Summer was doing a very fine job of hanging into autumn.

We walked past the high school, talking intermittently until we reached a small covered bridge by a wall, where we stopped to look across an open field. Beyond it was a path to Triphammer Pond. I breathed in the air, full of sweet smelling hay.

The sky turned pink. The sun came down, and a line of trees along the hedgerow in the distance, showed against the sky like ink painted, fine-drawn lines. Together we crossed the grass to the middle of the field. The air was warm. So we sat and then lay down side by side, looking at the sky.

"What clouds!" They were rose-tinged, as the sky behind them darkened. I sensed James's body lying close to mine, the woody scent of his jacket. But there was a kind of force field between us, stopping me from reaching out. "I liked the sound of your research," he said.

"Oh, I have a long way to go with it, though." Our silences were separated by the width of an untaken kiss. The larger part of my consciousness was cautious of his shyness and I was afraid to miscalculate. Our arms barely touched, but I heard his breath catch slightly, as we gazed at the faraway sky.

Lights burned in the windows of the house, as we came up my family driveway. We stood on the doorstep and something ruffled behind the living room curtains.

"That will be my grandfather. He can be rather odd," I said.

"What do you mean?"

"He throws his teabags out of the bedroom window, just for a joke," I said. "And he thinks that the sun is a planet. He asked my father if the sun was inhabited. That kind of thing."

We faced each other on the doorstep. James laughed, making that funny clicking sound at the back of his throat. "I'm going to write that down," he said.

I rocked back and forth on my heels. My glances kept returning to the curtains, then before I could kiss him goodbye, he made a funny 'tock tock' sound with his tongue on the roof of his mouth. So I turned away and went inside. My face felt hot – but I hoped they'd attribute that to the walk. I piled my coat on my lap, and watched Freddy pouring batter on the griddle.

"Timothy and Sorrel have gone with Nora to her play rehearsal," Freddy said, as he worked his spatula. "And I'm making pancakes. You want some, Rube?"

Grandpa lurked, putting his eye to the crack in the door, his shadow moving away. "Hi Grandpa!" I called out.

"Who is it?"

"Only us," I said.

The wispy sound of slippers shuffled across the hardwood floor. "Where's Mum? Where've they gone? Who was at the door? When are they coming back?"

"Gone to rehearsal," Freddy annunciated.

"What?"

"Rehearsal," he said in a louder voice.

"Oh dear. Doddup. Off in their world of make believe," said Grandpa. "Oh oh oh. When's supper."

"We're making supper now."

"All right. You needn't shout." A check of his wristwatch. "Dear oh dear. Doddup. Oh oh oh..." in a sing song at the end, as he wandered back to the living room.

James didn't come to the bookshop the following week, though I waited for him to appear each day. It wasn't until I'd almost written him off that he suddenly showed up between the stacks, wearing a black wool coat with a scarlet belt. I waved self-consciously through the door of Oliver's office and Oliver, perceiving my hesitation, looked at me from beneath his bushy eyebrows. "Go out and see if you can help him."

"Where did you get this wonderful coat?" I asked, when I was standing beside him.

"I brought it back from Nepal."

I turned his wrist, his skin was cool, to read the titles of the books he was holding – Alain Robbe-Grillet and Walter Benjamin. "A little light reading, eh?"

"Would you like to go out for lunch, Ruby? Because I know of an interesting place."

A frosted diffusion of sunlight lay across the bricks of Brattle Street signaling that autumn had finally arrived. We walked beyond the crowd of bareheaded students carrying book bags, and shoppers hurrying past in gloves and hats. "So," I said. "You haven't been round in a while."

"I was out on the water. There's a lobster fisherman I sometimes do a bit of work for." We passed the shop windows I usually liked, with tiny crystal sherry glasses, Russian shawls and Japanese netsukes.

"So you're a fisherman?"

"Uh, not really." We'd reached the really boring part of the street up near the post office when James stopped in front of a door. "Wow. Look at this." He was staring at a wooden front door, which had been repainted many times, without being sanded. His hands were in his pockets, as he gazed at the door with admiration, at the chipped and stippled paint, map-like and overlaid with thick black lacquer, an old tarnished knocker in the center.

We seemed to have walked too far. We crossed a highway bridge with traffic barreling beneath us. The trendy cafés had thinned out entirely and the shops on this side of the bridge had a desperate, abandoned look, more about repairing things than selling them.

"So where is this interesting place of yours?" My feet were beginning to hurt, but at last he led me into a pub, empty inside, except for a bartender filling up the paper napkin dispensers. The bartender looked up.

"What do you have in the way of lunch?" I asked.

"Sorry. We don't serve food until six," the bartender threw out in our general direction.

"You mean we walked all this way and they don't serve food?"

"How about a pint?" James suggested. And when I saw how lost he looked, I wanted to protect him from his own social ineptitude.

"But I have to go back to work, remember?" I said.

Then the bartender, irritated for his own reasons, tossed me a bag of potato chips, and began to slap together a roll with a bit of cheese inside, as if we were a nuisance, we paying customers, a bit of an interruption to the stocking up of his napkin dispensers.

We shouldn't have walked so far. My feet were killing me. I sat at a table and watched him order a pint for himself and a Coke for me. Then he carried my cheese roll to the table, and sat down beside me, and a wave of tenderness washed over me. So this was his interesting place. If only he wasn't so full of blank spaces I couldn't seem to fill, of conversations, which died on the vine as though he was swallowing thoughts. It was as though somewhere deep inside us both there might be taking place a conversation we would not or could not have.

We finished our drinks. I got through the sandwich. We ate the chips between us. But any hope of deeper familiarity eluded us since he kept avoiding my eyes. It was a long way back to the bookshop, and if I hadn't babbled on about my classes and Oliver Gordon's cats, the silence would surely have eaten us both alive.

Ten

Days grew colder. Weekdays of drizzle, college classes and bookshop afternoons grew into Hingham weekends, with chrysanthemums in pots and pumpkins on the porch. Ari had fallen in love with a clarinet player and wasn't available to me as often as before. On Friday evenings I sometimes took the bus to Hingham and chatted with James on the bus. "There's a reading you might be interested in," he told me. "At the Widener Library. Seamus Heaney."

"Shall we go together?"

"I mean," he stammered. "We could meet there."

I stood up. "Sounds good. Well, my stop, so bye for now," and I headed down the aisle, got off the bus and walked back home.

It was six p.m. on Halloween night. Freddy under the kitchen lights ironed his shirt for a gig out in Fitchburg. Lydia had been invited to a party and was planning her costume as Pebbles Flintstone, complete with a plastic dog bone in her hair. Timothy was on the telephone ordering pizzas. "Two, Nora? Extra cheese and pepperoni?"

"Lovely, darling," Nora said, dashing off with a bag full of chocolate to dole out to a small cluster of shy ghouls and skeletons who had congregated in the doorway.

"Trick or treat!"

"Don't you all look wonderful!" she cried, dropping chocolates into everybody's open bag.

"When are we going trick or treating?" Sorrel, dressed as a clown, with white face, and black triangles painted over her eyes, sat on the floor of the kitchen looking cross and rolling up the legs of a pair of Freddy's trousers. "This is never going to work!"

Nora buttoned her coat. She was going along with Sorrel to stand at the bottom of every path and keep a watchful eye. "If you find yourself running out of Mars bars," she instructed, "there are raisins and granola bars in that cupboard."

Grandpa stood at the window humming and grumbling under his breath and waiting for the pizzas to arrive. Lydia went upstairs to have a bubble bath and dress for her party. The doorbell rang. A couple of teenagers stood on the doorstep, glum behind their monster masks. A princess arrived with a tiny witch and a little boy dressed as a super hero.

"Doorbell!" Grandpa called as it rang out again. "Oh oh oh. Doddup."

There was a sudden split in the energy. I went to answer the door. Hetty the dog was wagging and barking raucously. There stood a small assembly of characters. A ghost, a witch, a vampire. A robot dressed in grey. And at the back was another figure. He was tall, broad-shouldered and handsome. His hair was dark and well cut. He was dressed in a blue wool coat. He was radiant with smiles and he filled the door with his presence. "Angus!" I cried. "Angus, my God!"

Eleven

What epic rejoicings accompanied that reunion! Four years away had mellowed and deepened Angus. He appeared to have grown more fully into himself. Now he exuded a refinement and restraint that suggested some hard experiences had knocked the arrogance out of his sails. He'd been living out in Arizona since his prison release, racing bikes and working on them. Then one day, he told us, he'd simply had enough. So he got in his Mustang convertible, and drove straight back to Massachusetts.

When Nora returned and found Angus there, she threw up her arms and held him close, with tears in her eyes, as though she were greeting a long lost son. Sorrel counted out her Halloween candy on the living room carpet, as we sat together talking. The place came alive with laughter and chatter. A sweet expectation sparkled between us. But there was no mistaking his awareness of me, nor my rekindled interest in him, and over the next several days, even when he had court appearances, to overturn his broken probation, and when I had research and writing to do, a still small current flowed between Angus and me, stopping my focus on anything but the joy of having him home.

I finished my paper about the metaphysical poets and began reading Ralph Ellison's *Invisible Man*, for my Afro American Literature class. That's when Angus came in with Freddy from an excursion to the guitar shop in Quincy.

"Let's see," he said, taking the book from my hands. I had got to a passage about an old food vender, cooking yams on a street corner. Angus took it up slowly and smoothly, falling in with the mood of the selection. He was putting it on for amusement's sake, pronouncing the word 'yam' as though it was succulent. He read about the smell of the yams, and how it transported Ellison back to his childhood days, and as Angus read the passage, a smile played out at the edge of his lips. He put on the voice of the yam-vender. I watched the drop of his eyelids, the thick dark row of eyelashes, and knew I was falling in love.

∼

Oliver scheduled a poetry reading at the bookshop that week and I was enlisted to help set it up. I also had to work on my Ralph Ellison paper and Angus was busy meeting with lawyers, and making amends with the Aleshire family.

Tango's was packed with poets and book dealers, students and would be writers, all assembled to hear a famous poet from New York. Everyone was there, including James Gillespie. I saw him at once; or perhaps it was more that I sensed him, straight across the room from me, distant and inaccessible, resting his chin in his hands.

The poet who read that night was dressed in an old leather jacket and alligator boots with a hole in the toe. He linked his syllables, and between the words that formed, he left the impression that if you understood, you understood it wrong. His poems led the listeners to a back alley of consciousness where the landscape was disconcerting and possibly even hostile. Simple words had so much power to alienate, I realized. As did empty silences. Yet there was Adrian Skinner, the big gangly fellow I was so fond of, frowning slightly as he listened, twisting his mouth, drawing on cigarettes, nodding as he took in the poetry, or else shaking his head.

And all this was backdrop. Everything was backdrop now to Angus Aleshire's return, what was happening between us, and what we might do in the future. I barely heard a word the poet spoke. Even afterwards when there was milling around to be had, with plastic cups of wine, I couldn't be bothered to focus. I had helped Oliver set everything up before hand, had a stake in the evening's success. But now it didn't matter. Oliver nodded quietly, pinched his nose and smoothed his moustache. "Well?" watching me from under his eyebrows and adjusting his glasses. "What did you think?"

"Not much," I said.

Oliver waited for more. Then, "'Sometimes the magic works and sometimes it doesn't.' Gordon," he said. I looked up to see James heading towards us. "Ah!" cried Oliver, full of goodwill for young poets who might be ready to fall in love. "Here he is."

"Hey!" as I pecked his cheek.

"What did you think of the reading?" James asked.

"Didn't understand a word of it. You?"

"I thought it was very evocative," he replied.

Adrian Skinner hovered nearby, digging in his pocket for cigarettes, knocking the packet against his palm. "He's setting something in motion and you as the listener are supposed to complete it," he explained.

"Well, I must not like the way I'm completing it, then." I turned to sip some wine from my plastic cup. Across the room the poet sat at a table, signing copies of his book for a small group of doting students. "I don't think that poet is entirely on the up and up," I said.

James chuckled. "The stuff your grandfather comes up with is better."

"If I was born before Christ," I said, putting on my grandfather's voice. "It wasn't B.C. So when was I born. When was I born, eh? 'They used a different calendar, Grandpa.' I know I know. But when was I born. It wasn't B.C. So when was I born?"

James laughed. "Tell Adrian about the teabags."

So I told the story of how Nora had found a pile of moldy teabags under Grandpa's bedroom window, and how he said he had thrown them out there "just for a joke." Adrian didn't find it as funny as James did. Perhaps losing your mind was less terrifying to James than I was, or poetry I didn't understand.

"You didn't come to the other reading," James said later, as we rode back out to the South Shore, on the Plymouth and Brockton bus. I wanted to be back in Hingham rather than in my room on Beacon Street, because that's where Angus would be.

"Other reading...?"

"Seamus Heaney at the Widener."

"Oh, no! I completely forgot." He faced the window. I couldn't see his expression. It was dark outside and the bus smelled particularly stale. "I'm sorry," I said, "I guess I've been distracted."

He didn't reply.

"It's because an old friend has come back to town. His name is Angus Aleshire. He lived with us for about a year when I was in high school."

"Ah huh."

"But he got involved in the wrong kinds of things. He's very intelligent. He moved out west and ended up doing time in Arizona. He evidently stole a piano from a country club, which I agree is a bit of a strange sort of crime..."

James cleared his throat. "So he's not a serious...." Silence.

"Criminal?" I offered. "No. I believe he was bored. Wasn't stimulated by the right things. Although to be honest, they got him on other charges too – drug possession." And here I sighed. This new piece of information was rather inconvenient. "Anyway, it's a long story. He also has a few unresolved charges against him here in Massachusetts, but that's why he moved out west." There was a hint of pride in my voice as I described all this, but when James laughed I felt exposed and annoyed by him. "Your reactions are so bizarre," I said. "I can't imagine what's funny about it."

"The details," he said.

"The reason I'm telling you," I said through my irritation, "is that he needs good influences in his life. He'll never make it unless good people believe in him, unless good people stimulate him. It's no use being nice with Angus. He needs intelligent and stimulating friends."

James stared at the back of the seat in front of him. "It sounds," he said. "I'm not convinced..."

"That someone can start a new life? Well, that is where you are wrong."

Angus was at the house when I arrived, and as I came through the door, he drew me into his arms. His solid, uplifting presence filled the room. "What's this you're wearing?" he asked. It was a vintage petticoat from a thrift store, and a pair of laced black boots. "Look at you! It's perfect! You're perfect!" hugging and kissing me, holding me round the waist with those beautiful hands of his, as if he might lift me right off my feet.

Lydia and Nora sat at the kitchen table. "Is something going on between you and Angus?" Lydia asked. I flushed to the roots of my hair.

"I knew it!" Nora cried. "It's probably very naughty of me, but I've always thought you'd be good for each other."

"Really?"

"Once he sorted himself out, of course."

"Ruby, it's wonderful," said Lydia. "It all makes so much sense."

Angus and I stayed up after everyone else had gone to bed, late into that night, in the sitting room, and then we were entangled on the sofa, kissing and talking until it was early, and a new sun came up. We couldn't get enough of one another.

Then we heard Timothy waking upstairs, his electric razor going and Timothy dressing for work and we stood at the door, kissing for several more minutes, until Angus finally tore himself away, to go back home to the Aleshires.

He returned a few hours later and drove me into town, so we could be together, so I didn't have to take the bus. But rather than going to class, I decided to skip. Instead we went to Saks Fifth Avenue. He wanted to buy me a pair of gloves. We sat at the glove counter grinning at each other like fools, while the salesgirl smoothed the glove over my waiting fingers. "These are beautiful," he said. "These are the ones for you."

No one had ever bought me a pair of gloves before. I'd never wanted a pair of expensive gloves. But now for some reason, my smile was splitting my face.

My Afro American literature teacher said that blindness was a recurring theme in black fiction. White people were blind in black fiction. She also said that one of the mistakes that people made was that they lived their lives as if there was a spare one in the trunk.

Angus showed up at my class and stood in the doorway, tall, dark and handsome in his navy blue wool coat. He could barely let me out of his sight, even for a couple of hours. The other students glanced up expectantly at the interruption.

The professor was a small plain woman, furious at being marginalized racially, sexually and intellectually. "Can I help you?" she asked.

"I'm looking for Ruby Lambert." The students perked right up at that, all of them listening in. "I'll see you after your second class at that place on Newbury Street, all right, Ruby?" he said, as if we were the only ones there.

My face burned. "Fine."

The teacher glared as Angus stood in the doorway. "Don't ever interrupt my class like that again."

"Sorry," he said. And stepped away from the door.

We met every day for lunch at a place that became our favorite, where they made big salads with sugar in the dressing. He stood out front on the bleached out pavement, full of expectation, new each time I saw him, fully himself, drawing me into his arms, smiling and beautiful and worthy of love.

We sat by the window, grinning and holding hands across the table. The waitress called us the lovebirds. What can I get for the lovebirds today? And we were always starving, eating every morsel in the breadbasket before ordering a meal and their special sugary salad. "My professor didn't like you interrupting my class like that," I said.

"Yeah? Well, I didn't like her."

"Don't do that again," I said.

"Okay," he said. "I'm sorry."

"It was very disrespectful."

"I apologize," he said. "But I had important news. The old charges against me have been dropped. I got the official letter today. So I'm not on probation any more, Ruby. My record's clean! We can start a new life!"

"We can?"

"Sure we can. I can even enroll in college if I want. I was thinking of enrolling at Suffolk University!" he said. "I'm going to study philosophy. What do you think? Enrolling in Suffolk University! My grandmother has agreed to pay. I've got the registration fee. I'm going to go and get the rest of the money from her to pay for the classes."

"You don't mean to separate an old lady from her money, Angus?"

"Not at all. This money was left in a trust fund by my birth mother when she died. So I need to go out to Pittsfield because that's where my grandmother lives. Maybe you can come along. It will be great. We'll spend the night together in a hotel.

Twelve

I clutched a hot water bottle underneath the quilt as we headed out in Angus's old Mustang past the South Shore Plaza. Christmas was in a few weeks' time, and we wanted to visit his grandmother and sort out the transfer of money so he could pay for college. But the drive would be long in winter and his car heater didn't work. "Tell me about your grandmother," I asked as we headed out.

"She's an odd duck. You'll see. She's picky. And possessive. And I'm all she has in the world."

"Give her a little bit of credit why don't you."

Angus looked surprised. "Credit?"

"For being old. Raising you by herself when her daughter was dying. That can't have been easy. And for the money she's giving you to complete your education."

"That's where you're wrong, Ruby. Think about it. My mother died when I was two. Then my grandmother gave me up for adoption three years later," he said.

Beyond the car window the world was lit for Christmas. Lights were draped in the trees, and I pictured the adorable little dark haired orphan that must have been Angus. "I wonder why she did that," I said. "And what became of your father?"

"Don't know," Angus said. "I never met him."

We got beyond the rush hour traffic and out to the Mass Pike, slowing down at a tollbooth to put money into the hand of the collector who was wearing a Santa hat. There was slush and snow along the road. It was not even six o'clock but already it was dark. There was an impoverished feel, and a gloomy atmosphere to the place. "It's freezing in this car," I said, adjusting my hot water bottle. Angus turned up the radio, as though sheer volume might warm us up. Credence Clearwater Revival blasted into the car. He drove steadily. We were bundled in gloves and hats, and he had a scarf wrapped round his neck.

As we sped down the highway, the tires shushed against the wetted road. It began to drizzle and Angus turned on the wipers as the car grew steadily colder. Soon it was so icy that I had to turn around in my seat to face the wrong direction, and huddle there. "Please," I cried desperately. "Please stop! It's freezing!" both of us laughing.

Patches of melted snow dotted the parking lot of a Friendly's Family Restaurant. The restaurant smelled of grilled hamburgers, and radiated heat. A row of booths and Formica tables surrounded the cooking area. Plastic cards propped up on the tables recommended ice cream sundaes with cookies wedged into them. The place was packed. Husbands in down vests sat across from wives. They looked overweight. They all had bad complexions. They were dressed like children, in casual shapeless clothes.

I was bursting to pee. I went into the ladies room and Angus went into the men's room and when we rejoined each other we sat in a booth and ate "Fishamajig" sandwiches and drank coffee out of fat creamy mugs.

He said, "Just now when I ran my hands under the tap in the men's room it felt scalding hot, because of how cold my hands were." His eyes glistened. "But when I finished washing them, I realized it was the cold tap!"

We finished the sandwiches, asked for coffee refills. Ordered a side of french-fries. "And does your grandmother call you Angus?" I asked.

"Why wouldn't she?"

"I thought she might call you David," I said. "The name you were given at birth."

"Yeah, well, she doesn't."

"And do you remember much from those early years?" It seemed strange that I'd never asked him any of these things before, all that time he lived with us.

"I remember my new dad holding my hand the first day. And I remember standing on the platform watching my grandmother's train pull away. Then he said, 'we thought we'd call you Angus, if that's all right by you.' And I said fine."

"That must have been so hard."

"And you know, I never fit in with my new family. I always felt like a different kind of person. One thing I particularly hated – the nickname my dad gave me: Gus." We finished off the French fries. "I guess I was difficult and I can see that now. But by the time I left to live with my grandmother, I was really screwed up."

"Who could blame you for wanting to reconnect with her?" I said. Then another thought occurred to me. "While you lived with us, you stayed out of trouble most of the time, didn't you?"

"It's more that I didn't get caught. When your parents gave me the place to stay, and Timothy spoke with the probation officer, it helped get me out of the hole. But don't you remember the way I was back then? Those crazy guys I hung out with all the time, Nacho and Kevin 'Crime Wave'. Can you believe the name? Crime Wave!" and he lingered on the 'I' sound in 'crime'. "We called him Crime Wave! It really fit him too."

"I remember the hash that Nora found and flushed down the toilet..." I prompted.

"There's more to the story about the hash. And to the story about the Linda Ronstadt concert. Jeez," he said. "Let's not even talk about it. It was all bad. All bad. But not anymore. I'm not a criminal anymore." Tears sprung suddenly into his eyes. It hurt me to see them.

"Are you mine, for better and worse?" he asked.

"As in the marriage vows?"

"Maybe not yet. But in a few years. What do you think?"

"I think we may do it!"

"Only, you won't like my grandmother much. She'll ignore you. She's the kind of woman who only talks to one person at the table. Can't engage a group. She directs all her conversation towards one person, as though the rest aren't there."

"Come on."

"It's true. She's very bitter and I don't know why. She's the kind of woman who had something mean spirited to say about everybody."

"Oh, I'm sure I'll win her over. Won't I win her over?"

"It's strange," he said, turning suddenly wistful. "I always feel so right with you."

We paid for the meal and returned to the car, where the hot water bottle had gone lukewarm. By the end of the journey it would be frozen solid. But I wrapped myself up like a mummy in the quilt and Angus got behind the wheel. He looked at me mischievously. "Ready?"

Thirteen

His grandmother lived in a complex of high-rise apartment buildings. Tinsel Christmas trees stood in the windows. "Happy Holidays" was spelled out in gold letters across the doors and windows. Lights blinked on and off. Plastic reindeer stood on snow-covered verges. Santas and plastic snowmen waved to us from windows.

We walked up a path and stood on a doorstep where Angus went down a series of names in the entry hall roster, then tapped in the apartment number on a telephone pad, and waited for a crackly voice to come out of the speaker.

"Is that you?" Before we could answer, the door buzzed open. Then, "I'm on the fourth floor."

The lobby was vacant and smelled of boiled cabbage. We got into the elevator. We leaned against the wall and kissed all the way to the fourth floor, and then the doors opened onto an artificial Christmas tree with a few red balls and an old woman with a freeze-dried look, was standing in an open door.

She wore a housedress and slippers, her hair a helmet of gray waves. "What took you so long?" she wanted to know.

Angus bent to embrace her. "Hi Nana, this is my girlfriend, Ruby."

"You didn't say you'd be bringing a girl."

"I wanted to surprise you. Ruby and I are in love."

"Well, isn't that nice," she said at last. Her hand was dry and warm as I clasped it. "Call me Margaret," she said, leading the way to the living room. The parquet floor was empty of carpets. Junk crammed every surface – photo albums, ceramic lamps, bowls with beads inside them, a silver pitcher, framed pictures, and along the window ledge small pots of African violets. A pile of recently sorted photographs and letters sat on the table before a chair. The air had the smell of a place that nobody entered. A place with cheap parquet floors but too much heavy furniture, left over from a more prosperous era. "I've been sorting through some heirlooms," she explained. "I thought you might like to take things back." She sat on the chair, which was evidently her favorite spot. Her hands were ancient, blue veined, the skin like crepe paper, and on her fingers she wore several rings.

Angus and I sat on a sofa holding hands. I moved aside the pleated cushions. Crystal ashtrays decorated the coffee table, a brass lamp with a yellowed linen lampshade. "Look at the pair of you," his grandmother said with a thin smile. She asked what he wanted to study in college, when he was going to enroll, and how the two of us had met, and before very long the conversation turned to deeper things. She wasn't as remote as Angus had described, but he was right that she was a little strange. Her face sagged in gentle tiers along her jaw line. Her teeth shifted oddly in her mouth. "I didn't want to give him away. I did it because I thought it would be best. How was I to know I'd live to this old age? Nobody knows how long they will live, and the Aleshires wanted him so much," she said. "He was a beautiful child. Just beautiful. I thought it would be best for him. How was I to know that woman would file a stubborn child complaint on him when he turned seventeen?"

"Look, Ruby." Angus picked up a china plate decorated round the edges with stylized green dragons. "It's hand painted. Lenox china. Isn't it beautiful?"

"What makes you so clever," his grandmother challenged, her croaky voice suddenly turning winsome.

"I've been surrounded by fine china and silverware all my life. And see this one Ruby," choosing another with an ornate floral design, "this is a Spode pattern."

"I have some good silver too, which you can have," Margaret put in. "Towle silver that belonged to your mother."

"It's not pronounced towel," Angus said scathingly. "It's Towle."

"That's what I said," she rejoindered flirtatiously. "I've always heard it pronounced Towel. In fact, there are many things that belonged to her and which you might like to take with you," she said. "When you have the space for it, of course."

"I'd love to hear more about Angus's mother," I interjected.

"She was a ceramic artist," Margaret said. "She made lamps for an exclusive shop on the Upper East Side. Oh yes. Sara Jane had a very promising career, and was just shy of her thirtieth birthday when she died of lung cancer." Her eyes travelled back a thousand miles while Angus appeared disinterested as he leafed through a volume of Hiawatha. "I never should have given him away," Margaret said again, almost to herself. "After Sara Jane went I had a lot on my mind. I was still grieving. And Angus was such a bright and active child. It broke my heart to let him go, but I thought it would be best for him to go with a family who could provide all the things for him that I couldn't."

Then, as if to shake off the melancholy, she took out the silver chest that had belonged to Angus's mother and after that she brought out a packet of photographs. She held them with steady hands. They were black and white glossy studio shots of a glamorous and severe young woman with very dark lips. I could see her resemblance to Angus. She leaned against a wall in a cloud of cigarette smoke. Silky hair hung to her shoulders, parted on the side, Lauren Bacall style. "This is Sara Jane," she said. "Angus's mother."

That night we checked into a hotel in downtown Pittsfield. I pulled him close in the elevator and kissed him deeply and then we kissed again in front of the door to our room. And then behind the door, we kicked off our shoes, and kissed as we peeled off our clothes, as we undid the buttons and clasps, and lay at last across a bed so enormous that we laughed at the distance between us.

Oh Angus, heart's darling. Our passion wasn't lust so much as reverence, a swim through crystal clear waters. Your body and the shape of your limbs seemed exotic and yet so dearly familiar. Your skin, soft and brown. Your hairless well-formed chest. I traced its several scars, the scar across your nipple, another like a raised welt down your ribs, where once you had flown through a barbed wire fence on a dirt bike, being chased by cops. I kissed your face. I held the thick dark hair of your head, and as you entered me, we entered the world of each other.

That first time we made love we cried with gratitude. Our love was the fusion of yin and yang, of parts that had always been seeking each other. I kissed your eyelids, and held your face in my hands. I hold you now in the language of my heart.

In the morning we made love again. Afterwards Angus produced his grandmother's volume of Hiawatha from the night before and read me the opening verses:

By the shores of Gitche Gume by the shining Big Sea Water
Stood the wigwam of Nokomis, daughter of the moon, Nokomis

I lay against the pillows listening to his voice, teasing my bare foot up his leg and watching his face, the drop of his eyelids, the smile playing over his lips – until he looked up at me with tears in his eyes. "I can't read any more," he whispered.

∼

After Christmas, Angus moved into a rented room near the State House. Most of the time though, he stayed with me on Beacon Street. We slept entangled, limbs knotted together in the bed. We cooked on a hot plate and kept our food in the tiny refrigerator beneath it. We ate apples and cream of wheat, spinach omelets with feta cheese and onion. Angus returned with supplies from the grocery store. "Come and see what I've bought," passing me a tin of devilled chicken, grapes, lettuce and French bread.

His father got him a job in the family china store on Newbury Street. While he was working I sat with my feet tucked underneath me in a big chair, finishing a paper on the Harlem Renaissance poets. It wasn't the grand oeuvre I had imagined when I conceived it, but I lowered my expectations and typed away on crinkly thesis paper at my Smith-Corona classic, stopping occasionally to white out mistakes.

The chair was covered with an Indian bedspread splashed with purple paisleys. The room was filled up with paper writing and love making, as though it was filled with flowers. From our loft bed we could see the trees outside, a pine tree caught in sun speckle, and the drooping of a late Christmas tree decorated with lights.

Occasionally we saw the neighbor who lived on the other side of the parlor partition, a dour man in pinstripes, heading off to work in the mornings. We heard his return in the evening too, his radio switching on. Those walls were paper-thin. Sometimes he left his soiled underpants hanging on a hook in the bathroom.

"It's disgusting!" I cried. "Why does he do it? He knows he has to share the bathroom! Oh, I wish we could afford to get our own apartment."

"When you graduate, we'll move in together, to a better place," said Angus.

"I wonder what my parents will make of that."

"They're happy we are together."

"They are, but they're also old fashioned. It has to do with the church. And what other people think. If Timothy knew we were practically living together now, he'd flip."

"So do you think we should get married? I mean, it kind of feels inevitable. In fact, I was going to keep this for later," he said. "But here. I have something for you."

He took my hand and folded something into its palm, and when I opened it up, I saw a little gold ring, with a setting of two star sapphires. "It belonged to my mother. My grandmother sent it to me and I want you to have it now. Go ahead. Put it on. Let me see it on your finger."

His expression was filled with shy and private pleasure as I slid it onto my finger. The setting was unusual and the stones were smooth and dark, unlike any I'd seen before. He smiled and watched my face. "We'll have to get it sized. Your fingers are too slender for it."

Then we heard the neighbor coming up the stairs with his latest pick up, the unlocking of the door, a bit of formal and awkward conversation between strangers before the rhythmic and quickening squeak of the next-door bedsprings. We heard our neighbor's voice cry out. "Take me!" while we lay in bed next door, muffling our laughter in the pillows.

The little old lady who lived on the floor above me sometimes came downstairs, clutching her towel and a bottle of shampoo. She squeezed past wordlessly and went into my bathroom.

"Why does she have to use our bathroom?" I grumbled. "It's bad enough having him next door."

"Come on, Ruby. It's her way of taking possession of the place," said Angus. It was an explanation so tender it made me feel mean spirited. "If she uses your bathroom she can feel like she's paying not only for her room, but also for the hallway and the stairs and the bathroom on this floor as well as the one upstairs."

A heavy smell of tar assailed us from the alleyway. We looked out of the half bay window to see two men standing on a flat roof, resurfacing it. The men moved around, shifting tools, picking things up and putting them down and Angus did a voiceover, speaking for the workmen, matching his words perfectly to the men's movements. "You wanna start here? Ah, let's see! No. Hows 'bout here. You got a hammer over there. Yup. Here you go... no wait. I think I got somethin' in my boot. Wait just a minute. Ah, that's right...Hey Brian. Come take a look at this for a second. Fuckin' A. What you got there? Jeez. I guess we should get started..."

∽

We lay in bed, after making love, out bodies erased like bubbles of air. Our voices in the dark were the only solid thing about us then. The rest of us had melted. It was in these moments that we talked of previous girlfriends and boyfriends, of how things had ended and who had hurt whom. "I have another story for you," he told me one day.

"Go on~"

"About this one time out in Arizona, when I was on work release."

"Yes~"

"...and these cops pulled me over for speeding. It was the car of a friend of mine, and there was something screwy about the registration. So they made me follow them to the station and then they held me in a room upstairs, while they tried to get the paperwork together. Who knows what they were doing. It was all just bullshit. But they left me in this empty room on the second floor of the building with a window. And I was thinking if I stay here they're going to find out I'm on work release and because of this car registration they're going to put me back in. I'm going to lose my work release and get locked up again for like five more months. Fuck that, I said. And I jumped."

"What! You mean you jumped out of the window?"

"Yup. I had to. I went over to the window and I escaped. But I really hurt my back when I landed. I landed on my feet and my back sort of popped and compressed. It hurt like hell. But I stood up and walked as easily as I could to the road. No one was out there and I was totally free. I got back in my car and drove it into the next town. I figured, why go back.

"So I'm driving down the highway," he said. "And no one is following me. Totally free. It was the most incredible feeling. So I stop at a gas station along the road to Tucson, in the middle of the desert, nothing going on. I get out of the car to pay the bill and all of a sudden I see this guy I know, the prison minister at the jail. Great old guy, with thick white hair. A guy as good as your dad, you know? He reminded me a lot of Timothy, in fact. A church guy."

"So what did you think when you saw him there?" I asked.

"He was paying for his gas. His car was on the next island over from mine. And I knew if he just looked up he'd see me standing there. I knew this was my chance. I knew it! I could turn myself in. I could go to him and tell him what had happened. I could come clean."

I turned to see his silhouette, the face I loved with the strong line of his nose, his gentle lips moving as he lay beside me on his back, staring at the ceiling. "So what did you do?" I asked.

He took in a breath. "I ignored it," he said. "I ignored the sign. I got in my car and drove away."

Fourteen

"We're being watched." We were sitting in an ice cream parlor, with cones of peppermint stick, the teenage staffers busy making banana splits and flipping burgers. I looked around to see what he meant. "Up there," he said, gesturing towards a small surveillance camera mounted in the corner of the ceiling.

"Oh, that."

"Do you realize how many people are kept in business by criminals?" he asked. "Not just law enforcement. The people who make those surveillance cameras; the locksmiths, banks, the insurance companies. The whole world is based on the fact that people can't be trusted."

"Not true," I said. "It's also because accidents happen."

"Criminals aren't accidents. They are just a normal part of a healthy society."

"I meant with insurance companies. There are natural disasters. There are mistakes..."

"Ruby:alarm system makers, alarm installers, the people who administer lie detector tests. The people who make the lie detector tests, detectives, social workers, probation officers, the police department, security companies, museum guards, prison guards, legal systems, even religious institutions...." His face was animated as he added to his list.

"Okay, okay. I get your point."

"If it wasn't for criminals, hundreds and thousands of people would be out of work. In fact criminals keep the economy healthy."

"I don't think it's helpful to think of it that way," I said. "Although speaking of being out of work, when I graduate I'll need a real job. What should I do with my B.A., do you think?"

He offered a teasing evaluation, as he finished off the rest of his cone. "Why don't you work at a bank?"

"Oh come on, I'd never do that!" I cried. "I'm terrible with numbers. I can't count. I was thinking more along the lines of editing for Oliver Gordon, while I think about graduate school.

Did you know that he once had a small press? I'm wondering if I can get him to start it up again."

"You behind the teller's window counting out money," Angus continued, enjoying himself. "Picture it. You with your curly hair and your hippie shirts. You'd be so good."

"Stop. It would be a total waste. I'd hate it."

"Why?" pleased with the picture he'd drawn and thoroughly amused by how cross I was at the suggestion.

"In a bank? You can't be serious! I want to do something inspiring, to begin an artistic career, and eventually get a master's in art history or the metaphysical poets."

"Art history and metaphysical poetry? There's a good career move."

"Well, I'd never do anything just for the money."

"Why not?" He looked at me critically, one eyebrow raised, and his expression reminded me of how I sometimes felt, listening to Ari talk about how artists suffered.

"I have ambitions," I explained. "But not about making money. I want to do something meaningful."

"Like what?"

"I don't know yet. Write something I can be proud of. Or work at The Atlantic Monthly on Arlington Street. Or, I don't know, work in a beautiful art gallery."

∽

I showed him the practice rooms at the student union and persuaded him to play through the Dolly Suite duets with me again. We sat in that tiny booth with its scuffed up walls and upright piano. Sometimes we played together; and sometimes Angus played alone, as if I wasn't there. At other times, I was the only thing there, and he stopped playing to kiss me, sliding me towards him, pushing aside the fabric of my skirt to stroke between my thighs, dropping to his knees to kiss me there.

If only I could return to that practice room now, and discover our ghosts inside. If only I could grab hold of this story and turn it firmly in a positive direction. I would slow things down and make a lot more of the piano – and those Fauré duets – especially *Berceuse* – of how Angus closed in on the phrasing, his eyebrows arched at the subtler sections, as he moved his arms and body with the narrative of the music; of how I leaned into the notes, complementing his. Because once we began to play that piece, it was like getting on a raft and floating over waves.

If only we could have journeyed through life as we journeyed through those pieces, through *Dolly's Garden*, with Angus's arm carrying the heft of the melody, so that the weight of the sound ran down his shoulder and into the fingertips. When the base line picked up the melody, I gave myself over, supporting his tenderness and confidence in my own echoes of the melody. Could we have done things differently? Was it possible to navigate life as we did those passages, through the darker stretches, picking through nettles, until we came out safely at the end.

Fauré's music suggested that life could be at once mischievous, dangerous, tender and lots of fun – that we could be those things, and more extraordinarily so together than alone.

He'd been accepted at Suffolk for September. In the meantime he continued working at the family store on Newbury Street. He brought me picnics while I studied for exams: French baguette, devilled ham, a tub of tapioca. He sat on the bed reading, with his feet up, while I wrote my final papers on my Smith-Corona typewriter.

When at last I graduated, he came along to the ceremony with the family, all of them so proud. Timothy with his super 8 camera stood on the steps and squinted through the eyepiece, as I held my up degree and grinned triumphantly.

∽

Cheryl Aleshire in the driveway of their home was unloading groceries from the back of her car when we floated the idea of a summer wedding. I don't know what reaction we expected. But she averted her eyes, straightened herself and allowed us to carry the bags to the house. "Aren't you going to congratulate us?"

Angus pressed her, when we put the bags on the kitchen table. She stalled, applying herself to unpacking the cans and cartons.

"I hope you aren't doing it just because you want to live together," she said at last from behind the open pantry door. Angus and I exchanged glances.

After we left he shook his head in disbelief. "Did you hear how cold and illogical she is? I mean, what the fuck, man! Of course we want to live together! That's why every couple marries."

But Cheryl's reaction wasn't our only disappointment. Even my friend Ari was doubtful. "What about your writing career?" he wanted to know. "I see you as more of a romantic."

"A wedding can be romantic," I said.

"But it's terribly conventional for you," he replied.

"I suppose you think I should be suffering away in a garret."

"Angus might drown out your creative drive."

"And how will he do that? That's ridiculous, Ari!" I said. "How could marriage to Angus ever be conventional? I mean, if anything that's why I want to do it. In marrying Angus I'll be taking a spectacular risk. From our wedding on, my life will never be boring."

Then there were my parents. "Why the rush?" Nora asked. "You're both so young. Are you sure you're ready for such a big step?"

"I've finished my degree and Angus is enrolled in university," I said. "He's holding down a job at his father's store, and we love each other. I can't believe that we're the ones convincing you about the virtues of marriage. With most of my friends it's the other way around."

"Sweetheart, it's wonderful that you love each other," said Timothy. "And I hope that things will go from strength to strength for Angus as well as for you. But I cannot walk my beautiful daughter down the aisle in good conscience, unless I'm sure you are ready for the commitment."

"We know it's a commitment," Angus said. "And I love your daughter more than anything else in the world." So Timothy said he would give us his blessing. Under one condition: that we talk it over with Pastor Jackson first.

Neither Angus nor I was big on the church at that point. But we made an appointment with Pastor Jackson, who greeted us warmly at the parish house door, with his smooth pink face and clear-eyed goodness. Then he ushered us into the parlor and we sat on straight-backed chairs in front of the empty fireplace.

Pastor Jackson had a tightly strung voice and a cheerful demeanor. "Well now, Angus and Ruby, I've been given to understand that congratulations are in order? I think that is simply delightful. One doesn't necessarily predict such felicitous unions to come out of Bible studies, don't you know." He laughed convivially, revealing a row of small teeth, which slanted slightly backwards into his mouth. "Splendid. But before settling on a date, I always like to have a little talk with the couple in question, about the seriousness of the marriage bond. So, tell me, Angus – you've had an interesting passage through the wilderness over the last several years, shall we say? Would you share your thoughts?"

Angus answered in measured sentences about the troubles of his past, and how people had given up on him over the years. Not that he blamed anyone. In fact, he didn't really expect anything from those he'd disappointed. But he had hit rock bottom out in Colorado. And all through that time he knew that we understood his potential, that we in the Lambert family held out hope and faith for his reform. "And what else can I say? I've loved Ruby for years." His eyes glistened. "As a friend as well as a girl. She will never let me destroy myself. In fact she brings out the best in me and I want to honor and cherish that with my life."

Oh, he might make mistakes along the way, he said. He wouldn't be human if he didn't acknowledge that. But the path forward was clear to him now. With me at his side, with his parents behind him and his college studies underway, not to mention Pastor Jackson's blessing, how could he fail. Wasn't forgiveness and redemption the very foundation of the Christian church?

I remembered one of my father's favorite verses, and now I trotted it out, without really considering its meaning, in order to drive the point further home. "It also says in the Bible that we have to be wise as serpents – but also as harmless as doves."

Pastor Jackson turned to me. "Go on," he said.

Angus and I locked eyes. His eyes fed mine, and with their lively expression, strengthened my resolve. "I think we must stay alert, but above all resist being cynical," I said. "It means we should take a leap of faith."

Fifteen

After finishing college I moved back home temporarily. And sometime in May of that year, Nora took me to pick up Sorrel from a play date with her friend Felicity Seabrook. I had no idea how the Seabrook house was to figure in our lives. I only went because, as Nora said, "You really have to see this house."

The Seabrook house sat at the tip of a small peninsular in Cohasset, Massachusetts. It was a three story colonial, with black shutters, and on the roof there was a railed widow's walk. To get to the property you crossed a bridge over a saltwater inlet.

Late spring blew through the car windows, carrying the aroma of fresh green things. After long rains the blossoms in the garden smelled especially fragrant. What a gorgeous setting it was: lilacs spilling over the wall like soft raspberry cushions, the scent of boxwood and mown grass floating on the breeze.

"Look, darling. Don't you love the archway? Oh, and that conservatory! What heaven!" She parked the car in the driveway. "Just you wait until you see inside," she told me with a wink. "You ain't seen nothin' yet!"

We were on a peninsula. Beyond a terraced flower garden and plantation birdhouse, a perfect lawn stretched towards the sea. The gentle peal of ropes could be heard in the distance, ringing against the mast of a sailboat. This was a privileged world, all right. Nothing to hurry for, nothing to grate on you.

"Isn't it incredible?" Nora gushed. "And they have their own private dock, darling." We walked up the path and rang the bell.

Ingrid Seabrook answered the door herself. Perhaps I'd expected a servant to answer in a house like that, but in spite of her incredible wealth, Ingrid appeared unassuming. She wore jeans and a t-shirt and her hair was cut simply, off her face.

"Ingrid, hello!" said Nora, as we stepped inside. "I'd like you to meet my eldest daughter, Ruby."

Ingrid smiled. "I didn't realize you had such a grown up daughter!" she said.

"Yes. Ruby has just finished college."

A crystal vase of cut flowers stood on the entrance hall table. A staircase wound towards the landing. A tastefully understated chandelier hung from the ceiling. The girls, Ingrid said, had been playing upstairs. "I'll go and see if I can find them."

It was then that I noticed the artwork. We had been left in the foyer and it was hung with 14th century gold leaf triptychs and diptychs. I peered into an adjacent room, which boasted renaissance paintings in heavy gilt frames: the adoration of the magi, the twelve apostles, a renaissance Madonna and child.

"What did I tell you?" Nora whispered, when she saw the look on my face.

"Wow!"

"Must be old money," she breathed, for it was impossible for us to imagine the kind of money evidenced here as the product of anything the Seabrooks actually did. People didn't earn this sort of money; they simply had it.

Ingrid reappeared. She looked at me strangely. I see you are impressed, the expression on her face seemed to say. But really, don't take it to heart. It made me embarrassed. Quickly I tucked my thoughts away – *Thou shalt not covet thy neighbor's triptychs* – as Sorrel bounded towards us. In that setting she seemed a bit thin and scruffy, a very minor player, eager to appear in her element. "Do we have to go?"

I saw Felicity Seabrook standing at the top of the stairs with her hand on the banister, solemn and watchful. "Go on, Sorrel. What do you say?" Nora prompted.

"Thank you for having me," she chanted.

Felicity remained mute and unsmiling. "Come along," said Nora. "We have a rehearsal to get to." Ingrid tilted her head. "A Noel Coward play," Nora explained. We too had cachet, after all. "*Blythe Spirit*. At the Community Center. You must come and see it."

We drove home along the coast, down Atlantic Avenue in Cohasset past all those beautiful mansions with their extensive lawns. "That was incredible. The *lives* those people lead," I said. "Isn't it amazing?" Nora replied.

"Why did you have to pick me up so early? We were just about to play on Felicity's trampoline," Sorrel whined from the back seat.

"Oh, and Ingrid," said Nora, "is such a nice woman."

"Where did they get all the artwork?"

"And Felicity is a sweet girl," Nora went on feelingly, for she wanted to feel generous about the Seabrooks, to consider Ingrid a friend. "She's very well brought up."

"Felicity likes quiet games," Sorrel chimed in. She was platting strips of colored plastic into a bracelet. She frowned but her cheeks were pink, as were the tips of her ears.

"I mean, I think I saw a Brueghel in there," I said. "And a Fillipo Lippi. One at least. Those paintings are incredible! They belong in a museum."

"I hate museums," Sorrel said. "I don't like walking down hallways really quietly and looking at pictures. I find that boring."

I wound down the car window, propping my elbow on the door. "It's actually rather obscene," I continued. "Imagine the responsibility of having all that stuff."

"Oh," said my mother. "I think it wears on Ingrid."

"I'll bet it does!"

"She finds it a burden. All those alarms in the house, which have to be activated. Her husband is firm on that." Our mood had turned. What stuffy old relics those paintings were. What old fuss pots, insisting on their care and respect, making a house full of children a solemn and gothic occasion! What sort of house was that to raise children in? No laughter here, please. Keep your fingers to yourselves!

It was then that Nora's voice dropped to a lower register. "I don't want to sound unkind," she said, "But I wouldn't tell Angus if I were you..."

I felt a little hurt. What could she mean by that? Did she think he was still a criminal? "Okay," I answered quietly. "I won't." And I kept my word.

∼

Our wedding plans gathered momentum, sweeping up misgivings, funneling and sucking on all forms of weaker energy. Lydia designed my dress. I stood still while she went around with a mouthful of pins, attaching bits of tulle into place. Nora arranged for the cake, for lilies and roses and madrigal music, and of course for a photographer. But would the reception take place at the Country Fare restaurant, or out on the lawn in a big marquis? And how was merriment to figure in a party that would certainly include all Timothy's church ladies as well as the aunts and uncles from out of town and the oddballs from Tango's bookshop?

Then came a surprising announcement. "James is joining the Navy," Oliver said. He and James were sitting on the sofa in Oliver's office surrounded by books and papers. My mouth fell open.

"Why are you doing that?" I asked.

"Honor, courage and commitment," James said and when they laughed, I felt excluded from the amusement. "Navy core values," he explained, looking down, his expression suffused with a private kind of modesty.

"He's off to Great Lakes Illinois in two weeks' time," Oliver explained, looking chuffed. "For eight weeks basic training."

"So you'll miss our wedding."

"I'm afraid so." But there was a lid pushed down on his feelings and I couldn't read his face.

∾

A series of gatherings led like stepping stones up to the wedding. Friends from Tango's took me for drinks at Grendel's. Ari cracked open a bottle of champagne and proposed a dramatic toast on the rooftop of his apartment, overlooking Back Bay. Well-wishers from the periphery also assembled. Lilly Pipping from church provided a shower at her little house near the duck pond. The congregation brought food: fudge brownies and fairy cakes, five-cup salads of mandarin orange, coconut, cream, marshmallow and pineapple and bestowed presents upon us of can openers, tea towels and corn on the cob holders and had a hymn sing around the piano in the living room.

Angus didn't want to invite anyone from his past – except for one ex-girlfriend, whom we sent an invitation to. But Nora held a special lunch for Angus's grandmother Margaret, who arrived in careful clothes and carried a square alligator handbag with a small gold clasp. We laid a buffet on the sun porch table. I privately hoped that Grandpa and Margaret might hit it off but Grandpa was unimpressed and kept his nose to the plate, scooping up his food. He had recently discovered that if he held his head downwards when he swallowed, he wouldn't be so liable to choke. When he was finished he got up and shuffled away inside to listen to his shortwave radio. "Good feed," he said as he departed.

"I was sixty-five when Sara Jane died," Margaret began.

"My goodness, you're marvelous for your age," Nora beamed. "Absolutely marvelous."

"Eighty-eight this October."

"Are you really? But look at her, Ruby! Don't you think she's marvelous?"

"Oh yes. Amazing," I said.

"I had no idea I would live this long," said Margaret, directing this now familiar commentary towards Angus, who sat uncomfortably at his end of the table. "I never supposed that I would be the last remaining member of my generation. After Sara Jane went I had a lot on my mind. It broke my heart to let him go, but I thought they would provide a life for him which I simply couldn't."

"Of course," Nora soothed her.

"I haven't had the chance yet to thank you for this beautiful ring, Margaret," I said.

Her face was empty of meaning but she watched as I held out my hand. "This one. The one you gave to Angus." Margaret looked at my hand without expression or investment.

"I've never seen that ring before," she said. I looked at Angus for help. He shook his head. Don't pursue it, his eyes said.

Sixteen

We had so many wedding presents and thank you notes to write. Dear yellow and orange and white breakfast china, Old Lace silver, crystal glasses, linens for the table and linens for the bed, silver breadbasket, blender, mixer and coffee pot, earthenware coffee set from relatives in England, crocheted caftan by a woman from church and step ladder, Hoover and dusters; antique American quilt, brown towels and cream towels, rag rugs and Spode china: Thank you all for starting us on our adventure. And Sara Jane's ring? Thank you most of all. "Why didn't Margaret remember the ring?" I asked Angus when we were finally alone.

"You misunderstood," he said. "It wasn't from her that the ring came, it was from my other grandmother. My father's mother."

"But I thought you said she gave it to you when we went to Pittsfield."

"No," he said.

"That's weird. I certainly got that impression. In fact, I thought you said it came from your mother."

"No," he said. "It came from my father's mother. Gloria Aleshire who lives down on the Cape."

Our wedding took place in the family church. Timothy walked me up the aisle followed by Lydia, Angus's sister Beth and little Sorrel, all of them dressed in mint green. We sang the hymns at the top of our lungs and Angus was so overcome at the recitation of vows that his voice shook and tears came to his eyes. Then Timothy read from Corinthians about the importance of charity and love, and it was clinched. If any union was blessed it was ours.

The reception took place at the Country Fare where Lydia looking beautiful, drank too much champagne and caught the bouquet. I wore Nora's bridal veil and a wreath of pale roses with orange blossoms. Grandpa stood about in his suit, facing the wrong direction when the family assembled for photographs. Duncan didn't attend the wedding because he was out in Wyoming, but Angus's sister Beth was in floods of tears, while

Cheryl stood strong and stoical, and Frank Aleshire clapped us on the back. "You kids are great."

Freddy danced with his new girlfriend June who wore pale pink and Freddy reminded me of Charles the Second with his mass of long hair. Angus's grandmother was more withered and washed out than ever in a scarlet floor length gown, scowling because she didn't care for the cake.

There was wedding cake and all of us had too much, wedding dancing and the wedding toast. Sorrel got dirt on the hem of her dress as she galloped barefoot across the grass. I was sorry to see that Angus's ex, the one guest from his past, had not shown up, but he didn't seem to notice. And at the end of the celebrations, Angus and I drove away in the old Mustang convertible, tin cans rattling on the road behind us.

∼

We honeymooned in Maine at the Aleshire's island cottage, renting a boat in Freeport and sailing across from the harbor. We docked in the bay, unloaded the boat and lugged our cooler and bags along the grassy path to the cottage. The walk took fifteen or twenty minutes.

The cottage stood on the banks of the water, all wood paneled Americana, rag rugs and cherry wood furniture. Cheryl and Beth had baked some brownies and left them under a glass dome in the kitchen. We sat on the porch with iced drinks. Angus tapped his foot as he leafed through a *Smithsonian* magazine. Water lapped at the shore. Smells of ferns and water, moss and greenery filled the air around us. "I was thinking of going to the harbor to pick up the sailboat and bring it back here," he said at last.

"Really?"

"Don't you like sailing?"

"I'd really prefer to swim."

"The water here is way too cold for swimming," he said. "No one swims in Maine water."

We listened to the water against the shore, and the chirping of birds. I was disappointed about the swimming. But we uncorked a bottle of wine, and napped under a blistering sky. When the sun went down, Angus made a fire and while it cracked and burned, we made quiet love on the carpet in front of it. So this was the pinnacle of harmony. Beneath it lay a nebulous blankness. If you looked down you could feel the pull of vertigo, and if you looked up you could see everything. Or nothing. At least, there was nothing to interrupt the sound of each other's thoughts, no schoolwork or part time jobs, no wedding plans or parties. We made love again upstairs and discovered the bed was screwed to the floorboards to stop its movement. Porcelain toiletries stood on a little Victorian washstand in the corner of the room. The sheets were cool and soft and the pillows were deep. Loons called out across the water.

But when the sun came up on our honeymoon bed, Angus had gone. I sat up, looked across the white-boarded floor, and got out of bed. "Angus?" I pulled on a sundress and went downstairs to make coffee. I looked out of the window and saw a deserted island out there, way across the water. But there was no sign of Angus, and seeing no note, I slipped on my sandals, left the cottage and went for a walk.

There were other vacationers on the island too. I passed a family in their little sunroom eating cornflakes from blue striped bowls. Someone had a boat up on struts and was crouched down on the grass beside it, with a can of varnish. "Hey there."

I smiled and continued walking, intent on looking deliberate, certainly not as if I was searching for a missing husband. A short distance later I found myself in a field of wildflowers and tall grasses. I lay in the grasses looking at the sky, trying to feel my way into timelessness. Lying in a scratchy field. I am a married woman. Gnats spiraling round. I am Mrs. Aleshire, as clouds made their passage across the slow morning sky.

When I returned to the cottage, Angus was out on the porch. "Where were you?" he challenged.

"Where were you? You were gone before I woke up."

"I went to get the boat from the harbor. Wasn't that what we decided?"

"Oh," I said. "I guess I forgot." In the kitchen, I hunted for a container, opening cupboards, which released a musty attic kind of smell. "Look at all these flowers I picked."

"Do you want to sail across the bay?" he asked.

"Now?" as I filled a jar with tap water.

"Sure. Why not?"

"Can't we go this evening? We could sail across to the deserted island over there."

"All right. Let's go this evening. We can even take a picnic."

That afternoon we went for a walk, and he showed me his favorite places, a clubhouse, and the view from the top of a hill. We walked beside the shore on wide flat rocks and across the bone of shells, past rosehips, dogwood, azalea. The whole place smelled of country and seaside. "What an amazing childhood you had, coming here every summer."

"I learned to sail and play tennis here. We went skiing, fishing. All of it," he replied in a flat unmusical voice.

The grass was covered in clover, dandelion and buttercup. The sun beat down and the sky was a blistering blue. We could see the deserted island across the water, the one we would sail to when the moon came up. "A few years back, some boys tried to walk across to that island in winter," he said, "when the harbor was frozen. But they only got half way. The ice cracked and they drowned."

"How awful!" The grasses tickled my legs as I scrambled down the hill behind him. "How old were the boys?"

"Ten or twelve, I think."

We found a shady path, which we walked along, single file. "Did you know them?"

"What?"

"The boys."

"Not really, no."

"It's very sad."

"Yes." I noticed a distance in his voice, the impression of something withheld. He was behind me as we walked. "I wonder what happens when you die," he said.

"I like to think you go on," I suggested. "Except in a different state of consciousness." The path had ended in a little clearing so we stopped and faced each other.

"Do you really believe all that stuff about heaven and hell?" he asked"Not necessarily in the Christian sense. But I think I believe in an afterlife. Otherwise why did Jesus come back? He came back from somewhere, right? There's also that character Enoch, who I always found to be fascinating."

"Enoch?"

"Angus! Don't you remember Enoch," I asked heartily, "from all those Sunday School classes? He was the guy who never died… he just disappeared. It says 'he walked with God and he was not.'" I slapped at a mosquito on my leg and started to talk about the Hindu concepts of afterlife, about the astral body, a less material body, one not made out of flesh and bone but one made out of thought.

"I think you rot when you die," he replied. "And return to the elements you're made of." Then he bent to pick something from the ground, which he popped into his mouth. "Wild strawberries," he said cheekily. "They grow everywhere here."

∼

The moon was full when we set sail. The boat rocked and bobbed, as it surged forwards into the dark. "Look," he said, when we were out in the bay.

"It's beautiful."

"Yes, but look at the sail." The water lapped against the boat as it rocked across the current.

"You really love to sail, don't you?" I said.

"Don't you?" Our voices seemed to fill the bay, to fill the whole world, as if we were the only things in it alive. "I think it has to do with escape," he said. "Escaping my troubles, I guess." The water surrounding us was black and deep. The moon shone high, and all we could hear was the sound of peace. Troubles, I thought? Were there still so many troubles, even here, on our honeymoon?

We docked at the deserted island and scrambled across the rocks. I watched his profile in the dark, underneath the moon.

We ate our chicken sandwiches. We'd brought a bottle of cider but forgotten about cups so we had to pass the bottle back and forth.

It was August 1977 and the future was all around us. The following August under a different moon, everything in our lives would change. Four years after that, an unnamed sailor would take a boat from Lewis Wharf and then jump ship at a different island. He would disappear like Enoch.

Seventeen

Our first apartment as a married couple was a one bedroom on Grove Street, the cheap side of Beacon Hill, with corner windows framing a view downhill. Sun streamed in. The galley kitchen had shabby wooden cupboards. The bathroom was tiled in pink and black.

The neighbors, like us, were temporary residents, all passing through. I befriended a botanist called Jenny who lived on the floor below us with her Lebanese boyfriend. She taught me how to make hummus and baba ganoush, mashing up eggplant, squeezing in lemon and garlic. Next door was Stetson, an architect who had recently come out of the closet, leaving a wife and ten-year-old son in Revere. But mostly there were students.

Angus and I badly wanted a piano, and Pastor Jackson who had always encouraged his musical gift, lent us a baby grand which had been in the church parlor, and which nobody used. Angus rented a van to drive the piano in town. He removed one of the windows of our second floor apartment and rigged up an elaborate pulley system. He disassembled the piano, and carried it up piece by piece: the legs, keyboard and piano lid. Afterwards, he and a couple of other friends wrapped the body of the piano in heavy canvas straps. He stared up at the window, making calculations, working deliberately and with confidence.

The piano hoisted through the air and a crowd gathered on the street below to watch. Everyone gasped as it lifted. We watched that prized possession swing precariously above the ground against a cloudless sky, until Angus appeared at the window upstairs and leaned out so far I thought he might fall. Instead he caught the rope and guided the instrument towards the window opening, at last easing it downwards, against the padded ledge.

∽

The muslin curtains stirred in the breeze of our bedroom. Angus studied philosophy books for his new college classes, while I sewed a cover for our hand-me-down loveseat. We took showers, stood beneath the water, smelling of almond soap, slippery with soap and filled up with each other. On weekends we made eggs and toast, and coffee in an hourglass pot. Piano notes sailed through the air, and down the street: Ecossaises in E Flat, jazz improvisations and Beethoven sonatas. On rainy evenings we went to the Exeter Street Theatre to see *The Rocky Horror Picture Show*, or took the T to the Orson Wells in Cambridge, where we saw classics like *The Shop around the Corner* and new French films like *Celine and Julie Go Boating*.

The corner store on Grove Street sold Duraflame logs, cocktail sticks, instant coffee, milk, Wonderbread and newspapers. Mildred, a fat toothless woman in men's work boots sat on the stoop out front. When I hurried past on my way to the Laundromat she heckled me. "How's the bride? Did you burn the biscuits yet?"

I combed through the *Boston Phoenix* and *Real Paper*, circling want ads: Administrative Assistant at Fisher Junior College; Researcher at Museum of Fine Arts; Piano Teacher for Mentally Handicapped Adult. No ads for writers, though. I wanted to be a writer or an artist. Absolutely anything but office work. But I was looking for meaning and connection, without any real sense of how I might find it. One thing was clear: It was going to be hard to make decent money doing anything decent. Nevertheless, I set up my apartment workspace, full of expectation, and when I came back from a morning at Tango's, and Angus was safely in class, I sat there diligently typing, gazing out of the window onto Grove Street, sipping my coffee and thinking, then typing out some more.

The first response to my job applications came from Shirley Stringfellow, who wanted a piano teacher for her son Melvin. "Ruby," said Angus, "you are crazy as a loon."

Undeterred, I took the train to Coolidge Corner to meet my new pupil. The Stringfellows lived in an apartment on a tree-lined street. My new pupil Melvin was partially blind and mentally handicapped, a large empty sack of a guy in his thirties. When you tried to engage him, his eyes fluttered off to the side, and the eyeballs strobed and flickered.

Shirley, his mother, was diminutive and wore a querulous expression. It soon became clear that caring for Melvin had become the central focus of her life. "Music brings out something very special in Melvin," she explained, as we trooped down a narrow hall into their living room. There were a great many doilies around the place, and lots of crochet.

"HelloRuby," Melvin repeated, in a single unmodulated stream. "Skinnie Minnie Fishtails," he added, rocking in his chair.

"That's his favorite song," Shirley explained. "You can play anything and he picks it right up. Anything you like."

I had brought along a beginners' volume called *Teaching Little Fingers to Play*. Melvin's fingers were like big fat sausages.

"Can you play something for us?" Shirley asked. I sat at their upright piano feeling slightly foolish, and by way of demonstration, played one of the few things I knew from memory, a Bach Invention, while Melvin stood beside me rocking gently back and forth.

"Maybe something more along these lines?" suggested Shirley, producing an ancient songbook with a broken binding. "*Oh You Beautiful Doll*? How about that?" And after I played it, Shirley asked me to come in once a week.

The job paid next to nothing, but anything was better than the kind of job that paid – which as far as I could see meant sitting in somebody's boring and important office, typing their letters and answering their phones.

Melvin waited on the porch each week, with the open door behind him and I was charmed by his simplicity, and my ability to connect with him through music. When I heard his "HelloRuby," it was as though he hadn't registered the passage of time between my visits.

We sat together at the piano. "Okay, Melvin. You see these two black notes and how they have a white one in the middle?" I began. "See how it looks like a dog in a kennel? Well, that's how you can remember the name of the note. Because D is for dog."

"Two black notes," said Melvin.

"The note next to D is called C," I persisted. "Do you know the alphabet?"

"Two black notes," he repeated.

"Look Melvin. Can you copy what my fingers do?"

"Two black notes," said Melvin.

Shirley peered at us thought the kitchen doorway. "You're gonna love this, honey. After you left last week he did that classy song you played, with all the little twinkles and everything."

"The Bach invention?"

"That's the one," said Shirley. "Mel, can you play it for Ruby?"

But Melvin simply rocked himself beside me and looked off to the side. "Don't be shy Melvin," I pleaded.

"Two black notes," he answered. "Don't be shy."

He brightened considerably when I opened up the songbook to *Skinnie Minnie Fishtails*. Then his eyes shifted, fluttering back and forth, as he sang.

When Melvin finally loosened up enough to play in my presence, I was flabbergasted. Shirley hadn't exaggerated. He could play Bach's 4th Invention. And he could play it exactly as I had, on the day we met.

I raced back home to share this news with Angus and see his reaction. But when I arrived, I found he had a friend with him, a guy from his philosophy class. They sat in the living room drinking bottled beer. The atmosphere in our apartment seemed stuffy and conspiratorial, and I felt their tension as soon as I entered.

"Hello. I'm Ruby, Angus's wife," with an outstretched hand.

"Mike Posey," he replied, shooting a glance towards Angus.

In telling Angus about Melvin, I gained a little ground. "It was incredible. He must be a savant," I said. "He never seems to watch that closely when I play. If you could have been there today, you would have been amazed. You see? My work is paying off!"

"But how is he doing it?" Angus asked, genuinely taken by the story.

"I have no idea."

"Man," he said. "That's wild." And he leaned on his elbows, mystified

"He hovers round, as if he's in his own world most of the time. But this has been inside him all the time, and it only needed bringing out."

Mike Posey waited for us to finish, gazing round the room, as though the ceiling molding held more interest than our conversation.

"But he isn't a genius," Angus put in, almost as though he needed to find a loophole. "It's more like he's parroting."

"So? Who said it was genius? It doesn't have to be genius to mean something."

"You know," he agreed, "that's true."

"And he could have died without anyone discovering his talent. He has this incredible gift! My God! When I think how he put up with my silly explanations about the two black notes and the dog in the kennel."

Mike Posey got to his feet. He shook out his shoulders. "I gotta go," he said. "Nice meeting you. And you," he looked at Angus, "I'll be seeing in class."

I watched from the window, as he exited to the street, then stood in front of our door, and lit a cigarette, before heading off down Grove Street.

"Who was that guy?" I asked.

"I'd like him to become a friend," said Angus.

"I think he's strange."

"Why do you say that?"

"I guess I felt like I was interrupting."

"As a matter of fact he's a really interesting guy. Don't you want me to have any friends?"

∽

We needed to paint the kitchen. I picked up some Duron paint samples on my way home from work and for several days, Angus and I pondered the different shades in the color pallet, pairing them together, holding them up against the wall. I worked at Tango's every morning, and when I came home and Angus was at class, or working his part time job at his father's business on Newbury Street, I sat at my portable typewriter, trying to write stories. Sometimes I sat on the sofa with my drawing pad, making pen and ink sketches, illustrations to go with my stories.

One evening when I came home from teaching Melvin, Angus was hanging a couple of shelving units on the wall behind the piano. "Where did you get those?" They were Victorian bric a brac, and not quite to my taste.

"I was out in Hingham helping my dad clear the barn, and they had these things in storage. Don't you like them?"

"They kind of make the apartment look like the Bologna Club," I said.

"The what?"

"*The Unpleasantness at the Bologna Club* is a book by Dorothy Sayers," I said.

Angus leaned backwards into his laughter, and soon I was laughing too. It was the word *unpleasantness* we found so funny.

But while I was at Tango's the following morning, Angus telephoned to tell me about a sudden cockroach infestation in the apartment, play by play from the front line. "It's like a fucking plague in here! They're all over the ceiling!" I stood in Oliver's office listening quietly as Angus raged down the telephone. "I can see them coming in. Jesus Christ- I think they're fumigating next door and now they're relocating. What the fuck, Ruby? Is this how we want to live?"

I stopped at the hardware store on my way home from Tango's to pick up some Roach Motels, and a few more Duron color strips of paint samples. I came up the street, past the hag on her door stoop. "Hey, Mildred."

"How's the bride?" she cried, and as I turned the key in our mailbox, magazines of all descriptions spilled forth.

Upstairs, I handed Angus a Smithsonian, Architectural Digest, Writer's Digest and Popular Mechanics. "Where did all these come from?" I asked.

"I found one of those cards where you can order what you want, and checked off the magazines that interested me," he said.

"You can't do that," I said.

"Sure I can. I already did it!"

"But how are we going to pay for them?" I sifted carefully through the rest of the mail. No news yet from the junior college where I'd applied for an administrative post. Nor from the

Museum of Fine Arts. Every day it was nothing but bills, and even more magazines: Time, Newsweek, Atlantic Monthly...

"How are we going to pay for all of these?" I wailed. "Subscriptions cost money. We'll have to cancel some of them."

"Yeah. I guess you have a point. I didn't realize I'd ordered quite so many."

"If I can just cobble a living together with Tango's and find some other part time work, I'll still have time to write," I said.

"As long as you're actually getting paid. What does Melvin pay you? How much do you think you're worth?"

I opened up the phone bill. "Hey! Wait a minute. This can't be right!" It was up in the hundreds, and full of long distance calls. "What are all these collect calls from Arizona?"

"Oh," he said. "That's Frenchie."

"Who the hell is Frenchie?"

"Don't worry about him. He owes me money which I'm trying to get back."

"Why does he owe you money?"

"He was in jail with me. It's a long story."

"So he's phoning you from jail?"

"Nope. Just Arizona."

"Why do you stay in touch with people like that?"

"Frenchie is a contact of mine. He plans to send a car from Roswell, New Mexico, as a way of settling a deal."

"But how is that going to settle the deal? It doesn't make sense. And anyway, what is the deal?"

"Don't worry, Rube, It makes perfect sense," Angus said. "Since the weather out west is so much better, you can get second hand cars in top condition for cheap. I'm getting an Audi. I'm having some people drive it across the country for me."

"I'm sorry. I still don't understand."

"I'll take care of it. And you are going to love this car when it gets here."

∼

The Roach Motels rattled with their occupants. Angus threw them out. He took great care in cleaning up the kitchen, sponging over the taps with soap, wiping down the counters, rinsing out the sink and the dishes, smoothing them under running water with the flat of his hand. He made us both sandwiches while I spread the floor with newspapers. Now that the cockroaches had all been killed, we planned to paint the wall a rich dark shade called Plum Burst.

I looked around for something to open the paint can with when I saw he had emptied the contents of his pockets onto the table. There was a handful of change, receipts and keys, as well as his Arizona driver's license. I peered at it, at first not understanding what I saw. "Angus?" He was busy eating his sandwich and reading a volume of Carl Jung. "This license says Angus Johnson instead of Angus Aleshire." He took a new bite of his enormous sandwich. Salami, cheese, tomato, lettuce and alfalfa sprouts, chewing slowly and deliberately. "Why is your license under a pseudonym?"

"Ruby," he said. "I don't want to argue with you about that."

"I don't want to argue either. I just want to know what it means."

"That happened years ago, and I never bothered to change it. I took the name Johnson when I lived in Arizona."

"Why?"

He looked at me steadily. "I was a criminal, remember?" Then, "Come on! Do you realize you're interrupting my college studies for us to have this conversation?" He looked back down at his book. "You should study Jungian thought, Rube. I think you'd find it fascinating. In fact, listen to this – he's talking here about how the psyche is not obliged to live in time and space..."

I'd made a big mistake. I'd painted the kitchen wall in Plum Burst when I should have chosen Iris Moon. The phone rang. It was a collect call from Frenchie.

"No I will not accept charges!" I barked into the telephone. "Get the hell out of our lives!" Angus watched from across the room, without reacting. I slammed down the phone, picked up a glass and hurled it at the newly painted wall. Angus stared at me, shocked. Then he got to his feet and went to fetch the broom.

The following day, I dressed and showered, and left for work without a word. The ugly residue of argument clung to me all morning. But my mood wore off as the day wore on. It always did, when books and the interesting flow of friends and acquaintances surrounded me – students and writers who were just like me, trying to make a living while they labored at their poetry. I chatted with Enid Aikin, who had shaved her head and recently participated in a training seminar called est. I had lunch with Ari, who was auditioning for a play called *Don Perlimplin and his Love for Belisa in the Garden*. Then after work, I ran into Sal Rosenblatt, a strange old guy who had a small recording company in Harvard Square. When he suggested drinks at the Harvest, I decided to accept.

I telephoned Angus several times throughout the day, hoping to make amends. But there was never an answer. Over drinks at the Harvest, Sal told me he wanted to make recordings of poets reading their work. Maybe I could work with him, he suggested. I knew about poetry, didn't I?

Afterwards, heading over the bridge on the T, I gazed at the Boston city lights reflected on the Charles River, and felt myself fully alive. It was 8:20 when I reached Charles Street Station, crossed the bridge, passed the gas station on the corner, and headed up Joy Street, which connected to Grove. Except it puzzled me to look up at our apartment, and see that the windows were dark.

I opened the living room door to see the answering machine blinking with all my uncollected messages. I turned on the lights. Angus was sitting on the sofa with his head in his hands. "What are you doing?" I asked.

He didn't look up. "Something really fucked up has happened." What he told me then turned everything on its head. He'd just returned from Hingham. Had gone out that morning to help his father clear the barn. Instead they ended up in juvenile court. Beth and her boyfriend Bone had been arrested. Bone was in possession of an illegal firearm, and Beth was running away from home. There had been a huge fight between Beth and the Aleshires, and Cheryl Aleshire was furious at Angus for taking his sister's side.

I sat beside him, still dressed in my coat. Their father, he told me, had a habit of waking Beth up every morning for school. He would flip on the lights without warning and then strip off the bed sheets. Now she was accusing him of making sexual advances.

"It was so fucked up in that courtroom," he said. "My mother at full throttle on one side, arguing with the judge. My dad sitting in silence, with his hands in his lap. And Beth on the other side of the courtroom, crying to a social worker." His expression retreated inwards. "I don't know what to do," he said at last.

My mind reeled. "That's horrifying," I said. "I mean, is that really how he wakes her up in the morning? It doesn't even make sense."

"Sure," said Angus, "He's done that for years. He's full of stuff like that. The way he used to punish us. He'd make us pull our pants down and bend over. And then he'd hit us with his belt."

"You're kidding me!"

"It was so humiliating."

"But have you talked openly about her accusations? What does he say?"

"He denies it," said Angus, "of course."

I tried to process the information. I tried to understand the truth. But thoughts wouldn't form. Only horrible images – snapshots of his family that didn't fit together with anything I knew. "But she's how old? Sixteen now?"

Angus shook his head. "And you know what? It doesn't really matter what the truth is. Because that house is poisonous. I have no choice but to help her move some stuff to Bone's."

"But what does your mother say?"

"She doesn't believe he's done anything wrong."

"But how is that possible? Does your mother think she'd be better off living with Bone?

"He may be a fuck up," said Angus. "But you want to know something weird? Bone is the only fuck up in this story you can trust."

Everything had tilted. I was looking at truth through a funhouse mirror. My worries about his fake license felt so naïve and petty. Nothing was clear anymore. I couldn't grab hold of anyone's motivations or make any sense of any of it.

Eighteen

Beth and her boyfriend Bone moved to an apartment in Hull. Angus made several trips out to help them, with the result that Cheryl and Frank were no longer talking to him. Meanwhile Frank maintained his absolute innocence. He refused to communicate with Beth or with Angus, so I telephoned one evening, hoping to get him on the line. Surprisingly, he came to the phone and listened in silence as I spoke. "Obviously this whole thing is terribly upsetting for everyone concerned," I said. "But there isn't any way forward unless you can all talk openly with each other."

"I know." His voice was barely audible.

"And Angus has looked up to you for years. He loves you. This is just devastating him. You do know that, I hope.

"Frank was hurt and deeply offended. "You know," he said. "I would do anything for my kids. Anything in the world. But when I'm accused of...something such as I am accused of here..." his voice trailed off. It was as though we teetered on the edge of a moral sinkhole that threatened to suck us all downwards.

If there hadn't been that split in the Aleshire family, maybe things wouldn't have taken the turn they did. But it was against this backdrop that Sal Rosenblatt invited me out again, this time to his office. Angus didn't trust him. "He sounds like a player, Ruby," he said. So he came along, and we walked there together from Tango's.

Sal invited us into his lair. Toulouse Lautrec posters decorated the walls. We sat opposite Sal on a black vinyl sofa, while Sal sat at his desk. "I think it's just great to see young kids like yourselves, getting married, setting up house..." he said in his nasally drawl. "It's very unusual."

He explained that he'd been through tough times himself. He was treated in Mclean Hospital the same time Silvia Plath was there. Oh yes, a lovely girl. He knew Kurt Vonnegut too. What a guy. He had connections and his friends made connections for him before he went on the wagon. Nothing like friends when you are down on your luck.

He poured us Johnny Walker highballs as the telephone rang. From Sal's end of the conversation we deduced that it was a woman, wanting to know if her husband was there. "No, Joanne," he said, "I haven't seen Harry in months."

A few minutes later, Harry himself called, to firm up Sal as his alibi. "Awe, Jeez," said Sal into the phone. "I'm awful sorry," because now the wife was onto him.

"He's with another woman," Angus murmured to me, as an aside. I found it terribly annoying. Afterwards, when we rode back home on the T, Angus said, "I was right, Ruby. That guy's an asshole. Stay away from him. I didn't like him at all."

By now Melvin was playing several pieces from his songbook, as well as the Bach Invention, and he played for me willingly while I sat beside him. I almost believed I had found a mission. Yet I was also conscious that I had taught him nothing. All I had done was encourage him to be himself. That, and given him something to copy: an example.

I sent out stories to small magazines with renewed commitment and vigor. The magazines had names like Calliope's Corner and Back Water Review. I slipped my stories into brown envelopes and posted them off to the world, and began amassing a pile of form rejection slips.

Then one morning in the office at Tango's, Oliver made an announcement. He had decided to revive his poetry imprint Tango's Press and wanted me to work as assistant editor, reading manuscripts and copyediting. It would mean more money and more responsibility. I was thrilled. There was so much I could learn under his tutelage, and not only about writing. Oliver knew how to think. He knew how to place his feelings circumspectly in the waistcoat pocket of his thoughts.

∼

Out in Hingham, Sorrel started ballet. Lydia had a new boyfriend from Barcelona and was thinking of traveling with him in Europe. Nora directed a production of *The Rivals* and Hetty the dog grew senile. She stood in the middle of the back yard, her legs like a tripod, barking at nothing. Timothy planned a lecture tour and Freddy moved to an apartment in Hull with some of his band members.

I consulted with Oliver about the authors he hoped to publish in his new chapbook series. "The idea would be a series of New England poets," he explained, "demonstrating a different kind of range. To show that New England poetry isn't just about sitting on a log in the middle of the woods." He pinched his nose and smoothed his moustache circumspectly."So, you want the selection to be careful, but not too experimental?"

"A black poet from Massachusetts, for instance; a lesbian from Connecticut..." He chuckled with a new thought. "Oh, by the way," he said, "last Saturday, I went to Suffolk Downs with James and I'm afraid we lost money, betting on the races."

"You mean James Gillespie?"

"If you must know, we lost twenty dollars," Oliver continued.

"But I thought he joined the Navy."

"Yeah, well, it didn't work out." There was an awkward pause, each of us thinking our own thoughts. I wiped my palms on my skirt. Oliver shifted on his cushions and focused on a pile of correspondence. "Yeah, Ruby," he said at length. "There are many walking wounded, especially at Suffolk Downs." He looked at me craftily then, as though he had me all sized up. The wall clock ticked and I turned my head, to stack my papers carefully. "He asked me to look over some poems," Oliver's voice continued. "He has a fascination for the counting out of syllables and the discovery of patterns, which lays aside all meaning. But it seems to me..." said Oliver, his meager voice gathering momentum, "it seems to me, in part, a misuse of language."

It was several weeks before James and I met face to face. He came up the stairs of our Grove Street apartment while Angus was in class. I leaned expectant, over the banister railing, my hair tied up in a colored scarf: Mrs. Aleshire, playing house, making an impression.

"You wretch!" he laughed, and when he reached the top of the stairs, he pulled me into his arms. He was more confident than the last time I'd seen him but we held each other nervously.

As I disengaged, I forced my face to a sociable smile. "What happened? Why are you back so soon?"

We stepped into the apartment. He looked handsome, dressed in a white shirt with the sleeves rolled up, and as always he carried a couple of books. "Medical problems," he told me.

"So you were, what? Discharged?"

"This place," he said, glancing round the living room. "How did you get the piano up?"

"Angus took out a window and hoisted it up on a pulley."

James nodded. "You have a good view from here," he said. His skin was tanned and as usual his hair was cut very short. It suited him.

"So," I said, "You left the Navy because...?"

"I wanted to get out, so I told them I was hearing voices."

"Voices. Wow."

"Which wasn't entirely untrue." We stared at each other a moment, then both our expressions went opaque. Something behind his eyes took a few steps back and disappeared.

"Would you like a drink?" I asked.

"Water?" he suggested. I went to the kitchen, shook out some ice cubes from a tray in the freezer and filled up a glass.

"You're looking very well," he remarked from the other room.

"So are you. Still writing, I hear?"

"I have a few finished poems," he said. "And I've filled up a couple of notebooks. I need to look through them more seriously though, and see what I've got."

James sipped his water while I told him that Oliver was reviving his press. Yes, he said, he had heard that. He put his glass on the table. "I'm actually looking for somewhere to rent."

"Great," I said. "Why don't you try our landlord? His office is on Charles Street." I scribbled the name on a piece of notebook paper, and James said he'd check it out. But after he'd gone, I saw he'd forgotten his books on the radiator, over by the windowsill.

Yellow notebook paper, torn and buried in the trash bin. It was the kind of paper Angus had used when he wrote that letter to me in Paris. I bent to scoop out the scraps, guiltily piecing them together on the table, to read his unmistakable half printed slant. *Dear Frenchie, I talked to Bone about the shipment...*

Oh my God. Not Frenchie again. But what the heck did he have to do with Bone? I stared at the yellow scraps, before tipping them back to the trash.

Some days later, Angus informed me that he'd arranged for two students from Rhode Island School of Design to drive his new Audi across the country. They were driving it back east because they were coming for college and needed the transportation. They were doing it for free.

"I beg you Angus," I pleaded, sitting on the carpet of our living room. "Do not get this car. For one thing, we don't even need one. And besides that, you said you would stop communicating with Frenchie. Please Angus. Cut off communication."

"By the way," he interrupted, "you didn't tell me Gillespie was back in the picture."

I sat on the carpet and stared at him, dumbfounded. "Yes, I did. I told you he left the Navy."

"Be honest. You didn't say he came round to see you."

"He didn't come round just to see me. And he was only here for twenty minutes."

"Are you suggesting he came to see me?"

"What's that supposed to mean? Maybe I forgot. But if you're trying to divert me, Angus, it isn't working. We were talking about the car. And James has nothing to do with that."

"Who's being devious now," he said.

"I just forgot to mention it."

"When I forget to mention things, you go ballistic."

"Because you have a history, Angus. I'm naturally wary when you leave important information out. I mean, what am I supposed to think when some guy named Frenchie phones collect from a jail cell?"

"So you get a free ride, when it comes to James Gillespie. But I have to answer every question you ask about what I'm doing and when I'm doing it. I can't even invite a friend from University round without you getting suspicious. Does that seem fair to you?"

"That guy from Suffolk was very weird," I said. "And he never once looked me in the eye the whole time he was here."

"...while James Gillespie is totally transparent."

"All right," I said. "So maybe I didn't mention James, because I thought it might upset you."

"Aha!"

"...but there's absolutely no need for suspicion."

"Well I feel the same. As I already told you, the deal is settled." Angus replied. He was utterly calm, handling my displeasure so reasonably, that even though I had a point, it confused me.

"I feel like you aren't being straight with me," I said. "You won't tell me what the deal is, or why Bone is suddenly involved."

"You didn't ask."

"I'm asking now."

"All right. I'm helping Bone to get some work," he said.

"Doing what? Dealing drugs?"

"Ruby," he said. "It's a sliding scale. And that's what you don't understand. Someone like Bone has limited options. Think about it. I mean really, use your mind and imagination! Think about the books you've read – think about *Les Miserables* or *Moll Flanders* or *Great Expectations*. Bone is like a character in one of those books. He needs the money, but he doesn't have any other skills."

"So you're setting him up as a dealer?"

"If you have a better idea, I'll be happy to hear it."

"I don't. At least, not yet. But that one is absolutely crazy."

"And what should I do about Beth, in your opinion? Should I send her back to my parents' house? No one else is helping her out, in case you haven't noticed. You aren't helping her. The church isn't helping her. Not even the court."

"Do you want her living with a drug dealer?"

"She is who she is, Ruby."

"She'll be living with Bone and dealing drugs..."

"First of all, Beth isn't like you. Not even remotely. She doesn't have your background and she has totally different problems. She's been smoking pot for years now. Do you think there's a moral difference between smoking pot and dealing it? As a matter of fact, it's a lot more honest this way."

"Oh my God, Angus, this is absolutely crazy! It's this kind of thinking that put you in jail."

"Try to understand that she doesn't have the same moral code as you."

"So you're going to help her lower her expectations..."

"I'm not the cops, Ruby. She knows what kind of guy Bone is..."

"And don't you think she should set her sights a bit higher..."

"You are living with *me*. Should you set your sights higher? Come on! Can't you see that it's a lot more complicated than how it appears on the surface?"

"You are a different case. You said you were trying to reform," I said. "At least that's what you told me you were doing..."

"And I am. I've promised you that. After this, I won't be involved with Frenchie again. He'll never phone here and you won't have to think about him. Isn't that what you want?"

∼

A week later, Angus waited on the Grove Street curbside as the RISD students pulled up in a powder blue Audi with coach doors that clicked gently when you shut them. It had cream leather seats, and a nut mahogany dashboard. He checked out every detail, his face creased into a frenzied smile. He was lit from within. Ecstatic.

The car was spectacular. I never in my life imagined us having a car like that. "Get in!" said Angus. And I slipped into the soft leather seat beside him and he drove us round the city. Everything was quiet outside the car and we were cushioned in a luxury world.

"It feels like we just won the lottery," I said.

"You see?" he beamed, "Wasn't this a great idea?" He hadn't looked so happy for weeks.

"I hope this is the end of it, though. I really don't want you getting involved in more scams after this."

"First of all, it's not a scam. It's money from a trust fund. And I can spend it any way I want. My mother left it for me before she died. You don't begrudge me that, do you?"

"Of course not. How can I begrudge you money from a trust fund? But surely that isn't the point."

"What is the point?"

"Priorities," I said. "It's a question of priorities."

But he stopped my questions with answers to questions I hadn't thought to ask, with new sexual intimacies and disclosures. We bore each other away on the switch rail of sex, in bed and on the living room floor, up against the front door, up against the piano, obscured from the window view. When we made love we returned to our elements. We turned into fire and water.

In the middle of the night, I woke up alone. "Angus?" No answer. I got out of bed and went into the living room. Streetlight played across the shadowed walls. I looked down to the barren city street, past the closed corner store, and the stoop where Mildred always sat. Nobody and nothing was out there now.

I grabbed my keys, threw on a robe and ventured into the hall. It smelled of mice and the stuff they used to fumigate. I tiptoed down the stairs, past Jenny the botanist's door, in the semi darkness. No sign of life there, and the main door downstairs was shut fast. Then, retracing my steps, I noticed a pair of Angus's shoes left by the open cellar door, at the top of the stairs. The picture of those shoes was utterly perplexing, side by side in the light which streamed up from the basement. Was he down there without his shoes? And if so, what was he doing? There may be rats down there, I thought, and God knows how many cockroaches!

It wasn't fear that gripped me then. It wasn't even panic. It was simply an awareness that I couldn't grasp hold of or use the information. It slid from me like mercury.

And to my shame, I let it. I let it slide away and didn't reason it through. I didn't want possession of it. I hated it so thoroughly that I needed to ward it off – to get as far away from it as possible.

I took the stairs back to our apartment, and in bed, I pulled the covers up, curling into a fetal position, with my eyes wide open. Everything fell silent. All except for my heart of course, which thudded so violently I felt it in my eardrums.

I remembered how Sorrel had a favorite bedtime story about Pecos Bill. At the end, Pecos Bill disappeared when he tried to lasso a tornado. Well, that's what it was like being married to Angus: like trying to lasso a tornado.

I lay in the dark, trying to shut down my conscious mind, trying to fall asleep. But like a mountain peak rising from the middle of a fog, a piece of my mind remained vigilant. Then I dreamed I was running. I had this urgent need to run as hard and fast as I could, except my limbs were paralyzed, liquefied weights without momentum. Panic. A cascade of terror. Something unknown pursued me but the only solid thing I knew was the need to run and hide. And yet I could not move.

Nineteen

I woke with a start to the ringing phone. Our bed in the early morning light was still smoothed flat and empty beside me. I snatched up the receiver to hear the background noise, a kind of echo and hum on the line. "Mrs. Aleshire? Officer Feeley here, down at the Cambridge Precinct..." My head felt empty and cold as a shell. My ears blocked. All the meaning in the conversation rained down and splashed away, so that it was only after I hung up that I understood Angus had been held in jail overnight, and that I could come and bail him out if I wanted.

Who could I call? Ari was in no position to help and calling James didn't seem a good idea. I considered Jenny from downstairs. Except I didn't want her thinking badly of Angus, especially when she liked him so much.

What was wrong with me? Angus's image had nothing to do with it. Yet at the time, upholding his image felt crucial. If he was succumbing to temptations that must be warded off, it wouldn't help his struggle if others began to distrust him. I had to protect everyone from this disruptive information, to keep it as far from their image of Angus as possible.

I telephoned home, waking Nora up. "Oh darling," in a thick sleepy voice, "I can't believe he's doing this. When did it all start? Oh, Lord. What can we do? Now, calm down. You have to calm down. Let's think this through. Would you like Timothy to drive in and fetch you?"

Timothy drove in, seeming to arrive from a reality now alien to me, a fresh and wholesome world, smelling of toothpaste and Ivory soap. "What's going on, honey?"

I threw myself into his arms and sobbed. I sobbed for my lost innocence, for Angus and Beth's lost innocence, for all the ways the world had crumbled around me. Timothy was my only hope, Timothy and his faith in God. Perhaps I would have disdained such faith if I hadn't so desperately needed it. I might have seen faith as hopelessly naïve. Now I clung to it, and when at last he had calmed me down, I asked if we could please drive to the police station where Angus was being held.

"You're absolutely sure about this?"

I told him that I was.

A golden morning light rose over Harvard University. Autumn leaves floated to the ground, newspapers were delivered in stacks, and a few early commuters trickled up the steps from the subway entrance. A woman walked her dog across the brick pavement. Morning routines had never looked more sparkling, or so inaccessible. It was as though a mental pane of glass, not just a physical windscreen, separated me from the rest of the world. I sat beside my father in the car, foolish, betrayed and conflicted, tears wetting my face.

We found a parking space in front of the Cambridge Police Station. Timothy pulled in, turned off the car, looked at me and sighed. His face was grave, but he was resolved. "Honey," he said. "Be strong. It's good that this has come out. And whatever you decide, we will stand by you. There's nothing hidden that shall not be revealed."

We learned that the stereo store above Sal Rosenblatt's office had been broken into. At least, the locks on Sal's office door had been tampered with, a window had been broken, and Angus had been apprehended as a suspect when running from the scene.

So we bailed him out, and drove back to Grove Street, where Timothy sat with us for more than an hour. He began quite sternly. But his deeper impact lay in the simple power of truth and gentle honesty on his side. "I urge you, Angus," Timothy said. "To return to God. He is an ever-present help and ready to forgive you. But you have got to hold fast. You cannot allow yourself to lapse like this. It will never pay off. There's simply too much to lose. The suffering you'll bring on yourself! Not to mention what it will do to Ruby." Angus sat on the piano stool, his face immobile. Every so often he shot a glance at me, and all the things that were going on inside him came up in the expression behind his eyes. "And what you will gain if you turn to good is immeasurable. Isaiah tells us to hearken diligently to God," Timothy continued. "He tells us to eat that which is good and let your soul delight itself in fatness. Incline your ear and come unto me,' he says. 'Hear, and your soul shall live.' This is the promise you've been given, this spiritual nourishment available to you if you will just turn in the right direction, with diligence, and trust it."

Angus looked at me. I looked back. "Won't you say something," he pleaded.

"I don't know what to say. I've gone so far out on a limb for you," I said.

"We've been through a lot these last few weeks," he said.

"But you are so ready to throw it away. You are taking it out of my hands. And for what?"

"Do you still love me?" he asked.

"Soon that won't even matter."

"What are you saying?"

"What will it matter how much I love you Angus, if the law catches up with you. You're sabotaging all our hopes and dreams. You're throwing us both away."

He dropped his face to his hands. It hurt to the bottom of my soul to hear his voice sobbing and cracking like that. We waited with the Plum Burst wall, the covered sofa, Pastor Jackson's piano and the Bologna Club shelves.

"It's like an addiction. I swear to God. I get nothing out of it," he managed at last. "I hate myself when I'm doing it." He looked up, red-eyed, exhausted, his face wet and nose dripping, lips swollen and distorted in anguish. "I hate doing it. I swear. My heart pounds and my muscles tense up and my palms get sweaty, and I can't breathe."

We sat in a stunned and exhausted silence. "Why did you do it? I can't even imagine what you thought you were going to get out of it."

He didn't reply.

"And this is nothing new. You've been here before I was with you. You were strong enough then to pull yourself through. And now you have me. So can't you do it for me? Can't you try? Because otherwise there's nothing I can do. We're doomed."

"I promise," he told me, "I'm going to make this up to you. Please don't leave me. Don't give up on me. Please."

∽

Three weeks later I sat at the back of the courtroom, feeling small and powerless. How useless we had been at this sapling of a marriage. We had got off to such a bad start. I didn't know how I'd survive if they sent him to jail. I didn't see how it would be good for either of us if they took him away from me. I looked into the yawning abyss of our future, and knew there was nothing to stop our fall.

The court appointed lawyer explained to the judge that Angus was going to Suffolk University and getting straight A's, that he was newly married, and had a part time job. The judge listened and leafed with evident indifference through the file on his desk. Then he looked up and handed down a suspended sentence, putting Angus on probation. He ordered weekly counseling sessions with a court appointed psychologist. Perhaps with renewed counseling, the judge said, "you can contribute in a meaningful way to society, and fulfill your obligations, not the least of which is to this young wife of yours."

We returned home, holding tightly to each other's hands. Utterly spent and weak with gratitude, we crawled into bed and held each other close. Reprieve was like sleep, like soft and gentle sheets, while the city world continued on without us. We slept and woke and then we made love. We had that slow reassuring injection of each other. The anesthetic of orgasm. The talk about the addictive nature of his behavior and the influences we allowed in our lives. He agreed that he needed better influences, that he needed to rewire himself somehow. "But I can't make friends with normal people," he explained. "I always have to edit myself and I'm always aware that they don't really get it. It's like there's an abyss, which they haven't looked into and probably never will. I'm aware of something they are not, and it marks me out as different."

"How about James?" I suggested. "He'd make a good friend. He's interesting and intelligent and different in his own ways. I think you might have things in common."

"If you think it would be good, I'll try," he said.

We also resolved to go to church. It was as though we thought we needed the discipline like alcoholics needed A.A. So we sat in a green velvet pew, Sunday by Sunday, the sanctuary soaring above us, as we listened to Bach cantatas, and sermons about Jesus.

Oh, living water. I wanted so much to believe in you, then. I wanted to drink you and never thirst again. I wanted a well of water, springing up to everlasting life. I wanted with all of my heart to believe that if a man had a hundred sheep, and one of them went astray, he would leave the ninety-nine, and go into the mountains, and find that stray. And that he would rejoice more in that single sheep, than in the ninety-nine, which never went astray.

Twenty

CASUALTIES
by Ruby Lambert-Aleshire

She woke in the middle of blue night to a bedroom with diaphanous curtains and her husband sleeping. Something outside, a screech God knows how fast, of tires and gravel traveled minutes in her head, and a thump made her jump from bed. Down the clean hallway she ran to the kitchen, with warm cats and washed dishes. Outside she ran, in her lavender nightgown. The clothes pegs stood like sentinels on the moonlit line. The Norton's house was tidy, its vegetable patches and woodpiles waiting usefully. She ran on the moist grass, crab apples interfering with her toes, ran towards the big sound.

Others stood in night clothes on Winter Street, white and bewildered, yanked from sleep. A car had buckled around a tree. Silent and black, while police flashed lights in the windows. In the garden she had tended that day, her hat protecting her face from the sun, she now stood alone, crying, unable to stop even in bed, where her husband curled until morning.

∼

I took the stairs to our apartment, two by two and burst into the living room, where Angus and James sat playing Risk. They both looked up with surprise. "Prose Poet Quarterly has accepted my piece! Look at this! Look, you guys! They're paying me fifty dollars!"

Angus lit up with pleasure. "You're a published writer!"

"That's good," said James as he swallowed a smile. "That's very good."

Christmas came and went. A new year marked another new start and Melvin's lessons came to an end. Shirley could no longer pay for them, but we promised to stay in touch. But in February, an epic blizzard hit New England. It fell steadily and furiously, covering the garbage of Grove Street, socking everyone in. The sea roared, biting deeply into the coast. Houses tore from their foundations as if they were lobster pots. Boats were beached and cracked. Sand, silt and snow washed through buildings. Residents evacuated. Others went into hibernation, venturing outside only to shovel the snow from their cars and driveways.

I telephoned the family in Hingham to make sure they were safe and had enough food, because in Boston the bread had run out, and delivery trucks couldn't pass into the city.

Freddy and his band members were evidently stranded in Hull, as were Beth and Bone, all living a high adventure. But Hingham was calmer because of the harbor. Nora and Timothy heaped banks of snow on either side of the driveway and Grandpa watched from the window, as the world became a labyrinth of icy paths. Snow covered the windows. Icicles hung down like swords from the gutters. The only spot of color in the landscape, according to Nora, was Sorrel in her pink snowpants and bobble hat, having a go with the shovel.

A snowplow rumbled up Grove Street in front of our apartment. The atmosphere buzzed and misted into a scrim of soft silver grey. When at last the snow stopped falling, we went out to explore, walking in our gloves and hats down the whitened roadways, awed by the silence. It was a festival of quiet, as far as Charles Street. All the corners were rounded and softened. Strangers acknowledged each other with smiles at the shared event and Angus called out down the sugar-iced street as we walked: "This is what it will be like when the oil runs out!"

To fill up the silent snowbound hours we played endless games of Scrabble. Angus practiced the piano, and learned a new sonata. He was thinking of taking lessons again. Since the bread had run out in the supermarkets, I phoned Nora for a scone recipe, not having any yeast in the house. Then I busily sifted flour in our tiny galley kitchen, greased pans, and turned the gas up high, while Angus played the piano. Then we ate the scones with butter and strawberry jam, in a room lit with candles.

James came round more frequently on those snowy days. He was living on a nearby street with his girlfriend, a poet called

Ann. Sometimes he came by alone, and we sat up talking into the night. I liked the way Angus drew him out of his silences, and how James began lending books to Angus: *Journey to the Edge of the Night* by Celine; and *Death on the Installment Plan*.

The electricity came back on. The snow melted, or else it turned black, and the city appeared worse than I recalled, full of slush and dirty corners. Angus got a temporary job with the HUD Disaster Office. He drove around the North Shore in his powder blue Audi, clipboard in hand, to assess damage, to walk through flooded living rooms and across crushed porches. I felt so proud of him when he reported back about the beachfront, full of broken wood, smashed boats, houses dashed upon the rocks, so much flotsam and jetsam. "You wouldn't believe it," he told me. "People have lost everything."

A new idea had been forming in my mind during those snowbound weeks: the idea that I might find work as an artist's model. I had modeled for Gilles when I stayed with him in Paris so I thought I knew what was involved. Also, Ari had done some life modeling at the Museum School and it paid very well. It would put me in an interesting environment of artists, and I could supplement my job at Tango's, still leaving time to write.

So on Ari's recommendation I took the T to the Museum School on the Fenway to check it out. It felt good to leave the confines of the apartment after so much bad weather, to travel down roads and sidewalks that were white and frozen cold. Tall, crusted banks of pockmarked snow rose against the curbside. I went up the newly shoveled path and through a set of big red doors.

The hallway was quiet. I wandered down a corridor, looking into studios, at large work surfaces and drafting tables and found myself in a sculpture studio. The floors were rough, the walls covered in shelves and stacked with supplies. Light streamed in from a skylight. The work was half finished, and because of that it felt more alive and authentic.

I examined a shelf of student work: a line of kneeling terra cotta girls, with their hands on their heads, differing only in execution -little bathers by a dried up stream. Wandering more deeply, I was taken by an angular installation of primary colored cubes – and the model of a head, with the planes of its face delineated; and a life-sized skeleton mounted on a stand. In this setting things were created, but words had no part in it.

"Are you looking for something?"

I jumped. A lanky grey haired woman stood beside me wearing a work apron. Her eyes were quick and direct, unembellished with makeup or artifice.

"I'm looking for the office," I replied. "Is there someone here who hires life models?

"That would be me," said the woman.

I explained about my friend Ari who had told me they might be hiring. I said I had modeled a little in the past, and was interested in joining a community of artists.

Her expression softened. "Maude Caruthers," she said. "I teach figurative sculpture. And yes, we are hiring models."

Back in our Grove Street apartment, Angus and James were poring over a set of blueprints spread across the table. "You'll never guess where I've just been," I said, taking off my scarf and mittens and unbuttoning my coat. Angus drummed his fingers, one knee jiggling up and down. He didn't look up. So I went to the kitchen, opened the fridge and stared inside. Nothing appealed. "Oh really, Ruby where have you been?" I said aloud to myself. "I've been to the Museum School. Oh wow, that sounds interesting." I lit the stove and put on the kettle, then returned to the living room, and stood in front of the piano, watching them. "Hello? Am I invisible?"

They both looked up and smiled briefly, as if only now realizing I was there. "What are you guys doing?"

"We're looking at plans for a sailboat," Angus explained. "Why were you at the Museum School?"

I leaned over his shoulder, trying to make sense of the diagrams, lines and notations on the blueprints spread before them. "Wow. Where did you get these?"

He stretched back in his chair, extending his arms, flinging one carelessly around my waist. "I ordered them through the mail. They're plans for a forty footer. I'm looking into building one."

"Building one?" I drew back. "You guys are kidding me, right?"

"Ruby," he said. "You're such a bummer sometimes."

James made a short embarrassed laugh.

"What happened at the Museum School," he prompted again.

"I spoke to a teacher of figurative sculpture..."

"And signed up for a class?"

"No. As a model. But can you please explain how you plan on building a sailboat? Surely I'm allowed to ask the question."

"You mean a nude model?"

"What about these blueprints?" I looked at James for help, but his face was closed; he was off limits.

"Ready?" Angus said and James stood stiffly, rocking awkwardly on the sides of his feet.

"Wait! We need to finish this conversation," I said.

"We'll talk later. Right now, we're driving to Cohasset. Do you want to come along?"

"Not really. I only just got home."

"That's what I thought."

James silently zipped up his parka. Angus picked up his jacket and went out the door with his head held high. He didn't even kiss me goodbye. I locked eyes briefly with James and he threw out another embarrassed laugh. "You're going to have to learn to roll with the punches, my dear," he said.

The kettle whistled from the kitchen. I took it off the boil and poured some water into a cup dunking a teabag angrily up and down. "Fuck him," I said to myself. "How dare he! Aren't I even allowed to ask questions?" I took out a manuscript Oliver had asked me to read, somebody's concrete poetry. I sipped my tea and although I turned several pages of the manuscript, I registered absolutely nothing, so I tossed it aside and dialed Ari's number.

"Hey Ruby. Can't talk now because I'm off to rehearse that Lorca play. *Don Perlimplin and his Love for Belisa in the Garden.* Can I call you back?"

"Sure," and I went downstairs to knock on Jenny the botanist's door.

"Hey!" Jenny poked her head round the door, and I saw she was dressed in a coat and woolen hat. "I was just heading out. Want to come for a little fresh air?"

Thickets of tree branches, glazed with ice showed a dusky pink against the whiteness. Jenny and I walked down Charles Street in the bitter cold almost as far as Beacon, and stopped at a corner café. It was buzzing with life. Little puddles of melted snow formed on the wooden floor between tables. We took off our coats and sat at a table against the wall in back and then we ordered carrot cake.

"That's pretty daring," she said, when I told her about the Museum School job, "if you don't mind taking off your clothes ..."

"Well, a friend of mine does it and sometimes it's portraiture work," I said. "Anyway, they're artists."

"What does Angus think?"

I sliced my cake with a fork, focusing on the plate with a frown. "He hasn't said. You know, Jenny, things with Angus are sometimes rather complicated." I had told her so little about his background, but now I opened up. I needed someone to talk to. So I explained about Sal Rosenblatt's office and the break-in, and finished with the blueprints. "And now he says he's planning on building a forty-foot boat. How can he be serious?"

Jenny listened, nodding and frowning. "Wow," she said at last. "It sounds to me like he needs psychiatric help. Someone who can prescribe medication. If he has a mental imbalance you need to know. It could be corrected quite simply. It might even be dietary."

"Actually, he is seeing someone. He gets counseling every week with a court appointed psychologist."

Jenny had a pert and pretty face and the air of someone who knew what she was talking about. She stared across the table. She was wearing a blue and red ski hat knitted with the word Bariloche. "It might be more serious than that. Maybe he is manic. He could need medication and psychologists can't prescribe medication. For that you need a psychiatrist. Shock treatment is also a possibility," she said.

"I think shock treatments are barbaric," I said.

Jenny shrugged. "I believe they've been helpful to some. You have to consider the alternative."

"You know, it's funny. I've always treated this like a moral issue," I told her. "Developing the ability to choose between right and wrong. Resisting old patterns of behavior. I've always thought his behavior was like an addiction and that he did these things as a kind of coping strategy."

Jenny sighed. "Behavior has all kinds of causes. Moral behavior can also be based on chemicals."

"Really? I thought it was based on ethics."

"No," she said. "It's chemical."

When I returned, Angus wasn't back. But I mulled over Jenny's words. The idea of Angus on medication didn't appeal to me at all. She seemed to see it as an obvious solution. I thought tranquilizers were a terrible idea. Such medication might alter something essential to his nature. I didn't want a lobotomized version of Angus. I couldn't imagine him with all his edges smoothed. I wanted a less criminal version of Angus, one who was less dangerous to himself, but not one wholly without danger.

Danger. I wondered what it meant. A fearless person didn't care about danger. I loved Angus's fearlessness. He seemed to see more possibilities in life because he was willing to question basic assumptions. He always took those dangerous steps that I would never dare.

Close to ten the telephone rang. They were at the Red Lion in Cohasset. Sorry, Angus said. He hadn't meant to argue. He'd be back soon. He just needed to get out of the house, was all. Cabin fever.

I took a long hot bath, put on a clean nightdress and went to bed with a pile of the magazines we'd recently had to cancel. I found myself reading about monarch butterflies. They flew for thousands of miles, in seasonal migrations. They laid their eggs under milkweed and then they died, the article said. Three generations lived and died in the same spot before the next migration. Then the great great grandchildren of the migrating butterflies journeyed back to where their ancestors had started.

It felt like I'd stumbled on an important and pertinent truth. I grabbed my journal and scribbled down some notes. And when at last I turned off the light, I slipped and flittered into dreams about butterflies.

I woke up suddenly and looked at the clock. 2:20 a.m. Still no sign of Angus. I got out of bed and went to the bathroom. My face staring back from the mirror was drained of color. Where was he? What was going on?

My features crumpled. Our wedding vows were only six months old. They had taken a terrible beating. Yet the idea of giving up seemed unendurable. I couldn't bear all those I told you so's from everyone we knew. It wasn't a question of weakness. It was more that I had an enormous sense of pride. I had invested so much of myself in Angus that there was a selfish demand to make him the fit the dream I had of him. The loss of that dream was greater for me, than any sense of self-preservation.

He returned at daybreak. He lay heavily on the bed in all of his clothes, and breathed out the sweet and sickly smell of booze. I barely moved, pinned as I was beneath the covers beside him. I couldn't sleep. At seven, I slipped out of the sheets and stood for longer than usual underneath the shower. Then I got out and toweled myself off, dressed in a vintage skirt, put on some red lipstick in an attempt to cheer myself up, and pulled on my boots. Then I hauled myself off to the subway for Tango's. It was an effort.

I stopped for an almond croissant in the square, but once I got to the bookshop all my resolve deserted me. I was exhausted. It was as much as I could do to sit on the sofa in Oliver's office, holding a mug of coffee. Oliver sorted through papers circumspectly while I told him what had transpired. "And when he finally returned," I said, "he fell asleep on top of the bed in his clothes. He didn't even put his pajamas on."

Oliver reached for his coffee cup, and took a thoughtful sip. "Well, Ruby. I wouldn't worry too much about pajamas." He put the cup back down again and pinched his nose. "Pajamas are a bourgeois concept. The fact that he doesn't sleep in pajamas... is no particular cause for concern." He adjusted his glasses. Picked up his cup once again. "A few late nights at the bar..."

"Sure," I said. "I understand." Oliver's words were comforting. They fed my sense that nothing was terribly wrong. Oliver himself had spent many nights of his youth carousing. It was some of those past experiences that made for his best anecdotes now.

We talked about monarch butterflies while Oliver sipped his second cup of coffee, about the primordial homing instinct passed down through generations. Except the garden butterflies had nothing in common with the journeyers, I told him. How could they? Some lived epic lives. Others were garden dwellers. And it seemed that when it came to butterflies, you couldn't have one without the other.

Oliver looked at me shrewdly. "Butterflies," he said, "are generally interesting. Nabokov was a lepidopterist and he discovered and wrote about butterflies out west. He spent weeks in Telluride looking for a particular blue butterfly on the trail, where he first documented it. Slept in his car and went out looking for them. Yeah..." said Oliver. "Nabokov was torn between literature and science. When he was writing the road trip in *Lolita*, he took time out to hunt for butterflies along with his wife Vera. Usually his book covers have a butterfly somewhere on them, if you look carefully."

That evening Angus and I had a serious talk. Okay, so the yacht might not be such a good idea, he conceded. But it was only an idea, after all. Why did I have to be so suspicious of him all the time? Surely I could see how it poisoned our relationship.

I disagreed. The poison came not from me but from a lack of trust. I wanted to trust him. But I was still smarting from the Sal Rosenblatt break in. And it wasn't fair of him to go out drinking all night, leaving me alone and worried back home.

Well, he said, he could understand that, but he couldn't do anything about it now. We just had to go forward, and I had to trust and see how things went. What he really needed was to do something with his hands, to release some pent up energy. He didn't want to rent an apartment in the city any more. What we needed was to buy. "It's money down the drain to pay for some crummy rental. I'm more of a country boy, I guess. I hate the idea of being ripped off by some stupid motherfucker who controls our life."

I rolled onto my stomach, propping myself on my elbows. "Once you are off probation, we could move anywhere we wanted. Think about it! We could even go to Europe. We could go to Paris. I'd love to show you Paris. And if we can't do that..."

"Paris? Get real!"

"I said, if we can't do that..." and of course I knew we couldn't, so long as he was on probation. "But until we move away from here I intend to learn as much as I can from Oliver. Oliver has connections. I don't think you appreciate that. He's also starting Tango's Press again and I want to contribute and learn about editing and meet some serious writers. It's very important."

"The South Shore is so much more beautiful than the city," he mused.

"But it stifles the mind."

"Do I stifle your mind?"

"I mean that people are different in the suburbs," I said. "They don't have such interesting thoughts. We won't find friends like Adrian Skinner or Oliver Gordon living on the South Shore. There'll be no more serendipity. I'll become a suburban onlooker. And besides which, how are you going to get into college? You'll have to commute."

"What's wrong with commuting? People do it all the time. We can commute in together," he said. "I can promise you I'll find a place out there that you will love. Something really interesting." He picked up my hand, and looked at it, threading his fingers between mine. "But first, tell me about this Museum job."

"The teacher is fascinating. Her name is Maude Caruthers."

"Okay..." with a gentle smile of amusement.

"Ari has worked with her too. She has this short grey hair and sharp features, and she wears a very old apron."

He kissed my hands and made a short laugh. "She sounds lovely."

"I'm supposed to hold the same pose for three class sessions."

"Without any clothes?"

"Does that bother you?"

"Actually I think it's kind of sexy," he said.

"Each class runs from 1:00 'til 4:00. I'll be modeling for twenty minutes with ten minute breaks in between. And I should bring a timer, Ari says, as well as a robe to wear during breaks."

"Hmm," he said. "Well, I guess it doesn't sound bad. So do we have a deal?"

"About what?"

"Finding a place on the South Shore."

Yes, I said. Fine. We had a deal. Arguing exhausted me. I had begun to believe he was right. City life was toxic for him. He required physical activity to stay sane and happy. So we had to get out of the city. Maybe if we lived by the water, where he could work with boats, he'd feel more at peace with his environment and all our problems would sort themselves out.

Twenty-One

Angus scoured the country lanes of Cohasset, the large and small houses, where the stars and stripes were aflutter, lawns were mown in perfect strips of green, walks were shaded with new spring leaves, and back roads wound past houses, each one different from the next, and each one equally charming. We saw a For Sale sign and he slowed down the car to take a look. "How about that little place. Can you see us there," meaning in a tiny Cape Cod, with pale yellow trim. Grape hyacinths lined a crooked brick path.

"It's kind of old fashioned. And it never occurred to me we could afford to buy."

"Ever hear the word mortgage, Ruby?"

"But we don't have any credit."

He turned the car off the main road into what looked like a private driveway. "You've got a point there. But if we explore a little we might find something really interesting," he said, as we bounced along a wood chipped driveway, between pine trees.

"Where are we going now?"

"I think I saw a barn somewhere round here," he said and slowed down in front of a small wooden structure with a slanted roof. "Yup. Here it is. We could fix up this place."

"That," I said, "is somebody's garden shed."

"But my God! Look at this land!" Pine trees surrounded us. The hillside dappled in shadow and sunlight sloped away endlessly on both sides. Even the air smelled privileged.

"This land belongs to some millionaire who has no interest in renting his shed out to people like us," I said.

"It's a barn, Ruby. Not a shed."

"Barn, shed..."

"It doesn't hurt to ask."

"But it feels so futile!" We had pulled into a circular driveway in front of an expensive white clapboard house. But we hadn't even stopped the car when a man came out, dressed in a crisp oxford shirt, linen slacks and topsiders. Angus got out of the car and shook the man's hand vigorously. I was ready to curl up in the corner and die of shame. I watched him point back up the driveway, gesticulating in his youthful and expansive way, to make his case. The listener's face seemed curious at first. Then, smilingly he shook his head.

"Well, that was embarrassing," I remarked as we drove back to the main road.

"We just need to look around some more. There are all kinds of places like that and sooner or later we're going to find one for us."

It sickened me how wealthy those people were. What did they need with all that money? It was almost obscene. I thought about the Seabrooks, and all their artwork that belonged in a museum. I thought of their alarm systems and all their splendid isolation. I said, "You're dreaming if you think we're going to find a place out here," as we drove along the waterfront where it smelled of ocean and seaweed. "Did you know the name Cohasset means big rocky place…"

"So I've been told."

"… and that this land once belonged to Indians. Can you imagine how irritating it must have been for the natives when all these strange white foreigners showed up and turned Shawmut into Boston? From now on this is called Boston, they said."

"Yeah. Well, the people who live in Cohasset these days are loaded."

"No kidding," I said. "This town has no doubts about itself," I continued, enjoying the sound of my commentary and embellishing the idea, as I went along. "They are so complacent here. There's no chaos."

"I thought you hated chaos."

"I do. But I still have doubts, and so do you, and that," I said, "is why we don't fit in."

"I thought you appreciated beauty. Don't you want to breathe fresh air? I mean, come on! Don't you think it's beautiful out here?"

"Of course," I said. "Blank and beautiful."

"I intend to own property out here someday. There's nothing to be ashamed of in that," he said.

I sat at the kitchen table in Hingham, looking over apartment listings in the weekend paper. It was Saturday. Timothy and Grandpa had returned from the dump, the dry cleaners and the purchase of Grandpa's weekly oranges and chocolate. Meanwhile, Angus was busily assembling a boat in the backyard. Freddy was out there too, stretching and lacing a canvas between the twin hulls of a brand new catamaran. "Good Lord!" Timothy cried when he saw it."Angus got a really good deal on it," I explained. "And he's wanted a boat like this for ages."\"But where did he get the money?"

"His grandmother gave it to him." The grass outside was a litter of ropes, hulls and shafts. Angus stepped over pieces of equipment, pausing only to assess his progress. Freddy grinned towards the window, giving us a thumbs up. Freddy and his vagabond levity infected me with joy, and I hoped that Timothy would catch the mood as well.

Instead, he cleared his throat. "Honey? How much do you think a boat like that costs?"

"Don't worry, Timothy. I heard him talking with the guy on the telephone," I explained, folding up the paper. "But I don't remember the specifics."

"Do you think you should find out?" "I could. But I'm so tired of fighting with him. Nagging does no good at all. And Angus needs more outdoor activity than we do. You saw how crazy he was living in the city. A lot of our problems may clear up if we just move back out here."

"Please do remember, sweetheart," Timothy said gently. "We have to be as wise as serpents. Not just as harmless as doves."

"Yes," I said, "but we also have to give him a chance. It isn't fair to assume the worst just at the point when he's trying to get his life on track."

Timothy looked doubtful, and just then Nora's car pulled into the driveway and she came into the kitchen with Sorrel in tow, dumping her bag on the table.

"Well," she said. "Again we couldn't get a run through. They had a rotary club meeting in the auditorium, so we went over the worst scenes (at least I hope they were the worst) in a tiny back room... no space to do moves, no progress on the set and frankly,

I almost give up." Then she looked out of the window and her mouth practically dropped to the floor. "What on earth...?"

"Wow oh wow!" Sorrel shrieked, as she scampered outside to join in the fun.

A glance passed between my parents then, which I wish I hadn't seen. It was a split second communication of concern and disbelief. "Apparently he got the money from his grandmother," Timothy said.

Nora's mouth was agape. "Oh, I don't believe it, Ruby. It's absolutely crazy. And where is he going to keep it, might I ask? Renting a mooring costs money. Not to mention the upkeep. It's crazy. Open your eyes!"

I opened them. Together with my parents I looked out of the window. I saw Freddy lacing the canvas, and Angus ruffling Sorrel's hair, all of them surrounded by pieces of boat. Angus brandished a tool in one hand as though it was an extension of his body. He was absolutely in harmony with the activity. "I know what you're thinking," I admitted. "But maybe you don't realize how many things I've already headed off. I've stopped him communicating with some very shady characters. There was a horrible guy called Frenchie once, who is now out of our lives for good."

"You must question him, darling."

"I do! I question him all the time. But I can't question absolutely everything he does, or I'll never stop."

"Then, where did he get this boat?"

"He got it up in Leominster."

"You have got to find out more! First it was the Audi, and now it's a boat. Find out exactly how he pays for these things."

Twenty-Two

Part of the trouble was our impatience with stillness. There were simply too many moving parts. That and the fact that a view can always be more than merely itself. Over time, the gentle roll of the grass out in Hingham, the white clover, the grape vine and the pergola embraced our story, our history. And when we saw each other, we also saw connotations, the ghosts of ourselves, augmenting ourselves.

Freddy at nineteen with his Stratocaster and Charles II ringlets was still my little brother strumming ukulele. Lydia continued making dramatic exits, running down the stairs with her boots half on, hairbrush in hand, except that now she was applying mascara in the rear view mirror and speeding off in a car with her boyfriend. And Angus to me, was still the ghost of his boyhood self, the foreshadowing too of his own potential. His questionable dealing on boats and cars was, for me, the least of Angus.

If Nora needed help striking the set from the previous production down at the Community Center, for instance, Angus recruited Freddy to go and pick up furniture for *She Stoops to Conquer*, on loan from Unicorn Antiques: a massive divan, a couple of landscape paintings in heavy frames and a stag's head to mount on the wall at center stage. Watching him move that furniture from the truck onto the stage, you couldn't help admiring his physical command, agility and gracefulness.

When Timothy went on a lecture tour, it was Angus who noticed that Nora wasn't her usual self. I worried it was on account of the catamaran, until Sorrel told us, "Something's going on with Hetty." She was seated on the steps, combing out the hair of her plastic ponies.

"What do you mean, Sorrel?" Angus and I sat next to her, and Sorrel kept her eyes on her work, wrapping florescent pony hair round her hand. "Hetty has a big red lump on her chest. It's very big and shiny and Nora is afraid. She doesn't want to take her to the vet."

"Oh dear," I said.

"She's scared that Hetty may be put to sleep," said Sorrel.

Angus went straight to the kitchen, where Nora was fixing macaroni and cheese. Her arm moved, stirring in the cheese and her back view was busy. But when she turned I saw that she was running the tip of her tongue along her upper lip, to stop herself from crying. Angus folded her into his arms. Nora, tiny and vulnerable, stood against his chest. "Do you want me to take Hetty to the vet for you?" he asked.

"Oh dear! I'm such a fool!" The wooden spoon from the cheese sauce was clutched in her hand, and jiggled about as she sobbed.

"You're not. You're not at all. You love her," Angus said, holding her while she cried. "We all do. She's a great dog. One of the very best."

Angus went with Nora to the vet after that, and stayed with her while they put Hetty to sleep. The end of an era, the end of permanence. Hetty had begun her life as the runt of the litter, one of the pups of a neighborhood dog. I remember how Freddy had picked her out. Perhaps he identified with Hetty, for he was also very small, sitting in the neighbor's garden at ten years old, with Hetty on his lap. Now we had seen her go from puppyhood, straight through youth and into middle age. Then she grew grey round the muzzle, her eyes clouded up, and now Hetty was gone for good.

The students in Maude Caruthers' sculpture class were somber and thin. They were mostly female, which put me at ease, although there was one guy dressed in a filthy sweater and mussed up hair, and a tall man with a ponytail. Maude showed me to the middle of the studio, where someone had draped an octagonal wooden platform in heavy cloth. "You don't need to disrobe yet," she said. "First we'll decide on the pose."

After a short debate about where I might position my arms and legs, it was decided I should lie on my back with my arms beneath my head and my left leg bent at the knee, left foot flat on the floor. I tried it out and it seemed a forgiving pose for an inexperienced model.

Maude marked the positions where my feet and hips should be, with masking tape. I then disappeared into the toilet and surreptitiously removed my clothes. I hurried with the buttons on my dress, folded up my underwear and stuffed it into the middle of the pile. Then, feeling shaky and self-conscious, I reappeared in my robe and stepped onto the stand.

But there was less reason for awkwardness than expected. Nobody paid much attention as I removed my robe and lay across the drapery because they were far too busy hauling out bags of clay, setting up stands, pounding out their bases, and cutting off chunks of clay with their wires.

"Let me know if you're cold," said Maude, leaning over kindly. "We have an electric heater." I lay on the blanket, one leg bent at the knee, the other long and strong. The temperature did feel cooler, but it wasn't unpleasant, and I stared up at an ornate light fixture, hanging above me from the ceiling. It was a kind of medallion made out of brass, cut into patterns, and the more I looked at it the further the students fell away.

I heard them pounding bases, talking casually amongst themselves, and the occasional instructions from Maude who appeared at my side repeatedly with a set of calipers, to measure various lengths of my body: forearm, thigh, the distance across the width of my hips, the distance from armpit to elbow. Vague driftings of conversation lulled me into a private mental space. Every ten minutes somebody loomed. "I'm turning you, all right?" And then they turned the base on which I lay, so that I felt like I'd become the arms on a clock face.

Sometimes my hands tingled uncomfortably and I longed to move them from under my head, or to bend my leg out of position. Taking off my clothes was the least of my worries. The difficult part was holding the pose. I counted the seconds and listened to the distant radio. Finally my timer went off and it was time for a break.

Out in Hingham, Nora was working on a spring production of *She Stoops to Conquer*. Ari was playing Marlow, and after the final performance there was to be a cast party at the home of Brenda Williams. Brenda was a local patron of the arts, glamorous in her forties and recently divorced. Since Angus had helped to build the set, Nora invited us along. "I think you'll like her," Nora said. "Such a friendly woman. And she lives out in Scituate in a wonderful old house on Hatherly Road."

Angus's face lit up. "Is it accessible by boat? Because if she lives on Hatherly, we could ride across the water on the catamaran."

I frowned. "Directly after the performance? Won't that make us late?"

"Not at all. It will be fun to ride across the water."

"Can't we save it for tomorrow? Do we have to do everything today."

"We can leave from Little Rocky Beach," he reasoned. "Brenda's house is right across the other side – a straight shot. Anyway," he said, "Don is coming."

"Don? Since when has Don been involved?"

"I invited him after the dress rehearsal. He said he'd like to come." Don had played Mr. Hardcastle in Nora's play. The suggestion of Don was the suggestion of authority.

So after the play, crew and cast members and other guests piled into cars, clutching bottles of wine, Tupperware containers of three bean salad and foil covered platters of brownies. Some of them still had stage makeup on, sitting on each other's laps, squashed into cars, flying off to the party eager to enjoy themselves at Brenda's waterfront home.

Meanwhile, Angus, Don and I hitched up the catamaran and towed it down to Little Rocky Beach. The beach was matted with black seaweed and shells. The boulder that Lydia and I had always swum to when we were girls, stood exposed, in low tide. But the air felt light, and the water was a ripple of pink glass under the setting sun. Angus pulled me up to the canvas. Seagulls wheeled above us and before we knew it we were bouncing out across to Scituate in the salty summer evening. The water glistened. "What a design!" Angus marveled, looking at the sail. "It's genius, you know? The way it meets wind and water, and manufactures power?"

Further out on the water, dusk turned imperceptibly to early night and the waves became boisterous. The sail ballooned as the twin hulls cut their way through the cold green water. The voyage was taking longer than I'd expected and the ocean splashed the canvas floor, carrying with it the salt smell of deep-sea things. Angus had never been more alert, pulling the line taut and leaning back against it, though I did notice Don looking troubled, as he white-knuckled the edge of the canvas and faced the horizon.

Water splashed beneath us. The boat rose up and I held tight, legs stretched out, released in the silent power of the elements as we flew across the water.

"It's times like these that I really feel like I'm using my life," Angus said. I felt such tenderness and longing for him then. This was when I loved him the most. When he constantly stimulated and challenged my complacency. With Angus, I could take nothing for granted. Our boat was precarious, but we would stay together, better as a couple than we'd ever be alone. Or so I thought.

The party was well underway at Brenda's house by the time we eventually arrived. Through the living room windows, we saw the guests line dancing to Bee Gees music. "More than a woman; more than a woman to me...."

Everyone had kicked off their shoes. Ari was in the thick of the dance, waving his arms and clapping his hands in the golden light of the living room. "More than a woman," clapping his hands, "more than a woman to me." He was nineteen years old, turning to the beat with Annie Swift who had played Miss Hardcastle in the play.

Timothy's face peered from the crowd. "They've arrived!" he cried. "And to prove it they're here!"

Sorrel hurtled towards us and flung her arms around Angus's waist.

"Come in my dears," Brenda gushed, glamorous in her cream-colored pantsuit, an enormous ivory medallion hanging from a blue silk cord round her neck. "Go upstairs and change, and then come down and have something to eat. There's plenty of food and drink."

I climbed the stairs, exhilarated. Until I overheard Don in the foyer below, talking to one of the stage managers. "Angus is fucking nuts, man. I thought the boat was going to tip over on one hull, and we were out there in the pitch dark. It was terrifying." I froze there, listening. Nobody in the circle below contradicted Don's interpretation. In fact, they seemed to concur. But I felt a tightening sensation in my throat, the sense of being betrayed.

After changing into warm dry clothes, I went downstairs to join the party. Everyone was still line dancing. "Ah ah ah ah staying alive. Staying Aliiiiive..." we sang. I danced with Ari and Annie while Angus and Brenda had a lively exchange on the other side of the room. Angus beckoned me to join them.

Brenda was attractive, with her hair in an up-do, a lively personality with gleaming white teeth. She flashed a smile, holding her wine glass off to one side like a stage prop. "Ruby my dear, you're radiant! And I hear you've been working as an artist's model."

"At the museum school," I told her.

"I know some of the faculty there quite well, you know, although the work I sell in my own gallery is mostly fauvist landscape painting." I nodded vaguely, and shot a look at Angus, whose manic smile was splitting his face.

"Guess what?" he beamed. "Brenda says we can keep the catamaran in her barn. She also has a studio out there, and I was telling her we might be interested in renting it."

"Except..." Brenda acquiesced, clearly enjoying her flirtation with him, "that was quite a few years ago, and as I told you, it needs considerable work."

"Brenda," he said. "If you're looking for ways to invest in the property and get yourself a rental unit, I do woodworking, plumbing, yard work..." he was ticking things off on his fingers, and Brenda interrupted with a brilliant smile of her own.

"Why not come out and take a look?"

So all of us, me and Angus, Nora and Timothy followed Brenda across the moonlit grass to the barn, with Sorrel running in front of us.

"What an interesting development," Timothy said.

"Anything I can do to help," said Brenda.

The downstairs of the barn was crammed with lawnmower, spades and garden tools and a car was parked in the back. "Disregard the mess please -" Brenda said, flicking on lights and leading the way upstairs. I watched the heels of her patent leather sandals as she climbed up in front of me, in a cloud of Halston perfume.

Nora squeezed my arm. "Lovely old paneling, darling," she murmured.

We found ourselves in an empty shell of a room, with a ladder reaching the hayloft. "Oh Brenda!" Nora gasped.

"Gosh," said Timothy.

"Nothing much, as you can see," said Brenda, "except for a lot of potential."

But Angus was already striding across the floor to check out the dimensions. He gestured to where an ancient rusted refrigerator hummed away in the corner. "You see this, Timothy. There are already enough electrical outlets. So that'll be our kitchen. Ruby, look," he said. "A hayloft! Imagine it," as he caught me around the waist, kissing the side of my neck. "That is where our bed will be."

"It was only a summer studio," Brenda warned us. "So there's no insulation yet, and no running water." I took in the skeleton structure doubtfully. It certainly had potential, but what you needed most with a place like this was vision. And wow. Just look at those cathedral ceilings!

"We can certainly all think about it," Brenda said. "Let's sleep on it, shall we? And you can phone me in the morning."

Why oh why didn't I head off this plan? What could I have been thinking! It was such a flight of fancy but at the same time, it fit so well with the spirit of that evening. Under the moonlight, Brenda's barn looked like a dream come true. Maybe Brenda was feeling magnanimous and a little bit drunk. Maybe I thought that she'd change her mind. On the other hand, my parents seemed to believe that Angus was up to the challenge of renovating Brenda's barn. All of us were swept up in a feeling of triumph – triumph over the elements, an exhilarating voyage across the harbor in a catamaran, the feeling of promise and boundless possibility. If I had doubts I tucked those doubts away. I thought this project would do him good. I wanted it to work. I wanted him to prove himself to myself and to all of our friends. I wanted vindication. *You see, I was right! Angus has reformed and he's made something out of himself!* But people are often most protective, when it comes to their pipedreams.

Twenty-Three

A phone call the following day assured us it wasn't just the white wine talking. Brenda had thought it over, and she was sincere with her offer. Not only did she like us both very much but she realized what a prudent investment it would be in her property, particularly since she was recently divorced. A rental property in a place like hers would turn into a gold mine. But rent would only kick in for us once the renovation work was done.

It was the end of May. Angus finished his exams at Suffolk, bringing in straight A's. Over the weeks that followed he went out to Scituate every chance he got, to work out all the details, while I continued at Tango's and finished my modeling stint for Maude, who was teaching a summer class and had slotted me in for another three sessions.

We gradually packed up our Grove Street apartment. I took down the Bologna Club shelves, and wrapped the knickknacks in tissue paper. I packed the china in boxes and folded the linens and sheets.

Everyone at Tango's seemed charmed by the concept of our barn conversion. "So great to breathe that fresh ocean air," mused Enid, a comment that seemed incongruous from one with a shaven head and body piercings. "I love nature," she said. "I'd swim every day if I could. I'd grow vegetables in my yard and start up a really cool herb garden."

"An herb garden sounds agreeable," Oliver put in. "The 17th century chemists were also alchemists and herbalists. That's the thing that excites me about John Winthrop Jr.," he said, as I finished unpacking a carton of books. "At some point I intend to go down to the New York Society to look through the remnants of his library. Winthrop was very interested in herbs. And of course the modern discovery of tranquilizers had part of its origins in the study of Indian plant lore..."

"Is it all right if I take some of these boxes," I asked, "to pack up the rest of our stuff?"

"You can have a beach party this summer," Enid said. "We can build a camp fire, smoke a little weed, toast a few marshmallows..."

The day before our lease expired, Ari and Enid came to help me with the move, and we worked for over an hour. Ari was like the white tornado, polishing every surface in the kitchen, while Enid packed up the sheets in plastic bags and told us about her est training and how we should live in the present moment and release ourselves from the burdens of the past.

But there was still no sign of Angus and now it was after 7:00. All our furniture, including Pastor Jackson's piano had to be moved the following day, and the place was still a mess of boxes and bags. The closet needed cleaning. I began pulling out all the picture hooks from the walls with a hammer. Next I'd clean the refrigerator. Enid lit a joint and passed it to Ari who passed it to me. I shook my head. "So Enid, why exactly did you shave off your hair?" asked Ari.

Enid drew deeply on the joint. "Strangely, you're the first person who's asked me that question."

"Because they're afraid to know why," I said.

"Where's Angus?" Ari inquired.

It was past 8 o'clock, when at last he called. "Hey Rube. What's up?"

"What do you think is up? We're knee deep in packing boxes. Where are you?"

"Out in Scituate," he said lightly. "Brenda and I have just killed off a bottle of wine. She's been showing me slides from her gallery."

"Are you fucking kidding me? Ari and Enid are helping, it would be nice if you could join us in our own apartment."

"I was thinking I'd just spend the night out here."

"So you're not coming home at all?"

Enid stopped working and lent against the basin to stare at me, wide eyed. "I'm making this thing happen," Angus said on the other end of the line. "This is our dream house. I'm telling you we won't get another chance like this. When we've got this place fixed up it will be great. We won't find another one like it."

"Why do you do this to me!" I cried. "Tomorrow we're moving. We have to move the piano and if we want to get back our security deposit, the woodwork needs cleaning – it's still a mess in here."

"Tomorrow. We'll do it all tomorrow."

"But where will you sleep?"

"Brenda's attic. She says that you and I can stay in her attic bedroom until we fix up the barn. Believe me, Ruby, the barn won't get rebuilt overnight, and we may be very grateful for her attic room. What's wrong with that?"

A sudden foreboding. A new reality gleamed through the veneer of our plan, some gaudy undercoat I hadn't noticed before. "I don't believe this. You are such a goddamn liar. This whole 'dream house' thing is full of shit!"

"Ruby," he said. "You can't do this to me now."

"Why not? Look what you are doing to me! How long will we have to stay in Brenda's attic? Don't we want to have an independent existence?"

"That's why we're doing this, Ruby," he responded calmly. "So that we don't have to live in a shit hole in Boston and pay rent to a slumlord. So that we can live an independent existence. Calm down. Take a deep breath. Stop the packing for now. We'll just pile the stuff in the van James is borrowing."

"Like that's going to work. We'll just stuff our wedding china into the van..."

"Calm down! I told you James is going to help. And once we move out of Boston everything will get better. You will go to work on the bus. I don't have any classes in summer so I'll focus full time on the renovation. Go to sleep now. I love you."

I slammed down the phone. I was furious. I felt the corners of my mouth grow heavy and the tears well up in my eyes. Enid rubbed my back in slow deliberate circles. "In the end it will all work out," Ari said.

"I'm not so sure," I sobbed.

"Of course it will," he said. "That barn really does have enormous potential. And it's going to be fabulous for your writing."

I was so embarrassed for them to see me like that, but Enid had the kindness to make only positive comments the following morning at work, when I explained how James had driven in with Angus and a van, just as I was heading for the T.

After work I took the bus to Scituate. I was still smarting from the night before. I doubted very much that Angus had finished the move successfully. But he picked me up at the little bus stop in Scituate, smiling broadly. "Did you finish the move?" I challenged.

"Of course," he said, as he drove me to Brenda's with the ocean breeze blowing through our open car windows.

"Did you give the landlord back his keys? Did they return the security deposit?"

"Yup," he said, handing me an envelope. Inside there was a check for our security deposit from our Boston landlord.

"You've done everything? The whole move?"

"You'll see," he said. It was a beautiful afternoon and as we pulled into the driveway, the barn was dappled in sunlight underneath the trees. I climbed the stairs and looked around at the jumble of kitchen equipment, throw pillows, pictures, clothes on hangers, and furniture. And at the end, one star item was also in its place: Pastor Jackson's piano, against the far wall, with sheet music open on the stand. Angus had been true to his word.

"How did you get it all done?"

"I told you I'd get it done!"

"You have been busy," I said, genuinely impressed.

"But it's been one hell of a day and we are fucking wiped."

"I bet."

"In fact, we were thinking of going for a swim now," he said.

"That sounds good. But I think I'll stay and do a bit of work here." I kissed him and then he and James headed down the wooden stairs for the beach.

While he was gone, I carried our clothes up to Brenda's attic bedroom, making several trips. I carried my yellow silk dress and Indian print skirts, the cocktail dress I had worn almost a year before as a going away dress after our wedding, and Angus's wedding suit. So I was the one who was out of sync. I was part of the problem. I had been at fault because I hadn't trusted him as much as I should. He had pulled through in spite of my doubts. I must remember this, and give him the chance to get things done in his own way. It was foolish to get too anxious about things that didn't matter. Perhaps if I tried harder, things would work out better. The barn would become our home soon enough. It already felt like Swiss Family Robinson. It was beautiful to be out in Scituate with all the green trees and the ocean views. For now we would take our showers and clean our teeth in Brenda's bathroom. We were very lucky that Brenda was so accommodating.

Angus drove me to the bus stop in the morning and I had to concede that it seemed a workable arrangement. The ride was an hour and twenty minutes, door to door. Once in town, I shelved books, and sat with Oliver over coffee while we went through the cataloguing. I ate lunch with Adrian Skinner and Enid. Adrian invited us round to his house in South Boston. The poet Ai was reading from her new book *The Killing Floor* and it was bound to be a stimulating evening. James would be there too, he said. So why not come along? Next time, I promised. But Angus and I had only just moved. For now, I must focus on the barn.

I stopped by briefly after work to see Jenny at the florist where she worked. I found her arranging and wrapping roses. "How's the dream house coming along?" she asked. The air around her was a tonic of freshly cut flowers.

"It's going to take time," I told her. "But it's beautiful out there and ultimately, I think it's good for Angus to cultivate his garden. You'll have to come out and see it."

Jenny shrugged. "Have you thought any more about getting him on medication?"

The idea had dropped entirely from my mind. "Getting tests and a serious doctor is terribly expensive," I said. "And for now things seem to be working out, so I figure we can wait a bit on that."

"Hmm." She was clean and straightforward as she sorted through her roses. Her life looked simple and beautiful. But I was determined to conceal any misgivings I might still have about the barn, to give it a chance and control my thoughts better. Angus needed me to be fully on his side. He was an entrepreneur. I loved that about him. I needed to entertain a more positive energy.

The first work he did in the barn was to cut a hole in the roof above the hayloft.

"Is Brenda okay with you cutting that hole in the roof?" I asked.

"Sure. It's going to be a skylight over our bed. I'll fit it with a window," he said. "But we'll leave it open for now. Don't you like looking at the stars?" He was tanned and shiny with sweat as he lay on the sofa drinking one of the Heinekens he had stacked up in the rusty refrigerator. I was still in my work clothes, sweeping the earwigs and cobwebs full of little white egg sacks, from what I hoped would one day be our kitchen. The barn smelled spicy, like warm wood with undertones of rot.

"Angus? How long will it take to insulate this place?" I lent on the broom and gazed at him through spirals of dust and sunlight.

"Not long. But next I'll get the water connected," he said. "Run a line from the house. Lay down pipes."

"It's really that simple?"

"You'll see."

I sat beside him. "We have such a long way to go, though."

He drew me close and kissed me deeply, tugging open my blouse. He bent to kiss my breasts. My hand smoothed the back of his neck and soon we had peeled off our clothes. At any given moment we were still never more than a step or two from lovemaking. Our hunger reached from the arches of his feet to the backs of my thighs, to the dark brown hair of his groin, and the golden crown of my head. Light streamed down from the open skylight and Angus and I were as hot as Brenda's attic. Everywhere we made love over those days was still and hot and sultry.

"It all sounds so complicated," I said afterwards, swigging on a Heineken. "I mean plumbing is complicated, isn't it. I know that it's expensive."

"Plumbers are the biggest rip-off artists of all, Ruby. But the fact of the matter is, the work they do isn't as complicated as they'd like you to think."

Oh, to spend a night in the barn! Neither of us could wait. Angus hoisted our mattress to the hayloft so we could sleep beneath the stars. It was heavenly in our loft bed, listening to the crickets and the night sounds, breathing the light open air. It felt like camping. The air had never been fresher or the sky so clear. We slept like logs, and in the morning woke to the sounds of thumping and scratching. We sat up in our hayloft and peered down into the barn. "Shhh," he said. "Look!"

I held my breath, transfixed by two raccoons cavorting in a silent mating dance on our living room carpet. They stood on their haunches wrestling playfully with their front paws. I saw in their fur the individual hairs of grey and black, the smutty marks around their eyes. Their noses and claws were as sharp as they were quiet, until suddenly the animals startled at something invisible, and disappeared downstairs.

Twenty-Four

Having a long commute means that you span two worlds. Country life on one side, city life on the other. The bus ride was my linkage. I decided to use it well by getting in some reading. I'd start off with a bang: with Solzhenitsyn's *Gulag Archipelago*. I'd heard him speak at the Harvard Commencement and now I'd have time to get through his books on the bus. It would become a reading project.

Maude's summer sculpture class began, and this time her students were older. Of the ten or twelve in the class perhaps only three were younger than me. The others were in their fifties and sixties and seemed to have known each other sometime.

They talked about their hearing aids and frozen shoulder injuries, about other sculptors and painters they knew, who was exhibiting their work and where. When my arm got pins and needles, or a cramp set in, I found it oddly heartening to make silly promises to myself: I will never again put my body in this position. After today I will never do this pose again.

Tango's was quieter in summer. People came in gentle waves so that Oliver and I had time to plan the next series of readings. Even in the heat we drank coffee, sitting on the sofa and talking about Solzhenitsyn. "He's trying to save us from ourselves," I said. "At the commencement he talked about how the Russians idolized the west. They were very disappointed to discover the truth about it."

"Well, Ruby, you are an idealist," Oliver said. "But I find him moralistic and patronizing. I am more of a realist, myself. I believe in know thyself." And he cocked his eyebrows and looked at me with amusement.

Oliver nourished and settled me. He objectified things and made them into a philosophy. When I talked about the barn, he answered in the abstract, as if it was an interesting story. "There's something to be said for having the wilderness right at your door. As you describe it, it might retain some of that quality."

Scituate turned to leafy green summer -with blossoms and lush green grass. Angus and I walked to the beach whenever we could. We crossed the rocks. The water was icy, and we swam out far and then trod water, looking at the land, and diving down, swimming underneath each other's legs. We liked to see the beach from there, and especially to see the wrecks of two houses, which sat where the blizzard had tossed them, out on the rocks like broken balsa wood models. We swam back under the bluest of skies and lay on the sand talking. Our skins were sticky. We didn't bother with towels. The sun could dry us so quickly.

One afternoon we walked to the broken houses, and climbed in through the windows. Nothing remained of their contents. A few wallpapered rooms, the top floor with a roof on. That was all. The first floor had been crushed in the storm.

We climbed into our loft bed. Limbs tangled on the white wrinkled sheets, with the smell of sex and each other's breath, the lazy indulgence of too much of each other. The leaves and shadows and filtered sun poured through the open skylight. We looked at the sky. "When are we going to get windows in here?" I asked. It was hard to renovate when we had so little money. Then Brenda lent Angus her charge card telling him to get all the materials he needed.

Every time I came home from Boston and nothing more had been done, I tried to bite my tongue. I practiced showing more patience. After all, he had a lot to do, and when I pointed this out, it threw him into a funk.

It reassured me to remember how quickly he had moved us out from Boston, even while I wondered how much was actually getting done on the renovation. But sometimes when I got home, he was out at the hardware store. Or else he'd gone swimming with James. Or gone for a sail on the catamaran.

One afternoon as my bus pulled up, I saw him beaming up at my window. His familiar brown-skinned figure in cut off shorts and old sneakers, his hair tousled and covered in dust told me he'd been working hard. His smile was relaxed and appreciative, his eyes fully focused. "I have something special to show you back home," he said. And when we got there, he made me close my eyes as he led me up the barn stairs. I was prepared for anything.

"Open your eyes!"

I opened them. I saw the dusty barn. The same old lack of insulation. Except now Angus had rigged up a wooden swing. It hung on very long ropes into the living room, and swung in a triangle of light, which streamed from the skylight in the roof – where he intended to, but hadn't yet put in a window. It was madness.

"You're kidding me."

"What do you mean?"

"That's all you've done?"

"Don't you like it?" His dark eyes shone.

"I like it," I said, "but..."

"I made it for you so you could sit here and swing!"

"I hope you don't mind us using your bathroom," I said to Brenda, as I filled up water bottles from her kitchen faucet.

"Don't worry about that, my dear," Brenda said, pouring out a glass of chardonnay. She was freckled from sunbathing, her hair was swept to a messy bun on top of her head, and she wore a kind of sailor top in blue and white, with an appliquéd anchor in the center. "I've just gone through a horrible divorce and it's good for morale to have you both around." She raised her glass. "Remember, Ruby. The first year of marriage is the hardest of all. After that, it's the nineteenth."

Except we had no food. All that was left in the rusted fridge in the corner of the barn was one tin of sweet corn and one box of Weetabix. I stood in the makeshift kitchen with the ever-replenishing spider webs, the smell of warm wood, and broke up the Weetabix, sprinkling the corn on top.

"Here," I said, passing the bowl to Angus. "It's your dinner."

He looked at it and grinned. "Ruby," he said. "You are out of your mind."

But as it happened we didn't have to worry about food that evening, because of the great excitement back at the family house in Hingham. Lydia and her boyfriend Gustavo had just returned from Spain and Nora invited us round for a celebratory meal. June was there as well, Freddy's girlfriend, sitting close to Freddy on the couch. Sorrel performed a mime walk she was learning. She couldn't get enough of it; across the porch and down the garden she slid across the air. Lydia was radiant, dressed in platform shoes and pleated pants and speaking Spanish with her boyfriend, who was, by the way, a knock out.

Gustavo was also an excellent cook. Much to Nora's delight, he'd appointed himself in charge of the meal preparation, and was grilling salmon, roasting potatoes and making an enormous salad, while Lydia opened one of several bottles of wine, which they had evidently brought back from Europe. Grandpa sat at the head of the table patting the sides of his cheeks. "What is it? Oh oh oh. I dunno."

"So Ruby, you're modeling for a sculptor and living in a converted barn?" Lydia asked when we were sitting together as sisters.

Yes, I told her. Although the renovation was slow.

"She thinks we're never going to finish it," Angus put in, as if to suggest that my fears were groundless.

"Oh, don't worry darlings," Nora said magnanimously, enjoying her glass of wine. "We'll all come along and help you with the barn. Won't we everyone?"

"Of course," Timothy added. "What can we do? Just say the word!"

So right then and there, Angus organized everyone in the family to come around the following weekend. He had shovels and pick axes galore. The entire family would help dig a trench for our water pipes.

Except when the time came, Timothy remembered he was terribly sorry but he had some important writing to do and afterwards was taking Grandpa on his much anticipated outing to the dump and to buy his oranges and chocolates. Then June and Freddy couldn't come either, since Freddy had a gig out in western Massachusetts and they would need to sleep in on the following day. It was just going to be Nora, Lydia, Gustavo and Sorrel.

"This is where you're living?" Lydia cried as I dusted away a spider's web from the doorway of the barn. "But this is fantastic, isn't it Gustavo. It's so bohemian! You should have seen the dump we've been living in. There was hardly enough room to turn round. And you have all this space, you lucky thing."

Oh, the endless earth! The bending and lifting, with blazing sunlight beating down on our backs, and the future line of imaginary pipe to be laid here.

"Where's Angus?" Lydia wondered. After an hour or so digging she felt sweaty and uncomfortable. Her nipples stuck out against her t-shirt.

"I think he went to Hingham Lumber Yard," I said.

"Why?"

"I don't remember. But he said he'd be back."

Gustavo was the first one to stop, to wander around Brenda's grounds, looking at the plants and then at his feet, as he smoked.

"To hell with this!" said Lydia, shoving her fork into the earth and leaving it there. "If Angus isn't going to help dig his own trench, I don't see why we should kill ourselves over it. Let's all go for a swim."

"I think that's a very good idea," said Nora, throwing down her shovel. We walked to the beach across the road; over the huge flat rocks. The tide was going out but that didn't matter. Besides, Nora had had the foresight to bring along a picnic.

Gustavo walked with Lydia across the sand to look at the broken houses, which were still waiting after the blizzard to be removed. I watched them climb through the windows, just as Angus and I had done. Then I walked out to the water's edge and swam. I lay on my back and splashed in the sea, and looked at the faraway sky. When I swam back I could see Nora on the shore with a flask of tea and the picnic basket. She was wearing her customary summer straw hat and big poet's shirt over her bathing suit. Sorrel beside her on the beach, picked raspberries out of a box and ate them, grains of sand stuck to her tiny brown legs.

Then Nora headed in for a swim, making a big show of how cold it was, tip toeing exaggeratedly into the waves, and pushing forth, her soprano shrieks of joy and mock outrage as she braved the icy water. We could see the line of coast from the water, and the roof of the barn amongst the trees.

"Have you been out to those broken houses, Ruby?" Lydia asked, when I was on the shore and she came back with Gustavo to sit on the blanket beside me.

"Of course. Did you notice how when you climb through the windows you're actually on the second floor?" I asked. "Because the first floor is crushed underneath."

"Ruby has always been lucky," Lydia told Gustavo. "She's always led such an interesting life. Look at you, Ruby: Modeling for sculptors, working for writers, getting your short stories published. And now you have this beautiful barn. I'm jealous."

"Really?" I said. "Because sometimes I wonder if I've made a huge mistake."

Gustavo reclined, lighting a cigarette as he and Lydia exchanged a fleeting look, which I didn't understand. "What do you mean by that?" she asked.

"I'm happy with my work, at least for now," I said. "And I have good friends. But I'm worried that we moved out here too soon, before we got this place habitable."

Sorrel was at the water's edge with her bucket, and Nora was now stepping gingerly towards us over the rocky beach on her white and tender feet. "That water was absolutely glorious after all our work."

"Do you think she's made a mistake, Nora?" Lydia asked.

Nora became grave. "You mean with the barn? Oh, I do understand, darling," Nora said, drying her face with a towel. "It does look like an awful lot of work."

"But do you think she's made a mistake?" Lydia took a drag of Gustavo's cigarette, while Gustavo lay with his head on Lydia's lap as she stroked his hair. They planned to move into an apartment in Cambridge – a little furnished sublet, with running water, heat, and air conditioning. She might have envied my life, but I began to envy theirs. Life for them looked so harmonious and simple.

"There's a lot of work ahead. Certainly. But look what we accomplished just this morning," Nora said.

"It take more than one morning to dig a trench," said Gustavo. "So the rest of the work...?" He shrugged, leaving us to guess at his meaning.

"I think you're very lucky," Lydia said. "Look at your overall life. Look at the bigger picture. You are going to be living in a dream house! You can come down to this beach and swim any time you want. At least you aren't like the poor people who own those houses on the rocks over there. Imagine how they feel about fixing up their places?"

We ate our cheese wedges, tomato slices, avocado and French bread in jovial spirits. Seagulls wheeled in the sky above and dived down to the sea. But when the family left that afternoon I wished with all my heart I could have been going along, instead of returning to Brenda's. As I came up the driveway and into the barn, I could smell freshly sawn wood. Planks of mahogany had been stacked downstairs. "What's all this?"

Angus was perturbed. "Where were you this afternoon? Did you enjoy your swim?"

"What's with all the wood?" I asked.

"It's for your bookshelves," he said.

"Bookshelves? I thought we were doing the plumbing."

"Don't you want bookshelves? I thought that's what you wanted."

"I do, but..."

"Are you a carpenter, Ruby? Are you a plumber? Then leave it up to me. All right?"

"But what's all this?" I inspected a band saw, a set of electric drills, a sewing machine... "Wait!" I said. "A sewing machine? How did you buy all this?"

"Don't you want to get involved? I thought you could make curtains." He slid his hands around my waist and kissed the side of my neck.

"But we still don't have any actual windows. Wait a minute, Angus. How did you buy all this stuff?"

"I told you," he said, disappointed in me. "Brenda lent me her charge card."

"But surely she didn't mean you to buy so much."

"Why not? We've got a lot of work to do. I told you, Ruby. Brenda and I are drawing up a contract and it would sure help out if you could get involved. All you do is complain. It's a real bummer," he said, turning crestfallen.

I went up to Brenda's and ran myself a bath, and soaked in Brenda's bath oil. Oh, wouldn't it be wonderful to have running water of our own out in the barn? Wouldn't it be grand when the barn was all fixed up and we had a bathroom and kitchen and it was insulated and Angus was finishing his degree, and making something good out of himself, feeling a well-deserved pride in his accomplishments.

When I came downstairs, Angus and Brenda were drinking white wine and conversing with great animation at the table. They seemed to have decided that what Brenda needed was a new shower designed to look like an old fashioned telephone booth. Angus was vowing to build her one and busily sketching the wooden doors on a paper napkin.

I went outside, walked down the gravel path, and sat alone on the stoop. Angus came out to find me. He sat beside me, kneading the back of my neck with his hand. "Ruby, what's wrong? We've had a good day. It's all been good. And I love you, all right? Just let me build the shower for Brenda. It will give her the idea that I can do this stuff. It will make her happy and then she'll be more ready to accept our other projects."

"But how much time will it take? And how much money? Winter will be coming before we know it..."

"Ruby," he said. "Get real. It's only the end of July."

ENID'S HAIR STORY
By Ruby Lambert-Aleshire

Of course my hair had meant something. I used to plait it with flowers. It flowed down rivers and sheets. I had many lovers. I would sweep it up, a mess. And I was as surprised as you that the time to cut it came so soon. I knew I'd cut it one day. I thought at thirty. Not to be a girl at thirty. Women are silly with long hair and I had decided I'd be ready then, but it turns out I was ready long before.

I had made twelve phone calls, and no one after another was there for me. I braided my hair, and lying in bed, I pulled on the braids, feeling the tight knots near my head. Then I got up and went into the bathroom. The lights were bright. I had good scissors and started to cut. It had to be done, simply that. A project was all it was, and I was behind that with no emotion, just the need to cut it away. Order, I wanted. There was no anger.

It took a long time for the scissors to cross each other, bare again, with no hair between. My hair had been thick, a tangle of dry love hair down my back. Now it was blunt and hung to my chin quite uselessly. I took an hour and a half and gave myself a beautiful haircut. I did it by feeling, cut all around the back layers short and shorn. I was there, and my face remained quite matter of fact between it in the mirror, looking forward and unsurprised at the sight, the smell of hair and water, and the ache of my arm bending with so much cutting.

The braids I placed after cutting, side by side in a box. Later, I sent them to a lover in Greece.

Afterwards I went back to sleep. I did not go outside, it happened, for two days because of the storm. But I wrote, thinking only of completing the work started. My neighbors saw it first and seemed to like it. Others were to say nothing. I shock them, perhaps. But I'm glad to know that beauty is bones. I feel orderly, clean. I have a good skull.

∼

Weeks passed. As I continued commuting from Scituate to Cambridge, I began to loathe the stuffy upholstered seats, the smell of exhaust fumes and depletion of energy the bus ride represented. I muscled through my reading list even though it often made me carsick. I hated the atmosphere on that bus. The other commuters were men and women, all dressed up for the business day, groggy because they were sleepy and bitchy and bored because they hate their jobs and their lives and because it was always the same routine. They depressed me exceedingly. Am I one of these people? Is this really me, I asked myself each day.

I walked with Oliver through Harvard Yard, as the summer session students poured onto the library steps. I told him about the barn, and how I intended to take Enid's suggestion and put in an herb garden. In those conversations, the barn felt like a lovely idea. "I'm thinking of planting some milkweed," I said. "To attract the monarch butterflies."

"Goody," Oliver informed me, off on a tack of his own, "That word is short for goodwife. You, Ruby, would be Goodwife Aleshire. Or Goody Aleshire."

It helped to feel good about the barn, to put my questions about the slow construction, about how James was supposed to help, but ended up being a distraction, into perspective; it helped if others supported the illusion, that when I returned to Scituate, I was becoming Goody Aleshire traveling home, not so much on a commuter bus, as on a stagecoach.

That evening when I got home, Angus had been true to his word and had finished building Brenda's shower. The wooden doors were assembled and ready to be painted, and Angus was crouched inside the shower, busy tiling it in a small turquoise mosaic. I got in beside him on my hands and knees. We had to smooth a grainy paste into the cracks between tiles, with a knife. We worked together on that project until the wee hours of the morning, until our backs ached and our fingers were covered in hangnails.

Twenty-Five

A few days before our first anniversary, Angus came into town with James and picked me up from the Museum School. It was the last of the first three sessions, and Maude had hired me to work another three weeks. As he entered the studio in his cut off shorts, to shake her hand and look around, he seemed a little alien to the environment. Meanwhile, James examined the sculpture in silence and I was struck by how Boston had become my terrain. Angus no longer belonged here. And James had become more his friend than mine. Things were working out. He had been in Scituate all summer long, and it suited him.

We got into the car and headed for Cohasset, with the windows down, the radio turned up loud, speeding down Route 3, Angus, James and I. It was beautiful and careless when we reached the summer country lanes. Day lilies nodded beside every road as we sped past boulders and the wide mown lawns of Jerusalem Road and Atlantic Avenue, overlooking the water. The sun set on the public beach where dwindling crowds traipsed to their cars across the sand, warm and tired with armloads of towels and folded chairs.

We stopped on a bridge, got out of the car and together leaned over the railing, watching the water froth below. The air smelled lightly of sea salt. I removed my sandals, and scrambled to a stretch of shore upstream, past beach plums, rose hips and sea grass. It was a little beach, a hundred yards or so from the bridge and when I looked up I saw James and Angus talking together. Angus rested his hands on the stone, and James with sun glinting off his hair, had his back towards me.

Then James turned, and as if on impulse, climbed down to join me on the beach. He tore off his shirt, and still in his jeans, waded out, to dip his head underwater. Then he came up. His hips were slender, his back long and narrow. "Coming?" he asked, facing me.

"Shouldn't we wait for Angus?" I was wearing my yellow silk dress and hadn't prepared for a swim.

The water was waist deep and running swiftly. James stood watching me. "I don't think he wants to come down."

I glanced at the bridge, to where Angus stood. I could see that he was thinking and wasn't going to join us on the beach. So after a minute, I pulled off my dress and laid it on the rocks. I stood before James in the shallows, dressed in my underwear, feeling his eyes on my body.

The water was clear, and my feet looked pale and unpracticed on the rocks, and when I dipped in, it was as much to cover myself, as it was to swim.

"Come out to the middle," he instructed. "We'll swim together, underneath the bridge. Pick your feet up, and drift with the current. And when you get underneath it, swim very hard to the right." He took my hand and pulled me towards him. "Ready?" he asked.

The current glided past us, sped with us, silent and free. I lifted my feet and it was beautiful like a dream is beautiful. The sky was enormous over our heads and the water was smooth. Angus called out as we traveled downstream towards the bridge. His voice flew away in the air as we approached. "Go Ruby!"

Then it changed. There was an abrupt turn. Beneath the bridge, the water frothed and thundered, and we were now in the thick of it. We no longer had anything in common with the glide of freedom. Now we must swim hard. And we did. We swam hard to fight against the current. James had told me to pull to the right. But I submerged, resurfacing briefly to cough up burning mouthfuls. Chaos. Until he grabbed my arm. "Swim..." he shouted.

I spluttered and forced myself forward. The seconds seemed to last forever, pushing and spluttering forwards without gaining ground. Until at last the scene came back to focus. I wiped the water away from my eyes. And suddenly everything calmed again.

Angus leaned over from the bridge above. James and I were in its shadow, breathing fast, our bodies pressed together. "Is she all right?" called Angus.

James's body pressed against mine. He was slippery, hard and forbidden. We held each other close, at first unthinkingly. Then

I held him in the water, an anapest too long. He let me go and I began to swim towards the shore without turning back. My yellow dress was on the beach. I saw it gleaming on the rocks where I'd left it, under a full white moon.

∽

And I knew nothing. Absolutely nothing. Even now it's hard to equate my view of that evening with what I later learned. It was about eight-thirty, I remember, and Angus wanted us to go to Blake Thackeray's house. I didn't care for Blake. He was an old school friend of James' and I'd met him before at one or two parties. But in my view, there was too much obvious damage in the guy to be comfortable in his company. It felt like we were either humoring him, or enjoying an inside joke at his expense. When I pictured Blake with his shag haircut, silver studded belt and black jeans, I was reminded of some cloven hoofed character out of Joyce Carol Oates.

"Come on. We'll just drop by," Angus said. "It won't be long, I promise."

Thackeray was out in back when we arrived, out by a tennis court and swimming pool, everything floodlit. He was fixing iced drinks in a little cabana, the central player to his own story of suburban privilege, beside the gentle heat of a tennis court. Red clay kicked up in the dusk, against the thwack of tennis balls and the sickly smell of honeysuckle. I imagined we would hang out for a while, and then go home.

But the night was hot and now my mind was conflicted. My thoughts kept returning to James and how he had held me in the water underneath the bridge. I hit the ball back and forth with Angus on the tennis court. The clay was dark, like powdered paint. Then I sat on the grass thinking private thoughts, while James was off somewhere else, avoiding me.

At one point I decided I should clean the tennis court. So I walked back and forth with the rake, and smoothed away our footprints in the clay. It satisfied me to do this. Meanwhile Angus chatted with Blake, sitting on a poolside chaise, sipping margaritas.

I remember a vague sense of boredom. I remember being fed up, especially with the sound of Angus and Blake blathering on about the CIA and how those guys always wore suits and expensive sunglasses. Angus began talking about some uncle of his – about how he was sure this uncle was in the CIA. There was no evidence for thinking so, as far as I was concerned. It was all a performance, and I didn't like it when he got like that. He was like that with Mike Posey too -doing a performance of someone brash and boasting. I could see him watching their reactions, gauging the effect of his posturing. I could see the signs of danger and normally I would have tried to head it off. Except then he threw out another curve. "Do you guys want to go to the Red Lion?"

"Sure. We could head down there if you like," said Blake.

"But I've got work in the morning, Angus." I was trying to talk to the real Angus – trying to talk to him as though I was unimpressed with his performance. *And you promised...* my tone attempted to suggest.

He brushed me off. "You don't have to come."

"Hey, Angus," James said. "Maybe." Long pause. "Maybe you should take Ruby home."

"She's a big girl. She can take the car," said Angus.

Liar, I thought. He said we would only stop by. I have work tomorrow. He's already drunk too much, and now this?

"But if I take the car, how will you get home?" I asked.

"I'll get a ride," he reasoned.

I didn't feel up to public disagreement. I was too tired. Besides, I felt distanced from Angus at that moment. Also empowered. The residue of excitement and sexual tension lingered from my swim with James. So I said goodbye, took his keys, got in the car and drove away.

The roads were dark and peaceful. It was the first time I had driven alone in the Audi, and there was a heady rush of independence about it. The barn, in spite of its disorder, seemed to hold forth the mirage of a home it might one day become, heralded with cricket chirps and the distant roar of the incoming tide.

I climbed into our loft bed, pulled up the covers and slept beneath the stars. Sometime later in the middle of my dreams, I heard the car pull up. I heard male voices. A car door slammed. Then Angus's warm muscled body slipped into bed beside me, and although I felt separated from him, I was relieved. I could sleep at last because he'd come back home.

Oliver and Adrian were already at Tango's when I arrived. The sun was dappled across the floor on a beautiful blue-skied morning. The door to the little patio was flung wide open, and as I spooned coffee into a paper filter, I could see a cat out there, curled on a director's chair fast asleep in the sun. The conversation between Oliver and Adrian drifted towards me in snippets; the new series of chapbooks on contemporary New England poets Oliver was producing "...to showcase poets of a different kind."

The smell of morning coffee filled the room. The telephone rang and I went to my desk to pick it up. To my surprise it was Nora. "Ruby darling, I hope you don't mind me phoning you at work. But there's something important I want to discuss. Have you seen this morning's paper? You remember the Seabrooks, don't you? Those people with the wonderful house? Ingrid Seabrook, the mother of Sorrel's friend? Well, they've been burgled."

I frowned into the telephone. I watched as Adrian lazily lit a cigarette on the other side of the room. Oliver sorted through books and papers, the coffee was ready, and I felt a kind of mental retreat coming on, a sort of hesitation in my consciousness. "The Seabrooks! Gosh. They were burgled?"

Oliver looked at me over his glasses.

"On Thursday night," said Nora's voice in my ear. I heard the rustle of her newspaper over the phone. "Four of their paintings were stolen. Listen to this ..." and I sat at my desk to do so.

There was a pot of paperclips, which someone always irritatingly linked together in a chain. So I began to unlink them idly as Nora spoke in my ear. "Ah yes...here: *Five paintings, including a portrait by Rembrandt and two 600 year old Ming vases were robbed on Thursday night from a home in Cohasset Massachusetts, in what police are calling the largest burglary ever from a private residence. Police conclude that the thieves made their way to the property by boat and broke in through a basement door. The owner of the property, Anthony Holland Seabrook, was not at home at the time of the break in. His wife was sleeping upstairs with her children. The artwork has been valued at over three million dollars. The thieves were able to get away, police say, because the burglar alarms had not been activated."*

I listened, and in my silence, hearing my mother's voice, it was as though somebody else, someone more capable than I, at the helm of my subconscious, was pulling down the blinds to a horribly unsightly roomful of thoughts. The aim, it seemed, was to contain me in a safer mental space.

Adrian caught my eye. "All right?" he mouthed in my direction. I nodded, frowning, and listened to Nora, as I continued unlinking the paperclip chain on the desk.

"I just telephoned and spoke with Ingrid and she's devastated," Nora continued. "What makes it worse is that she feels so guilty."

"What a strange reaction," I said. "Why would she feel guilty?"

"Because darling, she blames herself for leaving the alarm system off. She's been unwell, and Anthony was away, so she was sleeping upstairs with the children when the thieves broke in. Can you imagine?"

"It sounds terrible," I said.

"Darling," said Nora and I heard her sigh. "Oh Lord. How I hate this," she said, starting the sentence again. "Darling one, I really hate to have to ask. I know we're always hoping for the best..."

"Spit it out," I told her.

"You don't think Angus had anything to do with it, do you?"

The room stood still for a moment. I could feel Oliver and Adrian eavesdropping. My mind became a cubicle.

"I just have a sinking feeling..." Nora continued. "I hate to have to think it. But it just seems..."

I listened to her words, too horrible to contemplate. There had to be a way out. And the way out was to telescope reality down to the head of a pin. And on that pinhead were written two words: *Protect him.*

"It wouldn't have been possible," I said at last.

"Darling, are you sure?"

"He couldn't have," I said. "We were together all evening. We went swimming and then we went to a friend's house and then we both came home. Well, I came home before he did, but he was back in bed with me an hour or two later. And he drove me to the bus stop, as usual, that morning." My mind flew over the awful possibilities. Skimmed them really, without fully focusing. Angus had gone to the Red Lion Pub. I had driven home alone. When had he come home? Would there have been time to break into the Seabrooks? I couldn't know for sure. I had left around 11:00. But Angus had been in the company of James and Blake Thackeray. There couldn't have been time; and certainly he'd been perfectly normal when he drove me to the bus stop the following morning.

"Well, thank goodness for that," Nora said with relief. "It's horrible to ask, I know. And I hate having to think like this. But it's just the sort of crazy scheme ..."

"Don't worry Nora," I said to her then. My desire was to soothe her on the subject and that desire overtook any doubts, brushing them away, at least for the time being. "It would have been impossible," I repeated. "There wouldn't have been time. Besides, he'd have to be made of ice to pull off a heist like that and not show any warning signs."

And now I really had to go. The shop was back in motion, filling up with a morning's activity. Enid had come in, and there was a vagrant unpacking carrier bags in the doorway, whom someone needed to shoo away.

I hung up the phone and dropped my paper clip chain. I went to the coffee and poured myself a cup. My hand shook. I was numb. "Heist, Ruby?" Adrian asked. I turned to see him sitting on the sofa behind me, and his round reassuring face, which always reminded me of those Victorian illustrations of the North Wind, wore an expression of amused interest.

"There was a huge robbery out in Cohasset."

"Gee," said Oliver almost to himself.

"And my mother is a friend of the victim," I said. "It's really upset her." I tried turning back to my work. I'd have to think this through later. I wouldn't imagine it now. It couldn't have anything to do with Angus. It wouldn't have anything to do with him. Sure, he had left Blake Thackeray's after me. There was no getting round that one. But it was also true that I'd heard his return. That he'd driven me to the bus stop the following morning.

Twenty-Six

The next sculptural session for Maude was a standing pose, and far more challenging than the previous ones I'd held. It was hard to stay still, but they had me with one knee up on a step, my arms resting on a shelf. I had been in this position for almost fifteen minutes when conversation in the class turned to the Seabrook art theft. "It sounds implausible to me," said Maude, "I think the whole thing was a set up. I think the owners arranged for the robbery themselves."

"Of course! For the insurance money," said one of the students.

"Well, you can imagine how much they would get for work like that. The Rembrandt alone is worth millions."

"But the paper said the alarm was turned off. If it was off, that means they can't collect the insurance," another student reasoned.

"Why not? It's still their property."

"But how would the thieves be able to sell them?" someone else put in.

"Anything is possible," said Maude. "There are private collectors all over the world. Greed," she said, "works on all sides of this equation. It's pure greed – on all sides."

I shut my eyes to block out the vertigo that seemed to overpower me. I bowed my head to my hands and realized I was shivering. "Ruby dear, are you all right," Maude asked.

"Sorry," as my knees buckled. I sat on the platform, with my head in my hands. For the first time, I felt vulnerable in my nakedness.

"Maybe it's too hot in here," said Maude. "Why don't you take a few minutes? We certainly don't want to break our model."

I stumbled into the toilet and lent against the basin, breathing. My breath felt cold inside my mouth. I sat on the toilet and bowed my head. My bowels had turned to water. I flushed the toilet and rested my head on my arms, breathing hard and losing track of time. Then after several minutes, weak and still perspiring, I stood at the basin and drank a glass of water.

When I returned to the studio, conversation had turned to the subject of forgery, and how a good art forgery could be universally admired, even more than original work, sometimes even considered better. "It happened once with Giacometti," Maude remarked. "We should be so lucky."

I wandered round the sculpture stands trying to collect myself, and to see what they'd been doing. I couldn't see myself in their work. I never could. It was more about what they saw, and each of them saw things differently. One woman made the torso rather thicker than mine, and the arms more delicate in proportion. Some of the men made the breasts appear pendulous, while mine were rather small. Still another, the most skillful in the group, had embellished the form she was working on- adding a pair of wings to the middle of the back.

"All right, dear?" Maude said, taking me by the shoulders and looked at me directly. I felt she was seeing right through me. "Are you well enough to continue?" she asked.

I nodded. All the dizziness had passed. So I got back onto the stand, and listened as she critiqued their efforts and perused their workstations. "You see this line, from waist to hip bone? Try to get this curve, and remember there are no straight lines on the human body. You need to get some bulk in at the back of the head. But it's better to made the head too small, like the Greeks did, than to make it too big."

What was I looking at when I looked at Angus? Again, there was that self-serving desire to make his person fit my preconceived impressions. I had my own private vision of Angus, and I was fully invested in it. Like these sculptors, I was trying to make my vision work. I was looking at him, yes. But was I really seeing him.

"I'm going to kill him. I think I'm going to kill him." Brenda was in her bathrobe, hair wrapped up in a plush pink towel, as she darting about with buckets and bowls, placing them round the kitchen floor. I'd come in from the barn and looked up at the ceiling to see a huge damp spot widening out into a kind of map with brown stained edges. "It's that goddamn shower he built," she hissed, as I helped position the bowls, and water dripped from the plaster.

Just then, the plumber came downstairs with his tool kit. "Whole thing needs to be taken out," he said. "Nothin' done to code. You've got your shower membrane correctly joined in your shower pan. But because your sealant hasn't dried...."

"Ruby!" Brenda screamed. "Where the hell is Angus?"

I didn't know. He hadn't been there when I woke up, although I thought he might have gone to pick up supplies for the barn conversion. Or maybe he was busy with the catamaran.

A few days later Brenda called a meeting. We sat at the kitchen table, Angus and I, together with Brenda and her friend David Miller, who was also a lawyer, a lean fellow in a brown suit and tinted glasses. He sorted through a pile of receipts while Brenda sat meekly beside him, meek for the first time in her life, I might add, and very much mistaken. "Things here have come to a head," Miller began. "And the barn conversion is much more complicated than Brenda thought it would be. Added to which there are zoning laws and building codes which you seem to be violating."

Miller was taking charge, while Brenda, for her part, had become utterly mute. "The long and the short of it is that Brenda wants to call the project quits. She feels that Angus has bitten off more than he can chew."

Brenda wants. Brenda feels. Why couldn't Brenda speak for herself, I thought, just like she always did?

Angus leaned across the table, the perfect picture of outrage. "What? You can't do this to us! This is our lives we're talking about!"

"Maybe so. But the time has come to terminate this arrangement, before it gets any worse..."

"How can you say that! I've bought the wood, and the insulation. I've ordered all the pipes. We've dug a trench for water pipes. You can't just kick us onto the street. We had an agreement..."

"Except there was nothing in writing," Miller reminded us. "And even if there was, such an agreement would have been voided automatically by your shoddy workmanship. After the problems with the shower you built, how is Brenda to know..."

"Because she had my word! I thought that I had hers. You weren't part of our agreement. Brenda and I were... Brenda, Ruby and me. It was between the three of us. We started to draw up a contract in writing and Brenda was going to show it to you – and then she fucking sat on it for a whole month, and now – "

"Listen to what he is saying," Brenda put in wearily. It was like her face was dissolving and going slack, the force of her character all drained away.

Miller paused, sorting through receipts, and Angus glared at Miller while he continued. "In addition to her concerns about your workmanship, you have made numerous charges on her credit card, for items such as mahogany planks, a sewing machine, and a band saw, which Brenda didn't authorize."

"Bullshit! All those purchases were approved by Brenda," Angus broke in.

"When I told you I didn't own a sewing machine," Brenda said, "I didn't expect you to go out and buy one!" He leveled her then with an expression of such intense focus, I thought she might turn to stone. Instead she simply looked at the ceiling, towards the stain from the leaking shower, where the paint had bubbled to blisters.

Afterwards, back in the barn, we lay in bed under the open skylight. "She can't do this to us," Angus said, stymied, disconsolate and then suddenly furious. "Fuck," he muttered. "Fuck! How can she do this to us!"

"Well," I said. "She's doing it." I was perplexed by the way that Brenda was handling things, but Miller had made his points quite clear. Nevertheless part of me was proud of Angus. He had more conviction, was so much more imaginative and daring than a man like Miller.

But to be perfectly honest, my prevailing feeling was relief. "Maybe the time has come for us to move back into Boston," I suggested. "It won't be so bad. At least we'll have running water there. Not to mention heat."

"You know what, Ruby? You've never been behind this project," he said miserably. "Why are you never on my side?"

"Now that's unfair! I've been on your side all along. But the work you've done so far hasn't been very good..."

"Are you kidding me?"

"You heard them. The shower wasn't done to code."

"It *was* done to code. Brenda shouldn't have used it before the sealant dried."

"Now you're quibbling. You know she has a point. Aside from that, the colder weather is coming and we haven't even insulated the place. Even if she was in agreement, we'd never get it finished by winter."

"You were never on my side."

"I *was* on your side! It's because of my support that we're both in this mess!"

"Can you even hear yourself?"

"Well maybe I should have objected earlier. That was my mistake," I shouted back. "But at least I'm looking for a solution!"

"And your solution is to kiss this investment goodbye and move into town."

"At least we'll have heat there and plumbing!"

"We should fucking take her to court on this," he muttered.

"How, Angus? With what money? We don't have any leverage. And Miller is right about one thing: There was nothing in writing."

"Haven't you ever heard of a gentleman's agreement? Even in court that is binding."

"But Miller said your shoddy workmanship voided that agreement."

I'd said too much and hurt him. It wasn't the time to ask about the Seabrook robbery. And when we woke up in the middle of that night to the gentle rustle, followed by the steady downpour of rain, all thoughts of the Seabrooks had gone entirely from my mind. We sat up in bed as water rained down on us through the open skylight, streaming in from the midnight sky.

Angus jumped from the bed like a shot. He slipped down the ladder, picked up a flashlight and dashed outside. There was the hoot of an owl, the soft and gentle patter of rain. I sat in the white wet sheets, blued beneath the moon, and listened as Angus climbed onto the roof and secured a tarp in place.

Yes, I questioned his honesty. I knew his workmanship wasn't always up to par. But I never questioned his ability to climb onto a slick barn roof in the middle of the night, and stop the rain from falling.

Twenty-Seven

"What did he do?" Nora wanted to know. There had been a problem getting our possessions out of Brenda's barn. We were staying temporarily in Hingham and when we returned to pack up our stuff, we discovered that Brenda had confiscated some of our furniture and personal items as ransom, including our wedding album.

"He put too many things on her charge card," I said, "to pay for the barn conversion. And now she's claiming she didn't authorize it."

Timothy frowned. "But aren't any of these things itemized?"

"I don't know and neither one of them will discuss the details with me," I said.

"But why is there such animosity?" Timothy asked.

"I don't know," I said. "I wish it would just go away. All I want is to move on with our lives. I want to get our stuff back."

"She probably won't discuss it with you, darling, for your protection. And if I were you I wouldn't get involved," Nora advised. "Stay right out of it. This was between Brenda and Angus. You had nothing to do with it, and Brenda knows that."

The feud continued. A week later, Angus went back to Scituate alone. He waited until Brenda was out and then managed to extract a few of our remaining belongings from the barn. Afterwards Brenda retaliated with a phone call, threatening to take him to court.

Meanwhile, James had moved to Stillman Street in the North End of Boston, sharing with a sculptor called Russell Thorne. The North End, he told us, was full of low-priced apartments. The kitchens were big enough to set a table in them, and the Italians made friendly neighbors. They had lived in the North End for generations. It was quiet, civilized, welcoming and cheap. Why didn't we look for a place there too? In fact, he suggested, there was an interesting vacancy on Copps Hill Terrace near the pilgrim graveyard. The U.S.S Constitution, nicknamed 'Old Ironsides' was permanently docked across the water. You approached the building by means of steps to a narrow lane.

We went to take a look. The neighborhood looked sketchy, but the apartment was good and we liked the rooms, the hardwood floors and wainscoting, the enormous kitchen, and the simple bedroom, with its deep walk-in closet. It was clear why the place was so cheap when you stood at the living room window, though. The public terrace was strewn with broken bottles and rubbish. It looked like a dangerous hangout.

I stood at the window, looking at the old stone tables with broken inlaid chessboards positioned beneath the plane trees. Starlings sat on the telephone lines. I tried to imagine the courtyard as it must have been conceived, before the neighborhood went downhill. In my vision, old men sat here playing chess through the long afternoons. Children played hopscotch and mothers chatted beneath the trees.

"Copps Hill Graveyard," Oliver said, when I told him where we planned to move, "is where the Mathers are buried. I like the idea of graves overlooking a view. If I remember correctly, that one is on the rise and the church is on low ground. It's Increase's church, you know." He chuckled. "So Goody Aleshire's pilgrim life continues!"

Ari telephoned to say he had a part at the new repertory theatre close to where I worked. We arranged to meet at Tango's after his rehearsal. "It's wonderful having you back in town," he said. "We can meet up any time, and in fact, I'm taking fencing classes not very far from the North End."

I told him my plans for the new apartment, how I'd do my grocery shopping at the open market. I saw myself going home with brown bags of tomatoes, lettuce, avocado and big wet bunches of parsley. "With a kerchief tied round your head, I suppose!" he said.

We took the T to Boston Garden and wandered through the North End, stopping at a café on Hanover Street. Above the bar a row of bottles glistened. Sandwiches waited in a glass-fronted counter for consumption. We took our cappuccini and cannoli to a small marble table in the corner. Ari had rosy cheeks and seraphic good looks. He wore a hand knitted scarf, and old sandals with socks.

I told him about the series of very short stories I'd been writing, and about some little pen and ink drawings with which I'd illustrated them. I had also decided on a title: Little Stories of Loss. I said.

And how are you getting along with Maude?" he asked. "Isn't she fabulous?"

"She is," I said. "Yes. All of it is working out." I bit into the pastry, tasting its sweet ricotta and pistachio filling, and when I looked up, I saw Ari watching with a strange expression on his face.

"Is something wrong?" he asked.

"What could be wrong?"

"Your face in repose looked sad just now. Ruby," he said. "I *know* you."

"It's Brenda," I confessed. "We left her barn under a terrible cloud. I've never had an enemy in my life. But now with this Brenda thing going on, we've got a residue of defeat in our lives. Angus is always on edge. He made a mistake in the building of her shower and when I pointed it out, I wounded his pride. We had a fight. Now his pride is wounded, and so is his idealism."

Ari frowned. "Are you telling me that Angus is idealistic?" His legs were crossed at the side of the table as he stirred the foam on his coffee.

"You have to remember, he has very high standards," I explained.

"Standards for himself though, or for other people?"

"Both I think," I said. "It crushes him when he detects the flaws in people. If he sees someone trying to put themselves across as 'good' and then they fail, he tends to give up on the entire possibility of goodness."

I thought about his sister Beth. "He's easily disappointed," I continued. "Easily let down because so many people lack integrity. And if he discovers that absolute goodness doesn't exist, I'm afraid he might give up. That's my biggest fear. That he will give up entirely on goodness."

Ari frowned. "But absolutes don't exist, do they?"

"I'm not sure. The difficult thing about dealing with Angus is the way he looks for cracks in people's armor, and is then disappointed when he finds them," I went on, trying very hard to set the record straight. "But more than anything he wants to find something worth striving for."

"You are the idealist, I think, Ruby," Ari said. "And I love you for that." But instead of smiling, he frowned again, playing with his coffee spoon, stirring the foam that sat in the bottom of his cup.

While he was debating whether or not to continue the conversation, I saw my cue, and gathered my belongings. "Shall we?" I said.

We walked the narrow neighborhood streets, washing lines strung from windows above us. Ari laughed. "Gosh, Ruby," noticing a squat little door on a nearby terrace house. "Who lives in Number 27?" It was so small that it looked like the door to a hobbit's dwelling. "Dear oh dear," he said, laughing. "Is this where you're going to live? Because this is enchanting. Oh yes. I think you'll be very happy here."

Happy. The use of that word surprised me. I had almost forgotten about happy. I wasn't looking for happiness. What I wanted was meaning. Happiness took a back seat to that. It no longer mattered. I was on a mission to save Angus from the worst parts of himself and the hope of happiness had become good enough.

I fit my new key into the apartment door and opened it up to see our reclaimed furniture, surreptitiously removed from Brenda's barn, scattered about and waiting to be arranged. The radio blared and there was Angus, his back bent as he unpacked boxes of books. "Oh, you can do wonders with a place like this," said Ari.

Angus straightened himself. He was dressed in jeans and a tan v necked sweater. On the floor beside the books were a handful of tools, a hammer, a screwdriver, and several nuts and bolts. He saw the expression on my face at the same instant I noticed the bookcase. "Well?" he asked. "What do you think?"

My long anticipated bookcase! What was not to like? It was constructed out of mahogany planks, and perfectly proportioned.

Two ancillary units flanked a larger central one, and they stood together against an angled wall.

"It's beautiful, Angus. How did you build it so quickly?"

"You said you wanted a bookcase," he said, lifting a stack of LPs. "And once I planned it out, it went up very fast."

"Wait. You built this bookcase? Wow. Where did you get all the wood?" Ari asked.

"It's wood left over from the barn renovation," I explained. "It's great you managed to take this wood, Angus. And frankly it's only fair. Don't you think so, Ari? I mean, Brenda kicked us out without any notice at all. With nothing."

Angus had already filled up the central unit with books and record albums. Then I remembered something. "Wait a minute. I thought there was a closet on that wall."

His face darkened. "Not a very good one."

"So why don't we put the bookcase over there?"

It wasn't a good suggestion. It came across as ungrateful. Angus turned away and went on lifting books. "I built them to fit against these walls. And besides, it wasn't really a closet. It was just a wall with a door, left over from when they divided the apartment in two," he said. "And we have enough storage space already. We have that big walk in closet in the bedroom."

"But we could have used it to hang some coats."

"No," he said. "It was too narrow. And anyway it's damp inside." He turned to Ari. "Do you play chess, Ari?"

"Not very well," he said. "Why?"

"Because I'm looking for a chess partner."

"You used to play with Timothy," I said.

"I need a chess partner in town."

"As a matter of fact, I do know someone," Ari said. "My fencing master plays chess. He has a studio down near Lewis Wharf." He looked at me and laughed. "This location is looking better and better!"

I stood at the Duron paint counter while a bearded young man placed an open paint can underneath a spigot of color. He dialed up the pigments, and pulled a lever to release the colored droplets into the white. He banged the lid back on with a mallet, and positioned the can in a machine, which rattled and vibrated.

A three-minute mix and what had once been white turned into soft chalky blue. He pried up the corner of the lid to show me, and marked the top with a dab of color, smiling. There was a gap between his two front teeth. "There you go," he said. "Iris Moon."

I sat in the front window with the radio on, scrubbing grime from the glass. Angus polished the bathroom mirror with wads of newspaper. The place was filthy, but at least there was running water and a roof in this place. At least the windows had glass in them. The basics elements went to my head. Suddenly having the basics was everything to me. We could build on basics. We could make this pig's ear into a silk purse, sand the wainscoting, and finally paint it. I sat in the pile of redecorating things, with scrubbing brush and bucket, and after an hour or so of very hard work, I sat, catatonic, and stared across the expanse of floor, at all the things that needed to be arranged and unpacked.

Brenda had confiscated our wedding photos along with the sofa and a carpet that had belonged to Angus's grandmother. We still hadn't been able to get those remaining things back. Then it came in the mail: a summons to small claims court. Brenda was following through with her threats.

"How can she do this to us?" I cried.

"Don't worry," Angus said. He was dashing out the door to register for classes at Suffolk for the Fall Semester.

"What about your probation? Won't this overturn it?"

"Not at all. This is civil court and I'll take care of it. Don't you worry."

I tried not to worry. I tried not to dwell on unpleasantries. I made an effort to trust him because that was the key to going forward.

Angus resumed his classes. He had signed up for Western Philosophy, American Literature and General Psychology. He was thrilled with all the new reading lists – especially the Mark Twain and Walt Whitman, and took to reading passages aloud to me when we lay in bed at night.

While I listened, I imagined how we'd decorate the new apartment. The bathroom had possibilities. The bathtub was tiny, on clawed feet, its underside mottled in rust. I decided I would paint it orange. I'd also paper the walls in peacock hues. Yes, and then I'd place candles about the room, and pile towels on a wooden stool. Since Brenda had taken our sofa, I would string up a hammock in the living room and fill it with cushions, to make a kind of low lying sitting area. I'd drape the bedroom windows in melon colored saris.

The railings of the courtyard, the shade of plane trees, cast a sweep of shadow on the floor, where Angus sat in an old pair of track pants, carefully painting the apartment door. The radio was tuned to *Morning Pro Musica*. The courtyard outside had a forsaken quality by day. Nighttime was the problem because then the terrace turned into a hangout. We heard the sound of smashing glass. Beer drinking kids played disco on a boom box. Cars were broken into on the street out front, their tires randomly slashed. One morning I saw our neighbor, crestfallen, standing hopeless before his car because someone had taken a key and scratched along the finish.

Twenty-Eight

September meant new beginnings. In addition to resuming classes, Angus took up chess with Ari's fencing master down near Lewis Wharf. He went there occasionally in the evenings, if he didn't have papers to write, and if I wasn't going to a reading or hanging out with friends, I sometimes went along.

Nigel reminded me of the knight in Chaucer's *Canterbury Tales*. He sat on an upright chair at this ornately carved table and sometimes he took out a pipe and puffed on it while he considered the board. Their games were deliberate and measured, just like every other aspect of his place, witty in an understated way, full of the chivalrous interplays of strategy, grace and cunning. Attention was paid to one thing at a time. There was no such thing as multi-tasking at Nigel's. The studio was silent, the walls hung with sabers and foils.

After a few weeks, Angus found a part time job, which fit in well with his college schedule, playing the organ for a tiny church in Hyde Park. Timothy and Pastor Jackson both wrote recommendations and he drove out there in the Audi three times a week, once for practice and twice for services, where he played three hymns and a solo, the music for the offertory, a prelude and a postlude.

I accompanied him to that church every Sunday. We made our way down the broken streets. Trains rattled on the bridge above, and the walls were covered in graffiti. The church was a refuge only for a dying community of little old ladies. They smelled like violet cashews and clasped me by the hands whenever they saw me. "So lovely to see you, dear."

"Are those the people of God?" Angus asked, throwing me a sidelong glance of amusement as we headed home.

"I agree. It's depressing."

"Is that where it leads? The bad wigs, the fake smiles, that young guy with gum disease?"

"I guess they must be the lost sheep," I said. "And that's what the lost sheep look like."

"But you aren't one of them. And neither am I. You must be able to see that."

"I do, and it confuses me," I said. Then, "Maybe believing in God is naïve."

"It's possible that God is a beautiful lie," he said.

"Except that holding to spiritual precepts does people good," I said.

"Oh sure. Look at your father. He really believes in God."

"And Pastor Jackson too. He believes. And they are good. They are the best people. Believing in God makes them who they are."

"You may be right," he said. " But most of the people in church are hypocrites in my opinion."

"Do you think that it's better to be naïve than hypocritical?"

"Is that what you think?"

I shrugged. "I don't know. You tell me." He didn't respond. "I'm trying to work it out. I just don't understand why there are never any people like us in the church. I don't understand why we never fit in."

He got a second part time job during the week: Meryl's Kitchen in Quincy Market. They made sandwiches with natural ingredients – whole wheat with natural peanut butter, bananas, raspberries and raisins. They made smoothies, with yogurt and fruit in a blender. And soup: cucumber dill, tomato and basil. Meryl was a fat hippie who talked too much, with a bubble of spit at the corner of her mouth. She practically let Angus run the place, working the counter all shift long.

"Hey Ruby, listen to this! There's this booth across the way that sells Chinese herbs. And they have this chalkboard sign out front listing the benefits of ginseng. I was so bored today, I swear to God, that I snuck over when no one was looking and I wrote 'cures homosexuality' at the bottom of their list, in neat chalk writing."

"You did not!"

"And she never even noticed."

"I hope you told her, after you'd had your little joke."

"Sure. Later on I did. I said, do you realize what it says at the bottom of this list? You should have seen her face." He paused and his expression turned from triumphant to defeated. "Jesus," he said. "This kind of crap work isn't a life."

"But it isn't your life. It's only a way to make money while you finish your studies," I said.

"I know, but I need something more. I could do better than this."

"And I'm sure you will."

"I mean, what would you think if I rented a warehouse out in Jamaica Plain."

"What do you need a warehouse for?"

"I could keep the catamaran in there, and maybe I could start a business building boats. Kayaks," he said. "Little fourteen foot skiffs. I'll build them with cedar. I'll get the plans for wood and epoxy kits, and make one at a time and start my own business. I'll learn as I go. I need to do things with my hands. You know that."

"But how would you learn?"

"I'd learn as I go. I would teach myself."

"I don't know," I said. "It sounds shady."

"Anyone who takes a risk and tries something different sounds shady until they become a success. That's the whole point."

"But won't it be expensive renting a warehouse?"

"The place I have in mind is cheap. And as a matter of fact this guy I know at Suffolk has an Airstream trailer and he's looking for someplace to keep it."

"This guy you know? Who is that?"

"Michael Posey. You met him last year."

"Oh come on! You mean that weirdo who dresses in leisure suits."

"First of all he's not a weirdo. He's a psychology major. Second of all, he's agreed to sublet the space from me, and that's a good thing because then the place will pay for itself."

"Can I come and see it?"

"I haven't rented it yet."

"Before you rent it. Can I come and see and then we can decide?"

"But there's nothing in it yet. It's just an empty room."

"When can we go?"

"When it's all set up," he said.

THE STORY OF EVE
by Ruby Lambert-Aleshire

Eve arrived in the walled up garden called Eden at the coming down of daylight, when Adam was not in possession of his faculties.

And she saw him under the pear tree, pen over ear and notebook in hand, filling out grids with the neatest of writing. He had a fondness for nomenclature, for if he could give it a category Adam supposed he could own it.

Eve didn't share such passion for catalogues. She cared about the heart of the matter, and wanted to know what made him tick.

So they shared a meal – half an avocado each, followed by apple. She watched his steady hand as he capped off the end of the apple, and began with a deft curl of the knife, to peel the skin in a single, thickening spiral.

She imagined this as seduction. Here was Adam, the picture of boredom, everything systematical. She began to feed him segments of the fruit, hoping to split apart the code and find what lay beyond it.

Lovemaking started with eyes. Finger to finger, palm to palm, belly against belly, each step in its place, each body part locked in its sequence. She wanted to jumble the sequence a bit, but she bent like a willow to please him.

The part about the serpent was a lie. It was all in Eve's mind, played out in her deepest contemplations. And when at last she lay in Adam's arms, watching him watch her watching him watch, she knew it all came down to what they two were doing. Nothing beside this mattered.

Flesh of flesh and bone of bone, desired to be more than a rib and the art of yielding seemed to count too much. Complexity was Eve's curse. Adam's was simplicity.

And God said this would not do. Who was this woman? He had never called her Eve by name. So Adam denounced her, and Eve became brittle as a single bone. She'd taken it all too seriously, forgetting she was only Adam's dream.

The apartment was dark. Evening came down. The streetlights went on outside, and local delinquents congregated on Copps Hill Terrace. But Angus was nowhere around. I sat on the floor, phoning various friends. I even phoned Michael Posey.

"Hello, Mike? It's Ruby, Angus's wife. Is Angus there, by any chance? Oh. When did he leave? Did he say where he was going?"

I went to bed anxious and lonely and then woke up to the sound of breaking glass. I lay in bed looking onto the derelict terrace. A lot of hooting was going on, catcalls and the steady thump of a base line on the boom box they were playing.

I closed the curtains and lay alone in the dark. My heart pulsed in every inch of my body. Where was Angus and what was Angus doing? And why? But more to the point, who would stand up for the man he might become, if it wasn't me?

How do we learn about blindness by living in rooms full of color? How do we conceal the ugly truth of the obvious: Rembrandt's *Portrait of a Lady* a wall's thickness away, an El Greco, two Ming vases and a Brueghel, stolen from the Seabrooks and stacked in the closet behind my new mahogany bookcase.

I neither knew nor suspected they were there. It sounds foolish in retrospect, but it never occurred to me that something was stashed in that closet. It wasn't a real closet. It was only a wall with a door in front of it. And once I had my bookcase, I forgot about it entirely. I've concluded that it all comes down to selective blindness.

There's an optical illusion, which demonstrates the mind's selective blindness. Three steady yellow spots stand in a field of moving blue speckles. When you focus on the space in the center of the spots, they seem to disappear and reappear at random. This, neurologists explain, is because too many peripheral messages, in the field of blue speckles, prevent the mind from absorbing them.

There's another mind trick: a video of six or eight people throwing a basketball between them. The viewer is instructed to count the number of times the ball is passed. Meanwhile, a man in a gorilla suit walks across the screen, waves at the camera and moves off. But the viewer, intent on watching the moving ball, never so much as notices him.

At the time, I was troubled by other things. Sex, for instance. Sex with Angus had changed. We didn't feel like it as often as before, but when we did there was a different kind of hunger to it, an emotional disconnect akin to gluttony. When we climaxed it was like explosion, exposing the violent glow of the earth's core. It left us exhausted.

But when he played the piano, and that became more and more rare, when I watched his strong brown hands coaxing music from the keys, I longed for his former tenderness, for intimacy and truth. I longed for the heartache we felt in the earliest days, for the painful feeling of loving each other too much. We no longer played our duets. That would have been too painful. All of that had been stripped away, leaving us like exposed electrical wires.

He drove to the Hyde Park church to practice the organ. During the Sunday services, I sometimes caught his eye from where I sat in the front pew. I lived for those shared looks of amusement and conspiracy, his eyes dark with feeling. We knew we didn't belong in that church. But I began to suspect I'd fallen for a magician. The magician gave me both what I asked for and what I couldn't understand: the mental puzzle, the effortless illusion. I had been enchanted. Now I wanted to know what lay behind his tricks. Now, more often than not, I found myself perplexed, lost or left behind, as Angus obscured detection, with constantly new and inventive tricks.

The continuous buzz of unnecessary information had me awake at night, and worried. I confided my concerns to Nora on the phone. "Yes," she said. "I see your point. I agree that you've got to find out about this warehouse, Ruby. Why don't you tell the therapist he's seeing? Or better yet, can't you go out and see the place yourself?"

"If only the therapist was good. But he's just a court appointed psychologist, and I'm sure that Angus has him hoodwinked."

"Get the address of the warehouse, darling. I'll take you out there if necessary," Nora said.

So I asked Angus for the address and he scribbled something on the back of an envelope. "But if you really want to see it, I'll take you tomorrow. It's just there's nothing in it yet. I'm going to start building the first skiff soon, and then I'll take you to see."

"But I wanted to see it now."

"Not today," he said.

"Why won't you take me?"

"I can't."

"Why not?"

"Because I have a paper to write about Walt Whitman."

"Bullshit," I said. I sat in a chair in front of the bookcase he'd built me, my arms folded across my chest, my features tightened with suppressed rage. I felt like a bitch. I hated myself. "What do you need a warehouse for?"

"To store the catamaran," he said.

"I'm beginning to wonder if you're still taking classes," I said. "I think you're lying." The expression on his face was one I'd seen before: Disappointment, pity and an overlay of repulsion. He looked at his mother Cheryl like that. I had turned into his mother. "You aren't going to college," I continued into the hostile silence. "You're doing something else. You don't even smell like college. You don't smell like books or cigarettes or coffee. Your clothing smells like the open air."

He stood there staring at me, with a blank and calm expression on his face. Nothing I said seemed to penetrate.

"I hate you!" I screamed. "You never write papers. You never read books. You don't have friends..." The poison spewed forth freely. I was on a roll.

Until he broke in. "Why would I bring friends in here? Do you think they'd feel comfortable with you?" he asked. "I mean look at you?"

What had I become? What would my parents make of me now?

Angus turned his back. He picked up the phone and began to dial numbers, and now he was listening and talking to someone I didn't know, standing at a distance from me, preparing himself to leave and get on with his life.

"Where are you going now?" I hated myself as much as I hated him in that moment. I hated the person he was turning me into. "I said *where are you going!*"

He looked at me steadily, calmly, even sadly. "I'm going to play chess with Nigel," he replied.

"You are NOT!" Then he turned and left without a word. He didn't take me to see the warehouse, of course. He didn't take me then, or the following week, or the week after that. Still I held my ground. "Take me to the warehouse. You said you'd take me last week. Why keep putting it off?"

"I don't want to argue with you, Ruby."

"I don't want to argue either. All I want is the truth, goddamn it!"

"Yeah," he said. "Right."

"I want to put my mind at rest."

"At rest about what?"

"What do you need with a warehouse? You're supposed to be a student! You are supposed to be a guy with part time jobs. If you're a student, that means you need to spend most of your time on your studies. I never see you studying. You never even talk about you classes."

"You aren't interested in my classes."

"*You* aren't interested in your classes! It doesn't make any difference if I'm interested or not! This warehouse is a front. What are you doing in the warehouse?"

"What do you think I'm doing?"

"Have you forgotten that you're still on probation for breaking into Sal Rosenblatt's office?"

The hollow of his cheek pulsed gently, as if he believed my purpose was to hurt him. "And your point is...?" He made me out as obnoxious and unreasonable, my own worst nightmare, a nagging, bitchy wife. "What do you want me to say?" he asked. "I'm seeing the probation officer every month. I go to the psychologist every other week."

"But what do you talk about with the psychologist? Is he helping you?"

"We talk about a lot of things."

"I bet he doesn't agree with this warehouse..."

"As a matter of fact he thinks it's good."

"That is a fucking lie!"

"All right. Talk to him yourself if you'd like."

"Cast your mind back, Angus. Don't you remember how you felt when you said you wanted to rewire yourself? Don't you remember that conversation after you were arrested? After Timothy and I bailed you out? You cried after you were arrested that time. You said you wanted me to stop you from doing this kind of stuff."

"That was different. But there isn't anything wrong with this."

"Have you told the probation officer about the warehouse? Because if you haven't, I will."

"You will not."

And even as I threatened him I felt like I was the one in the wrong. He had turned me into a bitch and a nag. "I will turn you in to the authorities," I persisted, listening to my hateful voice, sounding like his mother. "I will fucking turn you in."

"Well, that sounds quite dramatic, Ruby, and it's very good to know," he said. "The only hitch is there's nothing going on. I have to do things with my hands. That's it. I want to build. It gives me peace of mind. You can't deny me peace of mind, can you?"

"All right," I said. "If you are looking for peace of mind, why are we always fighting?"

"I don't want to fight."

"Oh my GOD! I don't want to fight either! Don't you see that I'm trying appeal to your true self – the one I fell in love with?"

"If that's the case, why do you talk to me as if I'm a criminal," he said.

"I talk to you as if I'm trying to wake you up."

"Yeah, well. It feels like you're bringing me down."

Twenty-Nine

Nora showed up wearing a checkered top with flowery trousers and desert boots. It was a week or two before Christmas and we'd arranged to go out and find the warehouse. Angus was out, so I left a note, saying that we were doing some holiday shopping. Then we set off for Jamaica Plain, following the map beyond residential streets to a long winding stretch through an industrial area of town. This was to be our own private investigation. Maybe we'd surprise him in the warehouse; we didn't know. But if we did, he would have no choice but to show us inside.

We found the wide fronted buildings, all right. They were out in the middle of nowhere. Some were derelict, with broken windows, scrubby hedges and weeds. We passed an empty lot that contained a crane, heaps of sand and gravel. "What did you say the number was?"

"1411," I said, as I squinted out the window. Nora slowed the car before a huge brick edifice, with a metal grill pulled down the front, and no windows. "That's 1412. But where is 1411?"

There was a garage to the back of the lot. Was that 1411? Surely not! It was so nondescript we'd almost missed it, and it lacked the sinister feeling I'd imagined. It was closer to nothing at all than to something noteworthy. "Is that it? Do you think that's the one?"

"Should we get out and see if there's a door?"

"But there aren't any doors."

"There must be a *door*, darling. There's a door in the grid, I expect." Nora parked in front, and together we got out, and stood in the dark. The building was a garage in the middle of nowhere. There was no sign of life. But for good measure we took a brief walk around the building, and finding it unrewarding, decided the door must be in the grid itself. The place was cold and abandoned. But that was it. We returned to the car.

We drove back to Boston in silence, at first defeated, having not faced the insurmountable after all. Not having cracked our case. But soon that feeling ebbed away when we were back to the familiar haunts of the North End. We even had a bit of a giggle trying to park the car, and we ended up at Quincy Market wandering through the food court. Lydia had a job there selling apple pies at Johnny Appleseed's. We met her in the atrium. She worked on a pushcart, next to a man who had another pushcart, where he sold black and white photographs of Boston. They sat on high wooden stools, chitchatting all evening long.

The atrium was packed with shoppers and echoed with voices and holiday music. Enormous velvet ribbons hung against the walls, with gold bells and angels decorating them. A cacophony of aromas flooded our senses: chocolate chip cookies, Chinese takeaway, cinnamon candles, barbequed spareribs, pine and mistletoe.

Lydia finished her shift, so we settled on Cityside restaurant to order sandwiches. Back in a safe commercial dream world, white lights twinkled in every tree, wrapped around the trunks and wound around branches. Pavements and storefronts gleamed with holiday displays and carolers assembled in the courtyard to serenade shoppers.

Our sandwiches arrived and I realized I was ravenous. We talked about the warehouse. "I do wish we'd been able to see inside, though," Nora reflected.

"I hate doing things behind his back," I said. "But then I think about all the things he's doing behind my back."

"Well, that's exactly it. What have you got if you don't have trust?" Lydia put in.

"Right now, nothing. Only the raw material of Angus," I said.

"But how can you trust what he's doing with the raw material?" Lydia continued.

"I don't."

"Well," said Lydia. "It takes two to tango, and he's not being straight with you, Ruby."

Nora was lost in thoughts of her own and had eaten most of her sandwich before she spoke again. "There are so many layers to a marriage," she said. "And a complex relationship requires not only that you accept the person as they are, but that you accept the person they have chosen to be. Perhaps when you were younger, that wasn't such a factor."

A busboy stood at the counter, with a stupid pork pie hat on his head. He had dark brown hair, beautiful eyes and a clean generous mouth. He caught my eye and both of us grinned. I know this hat is stupid, his expression seemed to say, but I'm still cute and charming and you are cute as well.

If only I could fall in love simply, with somebody normal like him. But here is the deep down truth of the matter, and it's rather hard to accept. I had a very real pride in my illusion, although I didn't recognize it as illusion at the time. There was a sense of pride in knowing that although loving Angus was terribly difficult, I was able to manage it. I suppose you could compare it to the adrenaline rush some people get when riding a difficult horse. It may be frightening, it might even be dangerous, but it's much more fun than sitting on a placid old mare.

By the end of our meal, the holiday crowds had dwindled somewhat, and we managed to get in some Christmas shopping. I bought a set of Japanese plates as a gift for the Aleshires, and a record of summer birdsong. Then we found some printed maps for Timothy. Afterwards, Nora dropped me off, kissing me goodbye. "I won't come in," she told me. "But do cheer up, chicken."

I was proud. I was also ashamed. I didn't want her coming in. I didn't want her eyes on the mess of my apartment. I couldn't bear her unspoken pity and concern.

But when I ascended the steps to Copps Hill Terrace, I forgot about my shame. I was too busy wondering who had strung up all the colorful Christmas lights, which twinkled through my living room windows. I opened the door, to the heady smell of pine. The room was dark, except for the lights on a newly bought and decorated Christmas tree, and there sat Angus with a table beside him, and on the table was a bottle of champagne and two champagne flutes. Then I saw the present he'd put for me underneath the tree: a pair of skis and ski boots.

~

We attended church in Hyde Park on Christmas Eve. As usual, Angus played the organ. He played Ave Maria and a young soloist from Dorchester sung it feelingly. The church was old and warm, its heater humming in welcome. A lopsided holiday arrangement of poinsettias stood before the altar. The congregation was sparse, and everyone was cheerful in that church; everyone was also a stranger. There in the so-called house of the Lord I felt such a painful distance between myself and their perception of me. I was my most artificial, my most despairing in that church – wife of the organist, upstanding citizen, hypocrite. They knew absolutely nothing about me, and even less about Angus. But they didn't care to know. They wanted us to be sorted out. But we were the sinners within their gates and I would never feel comfortable asking for their help.

Angus sat behind the organ while I sat alone in my pew. In front of me nodded the ancient heads of several little old ladies. During the readings, I noticed Angus in repose. It shocked me to realize he wasn't looking good. Over the months his skin had begun to break out and his eyes had lost their luster. It was true that he bought tubes of Clearasil, and often stood in front of the medicine cabinet smoothing ointment over his pimples. "My face has erupted," he'd moan. "I look like a monster. Look at me!"

"Yes," I said. "I'm looking." Always looking; never really seeing him. I was looking at him now. I don't know what I saw.

Thirty

So according to the Bible, Jesus told a story about the tares and the wheat. The tares are another word for weeds. There was a farmer who owned some fields of wheat. And while he was sleeping, his enemy came to the field and sowed it with weeds. When the crop sprung up, along came the weeds with the wheat. The servants of the farmer didn't understand. How come this field is full of weeds, they asked. I thought we sowed good seed in this field. An enemy has done this, the farmer said. We'll weed the field, said the servants. No, said the farmer. Let them grow up together until the harvest. And at the time of harvest I will tell the reapers first to gather the weeds and burn them. Then, after that, they can gather the wheat and store it in the barn.

It was this sort of story that had me thoroughly stuck. I was also stuck on fear and the function of fear. Sometimes fear heightened awareness. It made you sharper and more alert. It protected you and because of that it must be a useful emotion.

But when I compared my own fears to Angus's fearlessness, I wondered if I was any better off than him. I was afraid of breaking the law. But not because it was wrong, so much as because of the reprisal. Angus didn't care about reprisal. He had more courage than I did, and probably less hypocrisy. His lack of fear, bordering on danger, was enormously compelling.

∼

Enid and I stood in the courtyard behind Tango's, wrapped in our coats. It was freezing out and Enid was smoking a cigarette. "He must have stolen those skis," I told her. I trusted Enid more than I trusted the milquetoast ladies at church. I trusted her because she was damaged. Perhaps everyone is damaged, in the end. But Enid was honest about her damage and therefore I could trust her and expect compassionate answers.

"I've never been skiing myself," she mused. "Do you like skiing?"

"I've only been once and that was back in high school."

She laughed. "I guess he must really want to take you," she said.

"But how can I go with him on stolen skis? Where did he get them? I have to put my foot down at some point, don't you think?"

Enid held her cigarette, nodding her head, and squinting as she drew on a final puff and exhaled. "Righteousness kills all joy," she said.

I frowned as she dropped the butt to the ground and scrubbed it out with the heel of her boot. "What do you mean by that?" I asked.

"It's one of the main principles in est training. The hardest thing to do in life is to give up your own sense of righteousness. But it gets in the way of every relationship, and it gets in the way of healing."

∼

Angus and I went skiing that February. The slopes were packed with athletic people dressed in colorful clothes. The car parks were full and the lines were long. I looked with trepidation at the icy tracks, cutting deeply into the mountain. Small children whizzed past fearlessly as we took a chairlift straight to the top.

Frozen air peppered our faces. Snow studded pine trees rose up around us, and something further inside me gave away and dropped out of sight once we got off the chairlift.

A sickly allure. The overpowering sensation of vertigo pulled me over the edge. Angus skied ahead, and curved off to one side. He turned and waited, watching me snowplow slowly towards a bank of trees. I glided forwards in a hunched position. I came to a stop and tipped over on one side.

I could see him laughing as I lay there in the snow. His eyes creased, his mouth was wide. He skied towards me and pulled me to my feet, positioning his skis outside mine. Then he pushed us off together across the frozen blanket of snow. Pine trees stood out against a lavender sky as we cruised together down the mountainside. Cold air whipped past, and other skiers smiled.

They all approved. They liked what they saw. They liked us together. Angus skied us down the trail, his skis on the outside of mine, his arm wrapped around me, and I was protected from every obstacle in the physical world.

Angus was mine, and in moments like that, the world became what I always knew it could be with him: intense and more intensely experienced. The good times with him held so much more promise and reward than good times with anyone else. There was no intensity equal to his. He filled me up with the eternal now, navigating a knife-edge, razor sharp, which felt sublime in its precision and clarity. He took me out to the borders of myself and dropped me over the edge.

~

But back in our apartment I hunted for clues, looking for ways to sabotage his criminal efforts. I knew there must be something to find. So whenever he went out I opened up the walk-in closet of our bedroom, and extracted things methodically. I emptied shelves, removed his papers and college books. I opened his briefcase, snooping and sifting through every last paper to see what I could unearth. I was sure there was evidence somewhere, as I looked into the closet, as I looked into the blankness.

I discovered several unrelated things. None of them seemed to line up. I didn't know what to make of the five or six unstrung tennis rackets in the trunk we used as a coffee table. It wasn't the whole story. It was only evidence, and it seemed so random. I couldn't discover any pattern to the stolen goods I found. Yet I kept trying to fit the pieces together into a neat little narrative, as if I were Sherlock Holmes.

I found a stolen stereo. That discovery seemed like a step along the way to filling out the bigger picture, but it didn't satisfy my conviction that there was more to be found. Later, some neighborhood kids stole that stereo out of our car. I remember thinking there was a lesson for him in that. "What goes around comes around," I said, when Angus heard them playing the stereo and dancing to it down at the park in front of Old Ironsides.

I asked questions but I tried not to make assumptions. It was all a kind of fog. Like a story with too many threads to it, that didn't tie together. I wasn't afraid. Perhaps you'll conclude I was hypnotized, weak or spineless, that I should have drawn the line much earlier on. But although I wasn't his partner in crime, I considered myself his partner in life. I took those marriage vows absolutely literally. And I didn't see myself as a snitch.

When Angus switched cars, trading in the blue Audi for a brown Audi and later acquired a large black Cadillac with a plush red interior, I knew it was preposterous. Of course! The idea of all that contraband was thoroughly preposterous one moment, and thoroughly tedious the next. But I was looking for a larger picture to emerge as I listened to his explanation, about how he got the Cadillac at an auction of repossessed cars.

If I could only get him away from the influences of people like Mike Posey, I thought. Then we might stand more of a chance, and he would stop being a criminal. Bad influences lay at the heart of the matter. Of this I was convinced. He was surely a bad influence in his turn, but what became of other people wasn't my concern.

Mike Posey came to pick him up. Then they'd go to the warehouse. Mike was always dressed in a camel hair coat and new loafers. He wore an expensive watch. He took a look around our apartment and shook his head. "This place needs work," he said, grinning at Angus, as if at an inside joke.

"Why is he always so pleasantly attired and sly?" I asked. "Do you realize that Mike has never once looked me in the eye. Who the hell is he? I don't understand the attraction."

"I'm sorry you feel like that," Angus replied evenly. "Because he and I are good friends."

"Bullshit! What do you do when you go to the warehouse?"

"We play chess." And by the way, it isn't true that people who lie will not look you in the eye, because Angus always stared me down.

I almost laughed. "Oh come on! And where do you play chess?"

"In the Airstream trailer," Angus said, holding my eyes with his.

"Oh really? Parked inside the warehouse?"

"Why don't you make friends with his wife. She works for Little Brown. You two would definitely get along."

"If she's so good, how come she doesn't mind him going to the warehouse all the time?"

Angus turned his head. His profile looked sharp – the strong nose and twist of his mouth seemed arrogant to me then, and the back of his head annoyed me. It looked strangely flat from that angle.

"Don't go, Angus. Please." I might have been talking to a heroin addict. It was just as useless and just as urgent.

He turned and stared at me, stony faced. "You know what Ruby? Sometimes you're like a burr. You just stick to me to give me shit."

I dialed Ari's number after he'd gone. "Why are you doing this to yourself?" Ari asked.

"I don't think I can any more," I said.

"Do you want to stay here for a night or two? My mother agrees. Come here right away. It's important, if only for your pride, Ruby. You can't let him walk all over you like that."

I packed up a bag, and took a cab to the Fenway. Ari met me on the steps of the Montessori School where his mother was the director. They had an apartment on the very top floor. And as soon as I stepped through the door, his mother embraced me. She was dressed in a heavy cotton muumuu, her hair wrapped up in a scarf.

"You must always feel free to come here," she said warmly. "You don't have to call. Remember that. Just come if you need to. Ari and I will always welcome you here."

I needed a big dose of sanity. Ari talked to me and listened to me, and he made me laugh at the absurdity of my predicament. At one stage he gave me a postcard. It showed a man kneeling on a doormat, pleading in front of a slammed door. "Wait, come back!" read the caption. "There's a part of my face you haven't stepped on yet!"

"I'm putting this on my refrigerator door," I said, "where I can see it every day."

"You can't go back to him," Ari said. "You've got to get out of that marriage."

And so for the next several days I went to work, returning at night to Ari's apartment. We walked down to the Christian Science Center and visited a strange and wonderful room called The Mapparium. It was made of stained glass and shaped like a globe, with a bridge running through its center. We stood in the middle of that bridge and listened to the echo of our voices.

On the way home, we passed a Brighams Ice cream parlor up near Symphony Hall. Then I saw a familiar figure sitting in a booth. "Oh my goodness, Ari – remember that guy I told you about who I used to teach piano?"

"The idiot savant?" he asked.

"Melvin Stringfellow. That's him, right there. The guy with the big head, wearing a raincoat?" We stood in front of the window while I waved toward the table where Melvin sat with several others, all of them holding white canes. A woman in pointy glasses bustled around them chattily.

"He's blind, Ruby. Surely he won't see you waving," Ari pointed out.

"Oh, of course! Let's go in. I'd love for you to meet him."

We went through the doors and approached Melvin who was steadily licking an ice cream cone. "HelloRuby," he said in his usual monotone. There was no surprise in his greeting, although it had been almost a year since we'd met.

"Melvin, how are you? How wonderful it is to see you again!"

"Yes," said Melvin, his eyes shifting off to one side.

"Melvin, this is my friend Ari," I said.

"Yes," said Melvin.

"Are you on an outing with your friends?" I asked.

The capable woman with pointy glasses answered on his behalf. "Hi!" she said. "Do you know Melvin? This is our ice cream social. Melvin has been joining us for almost a year now." Then in a loud bossy voice she added: "Great to see old friends, huh, Melvin?"

"HelloRuby," said Melvin. "Two black notes."

"Are you still playing the piano?" I asked.

"Two black notes," he answered.

"I taught him to play," I explained to the woman with pointy glasses. "He's extremely talented."

"Is that right," she said. But I could see she didn't care.

"You do know that he plays, don't you? He's amazing at it. Aren't you Melvin?"

"Yes," said Melvin.

We stood for a moment smiling at each other awkwardly, and then it seemed I was holding them up and so I said goodbye. "Send my regards to your mother. And tell her I'll come and see you soon," I said. And with that, we headed outside.

"What an incredible character!" Ari exclaimed. "How on earth did you ever get through to him?" And for a moment I couldn't seem to answer. For some stupid reason the tears had filled my eyes.

I couldn't do it. I couldn't stay away from Angus. I couldn't give up and it wasn't about me. It wasn't about happiness. It was about my stubborn compulsions. I wish I could say here that I went back to Angus because of my desire to find meaning. But the truth is probably simpler. Life without him felt flat and meaningless. Just as Angus was addicted to his criminal behavior, I was addicted to Angus.

But when I returned to Copps Hill Terrace and opened the door to our apartment, I knew it was a mistake. The radio was on and I heard the sound of sizzling food. When Angus peered round the kitchen door, he looked absolutely terrible. He had cut his hair and parted it on one side. It made him look like somebody else. For one split second I realized he was disappearing right before my eyes. "Ruby, you're back," he said. "Would you like some spaghetti?" But if he was disappearing, I needed to call him back – like Orpheus calling into the underworld.

The following Friday I went to Quincy Market with Lydia and Ari. Ari had just got a part as Snug the joiner in a new production of *A Midsummer Night's Dream* and rehearsals started the following week. But Lydia was in a quandary. Her boyfriend Gustavo had returned to Spain, and now she was taking up with a lawyer called William Dupont, who had a suite of offices at Government Center.

She'd met him at Quincy Market while buying baguette sandwiches. He'd taken her out to dinner at expensive places near the Waterfront Park, smooth-talked her into his bed saying he was separated, and then she discovered that no, he was in fact still living with his wife.

We ended up in Cityside and ate tuna melts for supper, and afterwards we walked back to my apartment. I had only been back there a couple of nights. Inviting them into the mess of that apartment, I felt deeply embarrassed. So this was my so-called home. Was I really going to stay here, they wanted to know. It was still full of redecorating things, of ladder, newspaper and paint rollers, unwashed dishes and unfolded laundry. It would cost so much to move out. It would cost so much to stay. Whatever path I took seemed to require more reserves than I had.

"Why don't you clear these away? Let's at least arrange the furniture. Here. Come on Ari, let's help her," Lydia said, as she pushed chairs around the place and folded up a few drop cloths. She took out a broom and swept up the scraps. "You've tried to do too much in here," as she sprayed furniture polish onto Pastor Jackson's piano, and wiped away the dust with a strip of paper towel. "All you need is a place that feels safe. You don't need all this wallpaper."

Ari took the spray can of polish from Lydia and began to work on the bookcase. "Where is Angus now, do you think?" he asked.

"Probably the warehouse," I said. "You wouldn't believe how many arguments we've had about that damn warehouse." I went to the kitchen, looked around, and made an effort by filling the kettle, taking out teabags and honey.

Lydia lifted a pile of clothes and papers from a paint-speckled butterfly chair, sat down and lit a cigarette. "What do you think he's doing there?" she asked.

I rinsed out some cups and put them on a tray. Should I tell the truth? "He says he's storing the catamaran and an Airstream trailer."

"Do you think he paid for that catamaran?" Ari asked. I came in with the tea and set it on the trunk in front of the hammock. Ari was lying there, head propped up with throw pillows. The place looked better already.

"If only I could get him away from Michael Posey. He's such a horrible guy."

"But how did Angus get that car, Ruby?"

"Which one?"

"The Cadillac."

"Do you think they're dealing drugs?"

"I don't know. I hope not." My tone was filtered, my seriousness diluted with levity and the levity forced, as if through mesh, sifting the dross of unhappiness. It was hard to remove the sting of disillusion. "What do you think I should do?"

"I think you should move," said Lydia.

It may sound foolish, but it's the small logistics of such decisions that often stop us making them. "Where will I go?" I asked them. "I'm the one who pays the rent. My name is on the lease. And if I move out and Angus doesn't pay, I'll be the one who ends up in court."

"Where did he get all those tennis rackets?" Lydia wanted to know.

Ari shrugged. "He's been playing chess a lot with my fencing master. Nigel really likes him."

"Of course Nigel likes him," Lydia said. "Lots of people like him. That isn't the point. He's very popular with my friends at Tannery West as well. Ruby, do you know that he gave away some tennis rackets to the people at Tannery West? That was the same week Meryl fired him."

"I think I should tell his probation officer about the warehouse," I said.

"Yes," said Ari. "Turn him in."

"I don't want to be a snitch, though."

"You won't have to snitch," said Lydia. "Just tell them about it and let them find out for themselves." And the following week I had the opportunity.

Thirty-One

The probation officer, Keith Lavern, was a smooth faced fellow with good intentions and a very heavy workload. He visited our apartment at Copps Hill Terrace and sat in a red armchair in front of the mahogany bookcase. Angus was out. But that didn't matter. Lavern had come to speak with me.

So... he began. Angus had a new job in Quincy Market. Wasn't he also taking classes at Suffolk? According to his records, Angus was meeting the psychologist regularly; so no problems there; consultations going well. Home stable. Rent paid on time.

I sat while Lavern ticked off boxes on his evaluation sheet. "Do you have anything to add, Mrs. Aleshire?"

"There are several things that worry me," I told him. "But one thing in particular. Do you know he has a warehouse out in Jamaica Plain?"

"He mentioned something about that, yes," said Lavern.

"I think you need to check it out."

Lavern had a gentle expression and a short military haircut. As he listened his face went slightly askew. He bit the end of his pencil, thumbing through his papers. "Well, Mrs. Aleshire, he and I have talked about the warehouse," he said at last, putting his papers into a manila file. "And it sounds like it's all above board. I'll try to get out there if you want, but to tell you the truth, I've got many cases far worse than your husband's."

But he never checked out the warehouse. Somehow it slipped through the cracks. Instead he signed off on the case, and our lives continued into the spring and the summer. The law had abandoned me and I gave up all hope of its uncovering his schemes. *Give up*, came the message, loud and clear. *You cannot save him from himself. Your standards are too high, even for the law*. But yet I was like a bird mesmerized by a rattlesnake, unable to lift my wings and fly away.

I returned to my tiny cubicle of thought, a life the size of the piano practice room at Boston University. I continued to live my life with him, as though Angus was a roommate. I lived in the poetry I read and in the little stories I wrote. I lived inside books and walks through the park, in drinks and sandwiches with Lydia at Cityside and meaningless light conversations. Unless they were conversations with Oliver and the poets, those conversations being mostly theoretical. I lived in a world constructed by myself, where the glass half full was never also half empty.

"Ruby," said Angus, one evening. "I have an interesting proposition."

I'd been sitting quietly in the bedroom reading and he was standing in the doorway. "How would you like to get away from here? To start all over again."

"What do you mean?" I asked.

"I mean I'm not on probation any more. That means I'm free to leave the state. What would you say to a trip across the country? We can go in Mike's Airstream trailer. He said I can use it this summer. We could drive down the TransCanada highway, and out to the West Coast. Think about it. The biggest expense will be gas. Everything else we can do on the cheap."

The chance to get away. The chance to start life over. Things might change if we had some time by ourselves. Once we got far away from Boston, perhaps it would feel easier to make a change.

We planned it out carefully. I took the time off work. We packed up the Cadillac and hitched Mike's 40-foot Airstream trailer onto the back. We said our goodbyes and off we set, driving to Northern Massachusetts and up through Vermont. Crossing the Canadian border, Angus was ecstatic. His joy carried us all the way to Sherbrook, Quebec where we got a flat tire. There we pulled over to a wilderness garage where I held the flashlight so that he could see.

Mile after mile we traveled a highway lined with slender pine trees. Deer country. That part of the journey was less inspiring than it was tiresome. Then we crossed into Ontario, heading for the desolate plains of Winnipeg, endless grassland, sky and lakes. You got the sense that the main objective there was to endure, to prepare for or recover from winter.

We walked down wide flat pathways, populated by nobody, civilized with the nicety of flowerbeds and the occasional duck pond. We were by ourselves. Nobody knew us. We were driving away, reinventing ourselves. On the road to Saskatchewan, I sat beside Angus, looking at a map. "We're missing all the high points," I said. "We missed out on Moose Jaw and Regina."

"Moose Jaw," he said, pronouncing it with care.

"Yes. I was really looking forward to Moose Jaw."

"There's a place called Long Lac that looks more interesting," he said.

"I think we already passed it."

"No way. We aren't even close."

"I think we must have passed it already."

"We haven't," he said. "Do you see any lakes around here?"

"No, but we passed a lake back there."

"That was only a pond."

"I bet you anything, that was it," I said.

"All right," he said. "I bet you fourteen piggyback rides. And the deal is I can get one any time I want one."

"If you win, that is."

We drove for miles. "What do they do in Long Lac?" I asked.

"I think they cut down trees," he said. "And they fish." Then, "You see!" he cried. "I won! I won the bet," As we passed a road sign: Long Lac.

We never stopped in Thunder Bay. We zipped right past, continuing on highways so clear and remote that we fancied we saw the curve of the globe in the endless expanse of nothingness. Hundreds of miles of nothing lay before us: grass, horizon, rainstorms in the distance like a dream, low and square, against an enormous sky.

People actually lived her. We could hardly believe it. We marveled at how the houses had all been built together in a cluster. Why did they do it like that, we asked, when on the other side of them there was all that nothingness.

We camped under the stars. Cooked sausages on a grill. We cuddled up in sleeping bags, not knowing where we were, until the morning light revealed it to be an even emptier and simpler place than we ever imagined.

Angus sat on a canvas chair facing the view while I cut his hair. Hair blew away in thick black tufts, tumbling into the wilderness. Then we threw away our picnic rubbish, got back into the car and headed back on the road, drinking cold bottles of Coca Cola, driving to Manitoba, through Medicine Hat and Edmonton, heading for the Canadian Rockies, destination: Banff.

On my twenty-fourth birthday in the middle of June, it snowed. Banff National Park was a place where you bundled in sweaters and walked or biked the road to Lake Louise, past streams of non-potable waters. Deer country turned into bear country. We took tourist snaps with my birthday present, a stolen Nikon camera. Banff was a gingerbread town, nestled beneath mountains. "This reminds me of Aspen," he said. "I could stay in a place like this."

"Yes," I said. "It's lovely."

"Hey Ruby, how about one of those piggyback rides?"

"Now?"

We were standing in the middle of the street, in front of a chalet that sold sporting goods. His face creased up. "You're not getting out of this! It was part of the deal that I can demand a piggyback any time I want one." He climbed on top of me, both of us laughing until we almost collapsed, as I staggered forward one or two steps, with his legs dangling almost to the ground.

"Let me take your picture," I said at an overlook, on the way to Lake Louise.

"Not now."

"But it's beautiful here, and I want to capture the moment. Take off your sunglasses."

"Just take the picture," he said. But he wasn't posing properly. He only stood waiting, his hands in the pockets of his straight-legged corduroys, a tight smile stretched across his face. I snapped my shot.

Those nights and days have blended now into the haze of a holiday built on so many lies it was destined to collapse from within. And yet for a time, it held us suspended, like cartoon animals running off the edge of a cliff, who don't yet know they are walking on air.

The country rolled up behind us and the future stretched before us as we headed across the Puget Sound by ferry, for Vancouver Island. The summer breeze was tinged with ice, but the island was sunny and both of us liked Victoria. It was an obedient old-fashioned town, which sloped and meandered. We peered into shops that sold Spode and Lenox china, and we contemplated augmenting our wedding collection.

"Can't you see us moving here?" Angus asked. We were sitting in the trailer, surrounded by trees and the smell of sap. It was the time of afternoon that seems to last forever, that special hour before the sun goes down, when the earth is still full of the heat of the day, but the air is growing colder.

"Wait," I said. "I need to finish this chapter." I was reading *The Collector* by John Fowles and it had me in a mood. "What a disturbing book," I said.

"I can see us moving here," he said.

"We're so far away," I said.

"From?"

"Everyone we know."

"And that could be good. We could start a whole new life out here."

"Oh, I would gladly live somewhere other than Boston, if I knew what we'd do."

"Anything we wanted."

"Not here, though. It seems too quiet. Don't you think this place is rather old fashioned?"

"Sure."

"I mean, I like it. But what would we do here?"

"What do you want to do?"

I put my book down. "I don't really know," I said. "But I'm willing to give it a try. Except we can't really stay, when this trailer belongs to Michael Posey."

"What about it?"

"We can't just keep his trailer. We can't steal it. We have to take it back to him," I said.

"We might be able to work something out," said Angus. Then he frowned. I could see he didn't like that observation. It put a big spanner in the workings of his plan. It was then I knew for sure that the trailer must be stolen. It didn't belong to Mike Posey.

"As a matter of fact," he told me, after a moment or two, "I don't think I'd like to live here. I want you to see Arizona first. So let's make a deal," he said. "If we find a place we feel we could live in, we should seriously consider staying."

We ferried across to Washington State where there were lupins and orchards. All the way down the west coast we listened to the same several radio songs – *Up on the Roof* by James Taylor, and Supertramp's *Logical Song*. Life was good and we were heading for northern California.

In less than a week we were driving the magnificent Pacific Coast Highway, straight for San Francisco. We were entering heaven. We wound round the hairpin cliffs, to ever more stunning vistas, out across the turquoise, out across the cliffs, the beach and the shore and the grand redwoods. Those trees were kings, with their wise robes of undulating bark. We lay laid beneath them and fell into eternity, staring up at the branches, up to the heavy blue sky and into forever.

We picnicked at an overlook and hiked down cliffs to the sand and then we tore off our clothes and swam. It was like you wanted to become the water, to become the actual landscape, to blend your identity with the place itself.

I telephoned a college friend in Berkeley, who lived there with her boyfriend and a golden retriever. Sure, they said. Come visit.

Berkeley smelled of eucalyptus. My friend Cara had hair down to her waist. She wore Indian dresses and earth shoes, and had a fondness for magic mushrooms. Her boyfriend was a sweet James Taylor look alike, except without the talent. They had a roommate who wanted to be a model. She was five foot nine but needed to grow at least another inch. She was contemplating getting herself stretched. There was this special process, she explained, whereby she could add an inch to her height. Even half an inch, even a quarter, would make all the difference in the world, she told us.

We sat in sunny cafés and ate salads of alfalfa, mung bean sprouts, and marinated tofu. For about a week, we talked about our college days with college friends, and planned what we would do with our lives now that college was over. We took winding paths up hills full of boxwood and birdsong. We sat on steps outside stucco houses, smoking weed and admiring the view. But did we want to live there?

"I don't know, Ruby," Angus said. "It seems kind of self-conscious here."

"What's self-conscious about it?"

"You know what I mean. It's too 'enlightened,'" he said, making quotation marks in the air with his fingers. "Like they've got it all figured out."

"Anyway," I said, taking up the joke, "what do they do in California? Every day is a day you want to take off."

We went to Laguna Beach after that, a town of blistering skies. The idea was that we would visit Angus's friend Nacho Gomez, a guy from Hingham who was now living out here. Angus was going to phone him in the morning. Then we would all meet up.

We parked the trailer in a dusty lot, across the street from a beautiful stretch of beach, and we went to sleep to the sound of the surf.

Thirty-Two

I woke up, in a hot and airless trailer, with the feeling that I must have overslept. I sat up in bed, realizing Angus was gone.

Ruby, said his note. *I've gone to see Nacho by myself. I don't think you and me and Nacho would make very good company. Nothing is going on, I just felt like seeing my old friend alone. There's a lot we have to catch up on, and I repeat, nothing is going on. You can be grumpy about it all you want. Or you can go to the beach. There's a beautiful beach across the street, so take full advantage of it. NOTHING IS GOING ON. I will be back in the early afternoon. I love you. A.*

I was furious. How dare he go off without taking me along! Of course something was going on. How dare he leave me here alone, giving me no choice but to go along with his wishes.

But after several minutes of fuming, I stopped. Even if he wasn't being straight with me, there was still nothing I could do. Either I was going to fret about what was going on – and I'd never know what it was – either I was going to sit here in the stinking hot trailer, or I was going to go to the beach and enjoy my morning in Laguna.

So I drank some orange juice, slathered on some sun block, put on a bathing suit and walked across the road in my flip-flops. The road was empty, lined with holiday souvenir shops. The palm trees were so ludicrously tall and with such small tops, they looked like Dr. Seuss had drawn them. But it wasn't as late in the day as I'd supposed. In fact, the beach was practically empty, except for a few early surfers.

I walked along the shore and waded in the sea. Then I turned and waded back to my starting point. The beach was golden and the water was blue. The place looked like paradise, except it wasn't paradise. It was more empty-headed than my vision of paradise, and far more superficial.

Finally I found a good place near a rock. I lay on the sand in my purple bikini, listening to the surf and smoothing my skin with lotions. We might live like this for the rest of our lives –

fugitives in stolen cars, living the nomadic life of hippie travelers. But was that the pinnacle of experience? Was it the life I wanted? It was good to be far from the warehouse, all right. It was much easier not to challenge him about it, but instead to fall in with the life he wanted to lead. It was also a relief to get Angus away from Michael Posey. But would we just move away from Michael Posey and into the hands of Nacho Gomez? Would Angus never change?

He was gone for hours. I dozed and then I tried to write a poem. I made a few sketches and got ink on my hands. Then my skin began feeling itchy and hot and I knew I'd been out in the sun too long. So I walked back to the trailer and tidied things up a bit. I threw out some trash and wiped a few surfaces. It felt stuffy and boring in the trailer. We'd been living in it too long. I made a salad, chopping up vegetables on a baby cutting board, in our tiny Airstream kitchen.

Where was he? I ate my salad with a plastic fork and sat on the door stoop watching the road, the cactus and the brown hills, and the tops of those silly palm trees. Then I drank a beer and watched the lizards scurry in the dirt. What kind of place was this to live? This wasn't a town; it was a wasteland. A paradise for fools. If Angus did wrong here, if he went off track, there would be nobody I could turn to for help. I would be completely alone out here. This was not the place for us. Nowhere was. Suddenly all I wanted was to do was to drive back home to Massachusetts.

Eventually I saw a speck moving towards me on a bike. It grew and grew until it turned into Angus. He was heading towards me with a bike. Where did he get that bike, I wondered.

"Where were you?" I said when he was within earshot.

He was covered in dust. He dismounted and washed his hands under a spigot, letting it splash on him, and on his clothes and on the dirt around him. The dirt grew darker as he tossed the water over himself, splashing water onto his face. Then he dried off and sat glumly in a deckchair. His knees stuck up, angular and athletic, and he rested his head on his brown hairless arms. "How was Nacho?" I taunted. I was determined not to get angry, mind you. Why give him the satisfaction. But I didn't mind it if he got a little bit annoyed. I didn't mind twisting the knife. "Did you enjoy yourself with him?"

"Not really," he said.

"Why not?"

"We didn't have much in common, I guess. He's changed. We talked for a while. But I didn't stay with him long."

"Oh," I said. "Too bad."

"So what did you do?" he asked me at length.

"I went to the beach. Can't you tell? I've caught too much sun. In fact, I feel kind of feverish."

He looked at me as if he suddenly recognized me, and his eyes softened. "You did catch the sun," he said. "But it suits you."

"What's wrong?" I asked him.

"Nothing. Why does something have to be wrong?"

"Oh come on. There is something wrong. What is it?" Silence. No, I thought. We can't keep this up. I've really decided, now. And we can certainly never live here. "Do you want a beer?" I asked.

"Sure."

He took the beer I passed him, twisted off the cap, sipped it and gazed into the middle distance. "I saw some guys hang gliding out across the dunes," he said.

"Oh. So that's where you were."

"I watched them for hours."

"Where did you get the bike?"

"Nacho lent it to me."

"Hmm." I took a swig of my own beer, and felt its cold sharp taste slide down my throat. We had to get home. I had to get back to my tribe of supporters.

"I'll never get to do that," he said.

"Do what?"

"Hang glide. I don't know. I can't explain. I hate it so much. I really want to try it, is all."

"That isn't it," I said. "What's really bothering you?" He looked towards the palm trees.

"It sounds to me like just the kind of thing you'd do," I said.

"All I want is freedom," he said. "That's all I'm looking for, I think."

I felt annoyance rise inside me, then. I'd been keeping it down, but now it turned into a physical presence, taking over my body. "And what's this?"

"This?"

"What's this if it isn't freedom? Isn't this freedom?"

"I guess."

"You always have to look at the downside of everything. Do you realize that? Look at what we're doing? Look at how we're living? What are you complaining about?" Frustration twisted inside my body, plummeting to my pelvis, and clenching the muscles there. "I've been doing exactly what you want this entire vacation. Do you ever think about what it's like," I asked. "Do you realize how much I've sacrificed? I've stopped asking about the stolen goods. I never ask you where you got the car or the trailer or any of that stuff. I just try to go along with you because I love you and I want to be together and because I'm hoping you'll reform some day and be the man I fell in love with."

"Stolen goods, Ruby?"

"Fuck you, Angus. Don't give me that."

"I told you, the trailer is Mike's."

"I know what you told me," I said. "I also know it's a lie. And I haven't asked anything about the Airstream trailer. I haven't asked about the car or where these things come from. And there's another strange thing about this trip. We never make love. We have all this freedom and yet we never touch each other. When did our love dry up? What is wrong with us?" I asked.

"It feels too weird to make love."

"Why?"

"I don't know."

"It's because there isn't any trust between us."

"I guess that might be true."

"I don't know how I stand myself anymore. Or you. What is supposed to keep me going at this point," I said. "Except for my fear of the future. Your future. And my fear of giving up on dreams."

"Why must you give up your dreams?"

"The day I give up on you is the day I give up on my dreams. I'm afraid that I've wasted all this time on a fantasy."

"And what's the fantasy?" he asked.

"It's about how I saw you when you were a boy, and the kind of person I thought you might become. It's a fantasy about you playing the piano, so intelligent and handsome, so capable of anything you put your mind to. How you know things that I have no clue about. How we complement each other."

He didn't speak for a while. He only opened another beer. And took a sip. "Here's the thing," I continued. "I love your fearlessness and courage. I need that in my life. But I have something equally important to give to you. And that's my fearfulness. And if you won't take any of that, it will be the end of you."

Thirty-Three

We headed down the road after that, and stopped in a place beneath the hills for veggie burgers. No one else was there, so the proprietor struck up conversation with us while we ate. He had a dark beard, and was a likeable enough fellow, but more of a mind to talk to Angus than to me. Angus did one of his usual performances for strangers. His clever stick, hail-fellow-well-met, bantering guy with a great philosophy on life and how well to live it. If only this stranger knew, I thought, as Angus blathered on about our trip across the country. If he only knew who he was talking to. If only he knew that everything we owned was stolen. But of course, he didn't know.

It turned out the guy fancied himself a painter. After our meal, he took us out to the barn to see his gallery. They were mostly watercolors of boats in harbors, and sunset scenes, the ultimate clichés. I suppose he wanted us to buy something.

But we got back on the road, and didn't properly stop again for any length of time until we reached Arizona where we intended to meet some of Angus's bike racing friends in Tucson. This was the highlight of the trip, in Angus's mind – as important as our stop in Banff. He loved this place, and wanted me to see it. He wanted me to meet these friends of his. These were not the same kinds of people as Nacho Gomez. In fact, Angus was sure I would love them.

But my first impression of Tucson wasn't very favorable. There wasn't a shrub in sight, nor a scrap of grass. Unless you counted Mount Lemon off in the distance, but that was like a mocking peak of greenery. Dry heat, no breeze, and when they cleaned the windscreen at the gas station, the water evaporated before they could wipe it off. I could never live there in a million years.

Angus, however, was in top gear. Ever since Laguna Beach, he'd been telling me about these amazing margaritas you could get at a particular Tucson café, and how much I was going to like his friends. When we arrived in town we drove down the main street with Angus oohing and ahhing at how some things had changed and how other things were just the same. Then we stopped in a trailer park and took a long cold shower. I changed for the evening into a new sundress. It was dark green with thin straps and it showed off my new tanned skin. I had never been tanned like that before – but the sun of Laguna Beach had done me good, after all. I was all set to meet his friends and make a good impression.

The most important friend I'd been told about was Matthew Steerforth. He was supposed to be an amazing bike rider, a juggler, and a bike builder – a salt of the earth kind of guy.

Well, I'll give him this much. He had an open smile and a lively personality. He charmed me because when we met he burst into laughter. "You're beautiful!" he cried, holding both my hands and gazing at me, arm's length. Then, to Angus, "She's beautiful!" so that Angus and I laughed as well.

We went out for Mexican food, and the famous margaritas, and then Matthew took us to meet his father, who lived in a stucco complex in the desert. I had run out of conversation by this point. They seemed to talk mostly about CB radios. Matthew's dad entertained himself with a CB radio, and his tag was Funky Monkey.

I went along with all of it. I tried to be one of the fellas. A day or so later, Matthew Steerforth drove with us over the border into Nogales and we had dinner in Mexico. Conversation was animated, but didn't touch on any subjects I could contribute to. Angus however, seemed ecstatic. We certainly all ate well. The Mexican food was delicious. Then Angus polished off the lettuce under the guacamole: big mistake. We drove back fast on the road, going at 120 in the Cadillac. The guys were in the back, having drunk too much, but I did all the driving.

By the time we arrived back in Tucson, Angus was bent double with Montezuma's Revenge. We checked into a motel because he needed a flushable toilet. For the next two days he lay in bed groaning, puking and shitting in the dark while I swam laps in the small blue square of a motel pool. It lay in the middle of a scorching expanse of cement that gave way to a desert landscape. The sun was blinding. Every now and again I got out of the pool, toweled myself off and padded back to the room to check on

Angus. The elevator had a sign above it. "Elevador," it said. What kind of place was this? But I'd go for a swim and then walk back down the carpeted hallway, and open the bedroom door to see him groaning in his sick bed.

"Can I get you anything Angus? Are you sure? Nothing?"

No. Nothing. He wanted nothing but the occasional glass of water, or flat ginger ale.

Two days later with Angus recovered, we left the motel and headed off for the Land of Enchantment, where huge jackrabbits bounded across the grassy desert. Then there was Texas. I was certainly glad to see the back of Arizona, but Texas was too massive for me. I saw only its bigness. Nothing specific, nothing I could latch onto. I could never live there. I didn't even contemplate the possibility. But it seemed like we were trying on lives as quickly as Angus tried on identities. And then before we knew it, we were in the strip malls of Oklahoma where, in a rainstorm, we took in the latest James Bond film. There was Kansas after that, another expanse of beautiful American land. After that came St Louis, Missouri with its majestic slinky arch.

∽

Greenville, I'll never forget you. Greenville Illinois with its common and library, pretty houses and country lanes. We followed one lane, which was lined in hedges until it ended with a view across the fields, and arrived at a field of green, a roll of land and country paths winding through the pasture. And this is where we had an important conversation.

"Could you live here?" I asked him. All our stops began like this. Could you live here, and then all the reasons we couldn't.

"Nope," he said. He could tell by the way I'd asked the question that I really liked it in Greenville, and I could tell he wasn't giving it any thought for that very reason. He wasn't playing along, because of my disappointing reaction to Tucson.

"You wanted me to like Arizona," I said.

"But Arizona didn't look the same to me with you in it."

"Why's that?"

"I don't know," he said. "Something about who I was back then, and who I have become, I guess."

"Were you better back then?"

"That depends what you mean by better."

"I mean did you like yourself more?"

He turned this question slowly in his mind. "I think I did," he said at last. "I guess I don't know how things have got so far off track. Because they have. You know they have. We both know that."

"I think it happened," I said, "when we stopped caring about the truth."

His face did a kind of collapse. "Ruby," he said. "I lie about everything. Even when I don't have to. And that is about the only true thing I've ever said."

Outside our trailer was a green field, full of corn. There was a fence, and a field, and a row of trees, and off to one side was a tractor, painted red. This is what I looked at while I talked to Angus. "Maybe I shouldn't ask you anything," I said. "Or at least I shouldn't respond to anything you tell me. That's what makes you tell lies, I think. You want me to respond in a certain way, and when I don't, you lie to me. It's the same with me. When I know there's something going on which I don't like, I lie to myself about it. Both of us lie. That's all we do anymore."

"What do you want?" His question was sincere. "I can't figure it out. What are you doing with me, anyway?"

"I'm your wife. And I want to work out our relationship," I said. "And stop you from destroying yourself."

"Oh Ruby." His sigh hung in the air between us, like a huge impossibility, like all the dashed hope of the last few years. "If there's one person in this world who I love," he said, "it's you. I feel as if you and I have a very close bond. But yet I don't know how that's possible, after all I've done."

"Soon it won't matter because we won't have anything," I said. "Not unless we make some serious changes. No. If we are going to stay together then we have to be honest with each other. You have to be honest with me. And I have to be honest with myself."

"I don't see how we'll do that."

"And I don't see how we can continue if we don't. Already," I said, "Our relationship has been poisoned. We've poisoned it."

"You're right," he said.

"Remember how much we were in love? That was only two years ago. We could have done anything then. And now, I feel there's this gulf between us. All this is going to come to an end. Because we can't keep living like this, on lies."

Maybe it was Greenville, the beauty and simplicity of the landscape, the green of it after all the brown desert, after all the strip malls of the Midwest and the blankness of the plains. But there was a window between us, a funnel of truth and light, and it was through this light that we spoke to each other now. "I don't know how to get myself out of all the shit I'm in," he said.

"Then why don't you let me help you?" We were sitting in the trailer, over the open table, the remains of our supper before us, and by now the sun was going down on the pastures outside.

"How can you help me?" he asked. I had the impression he was all emptied out. It was as though only the essence of him was left, and that essence was sincere.

"I'm your wife. Of course I can help you."

"You can't Ruby. You don't know the half of it."

"Then tell me," I pleaded. "Imagine what it would be like if you were completely honest with me."

"I can't imagine," he said.

"Then how about this," I said. "How about you tell me everything you do. And I won't do anything with the information. How about the only thing I do about it is to pray?"

He was stymied at that one. Even I was surprised by the idea of it. It was so revolutionary, and we'd had so many fights doing things the other way, that it sounded like it might work. We sat in silence for quite some time, and soon the sun was gone for the day, and all I could see was the outline of Angus. Only my imagination placed his features in their usual places. "You mean," he said. "I would tell you everything."

"Yes," I said. "Everything. You would tell me everything, and I would do nothing but pray. I wouldn't tell the cops. I wouldn't turn you in. But I would be a voice for goodness. By praying."

He looked as if the strings that had been holding him so tensely together had all been cut, releasing him. "Do you know what you're offering," he said, "I mean, that would be huge. Do you think you're strong enough to take it?"

"Anything's better than what we've been doing," I said.

That night we made the best love of our lives. We melted together, each sequence of our lovemaking playing its perfect part, in a seamless dance of music turned into flesh. His skin was soft and his body was hard and I knew and yielded to his every pressure, the weight of his body within me, the weight of his limbs, his torso, and his steady breath against my neck. Our bodies fit together in their singular dance, a dance that could only be done with love, and when we had finished we slept like babies in each other's arms.

This was our breakthrough. From now on things would be different. We had never made love like that before and it gave us a new beginning. When the sun came up, we looked out of the trailer window to a row of trees, and the green, green grass of Greenville, and then we just wanted the trip to be over. We wanted to be in our own home. So we drove fast, almost without stopping, unless it was to fill up on gas or to empty our bladders, until we got to Massachusetts.

Thirty-Four

We crossed the border into Massachusetts. "Let's go visit my grandmother," he said. He meant his grandmother Gloria, mother of Frank Aleshire, who lived in Wellfleet on Cape Cod. This was his adoptive grandmother, not his biological one, and a woman I'd met only twice. She had visited Angus when he lived with our family during my high school years. The other time was at our wedding, when we hardly spoke. Angus purported to be very fond of his paternal grandmother, and she, in turn, seemed fond of him.

So we got off the highway and made our way to Wellfleet and pulled the trailer into her little driveway. She wasn't expecting us – but that was Angus. He always loved to show up unannounced. When she answered the door she seemed surprised, a plain, overweight kind of woman in her early seventies. She invited us in immediately. There was nothing flustered about Gloria Aleshire. She was a no nonsense type. She had raised her sons, and seen them marry well, and then she had kept a respectable distance. She wasn't going to lecture us. She was just going to be there. Gloria Aleshire and her late husband had been the backbone of the family china business that was now being run by Frank Aleshire in Boston. Her older son, Frank's brother, had joined the State Department. Angus was enamored of that uncle. He was the one Angus had boasted about to Blake Thackeray, telling stories about him, because he was certain he'd been in the CIA.

We sat in the living room. A clock chimed. Gloria's parlor was decorated with rag rugs, antiques, and crocheted shawls. Family photographs hung on the walls. There were pictures of Frank and Cheryl and pictures of Frank's brother – and of the Aleshire kids when they were small, Angus looking just as I remembered him when I first encountered him in Sunday School class. There he was with Duncan, two little brothers, side by side, smiling for the camera.

We sat and talked politely. Before our arrival, Gloria had been doing some gardening, she told us. Would we like to walk around the flowerbeds?

"These are my hostas and my ferns," she said. "I planted some lily of the valley but it hasn't taken off as I hoped it would." After our walk round the garden we went back inside where Gloria served us tea.

"Straight across the country, you say. That must have been quite a trip." There wasn't much excitement in her voice. She spoke like it was a matter of fact. She didn't seem surprised by the Airstream trailer nor by the Cadillac. They were just things we had, and nothing to do with her.

Angus told her the route we had taken, emphasizing the high points along the way. He was performing again, but this performance was a different one – and I didn't find it disagreeable. He had it down to an art. He was more than well behaved, more than presenting himself like an upstanding grandson for his doting grandma. He was falling in with her mood, mirroring her tone and reinforcing it.

But I was also performing. I was playing the bright young wife, the pretty girl of virtue, who thoroughly believed in Angus. Butter wouldn't melt in our mouths. We were the young married couple with a promising future and nothing to fear.

"I never thanked you," I told her after about half an hour of this sort of conversation. "I never thanked you for the ring." And with that, I held out my hand, on which I wore the engagement ring, which Angus had told me she'd given to him.

Gloria Aleshire looked blankly at my hand. It was the same sort of look that Margaret had given me when I mistakenly thanked her for the ring. Her face took on a kind of washed out expression, as if the features had been worn down over time, and smoothed into the skin. "I never gave you a ring, dear," she said.

"Angus, didn't you tell me she gave you this ring? I thought you said she gave it to you to give to me."

"Well," said Gloria simply. "I've never seen it."

"That's because it was my other grandmother who gave it to me, Ruby," Angus put in. He was pouring himself another cup of tea, out of the silver teapot.

"Which grandmother was it, Angus?"

"Margaret," he said. "The one in Pittsfield."

We went out to dinner with Gloria to a local chowder house in Wellfleet. We sat in a dark booth with rounded edges and high backed benches. The ceiling was beamed. A waitress served iced water that was so cold you couldn't drink it without hurting your teeth. The clam chowder came with little cellophane packs of oyster crackers. Then there was fried fish, and small paper cups of coleslaw and ketchup on the side. All through dinner, Angus kept up his grandson role, his masterful performance. And I could only think about the ring.

Thirty-Five

I kept my word to Angus and I prayed. Maybe some people would call it meditation. It was that kind of discipline. Just as athletes must exercise and practice their sport regularly, or musicians must practice their instruments, I practiced praying regularly. I had to be strict about it. I had to make it a mental routine. I would pray in the morning while I showered. Then later, in my lunch hour, I prayed again. I walked through Harvard Yard to a particular tree in front of the Widener Library. Then I lay on the grass and look into the quiet of the branches. And I prayed. I prayed at the end of the day. And before I fell asleep, just as I'd done as a little girl, as Timothy had taught me, I prayed.

At first my prayers were general. It wasn't easy. But like an athlete, gradually building endurance with repeated physical exercise, I felt the practice fortify me.

"Are you going to keep your word?" I asked him when we'd been back in Boston for a couple of weeks.

"What word was that?"

"To tell me about the things you do. So that I can pray more specifically?"

"All right," he said, drawing in a breath. Then, he looked at me frankly and said, "I broke into a sporting goods store."

I don't know what I'd expected to hear but it wasn't this, and the heart seemed to drop from inside me.

"When was that?" I asked.

"Does it matter?"

I didn't know where I should rest my eyes, or how to disguise my shock. "Of course it matters. Please go on," I said.

"Well, the skis I gave you for Christmas came from that job," he said.

Job, I thought. A telling word. "The tennis rackets too, I suppose?"

"Yes. And all those ski sweaters."

That afternoon, I tried to pray. I tried to meditate, to find some mental calm within the chaos. We all do it, no matter our religion. No matter our lack of religion. We do it because we are desperate. We do it because we have no options, and not precisely because we believe. We do it in order to try and believe.

And in that spirit I prayed that God would not let Angus destroy himself. That Angus wouldn't miss his double life. Living at least two lives for so long would make it hard to cut that down to one. I prayed that he wouldn't miss the refuge of deception.

I prayed about my own motives too. I looked hard at my mistakes, at my inability and reluctance to hate his wrongdoing enough to let him go. That might have been my greatest fault. I wasn't good, and I knew that for sure. I had refused to turn him in. I hadn't said enough to that probation officer when I had the chance. No, I was just a coward, praying for courage. But I realized I wasn't responsible for Angus. I was only responsible for what I thought and that is why I prayed. I prayed to let him go, if necessary. I prayed to know that the results weren't up to me.

One evening after a peaceful dinner, Angus put on his jacket. "Where are you going now?" I asked

"The warehouse," he said.

I could hardly believe it. "But why? I thought we were changing things."

"You did?"

"Of course. Weren't we going to talk?"

"What do you want to talk about?"

"I thought you were going to tell me things and I was going to pray."

"So? I'm telling you things. I just told you. I'm going to the warehouse."

"And what are you going to do there?" Oh God. No. Why was he doing this again! "Don't go to the warehouse anymore! Please!" I stood against the door, trying to block his exit. "Don't go now. Please." I stepped in front of him, gripping onto his jacket sleeve. "Don't do it, Angus. Stop it. Don't go."

"Now you're making me late," he said.

"Late for what?"

"I told you. I'm meeting Michael there." The hollow of his cheek, the strong bones beneath the face that once I'd loved, were turned away from knowing me.

"I thought you were going to tell me the truth. That's what we agreed. We agreed that you would tell me the truth and that I would pray about it."

"Okay. That's what I'm doing."

"What's the fucking truth!" I screamed. "What's the fucking truth! If you don't tell me, I'm turning you in. Do you understand that?"

"I am telling you the truth," he said.

"You're *not* telling the truth~"

"What do you want to know?"

"I want the truth about my ring."

"Your ring? Why that?"

By now I was practically hysterical. "The ring. Where did you get the ring?"

"My grandmother gave it to me," he answered.

I flew at him then, hitting him hard. I screamed and beat my fists against his chest while he stood still with his eyes averted. "I hate you, Angus. I hate you!" And then he suddenly turned, tearing my fingers off his clothes. I grabbed again. I grabbed and clawed until he squeezed my wrists in one hand, restraining me, pinning my arm behind my back and locking it into place. Then he walked me to the bed like that, and when we were there he knelt on my back. My face was squashed to the pillows. "Do you give up?"

I couldn't see his face. I could hardly breathe. But I turned my head as best I could and spat. I was covered in snot and tears and spit and my arm was locked in place. I couldn't move. "Stop struggling. It won't hurt if you stop. Do you give up?"

At last he felt me weaken and threw me off. I sobbed into the bed. Even then, part of me was standing outside the situation, trying to draw down the blinds again – to get myself into that tiny mental cubicle of consciousness. But this wasn't drama. This was real. Then the door slammed behind him.

Thirty-Six

Mike Robbins was a wiry Boston Irishman in his early fifties who might once have been redheaded. He had a genial expression, a dry looking skin that freckled easily and a film of blond hair over his arms. Coleman was bigger and meaner looking, with an enormous barrel stomach and black moustache, and he smelled strongly of aftershave. They stood on the lane in front of Copps Hill Terrace, peering into the windows on the first floor, and flashing their badges at me.

"Boston Police." I didn't have time to think, but I opened the door, and since I'd been praying, I wasn't afraid. Instead I felt relief. I felt strong. Because everything that happened from now on, might be an answer to my prayers.

Also he had hurt me. My loyalty to Angus had been diminished because he had hurt me.

Robbins stepped inside and shook my hand. "Mike Robbins," he said. "And this is my partner, Gabe Coleman. We have your husband down the station. Been holding him since last night on charges of breaking and entering."

"Breaking and entering what?" I asked.

"Oh, we've been watching your husband for a very long time now," Robbins said. "And we'd like you to answer some questions."

It was early morning. I hadn't had time to put on any makeup. I felt exposed. But Coleman made himself comfortable in the red chair in front of the bookcase, while Robbins sat at the table.

"Please," I said. "Ask whatever you want."

"A sailboat was parked on a trailer out back here for several days last month. Know anything about that?" Robbins asked.

"No," I replied.

"How about a Cadillac? Black Cadillac sedan, license plate HRS 210 with red interior?" Coleman asked.

"That's ours. Angus got it at an auction, where they sell repossessed and unclaimed cars."

"Oh, he bought a car at auction all right," Robbins said. "An old wreck dredged from the harbor. All he took from that thing was the title."

"It would be in your interest to cooperate with us fully, Mrs. Aleshire," Coleman said, and he leaned deeply into the chair and adjusted the belt around his girth. "Unless you want to face charges of aiding and abetting."

Robbins scratched his cheek, and stretched his mouth. "Well, Mrs. Aleshire, your husband is probably hungry. He's been in the jail all night. Why don't you make him a sandwich or two and then we'll take you down the station to see him."

I went to the kitchen and looked through the fridge, while the detectives sat in the living room. I was feeling almost giddy. It was as if the fever had broken. This was it and I knew it. "Interesting place you got here," Robbins said, looking around the living room. "How much do you pay for it?"

I told them while I sliced up chicken, cheese and tomato, layering them into a sandwich. Then I became loose and chatty. "I work for a bookshop and a small press in Cambridge," I explained.

"Cambridge, huh. How d'ya get to work?" asked Coleman.

"On the T," I said.

"Never drive, in one of the cars?"

"We only have one car," I said. "And that's the Cadillac."

"You don't know anything about a rare Porsche automobile?" asked Robbins. "Sports car?"

"A Porsche? No."

"And your husband, what kind of work does he do?"

"He's had a series of part time jobs," I explained. "Nothing very steady. He's been studying philosophy at Suffolk. Also, right now he plays the organ for a church in Hyde Park." They both looked skeptical at that one. Then I took a breath. Here goes. "He also has a warehouse where he hopes one day to build boats," I said, pausing in my sandwich making. "I asked his probation officer to go and check it out, but he never went."

I sliced the sandwich in half.

"What kind of warehouse would this be?" Coleman asked offhandedly.

"The original plan was to build boats there. It's out in Jamaica Plain. I've never seen inside, but I told the probation officer to look into it, and I don't think he ever did."

"You about ready with that sandwich, Mrs. Aleshire?" Robbins asked.

I peered at Angus through the metal grid in the police station jail. The room was spartan. A guard sat in the corner. The skin around Angus's eyes had flushed, but the smile he brought to his face was dead on arrival. He clasped his hands on the counter before him.

"This might be the best thing for us," he said.

"I hate you for what you've done to us."

"Sorry," he said.

"What does it mean? The last time I saw you, you were twisting my arm behind my back and sitting on top of me."

"I'm sorry. What can I say?"

"What can you *say*? You can't *say* anything! I'm sick with anxiety and humiliation. I get no sleep. I have no peace. You sat on my back and twisted my arm, and then you left and never came back. Do you actually expect me to stick up for you and make sandwiches for you and defend you to these guys? Well fuck you, is all that *I* can say."

He didn't respond, so I continued. "They asked about a boat on a trailer, and a Porsche."

"Nothing I say will make it sound right. I hate this so much. I intend to come clean. I swear to God."

"Over a Cadillac and a boat? So you're going to come clean for a car, but you couldn't do it for me."

"The Cadillac," he said, "was a big mistake. I'll admit. But the owner of the boatyard won't want to press charges, he'll just want his boats back, and Ruby, I just want my life back. I want our lives, together..."

"*Boats?* How many boats are we talking about? "

"Listen, Ruby. Please. I don't know how much time we have to talk. There are some things I know which they are very interested in investigating—"

"Why did you get into all this shit? Why! I've been trying so hard to stop you. I've been begging you to come clean about this warehouse for a whole fucking year now-"

"I'm not talking about the warehouse, Ruby. This is something else. Something I know about. And please, don't mention the warehouse to them, all right?"

"Well," I said. "I already did."

He stared at me, incredulous.

"I already told them about the warehouse. I told you I was going to turn you in if you broke your promise. You wouldn't tell the truth, and so our deal was off."

He tried to impersonate a smile but didn't seem to be controlling the muscles in his face properly. "You didn't tell them about the warehouse," he said.

"I did," I said. "Of course. They came to me; I didn't go to them. Then they asked and I told them what I knew."

You might imagine that he broke down and cried after that. Except, he didn't. He simply sat in a stunned kind of way. He was like that man at the end of *The Rain Horse* by Ted Hughes: "staring at the ground, as if some important part had been cut out of his brain."

Thirty-Seven

For dinner, I ate a handful of crackers, which were shaped like stars. They were called Sociables, and I ate them because I felt unsociable. Then I drank a glass or two of wine. I could say that I kept myself sane by trying to pray, but I mostly stayed sane by playing with a new game Sorrel had lent me: the Rubik's Cube. I fiddled with the little squares into the evening and later the following morning on the train, and when I got to work, I played with it some more and got a sort of igloo going, an igloo of like-minded colors headed in the right direction. Oliver looked at me, in his usual circumspect manner, over the top of his glasses. "Trouble?" he asked.

If only he knew the half of it. But there was nothing he or anyone else could do. The world was separate from me now. The benevolence and possibility I used to associate with the future and my life had fallen completely away. "Why don't we go for a walk," he suggested. "Enid can watch the shop for a while."

We walked through Harvard Square. I filled him in on the necessary details. Oliver didn't look at my face while I talked. He simply fed the squirrels, with his pocketful of peanuts. "Gee," he said at last. "Well, Ruby. There is no more usual basis for union than a mutual misunderstanding." He tossed a peanut towards a squirrel, and finally caught my eye, with avuncular sagacity. "Henry James. *Portrait of a Lady*."

"Oh."

"You remind me of Isabel Archer, experiencing life with its suffering and intensity, determined to make an interesting choice."

"Hmm."

"As James saw it," Oliver continued, his voice taking on that theoretical attitude I always found so calming, "Isabel's refusal to set herself apart from suffering, though naïve, did suggest the desire for a deeper form of happiness."

Angus was released after less than a week. The police let him out on personal recognizance, pending trial, because he was cooperating fully. I didn't know what that meant: cooperating fully. But he told me there were things he knew, which he was helping the police pursue. Then he surrendered the Cadillac.

Next, the police got a warrant to search the warehouse. In the Jamaica Plain warehouse Detectives Robbins and Coleman found a rare Porsche automobile, two Audi sedans, an Airstream trailer, a catamaran and another small sailboat on a trailer, as well as various odd pieces of machinery, including power tools, key copying machines and an engravograph used for altering the serial numbers on vehicles. They also found a stockpile of sporting equipment: skis, tennis rackets, and fishing rods.

"How did you do it all? And how did you get all those cars?"

"Different ways," he told me, and then he explained how he'd test driven one in the Porsche Audi dealership – and struck up a rapport with the salesman. He had asked about an imagined engine noise, and when the salesman got out to check under the hood, he removed a few keys from the chain in the ignition.

We needed to move. Copps Hill Terrace had bad associations, and besides, we had to pay a lawyer now, and needed to find a good one.

Nigel Hargrove, Ari's fencing master, had mentioned that the floor below his studio was vacant. We went to see the empty space. The door was made of metal. Inside the rooms smelled like dust, and the place was oddly partitioned, covered in wall-to-wall carpet. "Look at all this room! It's massive," Angus said.

"There's too much work to do," I said.

"But you've seen what Nigel has done to his place, haven't you? Imagine when this is all fixed up. Can't you see it," he said. "These funky little windows?"

"There's no bath or shower in here, Angus."

"So? I can put one in."

"You didn't do so great on Brenda's shower."

"Which means I learned from my mistakes," he said. "Come on!"

"What about a kitchen?"

"I can put in a kitchen no problem, at all. This place is two blocks from Quincy Market! It's right near Waterfront Park. We'd be crazy not to snap it up."

I went for it. Once again, I went for it. Why, you may ask. Because I wanted to live an interesting life. I didn't want a conventional apartment. I wanted to live outside the box, dangerously yes, but not outside the law.

We walked back to Copps Hill Terrace. We wanted to start a new life. We passed a guy outside the subway entrance, selling Indian scarves and packets full of nylon socks, and dresses which hung on wire hooks under a makeshift awning. A woman begged for money, and another guy outside North Station was trying to palm off watches. That was their life. Ours was passing them by and saying no thank you, and wondering how the hell Angus was going to get off going to jail.

The preliminary hearing was scheduled for late October. I tried to focus. Of course I did. I went to work and to the market, getting bread and weighing pears, lemons and tomatoes, thinking about how I should do some real cooking. I decided I should make something comforting to eat, like apple crumble and custard. Then I thought to hell with apple crumble, why not get more wine.

Our move into Milk Street involved tearing out partitions, and ripping up old carpet, to reveal the wooden floor beneath. Ari helped for one whole afternoon. We pulled out the tacky tiles of the dropped down ceiling, chucked out the florescent light fixtures, and laid the space bare. I cleaned the windows while Angus worked on the bathroom.

Pope John Paul had come to town. He was touring the city in his Pope Mobile. I watched crowds of people flocking down Milk Street to catch glimpses. I heard cheering as the pope passed by. I went on cleaning windows.

Then I watched the people flocking back. A man on the street below gazed up to see me scrubbing. "What a thankless task that is," he called up.

Angus rented a floor sander and Nora came in with Sorrel to help. We spent an afternoon pushing the sander back and forth across the floor. "You could always move back home with us, darling," Nora said. "Don't you think you could use the moral support?" The pupils of her eyes moved back and forth across my face in concern.

I felt terrible for what I'd put them through, for all of the worries I seemed to have brought on their heads. "Oh Nora. I wouldn't have survived if it wasn't for you. But I will be all right," I said.Detective Robbins came around to Copps Hill Terrace. "When are you moving out of here?" Then he stopped in at Milk Street, and shook his head at the orange extension cords running across the floor. "This place looks like a gypsy camp," he said.

Sometimes Robbins phoned me at work. There was a hum on the line on both my home and work telephones these days. The line hissed, and every thirty seconds came a sharp and high-pitched beep.

"We might enroll you in the witness protection program," Robbins announced. "Give you new identities."

"New identities? Isn't that a little extreme?"

"We'll take it a step at a time," he said.

I sat in Tango's doing the Rubik's Cube, and talking to Rebecca Blackstone, a writer friend of Oliver's, who had writer's block because when she was in graduate school her thesis adviser plagiarized her novel. Now she wanted to move away. That was the only way she could continue. She had to get away.

Get away. Start a new life. Change your identity. Cooperate fully. Robbins phoned me again. "Do you know a guy by the name of Giuseppe Esposito?" he asked. There was that hiss on the phone again. I was sure they were tapping my line.

"Never heard of him. Why?"

"You sure about that, Mrs. Aleshire? Giuseppe Esposito? Never heard your husband mention a guy by that name?"

"No," I said. "Why?"

"Oh, we found his body down the Cape and we're looking for some leads."

It all seemed preposterous. A body down on the Cape had nothing whatever to do with me. Angus didn't know anyone named Giuseppe Esposito.

But I'd only just put down the telephone, when Angus called to say that under no circumstances was I to return to Copps Hill Terrace after work. "Go to the loft instead," he said. "It's too dangerous here. And just listen. Please. I need you to cooperate with me on this."

"But what's going on? How long do I have to stay away?"

"A few hours," he said. "Three hours. How about that? Go out with Ari or something."

"What is going on? Detective Robbins is talking about the witness protection program and some guy whose body they found on the Cape..."

"Don't ask, Ruby. Right now, I need you just to cooperate. This is serious. Do you understand? I'm doing this the best I can. I'm trying to go straight, but you need to help me on this."

Lillian Silverman came into the book store that afternoon- that odd woman who I thought of as the weird sister, and who had once been a beauty and a Russian scholar. Today she wanted a book by Boris Pasternak. Her face was daubed with matte powder the wrong shade for her face and she had on a neck brace.

"Lillian, what happened?" I asked. "Why are you wearing a neck brace?"

Nothing at all was wrong, she said. Certainly not with her neck, but the brace helped her feel more sturdy. Holding up her neck all day long felt a bit of a strain. And it worked really well, this neck brace. She felt great now.

I rang up her purchase, and as I did I wondered if one day I was going to end up like Lillian Silverman, an oddball eccentric with problems nobody understood.

Ari met me after work, and when he saw me, he took me into his arms. "Oh no," he said. "Oh dear. What's wrong now, my beautiful friend?" We walked to the Au Bon Pain on Brattle Street and sat at a table overlooking the square. I could only manage things in spurts: watching pigeons waddle between tables, sipping coffee, not because I wanted coffee, but to place me in the moment, for the gesture it afforded, as some tenuous claim to a casual afternoon.

"Why are you still beating yourself up like this? Why don't you leave," said Ari. "Leave him for good and go somewhere new. Go somewhere beautiful, like Paris. Let him figure it out by himself."

"Ari, I can't think of that. I can't think past this afternoon."

"Nora?"

"Oh Ruby darling, thank goodness you called. I've just had a very strange visit from a man called Detective Robbins."

"What? Now they're getting you involved?" I asked.

"Timothy and I simply told them everything we know. There's no point doing otherwise," she said. Then, "Are you sure you want to move into that loft space, darling?"

I was sure. I returned to the Milk Street loft, lugging groceries. We were moving stuff in gradually. The bottles were heavy and the plastic handles dug into my fingers. We needed a good lawyer. We needed to hold our necks up, to stick out our necks, like Lillian Silverman, I thought, as I climbed the stairs to the loft space.

It was an ugly building, with a travel agent on the ground floor – JJ Travel, and nothing else besides us except Nigel Hargrove's fencing studio. But I liked it better than Copps Hill Terrace. I sat in front of my newly cleaned windows and ate a cup of lemon yogurt, and looked at the office buildings across the street and the cars busying down the street, and the entrance of a bar on the corner, with its red and white door. A big bruiser of a guy stood in the doorway making sure everyone passed muster. I liked him.

And I had nearly figured out the Rubik's Cube. You were supposed to turn all the bad corners. Identify the good ones and turn the bad ones. There were eight corners on the cube, and you had to choose the bad from the good and then twiddle the bad ones back and forth, back and forth until you got it right. Please God, let me get through this. Let truth be our strength. Let the Rubik's cube teach me to be a logical person. Things will click into place. When I learn how to turn the bad corners.

The following week, Angus finished building a shower in the bathroom of the Milk Street loft. By now we had a makeshift kitchen down at the other end, next to a freight elevator, which opened onto our floor. But we had no kitchen sink. We had to carry the dirty dishes in a basin to the bathroom at the far end of the space.

Angus drove out to Hingham with me, to see the family and meet with Pastor Jackson. Pastor Jackson was ever wise in his counseling, ever receptive as he talked to us about being as wise as serpents and as harmless as doves. We conversed in the parish hall on dark blue chairs, and he gave us some Bible passages to consider – things about cleansing the double-minded.

Later he served us dry sherry from a crystal decanter. I watched the uncorking, the pouring out, the placing of glasses on a laminated placemat depicting scenes of London. I looked at the beautifully gabled roof and arched elegance of the church windows. There was a neat desk with the chair pushed beneath it, another chair by the door, where Pastor Jackson tied his shoes. He was a good person. He meant very well. All of us did. But I wondered if that was that enough. Was goodness enough, in the end?

Thirty-Eight

The recovery of the Seabrook paintings came out in the papers. The robbery was written up, not like a cold-hearted crime, but as the recap of an exciting escapade in a boat by moonlight, out to the Seabrook house. What a miracle that the paintings were completely unharmed. But who had returned them? The paper said something about the paintings being found in a wooded area, underneath a tarp that had been covered in autumn leaves. Nobody knew who had returned them and nobody had yet been charged.

I said at the beginning of this story that the truth is like God. You cannot see it face to face and live. So I saw the truth in small glances, gradually learning why the detectives had wanted to enroll us in the witness protection program. It was because Angus had made up a story and said the Italian mafia was involved in the stolen paintings.

But although the truth seeped out, the law came round reluctantly. It didn't hit hard like a judge's gavel until December. The law awaited proof: sifting evidence and alibis, scheduling hearings and investigations. People were given lie detector tests and summoned to court. Testimony was taken down and pieced together. Evidence was weighed against other witness testimony.

I went to work every day, leaving Angus in the loft, reading the newspaper. He talked with his lawyer, and the lawyer communicated to the prosecutor, and at length it became clear that Angus was to be charged with grand larceny. He said he was prepared to turn himself in as a show of good faith. The prosecutors were prepared to consider it, but an arrest warrant still hadn't been issued.

Weeks went by. We could have skipped town. Maybe we should have done that. Instead, I went to work. Angus spoke with Pastor Jackson on a regular basis and went for runs around the Aquarium every morning. He came home to the loft and played chess with Nigel upstairs. He went out to the Hyde Park church every week to play the organ for services. And we waited.

At last he was arrested and taken to the Charles Street Jail. He phoned Tango's to tell me they'd come for him. I in turn telephoned the church in Hyde Park and spoke to one of the little old ladies. "Angus won't be able to play the organ in your church anymore," I said. "You'll find out why later. But he won't be able to play this Sunday or any Sunday. Ever again."

"My dear, what is wrong?" said the voice on the phone.

"You'll find out. I'm sorry I can't say any more. Goodbye."

It was all that I could manage.

When Nora heard about the arrest, she immediately telephoned the Seabrooks to say how devastated she was that Angus had been involved. Ingrid Seabrook wasn't surprised. Yes, she said. They had known he was responsible since a week after the paintings were stolen, but they were waiting for positive proof.

The detectives filled me in on the case. James Gillespie had also taken a lie detector test, and told them about the events of that night in Cohasset, when he and I swam under. the bridge.

Angus and James had hatched the plan in that very spot a few weeks before, and then we had all three gone there on the night of the robbery. I had almost drowned, James said. He had been the one to catch hold of me and he felt that he had saved me.

On the night of the robbery there was a full moon. On the night of the robbery they had been at the Red Lion Inn. They had also been swimming in Blake Thackeray's pool. He remembered having to wait for Angus near our house – the barn in Scituate. He waited in a parking lot at a beach nearby. And Angus went back to the house with me until I fell asleep.

They had a problem with getting rid of Thackeray, because when they drove back into Cohasset on Boarder Street, his car was parked in the Hugo's Lighthouse parking lot, and he must have thought that something was up. At any rate, somehow they dodged him.

After hiding the car off a side road they walked out to the Seabrook house. The two of them waited and waited. There were no lights on in the house. There was no sign of movement, except a tiny red light in the basement window. Then, on the ocean side of the house, they saw they could walk out of the basement and onto the lawn.

At about two, they crossed the grass and stood at the basement door. Angus tried the handle and like a miracle it turned. The house was unlocked.

Supposing an alarm might go off, they then retreated to the other side of the bridge, to wait and see if the police would show. At last they returned across the lawn to the house. They opened the door. And this time they entered and climbed the cellar stairs.

The paintings hung in the north side of the house, in a room that must have been the living room. They took five paintings. Rembrandt's *Portrait of a Lady*, and an El Greco portrait, a Brueghel the Elder and two other paintings by lesser-known masters. They also took some Ming vases.

Angus and he walked past one another, moving the paintings out of the room on the north side of the house, which was where the paintings were.

Once they had the paintings outside the house, James carried some of them down over the rocks to the beach via a narrow path, and Angus took others across the bridge and the road to the car. There was some kind of lingering drunkenness, so that looking back over the events it didn't make much sense, but that is what happened. He was extremely careful carrying the paintings, the Rembrandt especially.

He said he remembered thinking how odd to be carrying it outside along the beach and water in the middle of the night, being able to see the figure of the lady in her exquisitely laced collar in the moonlight. He carried the Ming vases as well. Then they put the paintings in the car.

He and Angus wrapped the paintings in blankets for protection and took them to the old ruined mansion of the Elmwood Camp, which had been some kind of residential home. He told the prosecutor in a sworn statement that they had inspected this site earlier and found a place to hide the paintings temporarily. They then returned to the barn in Scituate where I was sleeping, so that Angus would be there when I woke up. James went into a shed in the yard. He lay down and tried to sleep on a table. He had only just dozed off, when he heard the sound of the car leaving. Angus was taking me to the bus stop. Then, when Angus came back, the two of them returned to the camp and retrieved the paintings.

They loaded the paintings back into the car. A police report corroborated later that this was around the time that they had been called about the theft. The police were already driving around looking for leads by then. In fact, they even drove part way up the dirt road to the Camp, but Angus and James must have got away just at the crucial moment.

They headed into Boston with the paintings and carried them up to James's small apartment on Stillman Street in the North End. Russell Thorne, a sculptor friend of James's, was staying there at the time and completely flipped out when he saw the paintings. Nevertheless they kept the paintings there for a week or two. And Russell immediately moved out.

Later, when Angus and I moved into Copps Hill Terrace, Angus put the paintings in the closet, nailed it completely shut, and built the bookcases in front of it.

Thirty-Nine

The Grand Jury interrogated everyone. They interrogated Nora and Timothy, and finally they interrogated me. I stepped into the Dedham Superior Courtroom at 2 p.m. on the afternoon of December 12, 1979. The sea of jury faces, a circus assembly, shifted in their seats and some of them coughed. I took the stand to answer preliminary questions about where I worked, and how long we'd been married. My voice, though clear and steady, came from somewhere distant in my consciousness, a separate file of awareness.

The District Attorney in that interrogation walked me through the evening of the robbery. Angus and me and our friend James swimming under the bridge where the water rushes in and out with the tide. Angus insisting we stop at Blake Thackeray's after the swim. I remember how it really annoyed me when the DA referred to the gathering at Blake's as 'a party'. It wasn't a party, I said. We just stopped by. Nothing was planned. It wasn't what he thought. In fact, I might have forgotten it altogether, if not for the swim we took under the bridge.

"Can you remember the conversation? What was discussed at this party?" the District Attorney wanted to know. An unforgiving man, Michael Kirby of Dedham Superior Court, and he was not in the mood to handle me gently.

"It wasn't anything important," I said.

"Isn't it true that you know the Seabrooks personally?"

I shook my head. "I don't know them. But my little sister is a friend of their daughter's."

"Was Aleshire interested in their art collection? Had you ever talked about it? Were you suspicious when he nailed up a closet in your apartment and built a bookcase in front of it...?"

Surely you knew, he said, that millions of dollars' worth of stolen paintings were walled up in a closet behind your bookcase.

Surely, they'd said.

Surely? But who would suspect a thing like that?

The barrage of questions went on and on until my head was pounding with all the subtle ways that truth could be distorted. But I knew the truth all right. And I knew I would lie to nobody about it.

To nobody except myself.

The District Attorney shuffled through his papers. "At what time did you leave the party at Blake Thackeray's?"

"It wasn't a party," I told him.

"A gathering then. Would you agree it was a gathering?"

"Yes. It was a gathering. I left around midnight."

"You left alone or with your husband?"

"I left alone because I was tired. I had to work the following morning, and Angus wanted to stay. I wasn't interested in hanging around."

"So why did Aleshire stay?"

"He said he'd get a ride. It wasn't very far."

The District Attorney cleared his throat. "You do realize, Mrs. Aleshire, that you are under oath? That anything you say can and will be used against you?"

I didn't care about things they could use against me. What would those be? I wasn't afraid of telling the truth. The whole truth, as I saw it then, was different from the truth they were trying to force from me. I stood apart from myself. I stood to the side, hearing my voice answer questions, thin and disembodied. This was all a projection of myself, a kind of sound and light show.

At one point when the tears started, I felt the alien weight of their pity. I didn't want the jury's pity. Nevertheless, it brought me up short.

"Did you discuss the robbery with you parents?" I closed my eyes in a long blink of darkness and reapplied myself to the question.

"My mother told me that the burglar alarms were disconnected at the time of the robbery. She said that Ingrid Seabrook felt uncomfortable having the alarms on while she was at home."

The interrogation lasted an interminable hour and a half. I looked at my lap, at my narrow fingers smoothing the fringe on a green scarf. I tried to control the quiver in my voice because it made me sound foolish.

"Are you saying that you never suspected your husband was involved?" asked Kirby.

The lights of the courtroom burned. The room was close and hot but the jury was far away in a grey distance.

"All the alarms had been turned off," I repeated, in a voice that frayed at the edges. "I believed my husband because I love him."

Everything Kirby said was true, of course. Ridiculous not to know about the paintings. But what he said was also a twist of truth, a few degrees off, making it a lie and a fiction. I had spoken honestly. I'd provided him with details. But just like his view, my idea of events came out as a distortion.

"You may step down now, Mrs. Aleshire," he said.

In the courtroom corridor, afternoon thickened to a soupy indoor tedium. People encamped with their coats and bags on benches, waiting to testify. They stirred with momentary interest as I passed through scattered knots of friends and acquaintances. Blake Thackeray was there, with his shag haircut and bellbottom jeans. I saw Brenda Williams too, dressed in a camelhair cape. They looked quite jolly, and hyper engaged in their banter, never so much as glancing in my direction. The Seabrook babysitter was there, as well as various other Cohasset people, sniffing at the trail of our scandal.

Timothy and Nora moved forward to embrace me. "You were in there a long time, darling."

I took up my coat and found the sleeves.

"I have a splitting headache," I said. "There's an appointment with the probation officer at 5:00. Will you come along?"

"Of course," said Nora.

But before we could exit, a triumphantly supportive Brenda Williams swooped towards us and embraced me. "My dears!" giving Nora a kiss, and grasping Timothy's arm. She put her arms around my parents' shoulders, as if to enclose and empower us with her courage. She had been one of the first to testify. "But they only asked for facts. How long had I known him and so forth," she said. "I told them that it didn't say much for my art collection because nothing of mine went missing!" She looked at me directly. "Ruby, my dear," she said, with a radiant smile, "above all, be strong!"

The weather outside was bleached and stifling, as if it might decide to snow. Or maybe it wouldn't decide. Slow suburban cars moved past office blocks and parking meters, against a bored horizon. Nora linked my arm. "You haven't had any lunch, darling."

"I'm not that hungry. And my head is just pounding." We crossed to a parking lot, and Timothy unlocked the car. "The D.A. was horrible," I said. "What a nasty man. He made me sound so dumb. Everything I said to explain about the closet being nailed up sounded so stupid. He wanted to know if I was suspicious. If I was aware the paintings were in our apartment. Did I think anyone else was involved."

"Yes," said Nora. "They asked me the same."

"People are really getting off on all this," I said. "Can't you tell? They want to make it dramatic, like a movie script. More dramatic than is already is."

"I'm absolutely furious with Angus," Nora said, as we drove to our meeting with the probation officer. "Well, I am, Tim. Don't look like that. What he's put her through." Her eyes brimmed up and reddened.

"I've been trying to assure him that it's never too late to repent," said Timothy.

"Well, as far as I'm concerned, he deserves whatever they dish out. Remember that, Ruby. I think it helps to remind ourselves what he's put us through."

I stared out of the back window onto the miserable streets. "I totally despise James Gillespie," I said.

"Now that I don't understand," said Nora.

"He betrayed me. I thought he was my friend. I actually thought he would help get Angus on track. "

Timothy cleared his throat. "I hear that he's making a statement against Angus."

"Against Angus?" Nora said.

"That's what I overheard, yes."

"But they're in the same boat," I said. "I know he's already testified that he did the robbery with Angus."

"Evidently not," said my father. "It's called a plea bargain, honey."

"But that's impossible! They did the robbery together! They were both responsible."

"Darling," said Nora. "You must be able to see the difference between them. Angus has a record. James doesn't. He would never have done it without the influence of Angus."

"So what? He still did it. They did the robbery together, and justice demands equal punishment."

Forty

I got off the train at Charles Street Station and crossed the icy footbridge to the jail. Angus was being held in lieu of $100,000 bail, and I was taking time off work to experience the grey and wrinkled river and the icy wind whipping round me. The old Romanesque stone jail was forbidding and out of place beside the high-rise hospitals of upper Storrow Drive. Charles Street Jail was a holding pen for those pending trial or sentence. The convicted were moved to larger facilities, Massachusetts Correctional Institute in Concord, which specialized in juvenile offenders, for instance, or to MCI Norfolk. Hardened criminals ended up in maximum security at Walpole.

In the waiting room several visitors sat on benches. A woman sorted through packages of clothing. Others smoked, with the dull hostility of resignation. At 9 a.m. sharp a guard came forward with a handful of pink slips. "Joseph, Anderson, Aleshire..."

Visitors followed through metal detectors, and stood before a huge iron door, waiting for the guard to press the button. A door clanged back on metal runners and we climbed the stairs to wait at another set of bars, where another guard released the lock.

In the visiting room a metal grid separated visitors from prisoners. The echo of metal slammed metal. Somebody shouted, every sound signaling disturbance. I took a seat at the counter.

The woman on my left was tapping her rings, jiggling her knee up and down and peering through the grid for her man. "I'm always waiting for him," she told me. "Always fuckin' waiting. Last time he was in the shower and didn't hear his name called. I told him, 'I can hear it out here for Christ sake.'"

Names were called on a loudspeaker, both deafening and inaudible. They reverberated like the announcements in a railway station. Lipstick marks stained the mesh partition as if they had been burned there. A sign on the wall in English and Spanish warned that any attempt to provide controlled substances to inmates was a felony punishable by a maximum of five years in jail.

Inmates trickled in, taking seats across from visitors on the other side of the grid. The woman next to me was already deep in conversation with her son. "All the guys are asking for you. Mitzi sends her love. But do you think I like this? It's killin' me and your father. You better pray to God I come back here. You think we can take this? It's killin' me I swear to God."

At last Angus stepped through the door, refined and misplaced, dressed in his own clothes, searching the faces for mine. "Angus!" I cried.

He turned and sat down opposite me and peered through the grid, hands cupped round his eyes in order to see me better. "I love you," he said.

"Where *were* you?" My voice was frantic and accusing, not the voice I'd expected to use. "Do you realize I'm taking time off work to be here? Why do you never come down when they call your name?"

"I know. I'm sorry. It takes so long because I have to come up from the annex."

"How are you feeling?"

"Okay," he said. "You?"

"Fine, I guess."

"So tell me about the hearing."

"It was terrible, Angus. Everything I said they twisted around. They made me sound so stupid. And then, at five we saw a court probation officer. He's absolutely terrible. Nora and I met with him. And we couldn't believe that a man like him has so much power. Delaney. That's his name. He's impossible to talk to. Nora and I tried to explain to him the simplest things and he didn't seem able to process them. He kept on talking in non sequiturs..."

"He's insignificant," Angus said. "Forget him."

"How can I forget him? He told us that he hadn't decided yet but that he may recommend a stiffer sentence than the D.A.'s. He may recommend you go to Walpole."

"Ruby," said Angus. "They'll probably give me a suspended sentence. Think about it. They wouldn't even have the paintings back unless I'd cooperated. And they know that. Delaney doesn't have as much power as you seem to think. Other things are much more important." I must have looked skeptical. "Tell me about the hearing," he said.

"I didn't get in until 2 o'clock. They called us for 9:00 and we had to wait in the hall until 2:00. Timothy testified at the end of the morning. Everyone was there," I told him. "Tons of people from Cohasset. Blake Thackeray and the Seabrook babysitter. Oh, and Brenda was there. She was very sweet."

"But what did they ask?"

"Everything. You name it. I was in there for more than an hour. The district attorney kept talking about how you must have gone across to the Seabrooks in a catamaran from the yacht club. Did you do that, Angus?"

"You know I didn't do that. I told you."

"But it's all so confusing. And they made me sound like a total idiot. And did you know that they are thinking of making the charge armed robbery?"

"What do you mean?"

"They said it was armed robbery because you cut the paintings down with a knife."

"Huh." He pulled back in his chair at that, with his elbows resting on his knees looking off to one side. Stymied. Then, "That isn't true. They were cut down with wire clippers. Jesus. I'd never carry arms."

"I didn't think you'd ever commit a crime like this, so how am I to know it wasn't armed robbery?"

"Take my word for it." He cupped his hands on either side of his eyes peering at me though the mesh. "It wasn't armed robbery. All right? We have enough problems without worrying about that kind of shit."

"But what if they charge you with armed robbery?"

"Then I'll plead not guilty, Rube. What do you want me to say?"

"Oh God, I wish this was over."

"I miss you," he said.

There was nothing to say in reply. What did I have to miss, except the illusion that things could improve?

"Did you talk to Jim?" he asked, meaning the lawyer.

"Not yet. He said he'd be coming in today to talk to you. Oh, and there's that friend of Lydia's, a lawyer who I'm meeting tomorrow. William Dupont. He has a few ideas which may help our case."

"Great…"

"Yesterday in court they asked me if I believed you could reform. And I said yes. They asked me if I loved you, and I said yes. I also told them I had no intention of leaving you."

"I love you," he said.

"How could you *do* this?" I cried again, with a shift to deeper despair, never knowing which mood would take over me next. "If you loved me you would never have done this."

"Ruby, I love you more than anything in this world. I promise you, when I get out of here I'm going to do everything I can to make you happy. I'll make this up to you," he said. "You'll see."

Poor Nora and Timothy. Like me, they had become the subject of terrible gossip. But their solution was to open up completely rather than close down. "We're just telling everyone. We aren't waiting for anyone to find out," said Nora, "or to wonder what they should say to us. We're giving people the chance to react with generosity and they are being wonderful."

Many were beguiled by the glamour of the heist. Maude Caruthers was one. "They must have done it as a prank," she said when I spoke with her about it. "I remember your husband quite well. I met him just once, and he didn't strike me as bad. Besides, paintings like those belong to everybody. There are much worse crimes than art theft," she said. And as I listened I felt reassured. Then, "What was it like," she asked me, "to have those paintings in your possession?"

I shook my head. "I never saw them."

"Well, that was a missed opportunity. I'm sure you must feel cheated."

This is the truth. Part of me did feel cheated. Perhaps even jealous. The idea that those paintings had been in my apartment for so long, hidden from view, seemed as Maude had suggested, a missed opportunity. Of course I felt sorry for the Seabrooks. But the part of my nature that wished to risk things in life was jealous at having been left out. If I had seen them, I am quite sure I wouldn't have enjoyed seeing them. On a conscious level, I wouldn't have had the courage for that. Subconsciously, I don't know.

I asked him endless questions. I wanted to know more about the paintings. I wanted all the details. "But there's nothing to tell. Once they were behind the bookcase, I never really thought about them," Angus insisted.

"I simply cannot wrap my mind around that. I don't get how you could do this. How could you could carry on, straight faced, when you knew the suffering you were causing the family. How could you go on normally? You must have thought about them all the time."

"Maybe you're right. I thought of it every now and again when I was with James. But only very distantly. Not as though it had happened to us."

"But when you saw the pictures in the paper, when you heard about the suffering you were causing the Seabrook family…" I persisted.

"It seemed very distant. I didn't feel it. You can't make it come out of me," he said. "Even now. You'll just have to believe that it didn't feel real."

The best kind of lie is a version of the truth, a fiction leaving some things out and embellishing others. What was truly real? My truth had been a lie, with its willful disregard of cars, boats, Nikon camera, skis and tennis rackets. What was the truth? Even as I recall facts now, I'm conscious of leaving things out. Too many details complicate the story. They muddy up the waters of truth.

Forty-One

I mulled incessantly over the particulars. I tried to make them tally with what I'd thought before. Why did the Seabrooks remain friendly with Nora and Sorrel, if they knew that Angus had taken the paintings? I learned from the two detectives that it was James who had left his fingerprints all over the Seabrook house. Angus had left none. I couldn't understand why this didn't matter to the prosecution, or why it wasn't in Angus's favor. Why had James been so careless? Above all, why had he done it?

Twice a week I went to the Charles Street Jail to visit Angus, before continuing on to work. He was quieter these days, sapped of courage and energy, often tearful and frightened.

"I need to hear the truth about my engagement ring," I said.

"What use will it do now," he answered.

"I asked you before and you said it was from your grandmother. Then I found out that it wasn't. So where did it come from?"

He groaned. "Let's not talk about that now."

"I need to know. To me it's very important."

"Why?"

"Because," I said, "it's symbolic."

He drew a breath, looked at his hands, then back up to my face. "It came from a girlfriend of mine in Arizona. Another girl. Nobody. Well, my girlfriend at the time..."

A punch in the solar plexus.

"She gave me the ring because I was going back east. I thought I might return but I never did. So I gave it to you. I'm sorry. She was nothing like as important as you... "

"Oh. My. God."

"Ruby, why are you doing this? It doesn't do any good to talk like this. Does it? It only makes things worse," he said. "I told you it came from my mother because I wished it did. I wanted to have a ring from my mother to give to you. But I didn't. So I told you what I wished was true."

I couldn't leave him. I wasn't brave enough to do that. Here we were at a turning point and since we were going to be separated anyway, I didn't see what would be lost by seeing it through. I was going to be free of him once he went to jail. And now he was down and out. Now he was at my mercy. At my request, Lydia spoke to her lawyer friend and ex-lover William Dupont about our case. He was far too expensive to hire in Angus's defense, but willing to consult with me off the record.

William Dupont had a suite of offices in Government Center. It was at the top of a skyscraper, with chrome furniture upholstered in caramel colored leather. Plate glass windows overlooked Waterfront Park.

"Well," he said, leaning back in his chair and evaluating me openly. "It was the biggest robbery from a private home in 1978. The paintings have been assessed at three million dollars. Quite a heist. On the other hand, they were returned unharmed months ago, and that is in his favor. The police are exploring all sorts of possibilities. Would you like me to lay some of them out for you? It might give you some idea..."

We sat across from one another on the wide leather chairs, in the middle of the room. He was a good-looking man in a well-cut suit, his hair slightly grey at the temples. "At this point they are not bringing any charges against Gillespie. I suppose you're aware of that?"

This was news to me. "Aren't they charging him with anything at all?"

He shook his head. "Gillespie's testimony is the evidence they need to put your husband away. As I see it, there are various options you might consider using in his defense. The first possibility," he said, "is that Ingrid Seabrook had a crush on your husband."

I wasn't sure I'd properly understood. "Let me explain," he continued. "Your husband is the son-in-law of her friend. Perhaps Angus was willingly allowed into the house. After all, there were no alarms on, and Seabrook was not at home at the time of the robbery. There were no locked doors to the living room. That's another important factor. Ingrid Seabrook's husband is much older than she is, while Angus is a very romantic figure. It's one of the possibilities they are exploring."

"But the Seabrooks never even met him," I said.

Dupont shrugged, and tipped his pen back and forwards between his fingers. "Well. It's an angle you might consider in his defense. Do you want me to go on?"

"Please."

"Another possibility. There's a second guy who's plea-bargaining. I don't know if you're aware of that. He was caught with an automatic weapon. Name's Dave Howard. These guys are all connected. They all know each other. All connected one way or another. Evidently your friend James Gillespie and this guy Howard were roommates at Amherst, and he's considering a plea bargain to get off a gun possession charge. He was found in possession of an automatic rifle, and he's willing to testify against Angus."

Oh, God.

Dupont continued. "Perhaps Gillespie and Howard had a homosexual relationship. Howard was jealous of Angus, knowing that Angus had returned the paintings and that Gillespie was the one who had left his fingerprints all over the house. Wanting to protect Gillespie and get rid of Angus..." said Dupont. "Do you see where I'm going with this?"

Things were going too fast. I could feel a headache coming on. "But James isn't gay. And that isn't the way it was," I said. "It's pure speculation."

"In my profession we call it making a case. If there's enough embarrassing speculation, it's possible the charges will be dropped. This isn't about being right. It's about making a case that holds up in court."

I needed to swallow, and when I did, it felt intrusive, an awkward interruption.

"Let me finish," Dupont said. "The third point, and this ties in with my second. Maybe Angus had nothing to do with the robbery. Maybe Gillespie took the paintings. He is the only one who left fingerprints in the Seabrook house. He might have given them to Angus to return. Perhaps Angus knew about it, and decided to plea bargain by returning the paintings. Dave Howard knew all about it too, and so this ties in with the second point..."

My mind tried on these theories, attempting to weigh their value, but in the few minutes I had to consider them, they seemed cockeyed. They were nothing but red herrings. And yet. It was, I saw now, possible to use them. Angus could go free. I suddenly saw how things could work out. I could use these lies and half-truths to get Angus out of jail.

Then I pictured Ingrid Seabrook. Not her person, but the symbol of Ingrid Seabrook. I barely remembered what she looked like now, but I did remember that she disliked alarm systems. Nora had told me that plainly. Perhaps she didn't like having the paintings in her house. Maybe she was living in a fortress. I recalled the look of discomfort that passed across her face when I went with Nora to pick up Sorrel from the play date that time. Perhaps subconsciously she wanted the paintings taken off her hands.

Dupont had juggled the facts for me. He had laid them down like a magician – pulling them out of his hat and his sleeves, piecing them together to conjure up a narrative that had never so much as occurred to me. He watched me with an expression now that combined sympathy and wisdom. But the most profound impression he made on me was confidence. No wonder Lydia had fallen for him. He was like Angus, with two more decades in his favor, and a lot more luck.

I shook my head. "I want justice," I said. "If he deserves to go to jail, I think he should go. He's got off the hook too often. I'm through with making excuses."

Dupont nodded.

"But will he definitely go to jail," I asked after a pause. "Is that definite?"

Dupont rose to his feet. "Not necessarily. There are work release programs and such."

"But if he goes to jail, which jail will it be?" I had saved this question until last, because it represented my worst fear. Please God. If he must go to jail, don't let him go to Walpole. Anything but that.

"Probably not Walpole," said Dupont. Said Lydia's lover. Said the man on the side of the law. "Walpole is for violent offenders. Angus isn't violent, is he? He might be sentenced to Concord – a small facility for younger people. They have work release programs. He might be able to get a job and return to Concord at night. There are all kinds of possibilities."

Forty-Two

I knew it was Angus as soon as I picked up the phone, because of the jailhouse noise in the background, the shouts and slamming metal doors, the echo of male voices. "Did you speak to that friend of Lydia's?"

"He told me that James is giving a statement. He isn't being charged. Not with anything."

"Oh..."

"And I don't know how important this is, but he mentioned something about a roommate of James'. David Howard. Do you know him?"

"What about him?"

"Evidently he has agreed to testify against you." Long pause. "He's going to testify that you took the paintings." I could hear the echo of shouting in the background, and as he said no more, I continued. "I guess he was charged with illegal possession of an automatic weapon. He had it in his apartment and didn't have a license. Apparently he collects guns."

"Are you sure of this. That he's testifying against me?"

"According to Lydia's friend he's entered a plea bargain. Testifying against you in order to get off the gun charge. But Angus, if that flies, then as far as I'm concerned, there really is no justice."

"Ruby," he said. "We're fucked." The din in the background subsided momentarily and it was as though there was a clearing for the agitated silence of his thinking.

I held the line.

"It didn't make much sense. A lot of what he said made no sense at all. I mean, do you really think they're going to let him off for illegal gun possession if they can send you to jail for art theft? Is that justice? And your fingerprints aren't even in the Seabrook house. The fingerprints were all from James."

I heard a few shouts in the background. "It's weird," he said. "I wasn't worried until now. I was going to plead not guilty. I thought they would recommend a suspended sentence..."

"That's still what our lawyer is pushing for."

"They're fucking me over, Ruby. Can't you see that?"

I couldn't see it then. But a few days later, Angus changed his plea to guilty.

I talked to Detective Robbins on the phone. "He may not serve the whole sentence," Robbins said. "At the most he might get five to seven. A lot of that will be on work release."

"But the probation officer said..."

"The probation officer has no say in the sentencing," Robbins said. "He was only trying to throw his weight around."

I was the main link now, between Angus and the world, although I knew others went to see him. That creep Michael Posey went. And Angus's father Frank. Angus was allowed three visits a week in the Charles Street Jail, as well as unlimited visits from his lawyer. But sometimes when I went to visit, Michael Posey had used up some of my weekly allowance and I was resentful of that.

Angus's grandmother Margaret got in touch by phone. "What will become of him," she moaned in her raspy voice. "If I had known when I gave him up for adoption, that he would end up like this..."

"He might be out in five years' time," I soothed her.

"I'll be gone before that," she said. "I may never see him again."

It was nearly Christmas. Oliver took me out to lunch at Grendel's Den as a treat. I watched a man standing on a ladder, stringing tinsel round the beams. The lunch was pleasant and distracted me briefly, but the sight of that guy on the ladder brought a wave of associations too sudden for me to guard against. It was the shape of his hairless brown arms, stretching up to work. It was because it was nearly Christmas. And Angus and I would spend it apart.

Oliver knew of everything from the papers as well as from me, and for all I knew he'd also heard things from James. But true to character, he was nothing but supportive. In fact he decided to change the status of my job so that my paycheck was larger, and he also arranged for me to teach a poetry workshop. People made sure I wasn't alone. They rallied around, Enid and Adrian, Oliver and the others. Except it was when I was with other people that I felt the most alone.

I continued to work steadily for Oliver, keeping my own counsel. One day I handed him the prose poems I'd been working on.

Oliver said he'd look them over, and for the next several days I didn't dare ask what he thought. "Well, Ruby," he said at last. "These pieces are taking shape and they intrigue me. They lick each other like kittens. But I wonder, are there some dark stairs to go down?"

In the weeks before the trial, Lydia moved into the loft with me. The space was long and deep with high ceilings and windows that looked onto an alley at the back. We kept the place neatly ordered. In the entrance across from the door, was a table with chairs, and in its center a huge vase of gladiolas. We slept on a divan, in the middle of the room, a cushioned futon under a kilm and an eiderdown. From the very start, everything was put away deliberately and tidily. Even the unevenness was deliberate; the stacks with books and tapes were purposeful. The pictures were not fussy. We had an Edward Hopper poster in the kitchen. We stocked up the new fridge, with bread, butter, marmalade, wine, biscuits and strawberries. Blue plastic crates on top of the fridge held dry food, rolled mats, a small watering can, pots neatly stacked.

I took my showers in the rickety stickety stall. Things were makeshift but I felt at peace with the energy. I liked the sound of Nigel fencing upstairs, the creak of the floorboards above and the sound of sword crossing sword, the occasional cry of "Touché!"

Sorrel and Nora came round to do some Christmas shopping and to see the newly refurbished loft. "Oh yes," said Nora. "This does have character!" as I filled the kettle in the bathroom and carried it across to the kitchen.

"I'm going to sell some of Angus's tools," I said. There was a shelf of tools, probably most of them stolen, against a wall near the bathroom. "Because we need the money to pay our lawyer."

"I think that's very wise. You'll be happy to get all that out of here," said Nora. I made us some tea and Nora and I sat at the table in the middle of the room drinking it.

"Does it worry you, Sorrel," I asked, "The thought of Angus being in jail?"

"No," said Sorrel bluntly. She was sitting on the futon, sipping apple juice from a miniature straw in a juice box. Her hair was in a French braid and she was dressed in a kilt. "But Nora says he has been in jail lots of times and I thought he would have learned his lesson." A new thought crossed her face. "Ruby?" she asked. "Did Angus steal Felicity's bike?"

HOW I DIED
By Ruby Lambert-Aleshire

I died at the point of a pen, trying to write a story that had nothing to do with truth.

I died cleaning a clay court at a house in Cohasset, walking back and forth as the sun came down on the pine trees, the pink sun and blue light on the shadow side of the magnolia. This is where I collapsed, and these were the last things I saw: a pair of discarded sneakers, a tiny crooked tree in a pot beside the cabana.

I died in a car crash. Crossing the road where there were no signs.

I died in an instant.

I died of flu. I died of long illness.

I died at the supermarket of heart attack. My wife was at work and I went to the store and never came back. Gone. Like a puff of smoke.

I died of old age, thinking the sun was a planet.

I was murdered in a barn. A rabid raccoon surprised me on the staircase and I contracted rabies.

I died of alcohol poisoning. While doing the Rubik's cube.

I was killed by my husband. He couldn't stand the arguments about his fucking warehouse. He didn't mean to kill me. But he did.

I died in an instant. I died of lies and thirst. I died of forgiveness and trying to live with a dangerous love.

~

Several workmen came to look at the tools. I sold them at a good price, but I could hardly bear to watch those men picked over the tools which Angus had handled with so much respect and understanding. I began sifting the things I loved in Angus from the things I hated. I found myself crying at silly things, when I couldn't open the orange juice lid, for instance, or when I couldn't unscrew things. I wanted him to hold me. I wanted to fall asleep in his arms.

In other moods I felt resentful for the people he had brought into my life: the probation officers; Bone and Frenchie with their Arizona scams, and Michael Posey. I prayed more earnestly than ever before and my parents supported me. "Well honey," said Timothy wistfully. "Jesus said we should forgive people seventy times seven. And my goodness, you've certainly done that."

Nora had a different approach. "You have to remember how rotten he had been to you. How you had to pay for everything. And all he put you through with that wretched warehouse."

I loved having Lydia around. She was very good company. We spent a lot of time in Quincy Market and hung out with her friends from Tannery West, and went to Cityside restaurant in the evenings. With Lydia, the city was free and alive. The lights were on and there were people she knew in the lighted cafés. These were also people who didn't know me in context, a crucial element.

I continued to organize files, bills and papers, which before had been a confusing mess. The very act of putting things in order had the effect of making me feel more orderly in my thinking.

Forty-Three

A week before the trial they moved Angus from Charles Street out to Dedham. I had begun to prefer talking by telephone to visiting him in person. If it continued like this when he was sentenced, I felt that I could cope. But I wondered if this was the easy part. Angus was close now and could phone quite frequently. I weighed these thoughts against the pleasing realization that when he was in a permanent place, I would be able to hold his hand. We would sit together, side by side, and that would be an extravagance.

I gradually eased into a new kind of buoyancy. For the first time in years, when Adrian Skinner took me out for coffee and cheesecake, or Enid wanted to smoke a joint in the tiny yard behind Tango's, I wasn't burdened by the background thought of lurking unknowns. When I went out to Hingham and we walked through Hingham forest to collect wood for a fire, I felt almost guilty for my effortless entrée to peace. At such times, it was a relief to be without Angus.

But when he telephoned and I heard his voice, a chasm opened inside me again. Suddenly I missed him, and wanted to make love with him.

"My evenings are so quiet," I told him over the phone. "I can't get over the quiet in my life. I did some writing and read a few reviews in the New York Review of Books. I took a couple of photographs. Oliver took me out to lunch at Grendel's. But still..."

"You know what," Angus said. "I think you and I have a very strong bond. And that's what's going to pull us through."

The night before the sentencing everybody telephoned: Nora and Timothy, Detective Robbins, Jenny Wakefield, Maude Caruthers, Adrian Skinner and Enid Aiken, Ari and Freddy and June. Even William Dupont. Everyone except James. And every time the phone rang, I hoped that it was Angus. I listened to see if the background was noisy, and if it was quiet, I knew it wasn't him.

We drove to Dedham on the day of the sentencing. My hands were cold and my stomach felt queasy. We met the lawyer, Jim Wilson, and I introduced him to Nora and Timothy. Frank Aleshire approached us, looking sheepish in his bomber jacket. "Hey, how's it goin'?" he said, as if we were assembled for a cheerful little party, instead of for a verdict which would put his son away.

"How are you, Frank?" I hadn't seen him face to face in a year and there was so much lying between us.

"Well, you know they've been holding poor Gus in the courthouse since 9 o'clock this morning," he said.

A 3 o'clock in the afternoon Angus was led through the courthouse corridor, his hands shackled, his ankles chained. He walked between two police escorts and held up his head and looked at nobody, certainly not at me. As I watched him pass I felt as if every particle making up my body had fused into a solid lump of agony.

The Seabrooks were in the courtroom for the sentencing. They sat together, somber and attentive and just like Angus, did not look at anyone. They did not turn in our direction, though we sat a few rows away. I waited between my parents. Nora's arm was linked through mine, and on the other side, Timothy clasped my hand.

Judge Dorothea Kendall presided. The court was called to order and the session began with a statement by Angus's lawyer, Jim Wilson. We listened as he expressed concern that the minutes of the grand jury investigation only included three of the testimonies. They did not included my testimony, Nora's, Timothy's or Brenda's, nor in fact any of the people who had spoken on Angus's behalf. "I am anxious that the court recognize that this is not all we have. The missing testimonies show that this was not a premeditated crime, and that Angus was intoxicated at the time. I also have here, your honor, many letters of support from family, Angus's professors and some members of their church. I would like to stress that Angus is not a violent person and that he does not deserve to be put into a maximum-security prison such as Walpole. I myself have got to know Angus very well over the past month, and there is no doubt at all in my mind but that he is sincere in his desire to reform."

Judge Kendall was a handsome woman in her fifties with salt and pepper hair and a calm intelligent demeanor. She listened to this statement without comment, as well as to the statement of Assistant District Attorney, Michael Kirby.

"Your honor," said Kirby. "I don't know what Mr. Wilson means when he says that the minutes are incomplete. This has been a complicated case, and there is a continued Grand Jury investigation into it, for which we still don't have all the records. Aleshire is a repeat offender. He has done time in Arizona and he's been on probation here in Massachusetts. He has shown no signs of reform, in spite of the court's previous leniency. My recommendation is a sentence of nine to twelve in Walpole."

Dorothea Kendall glanced down, to look through the papers before her. "What is the recommendation of the Probation officer?"

I held my breath. "In support of the Commonwealth's recommendation, Probation Officer William Delaney recommends six to fifteen in Walpole, your honor," said Kirby.

Jim Wilson stepped forward to pass a handful of letters to the judge, who said she would be glad to look them over. "Your honor, I would like to direct your attention to one of these letters in particular, from the two detectives on the case, Robbins and Coleman. The letter states that although they made no promises to Angus, he handed the artwork over to them of his own volition."

Kirby rose from his chair to object. "Your honor," he said. "The detectives deleted an important line in that statement before they signed it, a line that claimed Aleshire was cooperative in all his dealings with the Boston police. I would like to point out that the detectives refused to sign that statement."

There was a bit more paper shuffling from the judge. My heart was ready to thump its way out of my chest. Judge Kendall asked about the original statement, and Wilson stepped forward to give her a copy.

"Will the court please rise." The court rose. The judge stood up. She was taking a break to read the letters. Angus was then led to a holding cell outside the courtroom. I wanted nothing more than to be with him. I wanted to touch, to hold him. I hurried out to talk to him between the bars. It was the first time in months we had been allowed to touch each other. A guard allowed me into the cell and I rushed to him and he held me, a palpable joy in the midst of the agony. We clasped each other's hands, "I'll be all right, Ruby," soothed by the contact of skin against skin, both of us weeping. "I'm just so sorry that you had to go through this."

But the session was reconvening. We returned to our places and the court was asked to rise. The judge returned to the bench and sat down. She asked Angus to stand to receive his sentence. "I have read all letters and all the minutes," she began. "And I've reached my decision. In making this decision I have taken into consideration the defendant's past criminal record, which includes a sentence served in Arizona and the many opportunities he has been given for reform. I have considered all the good that has come his way and which he has not yet taken full advantage of. I have considered the recommendations of the court, and have read the letters fully.

"One thing I did not consider in reaching this decision was the wealth of the victims. If Mr. Aleshire had broken into another home and stolen something of little or no value, it would still amount to a symptom of the type of behavior, which must be seriously addressed. Therefore, I herewith sentence the defendant Angus Sidney Aleshire to thirteen years at MCI Concord.

"I want to point out that Concord is a juvenile facility and the possibility of parole will come up in eighteen months. There is also a possibility of a halfway house and work release programs in six months' time, and a chance for Mr. Aleshire to pursue his education. I believe that this sentence is a just one, and I do not think it so severe as to make the defendant give up all hope. In fact, I expect that with time to rehabilitate, he will be able to contribute in a real way to society."

I couldn't tear my eyes from his face. His expression was clean and poised as he stood to take the judge's pronouncement. Then he asked to speak. He leaned one hand against the banister before him. "I see that the Seabrooks are in the courtroom," he said, his voice trembling only slightly. "And although I know there is nothing I can do to take away the pain and unhappiness I've caused them, I want them to know that I feel I am capable of doing some real good for society. Although it isn't necessary, I'd like to think that knowing this, they might be able to find it in themselves to forgive me." His voice thickened with suppressed tears. "I want them to know that I'm sorry."

The Seabrooks remained deadpan. Ingrid Seabrook looked at her lap. Nora and Timothy did their best to conceal their emotion. But I was in agony. Thirteen years. *Thirteen years.* The thought was unendurable.

Judge Kendall answered quietly. "I am not so tough that I don't recognize remorse when I see it," she said. "I hope you will be true to your word."

Angus was taken directly to MCI Concord. I spent that first weekend in Hingham. We went for a walk on the beach on Saturday, and on Sunday, after church I went with Timothy and Grandpa to the dump. Grandpa brought his weekly rubbish of chocolate wrappings and orange peel to toss into the abyss. He stood grandly at the edge of the enormous pit, seagulls wheeling around overhead while Timothy busily disposed of garbage bags. "Look at it all," Grandpa exclaimed in awe. "The size!" Afterwards we went to the dry cleaners and the Fruit Center for Grandpa's weekly purchase of chocolate and oranges. "This will last me a month I expect," he said.

"Should we tell him about Angus?" I murmured.

Timothy shook his head decisively. "I wouldn't honey, no. He wouldn't know what to do with the information."

Forty-Four

Confinement and separation became routine. We were assured that thirteen years was the maximum sentence, and Angus would come up for parole in eighteen months. After two months, he was transferred to a correctional facility in Norfolk. It turned out that there was a nine month waiting list to get into Concord, and although it was further away, Norfolk was said to have better facilities.

I visited every Saturday, taking a highway towards Rhode Island and then various tree lined roads, through ordinary little towns, on a long straight road leading to immense walls, topped with razor wire. Nora sometimes drove me out and sometimes she came in to visit, depending on her mood. Sorrel liked to come as well. Other times Timothy drove me, and on the way home we'd stop at the Mug n Muffin for lunch.

The prison waiting room was decorated with string paintings, models made out of Popsicle sticks, and paintings of clowns on velvet – the handiwork of inmates, up for sale. The room smelled like pine cleaner. Heavy metal doors clanged shut.

After filling out a Request for Visit form, I passed through metal doors, and metal detectors, down a corridor and across a cement courtyard, round a corner and into the visiting room where a guard sat at a desk. The room was full of orange plastic chairs, linked together in rows, like a bus depot.

Families chatted, and couples sat together holding hands. There were many people of color. It was minimum security, so prisoners dressed in their own clothes. Angus usually wore jeans and a white shirt with a button down collar, and whenever I saw him I was struck by how remarkably healthy he looked. Over the months he thickened up. But then, the food in prison was surprisingly good, he said.

In fact once you got past the confinement, jail afforded many opportunities. There was time to listen to music and read all the books you could lay your hands on. He was working out in the gym and lifting weights and running laps around the prison track. He played a lot of chess. He had a job in the carpentry shop and was taking a computer correspondence course.

He wrote me letters almost every day and sometimes drew little pictures in his letters – portraits of the people in jail who he thought were really weird. One guy looked like a fetus. He drew a picture of the large head bent forward, a huge eye, a tiny tadpole body.

He described in detail his job in the woodworking shop, where he was learning carpentry. He worked with a guy who was doing time for murdering his wife and son. "The way he tells it, he doesn't deserve to be here. His wife was cheating on him. She turned the gun on him, and while he was wrestling it away from her, the gun went off and killed their son. He was so pissed off, he killed her too. But you really couldn't meet a nicer guy."

He made suggestions. Why didn't I start working out? What terrific shape I'd be in if I did a little running or lifted some weights. I could run around the New England Aquarium across the street from our loft. How sexy I would be with those well-toned muscles. What a new sense of wellbeing I would experience!

I sat in the visitor's room waiting and when he sat beside me we kissed for minutes on end. We didn't care how many people were around us. Afterwards we sat holding hands.

"How's the family? How's Lydia? Did you work out the problem with the overdue rent?"

I ran through the latest news. Lydia was great, but in her heart she wanted to move back to Barcelona and look up her old boyfriend Gustavo. Sorrel was turning seven. Nora was directing *See How They Run,* and Grandpa was having an operation for a cataract on his left eye.

Angus nodded. "Remember that guy I told you about who looks like a fetus," he said. "That's him, over there."

A pale rather ordinary looking fellow with a big head sat in an orange plastic chair talking to his family.

"That guy?"

Angus grinned. "Don't you think he looks like a fetus?" squeezing my hand and watching my reaction.

I laughed. "Not really, no."

"But it's the suggestion that makes it so disturbing," he said. "You know I'm right, Ruby."

He was always going to send some money to me. Money from his grandmother, and money he had earned working in the jail carpentry shop. It would help to pay for the heating bills in the new apartment, if Lydia moved out. But of course that money never came.

"Timothy is writing a series of articles about the women in the lineage of Jesus. He's writing about the spiritual significance of each of the women. Except that one of the women, Tamar, evidently tricked her father-in-law into having sex..."

"That's in the Bible?"

"Sure. She tricked him into it by pretending to be a whore..."

"You see that guy over there..." Angus interrupted, meaning a big fat baby-faced guy, flanked by two middle-aged women chatting merrily in a circle. "He likes to give blow jobs. They all line up and he sucks them off."

"Oh my God, Angus! That's disgusting."

"Yeah," he said. "It's pretty weird."

"How is it allowed?"

"It's not, Ruby. What are you thinking!"

"So how does he get away with it?"

"Some of the guys look out for the guard."

"Oh my God," I said.

A new thought flickered over his face and he allowed his hand to fold under the hem of my dress. "Oh Ruby. You feel so good. I miss you," moving his fingers under the edge of my panties. I felt myself getting wet.

"Hey buddy watch it over there!" The guard called out.

"I hate this place," Angus said, turning forlorn. "I'm horny as hell. I just can't wait to get out of here."

Then I started to laugh.

"What's so funny?"

"Nothing. Just that guy who looks like a fetus."

"I've thought of a way we can make love," he said, the next time I went in to see him. "You go into the ladies room when you come through to this building. And when they call my name I'll meet you in there."

"That would never work."
"Why not? It's easy."
"They probably have cameras everywhere."
"Not in the ladies room."
"I bet you they do."

Spring arrived and on warm days, we were allowed into an open courtyard. We sat on benches around the edge of a scrappy bit of grass, grateful for the blue sky above us. He told me there was going to be a picnic in summer for the inmates who had earned good behavior. They could invite their wives, families and girlfriends. It was going to be fantastic, he said.

I couldn't imagine it, and didn't want to go. But I didn't have the heart to say so.

Forty-Five

One day, on their way to work, Lydia and her new boyfriend Nicky picked up a dog in Harvard Square. He had been rescued from the pound. A woman sat in the square with the dog. The dog had a sign round his neck: Free to a Good Home, it said. That's when Lydia phoned me. "He's a beautiful dog, Ruby. This woman rescued him the day he was going to be put to sleep. The only drawback is he doesn't know who he belongs to."

"So have you already taken him?"

"I couldn't resist. He's a German Shepherd mix and he's beautiful. He sits with his front paws crossed. You'll see. The only warning she gave me was that you can't let him off the leash or he'll run away. Please, just take him for one afternoon? We'll figure out what to do with him later. Please..."

Lydia dropped off the dog. He was thin and golden, with a German Shepherd face and German Shepherd markings. He stood with his tail down. We didn't have a leash, but only a piece of rope. I decided to walk him to Boston Common. It was Saturday and the two of us, thin and sad, walked through the shopping crowds on Washington Street towards the park. He didn't pull me along. He was resigned to it, didn't have a stake in the outing.

We sat by the frog pond, underneath a tree. I was proud to be in his company, for he had the residue of pedigree, and had been through so much. I ate my baguette sandwich with Brie cheese and gave him a few pieces. He lay on the grass beside me and together we watched the ducks. We were a pair, both having lost the desire to thrive. We needed to find a purpose again. I hadn't been able to save my husband. But maybe I could save this dog.

I walked him home and on the way I saw Nigel Hargrove, the fencing master from upstairs. He pretended not to see me. I saw him duck into a doorway and wait until I had passed. What a coward, I thought to myself, as I walked my new dog and climbed the stairs to the loft. When we got inside, I gave him a bowl of water. He drank from it deeply and then lay down on the futon and slept.

The following week, I took him to a vet on Lewis Wharf and got him dewormed. Then I paid for all his shots and ordered him a license. I bought him special dog food down at the market beyond the overpass. I got him a new collar, black with chrome buckles. Lydia and I walked him round Waterfront Park, and sometimes Ari came along as well. The dog had become my protector. He wouldn't let anyone near me. He barked ferociously whenever a guy tried to pick me up. I named him Stjohn.

It was summer when Oliver scheduled the launching party for our new series of chapbooks by contemporary New England poets. It would be celebrated on Beacon Street, in Emerson College's Mahogany Room. On the morning of the event, I went with Oliver to the North End for fruit, bread, crackers and cheese. Adrian Stringer came along to purchase the wines. Then we wandered around the market stalls together, picking out fresh produce, tasting cherries and mango, comfortably conversing, and buying things for the party.

It was shaping up to be a hot day, and not exactly drinking weather. But after a light lunch we drove back in a taxi, loaded with paper bags of fruit and cheese and bread and wine, and at the Mahogany Room we set up for the party.

The Mahogany Room was a wood paneled drawing room with bow windows and a baby grand piano. Adrian and I set out plastic glasses and bottles, arranged the bunches of grapes, the Brie, the Stilton, the Sharp Irish Cheddar. We brought in bags of ice, soft drinks and cocktail napkins. Everyone at the bookshop was involved. Enid was prepared to take publicity photos; Rebecca Blackstone, who held writing workshops at the bookshop on Friday evenings, would act as official hostess. Oliver's wife Jackie set up a book display. Adrian and I were in charge of cleaning up, and Oliver was orchestrating all of it, as he stood near the piano looking chuffed and idly smoothing his moustache.

Guests trickled in from the city heat to stand bewildered in their rolled up sleeves and take relief in the air conditioning. They swarmed round the cheese board, and poured themselves glasses of wine. Oliver's wife Jackie looked elegantly disheveled in her linen dress, with her hair swept back. Rita Goldberg and Lillian Silverman arrived with Barry Priest.

I saw him by the window.

We hadn't spoken or seen each other since before the trial. Now here he was again, he who had contributed his fingers to the task, and his fingerprints, but never the necessary restraint. He stood in the sunlight, holding a glass of wine, and his face betrayed nothing at all, except his usual withdrawal to an inner life. He was never concerned with putting out impressions, was James Gillespie. He was hardly aware of making any. And yet he looked so handsome.

I turned away. Adrian uncorked the bottles at the drinks table, and I tried to listen while he rambled on about his foot fetish, and how he could tell the precise size of a woman's foot simply at a glance.

"Hi Ruby," James interrupted.

Enid wandered up with her camera. "Hey! Can I get a shot of you two, over by the piano?" That was so like Enid, oblivious to the awkwardness she was about to immortalize. She looked at us through the camera, and snapped her picture. "Thanks guys," as she rewound the film.

"How've you been?" James said. He was thin and tanned, but not, I was gratified to see, particularly comfortable.

"All right," I said.

"I tried contacting Angus," he said. "I even. I went to see him. But I did something foolish. They give you this, this form to fill out—" as if I didn't know "—and when I got to the part where they asked if I had been convicted of a felony I wrote down yes. Not surprisingly, they wouldn't let me in."

His face was evenly proportioned and symmetrical, almost the face of an honest man. "Angus doesn't want to see you anyway," I said.

"I wondered about that. How are you, Ruby?" he asked again.

"How do you expect me to be?"

"Did you know I'm getting married? Perhaps you heard? The wedding is next week."

"Had not heard that, no," I said, and frankly, I was stunned.

"Remember Ann?"

"Yes. Of course. Congratulations."

Rebecca interrupted. Oliver had bequeathed her as hostess for the event. Rebecca was vague and pretty, and she was striking an attitude of feigned helplessness, which she must have appropriated as a younger woman, to convey harmlessness and not insist on her brilliance. It probably worked in her younger days, but it looked foolish on a middle-aged woman. "Ruby? What exactly is the hostess supposed to do?" she asked.

"You greet people," I said. "Here. This is James. Let me introduce you." And with that I slipped away.

Adrian looked at me, his face as round as those illustrations of the North Wind. "Are you all right, Ruby?"

"A big glass of Blue Nun, please," I said.

"Not the Blue Nun; I bought it as a joke...."

A kind of fever was building up in the Mahogany Room. It was the fever pitch of making connections, of escaping the heat, and becoming too suddenly drunk. In that moment of the heat wave everyone seemed to have summoned the energy to put themselves forth. Everyone was launching themselves at the book launch party.

I was aware of the passage of time, of seeing people whose essence always remained the same, of the chemistry between people, the chemistry between James and me. Why was there always that draw and rejection.

Walking around the Mahogany Room, I came across Peter Dane looking rumpled and pale. He hovered by the piano, asking about a key. "We don't have a key," I said.

Adrian hovered as well, eager to put in a good word for Peter's acumen on the piano. Then Peter sat on the piano bench. He wedged his fingers underneath the closed lid. There was a tiny popping sound, as he lifted it. It was getting worse by the minute, this party. Now he had actually broken it.

"Don't worry," he told me positioning his hands at the keyboard.

"Oh, and he plays real well," Adrian soothed.

I had never been any good at stopping people from behaving badly. Who cared what I had to say about a broken piano lock, when Peter Dane was running his fingers up and down the keys with such aplomb. "Loved your book," I told him lamely. "*Play Time*."

"Uh hah. Thanks." Forget the broken lock. And James. Wall things off, I thought to myself.

"Mm hmm. I really liked *Play Time*," as he played his jazz riffs. His style of playing reminded me of Angus, and I tried to forget about James, but at the same time I was longing to talk with him. So I sipped my glass of Blue Nun and wandered around the fug of the party. After all, there were many interesting people. There was Rita Goldberg talking to Oliver about her book *March Baby*. Rita was very pretty with long brown hair and Oliver stood with his hands in his pockets and a smile on his face. "I've read your book Rita. Yeah yeah," almost to himself. "I've read your book."

Enid was flirting with Humphrey Stevens and Humphrey wanted to take her out to dinner and then he wanted to take me out to dinner too. And by the time that I was just about ready to surrender to the intelligent inanity of the book launch party, James was standing before me again, in a kind of funnel, as if he and I were the only ones there.

"Ruby. I think you should come with me. We haven't finished our conversation."

"I wish you'd go away," I said, as the party swirled around us. Except Humphrey Stevens and Enid were about to leave. "Are you coming with us Ruby or not?" they asked.

"Not," I said. Then James took my hand and led me up the winding stairs in the foyer of the Mahogany Room.

We found ourselves in a college dining hall, deserted for the summer. Immaculate stainless steel canisters had been lined up on the trestle table on the landing, and in the dining hall beyond, chairs were stacked on tables.

"Ann is expecting a baby," he said.

The news ran through me like a blade. "Congratulations. So life is really working out for you. That is grand. No really, I mean it. Congratulations all around."

"I didn't want you going with those other people," James said. "Because that would be a mistake."

"How dare you!" I cried.

"How...?"

"Dare you say that! You, who has ruined my life. Yes," I said. "That's right. I shouldn't even be with you. It was your plea bargain that put Angus behind bars."

"Angus didn't need any help from me to be put behind bars," he said.

"What are you talking about? You were the one who put him there!"

"Angus put himself there, Ruby. He was on probation for other offences. Then there was the warehouse, and all that loot—"

"You could have stopped him!" I cried. "You could have stopped him! You could have been loyal to me. You could have helped him reform instead of becoming his partner in crime."

"Ruby," he said. "If you couldn't stop him, how do you expect that I could? It's a good thing for you to get away from Angus. Both of us needed to get away. You seem to think that now is the hard time. Now that Angus is in jail. But, but actually. The hard time will be when he gets out."

"Really?" I cried. "Well, fuck you!" He stared at me then, as if he had been slapped. "How dare you," I said, trying to stop my mouth from trembling at the corners. "Getting married and having a baby! What's going to happen to me? Did you ever think about that?"

"You have your whole life ahead of you."

"Do I? Then why am I doing time? Because you clearly aren't. Where is your punishment? I am doing time, James. I'm in the best years of my life and I am waiting for Angus to get out of jail, and get his life sorted out, while you are getting married."

I was surprised by the tears that were streaming down my face. James took me into his arms and stroked the hair from my eyes while I wept into his shirt. Then he pulled up a chair and brought me to his lap. He held me close and stroked my cheek with his fingers, and he kissed my tears and then he kissed my lips. I had been wearing mascara and grey streaked tears slid down my face. I'd left some stains on his shirt as well. But he wiped my eyes and sat there, holding me.

At last there was one clear spot in the universe of chaos. And that spot was on a chair in a college dining hall, in the stinking hot summer, sitting on James's lap.

When we got downstairs the Mahogany Room was closed, and the building abandoned. Everyone had gone. I tried the door, and found that it was locked. "I was supposed to help clean up," I said.

"Don't worry about that. Oh, but wait," he said. "Actually, there is a problem." He stood silently, as if he was on hold. "Ruby. I've got to get back in. My wedding suit. The jacket was being altered and I picked it up before I came to the reception and I've left it there."

"Well I'm certainly not going to break the lock. Which reminds me: Peter Dane broke the lock on the piano and I'm going to get into trouble for it."

But James didn't care about such problems. He was only thinking of his suit. "Forget the suit," I said. "You'll just have to get it tomorrow."

So we left the building and walked up Beacon Street. It was so hot we might just as well have been roasting on spits. We passed the Hampshire House and crossed the road. The tarmac was soft, and gave beneath our steps. Then we walked through the Boston Common where the grass smelled like hay. We waded through the frog pond. Mothers and fathers were out with their kids and their dogs, trying in vain to cool off.

We sat beside the pond and cooled our feet in the water. Children's voices and splashing water filled up the rest of that dreadful afternoon, an afternoon of which everyone was tired. The entire city just wanted it to end.

"You know, it's strange. I remember you at a reading once, and Adrian Skinner was there," I said. "I cared about you then. I thought you were so beautiful and I was making you laugh. I don't remember what it was about."

"Your grandfather," he said.

"Something like that."

"Ruby," he said. "Listen to me. I've always loved you. When you married Angus, I was crushed."

"Why didn't you say anything at the time," I said. "I had no idea."

We continued walking through the park, and crossed the street in front of Park Street station. We walked down Washington Street past Filenes and Jordan Marsh, and we walked down Milk

Street through the financial district, and the further we walked the further the streets emptied out.

Finally we reached my building, the one with JJ Travel on the ground floor. I discovered a letter from Angus waiting in the mailbox. We climbed the stairs in the half-light.

The lights in the building were on a timer. The whole place would get pitch black a bit later on, but I felt safe in that building because I knew exactly where I was in the dark. I could walk up the stairs in the dark and know exactly where the door was. And at the end, I just held out my key and fit it right into the lock.

The door opened onto the loft space. Stjohn greeted me, wagging violently and we took him out for a walk in Waterfront Park. Then we came back and sat at a table at the far end of the loft near the kitchen. First I fed Stjohn. Then I opened Angus's letter.

"How often does he write?" asked James.

"Oh, several times a week. We both write." The fencing lessons were progressing upstairs. We could hear the sound of swords being crossed, the occasional cries of "Touché!"

"Do you want to hear what he has to say?" and I started reading aloud. The letter was all about a picnic in the jail, and how good it would be if I could come. Angus was looking forward to this picnic. It was going to be outside and there would be music. We could sit on the grass together eating watermelon and hamburgers. Maybe he would read to me. He still had that copy of Hiawatha. The one his grandmother gave him. It would almost be like freedom.

James stood and fumbled in his pockets for cigarettes and when he realized he didn't have any, he just stood there hopelessly. "I can't believe he has so much time on his hands to contemplate these kinds of details and, and put them down on paper."

"Why not? He's in jail. There's nothing else to do there. He always writes like this."

"Well, it tells me a lot about his mental state."

"He's all right," I said. "Forget about him. Come here and sit down." I pulled him by the hands. He sat back down. Our eyes met. Nigel was fencing upstairs. The floorboards creaked as the swordsmen jumped around, and as we listened, something came over us. "James," I said. "What are we doing?"

Oh James. I had so much to say to you. It wasn't really physical. It was about that courage of self-sabotage you always had. A way into the terrain where art can thrive, where you blow yourself up in order to examine the parts and see how they are put together. It was the way our selves were constructed, I suppose. We were writers, ready to reassemble the self in words. And that was how the word became God.

We wanted to have the courage and heartlessness to be true to ourselves. There was an utter selfishness required in that, and so we worked in the endless struggle not to do it, not to satisfy the craving, or to get that fix.

I suppose what I mean is, that this must have been what Angus lived with always.

My contact with James had always marked some downfall. Always. That is what I was to James: bad for him. But why was I so bad for him? Every time we came into each other's lives, and there would be more times when we did, even after this, it was at a terrible moment or had awful consequences. And yet I don't feel like I'm a bad person. Is that what Angus felt like too?

Maybe when I was with James, I felt conscious of my inadequacy, faced with too much that seemed insurmountable, too much intellect and ability to judge. So I had married someone whose weaknesses were more of an obvious inconvenience to other people. James's silences, I wasn't up to filling.

We decided to take a shower. We took off our clothes and stood under the water in that rickety makeshift stall. The whole apartment was makeshift. Water poured over us, and we crossed beyond the frontier of letters, sentences and equations. James was foreign territory, and so we crossed beyond the words of poems, and into that clean blank space of consciousness, to have the exchange we had always longed for.

There was never so tender a lover. His hips were narrow. His penis was foreign and beloved, his chest was broad as he pressed against me and through me, as we kissed, as I caressed and held him close.

Hunger, and yet not appetite. More a discovery of satiety. A familiar but foreign objective. "Ruby, I love you," he told me. "I've always loved you." And he lay on his back and pulled me forward to taste me, until I became like a sliver of gold under the crack of a door. A door we now had entered.

When I woke up in the middle of the night, he was propped on his elbow watching me. "Is it because you were drunk?" he asked.

"I only had two glasses of Blue Nun."

"I love you. Do you believe that?"

"No," I said. "I don't."

"Really?"

"Oh God, James, what have we done. How could we do this?"

"Do you believe that it's different with you?"

"I still don't get it. If you loved me, why did you let him sweep me off my feet? Why didn't we kiss in that field near Triphammer Pond?"

"I remember being disappointed at your lack of responsiveness. Or maybe. Maybe I was an innocent. I didn't understand about women then. I only know that when Angus came back, I didn't think I had any standing."

"What are we going to do now?"

"There's no guile in you," he said. "You have absolutely no guile." And he drew me into his arms, kissing and holding me. Then he mounted and entered me, and when we fell asleep, James was still inside me.

I woke up to find him standing in front of the bed, fully dressed, holding a glass of orange juice. "What time is it?"

"Time to get up. I'm just going to walk your dog."

So I drank the juice, and got up, and dressed while he was out with the dog, and when he came back we walked to Park Street in a kind of post-coital daze. We passed a corner grocery with a pyramid of oranges and grapefruits. James laughed. "It looks so sumptuous," he said. We stopped in at the Mahogany Room to pick up his suit and then we took the red line into Harvard Square. He was talking about a Beckett character, afraid in case someone attacked him at night in a lonely park, and realizing it was actually he that people were afraid of. He was the frightening stranger in the park.

We arrived at Tango's where I made coffee. "I still don't understand," I said. "Did you think the robbery would win me over? That putting Angus in jail would win me over?" We sat on the sofa in Oliver's office, waiting for the coffee pot to fill. Oliver himself was nowhere around.

"I guess I was intrigued by Angus's reputation," he said. "You have to realize, it all happened quickly, once the wait was over. And then. The whole year afterwards was one of terrible anxiety. As for motivation, I suppose that any motivation I had was mixed with the fact that he had you and I didn't."

Forty-Six

James got married the following Saturday. Ann was expecting his baby, and so their bond and future was cemented. On the day of his wedding, I went to the jailhouse picnic. Timothy drove me out to Norfolk and dropped me off at the back gate. "All right honey," and he gave me a kiss. "Have a lovely time."

I got out of the car, leaning in. "I love you, Timothy."

He drove away, dust kicking up on the ground, and I joined a crowd of visitors in front of the jail. We were the picnic guests, mostly women, and mostly black, in sling back shoes with kitten heels, our hair all done. It was evidently going to be quite the occasion.

We waited by a huge metal gate. Then there was a loud clang and the grinding sound of metal on metal as the gate drew up slowly, stopping a few feet above the ground. It had got no further before a few inventive women scrambled underneath it. Then the gate was lowered again.

There wasn't a scrap of shade. Some of the women started to argue. Every ten minutes we were let into prison, only three at a time. We waited for the gate to rise, and when it began its ascent, women pushed forward and rolled underneath. There was no line. No sense of organization.

Eventually I worked my way to the front, and got down on my knees. And when the gate began to rise, with the harsh clamor of grating metal, I ducked underneath it, stood up, and strode with dignity towards the waiting metal detectors. My bag was searched. I put my jewelry into a locker. I followed the guards down a corridor, and by the time I finally got through, my head was pounding so violently in my temples I thought I might throw up.

The picnic was set up in a large courtyard with a bit of grass, but not a single tree in sight. There was a trestle table covered in crepe paper and on it vats of chicken, potato salad, corn, watermelon, and barrels of Pepsi and ginger ale packed in ice. Motown exploded from the speakers. Couples and families, enjoying the reunion, stood in groups, introducing each other, all smiles and friendly banter.

A guard went about with a camera. The women clustered around their prisoner, and the women in front bent their knees and pointed their toes, to show off a bit of leg.

I sat on a picnic bench. Angus had brought out a book. "I thought maybe you'd like to read some poetry together."

"Sure," I said, massaging my temples.

"Or would you rather play chess."

"What do you want to do?"

"You look pale."

"I think I need some water." We sat on the bench holding hands, the party going on around us. The muscles ached in my hands, and in the arches of my feet, the onset of migraine.

He fetched me a Dixie cup of Kool Aid. "Sorry," he said. "They don't have any water left."

Timothy picked me up after the picnic at the front gates. I lay with my head against the back of the seat all the way home. We had to pull over twice for me to throw up. And when I got back to Hingham I went upstairs and lay in the dark of Sorrel's pink bedroom, with the fan on – in a soft bed, surrounded by teddy bears.

I had betrayed him. In sleeping with James I had untied the knot with Angus for good. At least that is how it seemed at the time, since Angus no longer had a physical hold on me. His physical presence had always exerted a kind of hypnotic influence, but now the connection was broken. I could see myself as separate from him.

The last time I visited Angus in prison was an evening. They had visiting hours on Wednesday nights so Nora drove me out there. But by the time I'd finished filling out forms and waiting for them to call my name, there was only half an hour left.

When Angus appeared in the visiting room he looked surprised. "Ruby! What are you doing here? You don't usually come in the evenings."

"What do you think I'm doing?"

"I thought it might be someone else."

"Someone like who?"

"I don't know. Michael, maybe."

"Posey? That creepy guy visits you here?"

"Sure he does."

"I cannot believe you're still in touch with him!"

"Why not? He's my friend. Don't you want me to have any friends? Anyway, his wife works for a publishing house, and she sometimes sends me books."

"I thought you weren't allowed to have packages."

"Hey. Why are you being so ornery this evening? They let you have packages if they come direct from the publishers."

"How very convenient," I said.

Angus looked at me strangely. "I have all kinds of reading material now," he continued. "You can't object to that, can you?"

Across the visiting room the lights were on and it was dark outside. I looked back into his eyes. "And what else does Michael's wife slip into those packages," I asked. I had a vision then. I could see the little baggies of cocaine lining the spines of the books she sent, and when Angus didn't speak, I knew I was right.

The visiting room had an evening coziness about it, and not so many people were there. "I've changed," I told him. "I've been living away from all the crime, and now I have a life. I don't worry anymore when I hear police sirens behind me. I'm not wondering if they're coming for us. And when I wake up in the night and find myself alone, I no longer panic. In fact I'm comfortable by myself. I like being alone."

"So what's your point?" he asked.

"That if I discover there's another scam, I will instantly leave you. Do you understand that I'm not going to do it anymore?"

He looked at our hands, our interwoven fingers, and then he slowly met my eyes. There was artifice in the gesture and both of us knew it. His eyes were hollow of meaning. "Of course," he said.

When I left, I found the waiting room was empty except for two young black women and their children. One was changing the baby. The baby lay on the bench kicking its legs free while the mother folded the diaper, and cooed. The other woman bought a bar of chocolate from the vending machine for her little boy while she waited for her friend to finish with the baby, and the two of them talked to each other quietly. They were gracious and unflustered and something about the way they took life as it came touched me deeply.

When they left, the guards watched me through the glass and I felt like I should leave as well. So I went outdoors and stood on the steps waiting for Nora to show up. It was chilly and dark and the visitor's parking lot was practically empty.

I started walking away from the jail, and away from Angus. There were reeds on the opposite side of the road, and up in the tower a guard kept watch. The jail behind me was all lit up, friendly looking and welcoming. Crickets chirped in the cool night air. There was a scurrying in the reeds by the side of the road. Then I saw approaching headlights. The car stopped and it was Nora.

"I thought it was you," she said. "But I couldn't believe it! As I was driving up I thought to myself, who would be walking here at night? And then I said that looks like Ruby. And then I said, it *is* Ruby!"

I laughed and got in beside her. I felt a peculiar resilience in that moment, the realization that I would get on better in a life without Angus. For the lights blazed in the jail behind, and the free world lay before me, down a long dark road.

Forty-Seven

I had to move forward from my bad investments, to get away and start something new. So I decided to take a job as a researcher and writer for Plimoth Plantation, a living museum where actors played the roles of Pilgrim Fathers. I would move out to Plymouth Massachusetts, and live with my dog by the sea. I gave my notice at Tango's, and Oliver threw me a party. They would all miss me, he said, but then, I wasn't very far away, and it was time I moved along. All of us realized this.

But the packing up of things was also the packing up of desires, the loss not so much of permanence, but of innocence. It was 1980. The new decade had already been seared by the Iranian hostage crisis, involving the siege of fifty-two American diplomats. Perhaps the world was also becoming less innocent. I only know that in my uprooting there lay a sudden shock, because so much that once had been was gone. The circumstances had shifted many months before, but now I understood that shift.

Freddy moved to the Milk Street loft and took over my lease. It was a good arrangement for all of us. He liked the space and I could leave behind the things that provided a link to Angus, a chain of possessions we had acquired and which Angus and I would divide when he got out.

I moved to a cottage on Billington Sea Road in Plymouth, forty miles from Boston. It was a summer studio belonging to Maude Caruthers and she was happy to rent it to me for as long as I liked. Plymouth was a town that thrived on its past but I tried to imagine the future around me as well. The sea breeze blew across me as I walked through the past and through the future along the paths of Brewster Gardens, over a little bridge across the creek, down to the Jenney Grist Mill and the herring run.

To reinvent the self. To start one's life anew. Reinvention of the self seemed to me the least desirable of states. But I discovered the self that had been buried beneath my persona. I found the town of Plymouth pleasant enough. It clearly didn't have the buzz of Boston, so I focused on another side of my nature, on buying plants, planting bulbs around Maude's cottage and putting them in pots, in picking over thrift shop spoils, and contemplating the indulgent purchase of a carousel pony. I did a lot of walking with the dog, along the paths of the forest, past cranberry bogs and down along the beaches. I enjoyed my work and at last I was being paid a living wage to write.

Then there were the people who worked as pilgrims for Plimoth Plantation and the Mayflower.

They were mostly a cheery group of academics and hippies and they liked to have fun. There were parties, and cookouts on the beach, but what I appreciated most: every gathering lacked the stony weight of blind ambition.

Sometimes though, I had difficulty sleeping. I remembered the Bible story of the seven virgins who kept trimming their lamps and waiting up for the bridegroom. Wakefulness, then. A kind of consolation prize for the lack of desire. Wakefulness in a rural community gave me the sense of being haunted, or if I was no longer haunted at least I was doing the haunting.

I lay in bed on my kilm looked at the fan on the ceiling: a daisy with the petals pulled off, five of them remaining. He loves me he loves me not he loves me he loves me not he loves me. But no, he doesn't love me.

I was twenty-six years old and had left Angus for logical reasons. I would never understand the principles that brought him to conclude: I will be this. I would never value the man he had chosen to become.

Sexual desire lay dormant for a time. My sexuality had fallen asleep and I didn't care to wake it. I felt no interest in or need for sex. Sex and love were memory and without them there was a leveling out, which made my life more bearable. I felt neither need nor hunger. Not even thoughts of Angus or James interested me now. It had all been so much bother; now it was even an embarrassment. To think I had been so agitated and so full of turmoil! It was right to forget about love, to leave love rotting like Miss Havisham in her bridal gowns.

There was a starkness to the pilgrim village, even with the tourists. Plymouth tore away my hunger. I found simplicity. There was no hunger, no pain and no desire. I had my dog Stjohn, and that was enough.

I started divorce proceedings. Angus didn't contest them. The papers were served to him in jail. The grounds, irretrievable breakdown of the marriage, required a year of separation, followed by a court hearing. Then it would be another year before the divorce was permanent. I was right to divorce him and at last I understood this. We would never have been able to live down the deception. What had happened would always lie between us, even in the most trivial of arguments. Even with my own betrayal, I would always be the one who had been wronged. And even if I hadn't been... My love had been too desperate for Angus. Nobody human can endure the burden of another's unconditional devotion.

I sat on my wooden deck, surrounded by beach plums and pine trees. I strung up fairy lights and Japanese lanterns round the deck, and walked Stjohn down to Billington Sea Pond, where we swam. The trees around the pond changed color. They reflected golden and green on the water and we swam out in the silky smoothness. The air was cold above us, and then we swam back, and I dressed, and walked back home. I put logs on the fire, and when I lay in bed at night, under heavy blankets, I looked into the branches of the pines, and let my mind wash clear. How could paradise exist, when you have an awareness of the suffering of others? The wind rustle, the moments of nothing, which weren't supposed to count, this is what nourished me now, as well as the principle of the pilgrim venture and the lives I was researching and writing about.

I researched the life of a Cape Cod witch called Goody Hallett, who had fallen in love with a pirate named Black Bellamy. He sounded a lot like Angus, did Black Bellamy, and I could identify with poor Goody Hallett. Bellamy never returned, although he had impregnated her. So Goody Hallett haunted Eastham Beach and supposedly caused many shipwrecks.

Stjohn thrived in Plymouth. I walked him along the beaches, and up the hill to the old graveyard. Sometimes there were storms in autumn and when there were storms the weather was terrific, with kettledrum thunder and driving rain. Stjohn lay on the kilm at the foot of my bed.

A long hard rain separates the dead from the living. The electric green of the reeds stood brighter against the lifeless briar. The grass glistened under a mat of fallen leaves. The grass was brilliant in sunlight. The dead branches of the dead trees were deader now than before the soaking rain. The living branches were quenched and nourished, and on the path lay tidemarks of dead pine needles.

It was on one of my walks with Stjohn that I first encountered Sam. He had a ponytail and he was a runner, jogging with his English setter out across the beach. Our two dogs drank water from the same spigot, a tap that people used in summer to wash the sand from their feet. "This dog," said Sam, breathing hard from his run, his face flushed and hands on his hips. "She loves to take a shower."

I laughed. "Oh really?"

"Yes," said Sam. "She stands beneath the water when she's hot and she sings in the shower. She goes under the spigot, and howls." I laughed again and we watched our dogs. "But she never goes in the ocean. Never."

"My dog loves to swim," I said.

"I think she's afraid of it." He met my eyes and I watched their subtle expanse, into a newly revealed interest. "Haven't I seen you before," he asked, "at the plantation?"

"I'm a writer and researcher there," I said.

"Ah, that's where I've seen you. Because I work in the village. I'm playing the part of George Soule." He put on a country accent: "Oim livin' pruf thaht gud things com to them thaht's willin' to weet a bit!" he said.

Sometimes after that, I met Sam on the beach, walking our dogs, and I smiled at him or greeted him. At first we mostly passed each other. Sometimes when we passed each other he would call as he ran on by, "It's the beauteous Ruby! How are you today? Everything going all right?"

Later we tended to meet on purpose, for lunch at the plantation. He'd come up the pilgrim street, in his pilgrim garb, his hobnail boots and burlap coat. All the villagers had to dress in pilgrim costumes, but Sam looked oddly sexy as a pilgrim, and he often smelled of wood smoke. He had to stoke fires in his pilgrim hut, and he kept pigs in the pilgrim village, and mucked them out. He had to pretend that life had stopped in 1627.

We walked the path to the cemetery together, and took to sitting on the bench at the top of Fort Hill where there was a wonderful view overlooking the harbor. It was the most beautiful hilltop. The weather was as clear as a bell and the church bell rang clear across the valley. The golden leaves turned brown and then they fell.

Sam lived near the gristmill, where Canada geese wandered near the water. He complained about the green swirls of goose crap on the grass in front of his house, and the freezing cold air that whistled through the window frames. We walked our dogs to a shack on the pier for clam chowder, and watched the boats. Mostly we talked. About genius, and how it could appear in people who were vulgar, unrefined or unpleasant, as in Shakespeare and Mozart. He defined genius as a balance between intelligence, skill and drive, which left out, as far as I was concerned, the crucial ingredient: the ease, lack of hard work, and often even the scorn, with which geniuses sometimes regarded their talent. "I think it comes out of nowhere," I said, and I told him about Melvin Stringfellow.

"That's an incredible story," he said.

Sam was an actor; he'd had a few good parts in Boston. To our amazement we realized our paths had crossed before. He had worked with Ari in the same production of *A Midsummer Night's Dream*. He was also interested to hear about Nora's theatrical ventures. He thought of his pilgrim role as an acting role, but really it was a stopgap, because his aim was to move to New York in the coming year.

We talked about dogs, and we talked about each other. When it was time to tell him about Angus, I told him. After that he told me about his mother's suicide, and his guilt for not being there more often. "Although in fact she didn't want me to come."

"The terrible thing about loss," I said, "is that even when you are in the company of other people you feel alone. Sometimes even more so."

Forty-Eight

I moved with Sam to New York City the following autumn. We took both dogs and rented an apartment in Crown Heights on Eastern Parkway in Brooklyn. We lived across the road from the Lubavitcher headquarters of Hasidic Jews, who dressed in black suits and wore hats and beards. The rest of the neighborhood was mostly black and West Indian. Our apartment was affordable, and it had those rare and essential commodities: light and space, and somewhere nearby to walk the dogs.

Sam auditioned for shows and did construction on the side. I found a temp job at NBC, and was later hired permanently in a programming division. I read and evaluated script submissions. I missed the intellectual life of the bookshop crowd, and even the writers and researchers in Plymouth. But that was all I missed about Massachusetts. Sam and I were in an easy love and most of all, we were happy. Truly happy.

I stopped talking about Angus so much, but when I did, Sam was generous. He was far too gentlemanly and confident in my love for him to pass any judgment on the subject, simply observing that Angus's was a very sad story.

Freddy telephoned with news that November: Angus was out on parole. He was standing in the middle of the living room when Freddy came home from practice one day. "He scared the hell out of me."

"But how did he get in?"

"This is Angus we're talking about," Freddy said. "He broke in, of course."

"But how does he look? What are his plans?"

"I think he wants to move back into the loft. I guess I'm fine with that. He's going to need some sort of support system or he's never going to make it."

"It doesn't sound like he's off to a very good start," I said. Then, "Come on, Freddy. Are you really prepared to be Angus's support system?"

"I think I can handle it. After all, he's the closest thing I have to a brother. " Freddy cleared his throat. "I told him about you and Sam."

"Oh? And what did he say?"

"He first went very quiet. And then he said you deserved a good man. But he really wants to see you, Rube."

So the next time I was up in Massachusetts, Angus and I arranged to meet. I took the usual bus from Hingham up to Boston and walked across Waterfront Park towards Quincy Market, my heart beating. We had planned to meet at the loft and then, I imagined, we would go out somewhere for lunch and talk. I was anxious about the effect his physical presence might have on me, but I needed to see him and find out for sure.

I got as far as the Black Rose pub, when I saw him coming towards me on the sidewalk. I saw him before he saw me. What a tumble of confusing feelings came upon me then. He looked so strange, so singular, as if he'd been let loose on a crowd of less aware pedestrians. He was strong and thick, both physically present and out of place. He was the memory of something good inside a much harder person.

We were coming face to face in the free world at last. I stood still and waited for him to see me, then I watched the smile stretch over his face and I moved forward to embrace him. "You've been working out," I said.

"Not much else to do in jail," he joked. His features were less mobile than I recalled, and seeing him so condensed called into question the essential elements of Angus.

"You've done something different with your hair," he said.

"Hennaed it," I said. "And let it grow."

"Want to grab lunch?"

"There's a place over there, on the corner. Friends and Company?"

"Sounds good," he said. And so, we sallied forth. It felt awkward. Then, "I'm moving back to the loft. Freddy's fine with it. I enjoy his company and I don't expect him to move out. But I have nowhere else to go. This is my home."

"Yes," I said. "I do see that."

Friends and Company was a cozy watering hole patronized by business people, and it had a pretty standard lunch menu. We sat at a table in the back. It was dark and wood paneled with maps hanging on the walls. We ordered a couple of beers, in the spirit of the occasion. For in other circumstances, this would have been our moment. There would have been rejoicing. And in our rejoicing we would have been immune to the social clumsiness that came upon us now.

Our beers arrived and we ordered food. "Are we divorced yet?" he asked with a grin.

"Not for another year," I said. "Haven't you been following it?"

"Not closely, no."

I sipped my beer, tasting its cold bitterness. "How do you feel, being in the world again?"

"Hard to explain," he said.

"I imagine it must be unsettling, in some ways."

"Not unsettling. Hyper real. Everything still seems novel." He marked a new thought with a gentle motion towards me, and reached for my hand. I took his cautiously as the waitress returned with our salads. We were trying to smile, even then. Even as the tears began. How silly to feel this way all of a sudden. Wasn't I glad to be free of him? He was also free. How silly it was to cry. How very cruel to feel like crying now.

His eyes brimmed. "It wasn't all bad, was it?"

"No," I said. "It isn't that."

"Don't explain," he said, wiping his eyes. Then I wiped mine and blew my nose in a paper napkin and we looked at each other and tried to laugh. "All right?" he asked.

"Yup," I said. "Sure."

After lunch we returned to the loft. We had to divide our possessions. Basically we just walked around the place, and stood in front of pieces of furniture and shelves of books. Do you want that? You can have it if you want. Do you want this china? How about I take the other stuff. How about these pictures? No. You can take them.

We fought over none of it, disagreed on nothing. It took us twenty minutes to go through everything we owned. After that we lay on the bed. We were mentally and emotionally exhausted.

Only the desire to sleep came over us now. So we fell asleep like brother and sister.

When we awoke, the day had gone on without us and we both felt dazed. "The bus back to Hingham is leaving in half an hour," I said.

"I'll walk you over there."

"No need."

"Okay. I'll walk you down stairs."

"My boyfriend Sam can come up from New York to help pick up the rest of my things," I said, realizing as I said it that I felt proud to bring up Sam's name, and to claim him as my boyfriend.

"I don't want to meet Sam," said Angus.

"Then Freddy could drive my things out to Hingham, and we could pick them up from there, if that's what you prefer."

"Fine." We headed downstairs and stood in front of JJ Travel. The sun gleamed bright between the office blocks, on its way down, and while we were standing there, Nigel Hargrove the fencing master turned the corner, heading our way. He looked like the ghost of Hamlet's father. I watched as he ducked into a different doorway, so as not to be seen.

"Oh God. Not this routine again. Pretend not to notice," I said.

Angus laughed in his customary way. "What?"

"Nigel always does this. He's hiding in that doorway over there. He always hides when he sees me coming."

"Why?"

"I have no idea. It's really silly."

I looked into Angus's face, and watched it soften into deeper familiarity. Knowledge and love: hard to let go of that combination. To be known and loved at once; isn't it what we all yearn for? The raw material of Angus impressed me, even then. I hated only the overlay, what he'd decided to become. It was this I walked away from on that final afternoon. I turned towards the future and a different kind of promise. I said goodbye, he said it back, and I never saw him again.

Forty-Nine

It was from a considerable remove that I heaped up remaining scraps of information about Angus. Lydia and Freddy kept me up to date. Lydia still lived in Boston and saw him occasionally, partying in Quincy Market and doing lines of coke. But after a few months of sharing the loft, Freddy grew weary of the stress and the constant bristle of negative energy that came along with Angus. He kept odd hours and his behavior was unpredictable. He took people up to the roof in the freight elevator and partied until daybreak, or walking across the rooftops and climbed in through skylights to steal stuff.

He even took to breaking into Nigel's loft. When he saw Nigel setting out across Milk Street in his shabby old raincoat, he'd go up in the freight elevator and walk around, picking things up and putting them down, looking at the swords and the books. It was astonishing, he told Freddy, the amount of weird stuff that guy had. The junk he had squirreled away. Freddy was disgusted by this behavior. So he moved in with his girlfriend, who wholeheartedly disapproved of Angus, and thus the contact was dropped.

Then there was a stabbing. Two musicians had moved into the loft to take Freddy's place, and they heard the whole thing. Nigel discovered Angus in his apartment, and they heard the confrontation, the scuffle – Nigel yelling that he had been asking for this, that he, Nigel, knew enough about swordsmanship to wound Angus badly without killing him. A few minutes later Angus was pounding on the door: "I've been stabbed, man," he cried. "Help me, I've been stabbed."

They took him to the emergency room and got him bandaged up. It was a clean wound beneath the heart, but required stitches and medication and the bandages had to be changed periodically. Angus grew weirder by the day, and the two musicians were up to here with it.

In mid-December he knocked on their door. The pupils of his eyes were like pinpricks. He had come to tell them that his boat was leaving. "Your boat? What boat?" they asked.

"My boat," he said. And when he left they asked no more questions. Why would they? They were that relieved to see the back of him.

Lydia was the last of us to see Angus. He showed up unannounced and looked through the windows of her cottage on Bank Avenue in Hingham. She had moved out there with her boyfriend Nicky.

"I think he must have been abusing the prescription pain killers on top of all the coke," she said.

"The guy was fucking crazy," Nicky put in. "I mean, how did you live with that guy? You were married to him? I can't get over it. Why?"

Lydia and Nicky were visiting us in New York after Christmas when I heard this story. We had been out and about all day long, and were sitting in the West Village drinking Irish coffee. Sam and I sat side by side, holding hands and we listened to the story, the kind of extraordinary story that anyone else would have soaked up in all its curious detail. But as I listened, I felt the distance widen between me and Angus. I was finally free. I had no personal investment.

So feelings weren't bottomless, after all. You could actually use them up, in spite of their intensity. I had finally flat lined.

Fifty

So that is all I know for a fact. The rest of this story is pure speculation. I was still living in New York, when in December Nora sent me a newspaper clipping. "Do you think this could be Angus?" she wrote at the top of the page.

The article was about a 40-foot sailboat stolen at night from Lewis Wharf, not very far from our Milk Street loft. Coast Guard helicopters had pursued the stolen sailboat as far as Peddocks Island in Boston Harbor, calling on bullhorns for the thief to surrender. But he had escaped, jumping into neck-deep waters, swimming to shore and then disappearing into the woods.

Peddocks Island had remained under surveillance for several days after that, but the thief had never been found. Police speculated that he might have got away in one of the rowing boats left at one of the summer cottages. It would have been too far to swim for the mainland, they said, and especially dangerous in the cold.

A month after that sailboat went missing from Lewis Wharf, a body washed up near Nantasket Beach. It was the body of a woman who had drowned. The police issued a description and her roommate speedily identified it.

Then there was a second body, less than twenty-four hours later. This was the body of a young white male, caught in the nets of a fishing boat just off Peddocks Island. It was reported like an afterthought, a postscript to the update on the woman who had drowned. The story of the second body would be easily missed. It was so badly decomposed that cause of death could not be determined. The coroner stated that it had been in the water between thirty and sixty days, and was mostly skeleton when they recovered it.

When Nora read that story in the paper, she got one of her sinking feelings, and at her urging, Freddy telephoned the Boston Police and was put through to the Detective unit. He asked to speak with either Detective Robbins or Coleman.

"Robbins is retired and Coleman is dead," came the answer.

Freddy was shaken. "No!" he cried.

"Yes!" the officer mimicked. Then, "What else can I do for you today?"

"I was hoping to get information about the body found on Nantasket Beach last week," said Freddy. "I think it might be my brother-in-law."

"That information is confidential," the officer said. Then paused. "How about you tell me the name of your brother-in-law, and I tell you if that name is correct?"

"All right," said Freddy. "His name was Angus Aleshire."

"No," said the officer. "It's not him."

For years, if someone asked me what had happened to Angus, I said I thought he'd returned to Arizona, to start another life. After time, I imagined he would turn into the man I always hoped that he could be.

That's what I maintained until March of 1990, when the Isabella Stewart Gardner Museum in Boston was burgled. When two thieves, disguised as police, entered the museum under the pretext of answering a security alert. They lured the guards away from the alarm, then handcuffed them in a basement room. They took a Rembrandt, a Vermeer and several drawings by Degas along with many other works. It was the biggest art heist ever pulled off and the value of the work was estimated at five hundred million dollars. The crime has never been solved.

In other moods, I believe it was Angus who escaped across Boston Harbor in the stolen 40-foot sailboat and then jumped into neck deep waters, pursued by the police. If he had died that night in 1982, the stab wound would have played a part. The gauze would have unraveled in his swim to shore. Hypothermia or cardiac arrest. The heart wound's delicate healing would tear in the stress of the swim, and at that moment it would have been pumping blood with the boost of adrenaline and cocaine. He wouldn't have been able to stop its flow.

I can picture him out on the ocean, the rowboat floating in the water's lull, as he lies back down – if only for a moment – to take cover and catch hold of one streaming thought, to gather strength before deciding what to do next.

He stares at the stars in that final moment in my mind. Why die in inches when you can do it all in one go. Does he remember me – feeling his way through a hole in the universe, finding his escape, in the most intimate of moments in which he now finds himself?

I never followed up on the coroner's report. Nor did I contact the police. I could also have inquired of the Aleshires. I didn't even do that. I didn't want to know. The truth is hard to look at face to face and the truth about Angus has always been so painful.

So then I picture the ear-buffeting thud of the helicopter blades, cutting through the quiet of Angus's solitary getaway. I imagine the glare of searchlights on the water, the helicopter thumping overhead, and the crackle of a voice calling him on a bullhorn. For most people that would be terrifying. But Angus would never have felt more alive. All the sensations of beauty and power and icy moonlit breezes would blend with the thump of helicopter blades and bullhorn warnings to stop, until the boat neared Peddocks Island and he saw his opportunity.

He always took nothing but chances. So he dropped anchor, stood on the edge of the deck, and not thinking further about it, jumped into the darkness.